ASHES
and DUST

PRAISE FOR *ASHES, WINE and DUST*

"Kanza Javed weaves a fine tapestry between two worlds, a past that is slipping away and a present that is at once frightening and intense. Yet there is hope. Definitely, one of the exciting new voices from Pakistan."

— Shrabani Basu,
author of *the Spy Princess*

"A reflective, thoughtful novel from a young and resonant new voice"

— Namita Gokhale

"In this debut novel, Kanza Javed weaves a hypnotic generational tale of old and new Pakistan, of new loyalties, half-loyalties and enduring love.
Javed's depiction of the love between Mariam and *Dadda*, her grandfather, is unforgettable. Her portrait of life in a country and culture rapidly changing and changed, along with the promise of forgiveness, healing and hope, show '*Ashes, Wine and Dust*' to be the achievement of a remarkable young novelist at the beginning of her stellar career."

— Melissa Pritchard,
author of *Palmerino* and *A Solemn Pleasure*

"Delicate and full of feeling, '*Ashes, Wine and Dust*' draws out the shape of things in a particular place and time in Pakistan, but also transcends that exactness and reaches out to all of us who are trapped by memories, both beautiful and unspeakable."

— Mayank Austen Soofi,
author of *Nobody Can Love You More:*
Life in Delhi's Red Light District

ASHES, WINE *and* DUST

Kanza Javed

tara
India Research Press

tara
India Research Press

Flat. 6, Khan Market, New Delhi - 110 003
Ph: 24694610; Fax : 24618637
www.indiaresearchpress.com
contact@indiaresearchpress.com

2015

ASHES, WINE *and* DUST
Kanza Javed

ISBN 13 : 978-81-8386-134-2

Printed for Tara-India Research Press at *Manipal Technologies Limited.*

For *nani*
for embracing, knowing, understanding and always, always,
believing in me.

and

to all the women in Pakistan who question.

Acknowledgements

I wish to thank the Tibor Jones South Asia Prize, and Anuj Bahri, Sharvani Pandit and Aanchal Malhotra from Red Ink Literary Agency, New Delhi for their generous support and guidance.

I'd like to mention Aanchal Malhotra once again, and offer my earnest gratitude for revising, understanding and preserving the essence of each character in *Ashes, Wine and Dust*.

I would also like to thank my parents, Muhammad Javed Anwar and Iffat Javed, for always encouraging me to pursue the written word.

Prologue

My grandfather was a quiet man. Desolate, he'd call himself, a simple desolate man of few words and many thoughts. When twilight would near and lavender skies finally decided to patrol the hollow earth, without a single word he would pull out his beige *charpoy* and place it adjacent to Hamida *baji's* rusty sewing machine.

With one hand tenderly caressing the hose of his reliable *hookah*, he would recline on his bed, staring ominously into the distance. Newspapers and old magazines would surround him, craving for his attention, but the flight of his contemplation seemed to take him to a world beyond the perception of an ordinary man. Leisurely exhaling ghastly white clouds into the air, he made queer symbols with his long, frail arms and sometimes his brittle body would sway mechanically from side to side.

"Deplorable!" my grandmother would softly cough and hide her face in her mauve *dupatta*, shielding herself from the smoke. My grandfather wouldn't respond, instead just close his eyes and emit longer swirls of grey. He was someplace else.

"Mariam?" he would suddenly say, so pensive. I would abandon whatever I was doing and sit nervously on the corner of his *charpoy* with my eyes fixed on the wooden cane he seldom used. My eyeballs would land on his dark irises, transfixed.

"Shall we go tomorrow?"

My face would suddenly bloom, "Promise me?"

His reply was always a brief nod, which required no elaboration. We were going.

The following afternoon, my grandfather took me to a

graveyard. I was eight, and this was the best memory of my childhood.

"*Dadda,* wait! Wait, wait!"

He ambled and then came to an abrupt halt, swinging his body to his left. He tsk-tsked. He wasn't pleased.

"He is never pleased," my grandmother would have said had she been there, making use of this sentence multiple times to bruise his fragile ego.

"No one has discipline," he murmured as I caught up to him.

I looked up at him, not quite sure who he was addressing, the dead or the waking. He held in his hands two rocks, once a part of a massive tombstone. He looked at the littered ground. My eyes, too, scanned the crammed dry graves. Wings of the dead pigeons, brilliant looming shadows, decaying flowers and crumbling tombstones. And the cold, moist earth.

We were trespassers.

"There is no order, Mariam."

He held my shoulders with a firm grip and said, "We must not abandon the people we love so easily, even after we lose them, even after they perish. We must always find love within us for all beings, for the frailest bird, the smallest insect and even the dead. We must never lose that warmth."

I nodded

"Even vultures don't relish on cold, hollow men," he added with finality.

ASHES

LAHORE 1994

CHAPTER ONE

It shook the elders inexpressibly. The children felt nothing.

In the autumn of '94, my grandfather passed away after a brief illness. The funeral was a grand affair of forty days. My sisters and I were the water bearers, for the mourners were always thirsty. At every day break, we would form a line and draw water from the hand pump outside the house in big steel jugs. They were too heavy for us to carry but we had to anyway. Water rushed out of the pipe like a fast raging river, drowning our toes and everything that the human eye cannot see. The squeaking sound of the machine echoed in the early mornings around the village that slept under a cover of stillness and sorrow.

This was my first memory of feeling pain.

Men crowded on the floor in rows, waiting for their turn to loudly express at least once how my grandfather was an epitome of social piety. I'd hear them say that he would be allowed an easy access to the highest ranked heaven. As a child, I believed that they were all intimate friends with God, and knew secrets of the mysterious universe. They also told me that I looked very much like my grandfather; I had his eyes and the arch of his eyebrows stamped on my face.

When my sisters and I poured out water for them, they asked us about that one precious memory of my grandfather that we were going to hold on to forever. The graveyard day was what I remembered:

It was afternoon, a lovely Thursday afternoon. The sky was calm and the clouds, unchanging. My grandfather and I stood in the family graveyard. His mind was submerged in memories of his mother and great grandmother, who lay before us under heaps of soil. He seemed to be absorbed in another world, removed from all the filth, all the banalities of daily life and social boundaries, away from all the lights and sounds, away from all human contact and away from his granddaughter. I watched the pigeons, dozens of them, breathing softly, bathing in a small pond nearby; some wrestling in the sunshine, speaking in a language of their own about subjects only they understood.

They scurried close to my feet. I drew out my hand. My eyes were wet.

I couldn't tell the mourners at his funeral the reason why I was crying that day at the graveyard, because I, myself, couldn't remember at the time. It only came back to me years later, like warm sunshine on bitter winter days. But despite the missing details, this memory with Grandfather remained my most cherished.

A drifting leaf fell on his lap and he recoiled from his daydream.

"I don't think it's any good crying now, my child," he said.

I sniffed. Dust, smoke, rose petals and incense, all homogenised into one heavy bittersweet scent.

"I'm not crying," I muttered, "Dadda? Thank you for the new shoes." I looked down at my brand new shoes.

"You're welcome, my darling. Now smile for me," he grinned. It was only then that his still face betrayed any emotion. I responded with an uneasy smile.

"You know, there's so much out there for you, like these new shoes," he said softly, "There are so many things that will bring you joy, like these blue shoes. Imagine all the new places you will see, all the books you will understand, all the music you will listen to, and all the men you will fall in love with."

I was silent for a moment. Then I said, "When?"

"Eventually, but you don't wish that now. You don't want to rush

into things. Childhood should be the best part of one's life."

The dusty wind blew. Stray incense ashes fell onto the grave. A heavy droplet fell from the sky, smothering the earth and the ash underneath its weight. Carefully, my dadda rose and took my hand in his. We set off walking straight out of the graveyard towards the white sky.

The mourners didn't understand the importance of that memory. They just shrugged and drank the water, unaware of his presence, but I looked outside the window and felt that any moment then, his shadow would appear as if it had never left. He would walk gently as he always did, not a care or worry in the world that could repress his heart. He would have the yellow sun on his back and a sugarcane stick on his shoulders, beaming, as he would grow closer. I imagined myself sitting on the steps outside his house, standing up eagerly, as his figure would approach. And if he were here, really here, he would have said, "Mariam, look what I have got for you."

The moment would have been perfect.

***

Funeral afternoons had little activity. My grandmother and I would sit in the *veranda*. The only conversation that the pair of us had was with the falling leaves. It was like watching the world collapse in shades of yellow, orange and brown. Often, she would heave a weary sigh and then look deeply outside the window, as if contemplating some captivating vision landing on the ground from the almost bare trees.

To pass the long dreary hours I drew on my small slate. I would sketch the side of her face with white chalk. First, her long and pointed nose and then, her small round eyes. Like an artist's patient subject, she remained perfectly rigid till the portrait was complete. She would then twist around to face me and smile softly.

Silent. Mindless. Struggling for the right words.

I think more than anything, the social disconnection was a terrible blow for my grandmother. This *Iddat*, the pre-determined grieving period, was to continue for forty days and nights. She wished to crawl inside a warm burrow and mourn quietly. She wished to mourn for the moments she spent with her partner, however small, however insignificant, before they escaped her for good.

When Father announced that it was time for us to leave for the city, my sisters couldn't contain their happiness.

No more work.

No more sounds of women wailing.

No more stillness.

I, on the other hand, wondered about *daddi*: *what was she to do alone? Whom was she to blame for all her solitary evenings and unhappiness?*

Mornings later, we bade goodbye to Grandmother, the thirsty mourners and the water pump. To our surprise, the bitter memory of the morning ritual of drawing water never stopped haunting us. We dreamed of water currents drowning people and Grandfather for a long, long time.

***

CHAPTER TWO

Unfortunately, school doesn't stop for children who have just lost somebody they love. The geography teacher was a middle-aged woman, stout and arrogant. She called me to her desk to ask where I had been for weeks. Resting her chin on her palm, her narrowed eyes revealed no real desire in learning about the sad story behind my prolonged absence. I looked down at my tennis shoes and then back at her disinterested face.

"It is not a perfect world; terrible things will keep on happening but you can't stop your education. All this country needs is yet another excuse for a girl to stop learning," she said as if I were eighteen, not eight.

I pondered over her philosophy.

"What was your name, again?"

"Mariam."

"Mariam what?"

"Mariam Ameen."

I watched her carelessly scribble my name in the corner of her notebook.

Mariam Ameen.

My father gave me that name, just like he gave the rest of my siblings their names – Anika Ameen. Aminah Ameen. Fatima Ameen. Mariam Ameen. Abdullah Ameen.

Our parents raised us as ordinary middle-class children in Lahore. An invisible chalk ring of moral and religious confines encircled us, but it didn't imprison us and our exposure was not constrained. My father, a landowner and businessman, was famous in the family for his truthfulness and kind nature. But it was always his father that I was close to, never him.

After my grandfather's death, my attention telescoped to Anika. She was four years older than me I, two years older than the twins, Aminah and Fatima, and eight years older than Abdullah. Anika was the silhouette of a heroine from an *Urdu* or a *Punjabi* folk story. Conventional. Modest. Courteous. If Jane Austen were requested to revise her definition of an "accomplished woman" and review Anika, she would have passed the test.

"Mariam, you have to make friends your own age," she would always say to me, "You can't spend all your time by yourself! You will grow up before you know it. There's nothing extraordinary about that. But you can't take a giant leap and skip childhood."

She was the good daughter.

She made little imperfect clothes for dolls when she was six, stitched covers for the guest room cushions by the time she was fifteen and could make every dish you requested when she turned twenty. She could spend hours gazing at the flickers of the fire in the hearth, and sometimes when deep in thought, she reminded me of Grandfather. I could tell that there was a lot more going on in her head other than sound of the salt and *masala* shakers, and the rhythmic music of the sewing machine.

A strong believer in love, magic and mystery, her library comprised dozens of books about romance and astrology. Rubbing her cold index finger over my tiny palm, she would tell me my future as it changed every day.

"Mariam!" said a shrill voice.

I was back in the classroom.

The twins towered over me. They had been standing near my seat for some time.

"A classroom is not a place for dreaming, everyone will run ahead of you," said Aminah, "We have to leave for home early today. We have asked your teacher. Father called the office, we have work to do."

I packed my bag and looked at the teacher. She folded her arms over her chest and sighed, disappointed to witness my early departure.

Soon, my sisters and I were walking fast on the main road. We passed a wide street with small shops selling fresh fruit juice and vegetables. The bus stop was always crowded with young flirty boys in blue uniforms and plump homemakers carrying plastic baskets full of groceries. When we reached the railway station, Anika met us by the main entrance.

"Come on, we can't be late," she said, "I think I heard the whistle."

We were bestowed upon another complicated task of receiving an unexpected guest from the railway station, our grandmother. It had only been a week since we last saw her but she called our father saying that she wanted to move in with us for a while. The house, the mourners, everything in the village made her sad. My father, being her only living child, was moved.

I held Anika's hand as she glided through the passengers in the waiting area. She looked back at me and smiled. This was my second favourite place after the graveyard. I liked it because my eldest sister did too; it formed a kind of spiritual and intimate relationship between us. She found the sound of the train's whistle and echoing footsteps on the platform peaceful and haunting. *There was a certain comfort in watching the lovers reunite and people escape*, she said.

The station itself was a rectangular, noisy building that had been modernised a few years ago, but it still held traces of British architectural pretensions. The spacious station must have been beautiful once, with its arched ceiling, skillfully crafted benches, multiple pillars and polished marble.

"No, sir, thank you," Anika said for the seventh time to a waiter dressed in an old khaki-coloured *shalwar-kameez*. His clothes bathed in the aroma of the golden crispy fries and *pakoras*. With his keen eyes resting on four young girls who fidgeted nervously under their black shawls, he kept trying to convince us that the food was promising.

"If he keeps persisting, I am afraid I will grow hungry," said Aminah, licking her thin pink lips.

I chuckled.

Then *chugchugchugchug*, came a sound, followed by loud exclamations from the people collected on the platform; the metal monster was approaching.

"It's mighty huge, isn't it?" exclaimed Anika.

"Of course, Anika, it's a train," replied one of the twins.

Dust, the sound of hooves, whistle, laughter, new faces and strange stories of faraway lands; the train had arrived, towering over us as. A figure suddenly seized my arm, giving my body no time to react to the sudden restraining action. Anika grinned and readjusted her *chadar*, it slithered off nevertheless and she held on to the corner so that at least some of it would stay in place.

"Why would you take a black shawl?" was the first question my grandmother imposed as her eyes met Anika's, "Is it some mourning we are supposedly attending? Rejoice, my girls! Let the celebrations begin! I have come back to the city to find myself again!"

We beamed.

Holding my shoulders, she rattled my body in excitement. She was pleased to meet us. After five brief minutes of greeting, counting her luggage and inquiring about her journey, we made for the house.

"How is my Abdullah? How is that naughty grandson of mine? *Mashallah Mashallah*!"

We noticed that her fair face had drooped and her chin possessed several new folds over the days. Giving a toothless grin, she narrowed her dark blue eyes, two crystal clear pools of blue, "*Aye aye,* Mariam, you have certainly grown weaker, my child."

"You, yourself look pale, *daddijan*."

"Oh, don't mind me, child, I have lived my life! I have a few more years anyway and then I'll be like the wind, I'll disappear, but you will feel my company even so," she gave a nervous giggle and then tapped my chest gently, "here, in your heart."

Our face turned grim at the prospect.

The dandy chip-seller, who had taken ample time to style and re-style his hair with a tiny brown comb, greeted our grandmother as if they had played hide and seek together back in her time. He offered assistance in carrying her luggage. Swinging her giant body in his direction, she shooed him as if trying to baffle a fly off a teacup. Her quivering hands moved steadily through the air, nearly hitting his head one time. He backed off in a hurry, bewildered as to what had issued him this level of hostility from my grandmother.

"Damn you! Rot in hell! I am well aware of your strategy. Trying to charm the girls! You snake!" she shook her fists at him as if they would punch the lights out of him. His smile died and his mouth engaged in muttering some alien curses. Shuffling his feet, he dashed out of our sight. Now *daddi* with her unsteady gait ambled out of the station and we followed, juggling her three large suitcases. She told us she wanted to bring her sewing machine but it was very heavy.

"It's no ordinary sewing machine, you see, not like those paper machines they sell in the markets now days. I stitched my wedding dress with that thing."

Then looking around us at the crowd, she made a sombre face

and began preaching, "Always be careful around such men. They are like snakes, their vibrant patterns might attract you but once you approach them, they inject their gleaming fangs into your skin."

She spoke as if from experience. Holding her two fingers in the air and slightly bending them to imitate fangs, she touched my arm as if trying to infuse poison into my veins.

"They put drugs in the food," her tone became intense, "Have you heard about women trafficking? They abduct young girls like you, rape them and then, sell them. Selling another human like yourself, how shameless!"

I gasped because I hadn't heard anything like that before. My sisters too stared at her, horrified. Rumours said that one of *daddijan's* sisters was raped when she was thirteen. It was a man they had trusted the most. It broke her family, caused them deep humiliation and moreover, it shattered their trust in any stranger.

"Don't you get lonely, *daddi*? Move in with us," Fatima struggled to change the subject.

"Nonsense! The city is nothing compared to my village," she had always been possessive about her home, "You can't imagine what luxuries you are missing out on."

On our way home, *daddi*, Anika and I shared a rickshaw. The twins hired another with the luggage. Throughout the ride she taught us how to toss red spices into the eyes of rickshaw and bus drivers if they tried to become what she called "too friendly". The poor driver who was driving us cleared his throat uneasily.

When we reached home, there was a stir of excitement as *daddijan* embraced our brother.

"Abdullah, Abdullah, Abdullah!" she chanted, squeezing his little body, "Have your sisters been nice to you?"

He let out a childish squeal and said that the family had been busy.

After she had freshened up, she sat down with all us children crowded around her. First began the stories of school and bullies and then *daddi* told us about her life after Grandfather. She told us stories about her house in the village, where she now resided with her blind sister, several ghosts and other inexplicable entities.

***

CHAPTER THREE

Strong winds ransacked the city all morning. At night, it finally rained.

Abdullah and I looked out of the window at a washed out wedding in the rose garden next door. Contrary to its name, the rose garden had never been a home to any flowers or bees or birds. It was just a piece of vacant land reserved for big weddings, school activities and religious seminars.

Abdullah giggled as the bridegroom picked up his red and golden turban from the ground and opened the door of a car decked with flowers. The teary-eyed bride, fenced by concerned relatives in fancy clothes, sat inside. I looked at my brother's face. He was only four then; an unusually quiet child with unusually quiet hobbies such as drawing, reading and nursing wounded animals.

We heard *daddi* clear her throat and flip through the pages of an *Urdu* romance digest. Like always, after reading, she was going to watch some television and sleep. Such distractions absorbed her pain.

"Come here, you," she called me, "Close the window on your way back. I feel cold."

She sat on the bed with her legs on the ground. I sat near her toes.

Abdullah skipped away.

She untied my braid and started massaging my scalp with almond oil.

"During my time, Mariam, we washed our hair with *lassi*. You have never seen the photos of my youth, have you? Skin, so flawless and hair so immaculate. My sisters were a work of art, too. It's a shame, these things are gradually dying. Women should be like ornaments, fragile and beautiful."

"Now we have shampoos for our hair, *daddi*."

"Oh, we had shampoos during our time, too, but we knew better," she said with a tone of irritation, "You should've asked your grandfather what a doll I was when he married me. His relatives couldn't take their eyes off me. They were kind people… at least for a while."

She told me that relatives, sometimes when together, unknowingly, impersonally, talk about useless things that trigger rumours. These rumours then echo back to the person they are spoken about, hurting them, impairing them in ways from which they can't recover. They collapse in social gatherings. Forever an outcast.

The rumour mill spun many stories about my grandparents throughout their adult lives; alarming stories, some true, some partially true and some unbelievably far from the truth. They stood up when they had the strength but sometimes their relatives, like a pack of wolves, retaliated and brutally severed their confidence, destroying their trust as a couple.

I had grown up hearing that my grandfather had an affair with an old lover who moved to Delhi after the great divide of 1947. The estranged lovers met again when he went to visit an old friend across the border. My grandmother left him for a month when she saw that he had brought her back with him. But eventually, he chose my grandmother and soon their second son, my uncle, who died in his forties, was born.

There were many other stories that spun around for decades but they didn't intrigue me as much as this particular one because this story, as I later discovered, was actually half true.

My grandfather was a solitary man and my grandmother, quite the opposite. During the early years of marriage, she had enjoyed the company of her hearty in-laws. Her own family lived in a different city. The news of my grandfather's supposed infidelity caused my grandmother to spend a few years in isolation. My grandfather celebrated his relatives' distant manners with a cold sneer. My grandmother, in turn, hired a young personal maid, Hamida, whose job was not only to assist her in the kitchen and laundry room, but also to engage in long discussions about life, its lessons and why men did the things they did.

I turned around and looked at *daddi*, who had tied my coal black hair into a neat braid.

"There you go," she said, "You've an ordinary face, Mariam. I do hope puberty is a blessing for you. If I am still alive when you're growing up, I will make you a goddess, like I made Hamida a goddess. She is like my daughter, you see. She has always been there for me."

I half-nodded.

"Do you miss everything back home?"

"Ah, what's to miss? This is only for a short while and I will go back to the village, now, wouldn't I?" she brushed off something invisible from my shoulder, "Besides, Hamida must be enjoying her time with Gulshan and the ghosts."

She waited for me to probe but instead I lay on the carpet and stared at the ceiling. This was not the first time someone had mentioned the existence of ghosts in *dadda's* house.

When the twins and I collected water from the pump, we remained extraordinarily quiet. Partly because it was early morning and none of us wanted to move a muscle, but mostly because the task itself was so wearisome that we wanted to just get it over with.

One morning amidst performing the duties, one of the twins had something interesting to share.

"Would you two believe me if I told you that there is a great chance that *daddajan's* spirit is still lingering in the very corridors of this house?"

The speaker was Aminah. She was sitting on the ground with her hands behind her back, staring up at our beautiful ancestral home.

"I wouldn't be surprised," replied Fatima as she placed a heavy jug on the bench.

I looked at both of them. They were very serious. Without a word, I loosened my grip on the cold steel handle and waited for Fatima to put another empty jug under the pipe.

"Look at this place. It's utterly depressing. Aren't we lucky that we only come here once or twice a month?"

"I think it's the unusual structure that gives it a depressing feeling."

I looked at the house. It was a little unusual but still, it had character, a vivid shape and soul. Ceilings were tall and grand. There was a pavement for horse chariots and big windows with coloured glass. It had seen things, one could tell. When we were young, Father said that a Raja built it sometime in the 1800s and my grandmother added that during the British Raj, the English rented part of the house as their offices. She described pale-skinned, dandy officers walking in and out of the corridors.

"They would come here in their dandy clothes and ask for iced tea," she used to tell us.

"Then one of us would come carrying a steel tray with tall English glasses," my grandfather would laugh.

We all knew the truth after a few years. It was a desperate imitation of a colonial house. No Raja or British official ever lived there, but my grandmother's knitted stories were so fascinating that it was hard to believe that they were not true!

"Won't you ask me about the ghosts?" *daddi's* voice brought me back to the present. I didn't respond because I knew she would have told me anyway.

"People get whisked away by *jinns* all the time but this feeling is different," she began, "Sometimes I feel like I am being followed in the dark corridors. I have given up climbing stairs to check if the door on the roof is locked or if the *haveli* guard has arrived or not."

She called the backyard the *haveli*. It was the *haveli* where the most dreaded water pump was built and where my sisters and I were compelled to spend the funeral mornings.

"Have you ever seen anything strange in the house, *daddi*?" I revealed my curiosity.

"Once I heard Gulshan talking to herself. I became vigilant and asked her about it. She sat up straight and said that she thought I was sitting next to her. But I wasn't, I had been in the kitchen the entire time!"

Raising my eyebrows I made a serious face, "Was she frightened?"

"Since she lost her eyes, she has stopped being scared. You don't know what it's like living in darkness, she says. What can be worse than losing such an integral sense?" she shook her head, "Sight. She doesn't mind being left alone in a forest for a tiger to pounce on her."

"Hmmm," I said, imagining myself in the same condition. Would blindness wipe out all fear of pain and foreboding doom? I wasn't really convinced.

"She has seen a lot in her days. I am surprised she is still surviving."

Suddenly, she stood up with a jerk, "Sometimes she swears she hears a man coughing in the living room."

"But that's where *dadda* sat in the evenings…" I gasped.

"Yes, and sometimes, she can smell the smoke of his *hookah*."

"Did you ever?"

"Dear God, no. I believe her though, but as our roofs are connected, it must be Bashir *sahib* smoking on his roof when the sun goes down," she stood in front of the mirror and removed her *jhumkas*. Through her elongated earlobes, I looked at her reflection as she prepared for bed.

The excitement accelerated. I lay back down on the carpet and thought about the house. The spirit, possibly Grandfather's, drifting ethereally, his gleaming silver hair combed to a side. Skin so pale and translucent. Gliding weightlessly through the halls, ascending up the stairs and revolving around the water pump. Calling our names. Calling me.

Mariam. Mariam. Mariam.

Calling me for one last conversation.

"Do you think we can talk to the spirits?" I suddenly spoke.

There was no reply. I got up to look at her.

Daddi had drowned in a deep slumber.

***

CHAPTER FOUR

"One realises the immortality of true love only after the lover dies," my father said.

Pain takes time to soften. People recover differently. Some change cities, some fall in love and some begin writing. *Daddi* transitioned hastily. She took off her all her jewellery and gifted it to my mother, who was taken aback by this warm gesture. Mother put a thin gold necklace, a ruby ring and antique bangles in a box away from everyone's sight.

"I will gift this to Anika at her wedding," she declared.

No matter how distorted the sketch of my grandparents' relationship was in our heads, a part of me realised only after his death that my *daddi* forgave her husband's supposed infidelity a long time ago. But it was something else he had done that she couldn't forgive him for, the fact that he had died before her.

How dare he die before her?

How could he leave her alone?

What was she to do alone?

After she gave away her possessions, she stood with her back towards me, looking out of the window at the rose garden. Her eyes absorbed, her face glowing from the many colours of sunlight, her hair thin and frailer than I remembered, falling down her back like a silver river.

"This is what I feared," she said, "Being alone at the end. He was not a bad man, your *dadda*. I had grown quite used to his presence."

The couple displayed their love in the oddest of ways. They never uttered a kind or affectionate word to each other, but Grandfather always brought sweet sugarcane for her when he returned in the evening from his adventures in the golden fields.

After his death, *daddi's* love also finally came out from under the ragged quilts. Though he was no longer there, she made sure that his bed was always made, his old fawn safari hat hung on the rusty hinges, greeting spiders, and his sunburnt *hookah* sat peacefully next to her *charpoy*. Even his brown leather *chappals* sat on the doormat, greeting every new pair of feet that entered or left the house. She felt less alone, I believe, knowing that some part of him was still around. His things gave her comfort, made life feel more normal, made the void he had left within her less visible.

When he had lived, she barely noticed me. Maybe because she felt that *dadda* gave me enough attention already. The twins had always been her favourite. They were taller for their age, slender and fair - in short, every South Asian boy's fantasy. Anika and I, on the other hand, possessed ordinary looks and a "wheatish" complexion - a term coined by our mother for our beige skin colour.

After the funeral though, a lot changed.

She said my "wheatish" complexion and raven black hair were beautiful. She said my eyes and the arch of my eyebrows reminded her of someone. She said she loved how, unlike the twins, I was neither conceited nor pretentious. She saw him through me, I could tell.

"You are silent like your grandfather, Mariam. The silent ones are the most dangerous, they say. They are the fiercest from the inside."

***

When winter came, *daddi* announced that she was ready to go back home to the village. We flocked around her luggage, discouraging her, asking her to stay for a little more time but she said, "I can't trust anyone with my house. Besides, I've to leave before the cold weather creeps in. Preparations need to be done."

Father, sentimental and saddened, asked Anika to accompany his feeble mother on the train ride back as he was going away for business.

"But Papa, my school?" Anika asked softly.

The winter holidays had just started and he assured her that it would only be a week or two until she settled back into her routine in the village. The night before the journey, Anika used all her strength to convince me that I should be the one accompanying her.

We sat with the Ludo board spread in front of us. She curled her lips and glanced at me.

"Mariam, what were you saying about the ghosts the other day?"

I rolled the dice.

"I said, *daddi* is going back home because Gulshan is petrified that the ghosts will eat her up."

"Do you think there are really ghosts there?"

"You said the women were old and lonely, that's why they invented such details, for amusement and attention."

"Yes, that's true, but I've started to think that Grandfather's spirit must be still hovering around."

My face turned serious. I leaned forward and whispered, "If you see it, will you promise to tell me about it?"

"Nah," she stretched her hands, "I'm not curious like you. I will probably ignore it and sleep."

"Don't you want to see him?" I gasped, "Didn't you love *dadda*?"

"Yes, of course, but Mariam, can you go with *daddi* instead of me...?"

She stopped and then sighed, "Look, I can't stay there, not even for a week. Besides, she won't enjoy my company at all. But you get along so well with her. Would you be a good little sister and go?"

My sister knew exactly what chords to play. I couldn't say no to her and the curiosity that she had cleverly aroused in my mind.

"Two weeks will pass before you even know it!" she said, smiling wide.

*** *** ***

So, before the sunshine laughed and struck every plant, wall and person, *daddi* and I were on our way to the railway station. She was ecstatic about the change of company and hugged me thrice to reveal her pleasure. But this excitement didn't last long. Her whining began as soon as we reached the station. Despite the change in seasons, the days were still a little hot. She fanned herself with a corner of her brown *dupatta*. I barely held onto the four suitcases that contained everything but her sewing machine.

Our porter, who was now drenched in dust and sweat, made a face and brushed some particles off with his red shirt. His face clearly read, "*A cantankerous old lady and an ignorant child, what a day!*"

"Water? Did you bring a water bottle?" drawing her eyebrows closer, she asked. I handed her a flask.

"When does the train come?"

"Train, *bhai*?"

"It's late, that's the government's fault, as usual. Money-sucking automatons. Pack of wolves feeding on people's blood!"

"Thank God, the *angraiz* were kind enough to lay down the tracks or else we all would've been riding carts."

At a distance, smoke rose, staining the blue sky followed by the much-awaited screeching sound; people stood up instantly with desperation and joy. The train was here and it was time.

"*Chalo, chalo, chalo! Aye bhai train aye!*" porters cried, suddenly becoming alive with the rhythm. It was time to make some extra money.

My grandmother held my arm, smiled and pointed at the emerging green monster. I smiled back. Arshad, our loyal coolie, pushed some men aside and presented to my *daddi* three iron stairs. Complicating the matters, she took one step and stopped midway, her bulky body hanging in thin air, "Oh, please, son, give me three seconds to decompress!"

The coolie now pictured the train moving with a woman hanging onto the steel handle and a young crying girl stranded on the platform with mountains of luggage and decided he wasn't comfortable with conceiving that thought. Panting, as if she had just climbed a snow-capped steep mountain, *daddi* shook her right hand dismissively.

"No time to relax! People are waiting! This train waits for none!" he said aloud and literally pushed her through the little doorway.

"The elephant's in!" someone joked from behind, followed by some "shhhhhh!"

Relieved that she didn't hear the offensive statement, I waited for her to turn and throw her arm out for me but, much to my surprise, she walked right inside, hunting for our compartment, oblivious, not worried, that she abandoned an eight-year-old, boxed between snake-like men. Meanwhile, I struggled with four suitcases.

"*Daddi!*" I wailed out, frightened.

"Oho, *beti!*" the porter sighed, handling the cases and assuring me that trusting a man I just met an hour ago would be perfectly normal. He would deliver them to our seats.

I found *daddi* already seated with her legs on the bench. She barely noticed me as I sat down beside her. She was no longer sweaty or frantic; her face was calm and serene, lost in thought. She looked out of the barred window at the platform and the people trotting with their bags.

"Goodbye, Lahore," she whispered as if telling a secret, "You've been a kind friend."

***

CHAPTER FIVE

I was fading into an undiscovered, wondrous blue sea. The bare trees paled and reduced into smudged grey blobs. The moon disappeared. Stars dwindled away. The world lapsed into nothingness as my tiny body sunk deeper and deeper, as though being pulled by an invisible force. My arms were swollen. My legs lost all their strength as the current washed over me. My heart did not beat.

This was the first time I dreamt of water.

Funny, I didn't remember sleeping at all; maybe it was the journey or maybe *daddi's* recurring fairytales. Anxious and frustrated, I woke up in her cushion arms. She had been fanning me with an old newspaper. Beads of sweet on my forehead. Heart racing. I was terrified.

Gulshan lay next to me, half-awake, muttering, "God have mercy on us all. Allah have mercy on us all."

The cold sunlight peered through the unclean glass window in the bedroom, creating a spectacle of dancing diamonds in the atmosphere.

"You look so lost and confused," Gulshan, *daddi's* blind sister, interrupted.

I sat straight on the bed, confused, scanning her marble skin and trembling lips. She raised her unplucked eyebrows, painted orange from the *henna*, and let out a cackle. *Daddi* woke up with a yank and her hands started working devotedly on the paper fan.

"I *can* see you. My third eye still works," Gulshan informed, "I'm Durga…Durga. Don't you see? I am Durga."

The three-eyed Hindu deity scampered about in my head. I gave her a nervous stare, imagining a third eye on her wrinkled white forehead. Without an indication she hugged me and lowered her lips to kiss my head.

"My child!" she released me, "You've come to rescue us, haven't you? Only you can save us from this loneliness and darkness."

"She's only here for two weeks," my *daddi* stroked my hair, "Oh, I'll make her stay for a long time."

The old women grinned as they shared a secret. I sat between them, holding Gulshan's soft hand and discussing the weather, old songs and stories about her childhood for a long time.

I didn't know much about her then. I had seen her for the first time only at Grandfather's funeral. She told the mourners that she had no home because she never married. Some relatives gave a room to stay. Her sister's widowhood was a blessing in disguise. She needed a new home and her sister, company.

"Ah, Hamida left the water tank running!" Gulshan said, hearing the sound of water flowing before any of us did.

"She did! She did!" my grandmother got to her feet, "Now where are my *chappals*?"

We went out of the bedroom to look at the spectacle. Like a glistening screen, a small waterfall cascaded from the lips of the water tank. *Daddi* rejected my help and went into the kitchen to find a plastic bucket.

"Would you like to take a bath? The water is very clean," she proposed as she looked at the excessive water in the bucket.

I craned my neck to look inside the bucket.

Small waves. Small, thunderous waves that could smother me. I remembered the funeral, the water, the buckets. I shuddered.

"No, thank you. I feel clean, *daddijan*."

"Do me a favour then, shower this water on the plants," her tone became mellow and she tried to lift it, "Go, pour this in the *haveli*."

"*Haveli*?"

She nodded and disappeared inside. I dragged the bucket to the backyard, leaving a messy trail of water on the ground.

Things were different when my grandparents were young; things breathed and walked differently on the surface of the village. The *haveli* was alive. There were many farm animals – two buffaloes, a couple of hens and an aggravated grey-black busy donkey.

Eid in the village was a treat; the aroma of the delectable *biryani*, at that time, my mother's, and now Anika's specialty, *Sheer Khurma* and my grandmother's *gajrela*. Erratic hens cackled and scurried around the kitchen, a thousand little hands trying to grab their firm bodies. The men of the house lounged in the *veranda* for long hours engaged in serious discussions of business and politics, oranges in their hands, the smell of citrus in the air, and their faces looking away from the piercing sun.

But now, my blue shoes stepped on a virgin land. The place held nothing but dry wind and mud. What plants was Grandmother referring to? Three unattractive trees and some brown shrubs? Nevertheless, obediently I dragged the bucket to the various assigned spots and fed the half-dead vegetation.

My eyes met a box-shaped room at the end of the courtyard. It conjured images from the past – *dadda* had it specifically designed for his friends during Eid. As I pushed open the door, the concentrated smell of cement and his *hookah* kissed me. To my disbelief, the black and white photographs from his college days, which hung in misshapen large silver frames on every wall, had been removed and all the room contained now were some old chairs and a table to cater to the spirits.

"This is very wrong," I said in a mocking tone, lecturing his invisible wife. She had always believed some suspicious developments took place behind these doors, constantly asking Hamida to inspect, "Take them some fresh juice and see what they are talking about."

Hamida would often return with nothing interesting to offer, "They are discussing politics and some war or the other…"

Sliding my hand on the low cement shelf, I drew ambiguous patterns with my dust-laden finger, just the way I had seen Grandfather draw in the thin smoke exhaled from his *hookah*.

"*Daddajan?*" I whispered hesitantly.

Dead silence.

"*Daddajan, daddajan, daddajan.*"

Everything remained still.

"*Dadda!*"

Finally, there was an answer. But it wasn't something I was expecting because it wasn't from him.

"*Om bhur bhuva swah…tat savitur varenyam*"

Somebody was chanting softly. Somebody not very far away.

My body gained motion. I quietly crept out of the room, finding an opportunity to implement my detective skills. It was heard again. It wasn't an ordinary whisper. It sounded like a prayer or a chant…a beautiful, reverential chant.

Upon discovering that the voice came from the house next door, I attached my ear to the wall. It grew louder. It was a woman. I wanted to look at her.

I found an old ladder lying on the ground. I climbed up the roof of *dadda's* guest room and crawled slowly. I could see her veranda but not her face. I crawled further and realised that her rooftop was indeed very close to ours. I could easily jump on it and get an aerial view.

This is one of the things I always remembered about my grandparents' village – one could easily make connections. There were fewer secrets. People seldom closed their doors and the rooftops were all connected. Everyone knew each other's name and life story. Anyone could run across anyone's vegetable patch and pluck apples from anyone's orchard.

"*Om bhur bhuva swah...*" the chant began again. The verse finished and I heard her walking about the *veranda*.

Permitting my ghoulish curiosity and burdening intuition to seize my body, I took off my sneakers to climb the roof. A shadow coughed and started humming an unfamiliar tune. Like a ghost, I hid from the singer's view.

"Oh, where did you go, oh lover
The earth still spins and I am here alone
Oh lover, have a heart!"

I coughed accidently and then pursed my lips hard after realising.

"Who's there?" questioned the authority.

Leaves crunched beneath my feet, she gasped and I mumbled a curse. Now slightly aggressive about this sudden uncalled intrusion, the singing woman attempted to attach a ladder to her roof to investigate herself.

Brave woman, I thought.

I could hear her climbing. I panicked and calculated the distance from her roof to mine.

"No, no, no!" I crawled in reverse.

What excuse can I pen down in my head? I was cleaning your roof? I was flying a kite? I misplaced my book? Surely, she sounded like a gracious woman who wouldn't grumble and threaten to notify *daddi* but it had hardly been four hours since I arrived in the village. I wasn't going to be making the most ideal impression.

"Please be merciful, please be merciful," I whispered prayers.

As I continued to crawl back, I bumped into something hard.

"It's no one but me, mother," said the object I had crashed into. I turned around, bewildered, alarmed, only to find a boy dressed in a blue school uniform towering over me. He didn't seem old, eleven or twelve maybe, with kind dark eyes and a round chubby face.

"Oho!" the woman laughed, "You could have spoken. Now come down, lunch waits. There's nothing worse than cholera or cold food."

After making sure that his mother had left, I stood up and hastily brushed dirt and leaves off my sweater. He folded his arms and raised his eyebrows, waiting for an explanation or perhaps an apology. I faked a nervous smile and made for the ladder.

What could I possibly offer as a reply? That I was mesmerised by your mother's voice? What was she chanting? What was the song? Who are you people?

I realised I didn't owe him any clarification while climbing down but still, he looked at me with a certain eagerness. I jumped to the ground.

"Hello, madam?"

I wore my shoes, ignoring him completely.

"I am Karan."

"Mariam," I said timidly and dashed out of the *haveli*.

"You forgot your bucket!" he called.

I ran away then, but we met days later.

Karan became my first friend after Anika and Grandfather.

***

CHAPTER SIX

In the mornings, they lounged under the sun in the *veranda* on polished *divans* next to Grandfather's *hookah*. *Daddi* tried to fix her old tape recorder and her blind sister stared blankly at the green plants. Sometimes, she counted her steps and watered them and sometimes she showed me ladybirds she caught on her fingertips. She would let the coloured insect crawl on her yellow fingernails and then by connecting her fingertips with mine, she would let it roam freely on my palm.

"Come on," she whispered, "speak to it."

Winter brings home its own stories and misery. Because of its open fields and houses, people froze easily in *daddijan's* village. All the lambs and cows were relocated to well-built rooms with low fire and food, and the houses would smell of fresh manure and ashes. During the afternoon, the men disappeared to work and the women came out of the houses with children on their backs and loose veils over their heads to sit in the sunshine and watch the trains ramble down the foreign rail lines.

The porters in their orange uniforms would appear like little dots of fire; squatting, smoking, roaring with laughter as they waited for the train to slowly arrive. Women, some dull, some bright, looked out of the barred windows at the dancing dots of fire and the men stood at the door of the train with their duffle bags over their shoulders. Excitement would trickle down the faces of children. It was the most majestic thing they had ever seen.

The water remained calm during the winters and the farmers seemed less angry. Scarecrows remained perched in the soil with an insensitive expectancy. Crows and sparrows sat on their shoulders and pecked at hollow heads.

Hamida said that the real activity happened where the men worked, far away from the railway station and the houses, in a huge biscuit factory with blue windows and a steel head. They gathered around the *angithi* with their deck of cards, behind which were the pictures of Bollywood actresses of the eighties in flattering poses. Their faces were uncanny and bitter as tension built in the game. Some went home lucky and the rest waited for another episode of drawing cards.

When the night came crashing down, the village folded instantly. The villagers slept. The insects cried. Toads conspired. The strays wailed. On one such night, *daddi* caressed my head to make me fall asleep. Her face was bathed in a golden light and it dazzled like an open flower. Her eyes burned with delight and happiness. Her hand was soft and her thin silver hair was tied back in a braid. She traced the moon with her hands and then pretended to have possessed it in the centre of her palm.

She brought the imaginary shape closer to my sleeping face and whispered, "Don't wake up, my darling. You're in dream world, where reality is metamorphosed and you're away from everything that is discomforting. Don't wake up yet."

Her glass bangles made a soft sound. I held her delicate hand and closed my eyes as the lovely night fell over me like a curtain.

"I hate my dreams, I'm sick of them," I heard her say, "But you, my child, have so much to see, so much to understand in life."

In that moment, I realised that inside me was a power that could take away her pain, an element that soothed her aching heart and I was afraid that if I went away, my power would fade away with it and her heart would stop beating. So when Father said that he couldn't pick me for another two weeks because of work, I did not mind.

***

Gulshan called me to her room one afternoon. I rubbed moisturiser on her back and noticed that her body was burnt. I traced my finger over the skin as if over a map but didn't have the courage to question her about the history of the bruise.

While wiping off spilled tea from the body of what my grandmother called, "dandy British tea cups", I explained to *daddi* what I had witnessed. She looked around and lowered her tone as if about to unravel some dirty secret.

"She was a bad child, a rebel, like you call it. She has done some terrible incomprehensible things in her past. That burn is from when our father hit her once. She fell into a tub of burning hot water."

I trembled as the episode flickered before my dark eyes.

"Why do you think she lost her eyesight? Do you believe in *karma*? The doctors couldn't tell how she lost her vision."

I turned around so she couldn't see the altering expressions on my face, and began wiping the tea stains from the counter.

"That's what God does if you meddle in his affairs. That's what He always does, and then He makes the entire family pay for it. One bad seed ruins the entire crop. Why else do you think I was married so late? God and His funny ways of vengeance," she shook her head as she compartmentalised the divine.

She didn't just stop there. She continued and told me that how my life would gradually change, too, and I might experience tremendous amount of pain, whether I liked it or not.

"*Chai* stains on the bed, puddles on the carpet, dirt on the wall, such things are transient. What is real is the inevitable pain every woman experiences in her life. By that I don't mean childbirth. Other kinds of pain, a heartbreak, death of a lover, infidelity, losing a child to various things, death…this world…a woman is built to endure great pains. But don't worry, a real woman never gives up…"

And then she left it, just like that, and continued to work in the kitchen.

That reminded me of what Grandfather once said.

"Pain transcends through an invisible crack in your body and slithers inside you. It travels in your vessels, befriends every organ and leaves a great impression as a souvenir. A shaped scar, a burning bruise, or a deep wound. This souvenir is a constant reminder of the excruciating past. The brutal wound throbs and it reminds you that the pain has not yet set you free. The tattoo still burns. The tattoo always burns. It leaves you only with two options," he had said to me, "Either restoring yourself or unravelling altogether. If you are able to restore yourself, the tattoo eventually fades away, leaving only a faint imprint, which too later dissolves."

I had only listened to him quietly. The same way I now listened to my grandmother.

Later that night, we all sat together in *daddi's* warm bedroom. Placing my head on my knee, I watched Gulshan sip tea in the ceramic saucer and pictured her falling slowly into a tub of hot water.

How young was she? How much did it hurt? Would my father ever do that?

She wiped her face with the sleeve of her sweater and slid under the blanket, concealing herself from the world. Then the sisters huddled together and talked about things that would remain opaque to me.

It was eleven at night. I poked the remaining dim embers with a stick and imagined a striking ranting tiger breeding behind the demonic flames, ready to wake up and engulf us all. After a while the fire died completely and there remained nothing but a blanket of black silk. I heaved a sigh, longing for a new diversion.

Lying back on the carpet, I sung to myself,
"Oh, where did you go, oh lover
The earth still spins and I am here alone
Oh lover, have a heart…"

"Sshh! There it was again!"

"What?" I sat up straight.

Daddi lightly removed the quilt from her legs and rose. Gulshan kept a hand under her chin and tried to listen to something.

"The sound, did you hear the sound?"

"Sound of what, *daddi*?"

Her frail hand only gestured towards my grandfather's cane, which leaned against the wall. A burglar perhaps, but we were in no shape to wrestle them. I wore my slippers and crept behind her, not sure what we were questing for.

"You go and see what it is," she pushed me out of the door, handing me the weapon, the thin cane, "Go, you will hear it too."

"But what is it?"

"You will know, Mariam! Now go, before Gulshan has a panic attack."

So I did.

Leaving the children behind, I walked along the long, poorly lit corridor. The idea of being visited by a spirit didn't seem gripping or adventurous anymore. The door creaked as *daddi* closed it and began pacifying her sister. My clasp tightened, as I stood alone in the deserted place.

"Go ahead and make your escape, Mariam," I said to myself, "Tell them it's a stray cat."

I slowly turned around and tip toed back but then I heard it.
I heard a man cough and it rattled every bone in my body.

***

CHAPTER SEVEN

Her fingertips were stained orange from the *henna* she applied into their white hair and eyebrows. Winking at me, Hamida chewed on sweet *paan* and hummed an old tune. *Daddi* stretched her legs and pretended to read a digest as she got her scalp massaged with mustard oil. Gulshan dipped a finger in some *henna* and tried to make a design on her palm. Blinking her eyes she asked me to study what she had drawn.

"You drew a circle and I think you tried to make fire around it."

"Silly girl! Those are flower petals."

Daddi bent over to look at the piece of art. She said she was impressed. Hamida asked if I was interested in staining my hair red-orange, I shook my head and giggled. Pushing the *henna* powder tray towards me so I might change my mind, she started narrating its benefits, telling me to smell the green powder. It smelt of fresh cut grass, stimulating indeed, but still I couldn't risk colouring my raven black hair.

"Didn't you like it?" she tsk-tsked, "Oho, Mariam *bibi*, I will bring black *henna* for you. It makes you hair so glossy and powerful."

That's what she said. Powerful. I snickered and hid my hair under a shawl.

"During my times, we used *lassi*," *daddi* said again, "Don't you remember, Gulshan?"

"Ah, yes the *lassi* treatment," she smiled, still worked on the design.

Placing a hand on my forehead, I tried to dodge the bright sunrays. I looked at Hamida's long dark shadow and smiled. It reminded me of the night before and the shadow in the corridor that had made my heart stop.

***

As the sound of the cough echoed in the long passageway, a strange feeling took over me. It was a certain delight and fear. With an unsteady grip on the cane, I imagined myself trying to hit a spirit on its invisible head. But if it was Grandfather's spirit lurking in the shadows, I didn't wish to startle it.

"Spirits and ghosts might be invincible but I am not afraid," I whispered to myself.

A yellow blob appeared in the other end of the corridor. Taking a sudden step backward, I wondered if it was still too late to run back and fall into *daddi's* arms.

"Wh-who...is it?" I asked, assembling some courage.

The blob refused to cooperate and instead transitioned into a brilliant flicker that now gave birth to an oblique shadow on the wall. I knew my grandfather and this wasn't his shadow, but the chances that a burglar might jump from the terrace and strangle us to death were plenty.

"Don't move," there was a husky whisper, but I did. Stumbling, I tried to run back towards the bedroom, dropping the cane somewhere during my grand escape. But before I could open the door, there was a recognisable laughter from the shadow.

"Calm down, it's me," with this the figure brought a light close to its face.

It was Karan, the neighbour's boy.

"What in God's name were you thinking?" I screamed, unleashing the fury that somersaulted in the pits of my stomach, "There are two old women petrified to death. How often do you sneak into people's houses at night? Shadows on the walls, a man's cough…now tell me you light cigars on the roof to frighten the poor old women?"

"No, in fact this is the very first time I have come," he said with great confidence.

"Why are you even here? And this better be good," I folded my arms in the dark. He kept the candle on the ground and his face finally appeared a little less ghastly. Taking a step forward, he said the most unexpected words.

"I was just here to see you."

My heart skipped a beat. I took a step backward and looked into the eyes of the stranger. He stood, expressionless.

"Whaa…" I began and then saw him sniggering again.

"I am just here to request your grandmother to seal the roof door."

"I…I don't buy a word," I stammered, failing to recover from the intensity of the joke.

"Oh, come on Mariam, have a heart. Go ask her, I am bound to perform this task every night, from house to house. I get tipped sometimes." He continued, "I am like a protector of this village. Tonight, I happened to notice that your grandmother has forgotten to fasten the door. So that's why I have come."

He explained slowly, with great gaps between his words as if I could not hear him the first time.

"Up, up!"

I hurried towards the stairs and he followed me submissively, "I'll lock it for her. Just leave from the roof."

He showed a victory sign and turned his back to leave.

"Don't get scared on the way back," I joked.

"At least shadows on the wall don't terrify me," he mocked,

smiling broadly and looking back. I stared into his eyes, two endless pits of darkness.

"Just leave," I whispered.

He pretended to cry but I did reveal my amusement.

"Good night, city girl. Get used to the shadows, for this village has many."

I didn't understand what he meant and bolted the door. I walked back with an uneasy grin on my face.

I didn't tell *daddi* that it was Karan. More than familiar with her hysterical nature, I thought I would protect the stranger. I returned with my heart furiously beating.

"I came back from the roof, checked every nook and crack, there is absolutely no one. You had left the door on the roof open, *daddi*."

With that, I killed the lights; the sisters didn't stop whispering throughout the night.

***

Still swimming in my thoughts from last night, I looked around the open courtyard. The *henna* was left on to dry for the day and the sisters were left lounging under the bright sunshine. I followed Hamida into the kitchen. With her slender fingers bedecked with odd cheap rings, she tried to untangle her dishevelled hair. Sitting on a low stool, I waited as she took out a small steel saucepan from the closet and began to boil some water for tea.

She gave me a glass of warm milk.

A cat glided silently from the roof into the *veranda* where the old women lay on the *charpoy*. Its amber–coloured eyes reduced to slits. Jumping over *daddi's* outstretched legs, it found itself a comfortable cushion on a chair and curled up.

"What are you hiding, Mariam *baji*? What are you not telling me? I love secrets. Everybody around here tells me their secrets," she danced her thin eyebrows. How did she do that?

"What would I hide?" I said, watching the stray drown into slumber.

"Poor soul, expects her husband would fly back to her anytime soon," she blew off a matchstick and brought it to her purple lips, pretending it was a cigarette and she was a heroine from a bold Bollywood film. I followed her gaze; she was talking about Gulshan, who sat soaking up the sun.

"What's her story?" I asked.

"Every day is a new chapter for this never-ending novel. It's like a journey she experiences every day, lives and relives her past," she sat next to me and whispered. "Her husband left her for another woman, someone much younger than she. The separation was final. She wanted to stay with him anyway, but fate sketched a different plan. The night she had to leave and make space for the new bride at their home, she cut his chest open…"

Milk sprouted from my mouth and nose, "She…what?"

Fuzzy images of the possible grotesque murder were unconceivable. She got up as if oblivious of my existence, casually lifted the waste basket and walked gracelessly out of the kitchen. I remained tangled in a web.

"She just ripped his chest like it was a piece of cloth…"

"What happened later?" following her out of the house, I asked in desperation.

"What do you think happened, Mariam *baji*?" she sat down and emptied the trash bin into an open sewer, "The poor man painted his bed red. The next morning, everyone found her soaked in blood, sitting in a corner of the room, away from her husband's body. She was hysterical."

"Who found her?"

"On not hearing from her bridegroom, the bride called his family. Brutal, brutal scene. They took her away, to those women centres in large cities for some treatment-*sheatment*. She faced prison too, for a year maybe. Only a year because they had connections."

"This can't be true," I said, finding it hard to believe all this new information.

"I told you what I know, child. Never asked you to believe it."

"Is this why her body is burnt? Did her father hit her because of it?"

A strange domineering smile was her only response. How could I not have believed it?

I maintained my distance when lunch was served, but almost fell from my stool when Gulshan picked a knife to split her meatball in half.

"Don't you think you should help her? I mean, with the knife and all," I whispered to *daddi*, who helped me shred my food.

"Nonsense. She is good with knives."

"Good with knives?" I could barely swallow now, "What do you mean, good with knives?"

"Yes, she just can't see, doesn't mean that she is paralysed."

When I met Karan again, it was on the rooftop. I told him about Gulshan. He roared with laughter.

"Hamida tells tales; don't tell me you believed her."

"But I saw her body…it was burned."

"I still don't believe in the murder story. Either you're very stupid or plain bored."

I looked at him angrily.

"Come on, living with two old women, it's not the best thing in the world."

"Thank you for worrying so much," I said mockingly, "I must tell you, I'm having a lot of fun."

"Oh, really? For how long do you intend to stay?"

"Why do you care?"

"Did your father forget to pick you from this mad house?"

I punched him in his stomach and he pretended to cry.

"I feel sad for Gulshan. Guess we will never find out if it's true or not."

"Well, there's one way to find out," he said, "Let's ask your grandfather."

"Who?'

He got up quickly and went towards the ladder.

"Meet me here tomorrow evening."

***

I watched the world from the roof, evaluating the indecisive outline of the secluded clouds. The sun started drowning and he still hadn't come. Fear digested me and I felt as if I were about to engage in some obscene venture. With the sudden sound of someone adjusting the ladder, I sat up straight.

"Hello, hello," Karan climbed on our roof with a piece of cardboard.

"What took you so long? Do you see that?" I pointed at the space where the sun was supposed to be, now the sky was shaded crimson with a tinge of purple and blue

"Oh, did you get scared?" he patted my head as if calming a scared child.

"Not scared, annoyed. My *daddi* would notice my absence any minute now."

"Don't be mad," he spread the board in-between us, "Behold and be overwhelmed, for I present to you my very precious *Ouija* board."

"Your…what?"

Before us lay a flat board painted with alphabets from A-Z, numbers from 0-9 and three basic words, 'Yes', 'No' and 'Goodbye'.

"This board is an answer to all your prayers. It's almost dark and the perfect time."

"Perfect time for what?"

"You know, when birds and other creatures leave for their abodes during sunset, the spirits hover around the sky. It is not safe for a beautiful young girl like you to be out during this time."

I could tell he wanted a reaction but I pretended to remain cool and collected.

"You don't really think this board can help us awaken the sprits, do you, Karan?" I asked half-mocking, half-scared.

He nodded vigorously, his eyes twinkling.

"Now, before we begin…wait, did you bring his shawl?"

"I couldn't get my hands on the shawl, would his pen do?"

"Wow, an army pen, your grandfather had class," he examined the nib of the twenty-year-old ink pen with great zeal. "So before we begin, I think you should be familiar with the rules. For beginners, we have to be very serious, no joking around with the spirits because that can lure potentially treacherous, negative energies…or evil spirits and things…"

"Are there evil spirits?"

"Oh yes, there are more negative spirits floating above you than you can imagine."

"What else?"

"Ever heard of a poltergeist?" he continued, assuming I didn't know the answer. "It's a mischievous loud entity, which manifests itself by wandering around humans and influencing objects. That would explain all the racket and bumps that your grandmother hears at night."

"No, my sister Anika says it's all in their head. It cannot be true. I've been here for more than two weeks, I never witnessed anything peculiar."

The thought of Grandfather's spirit performing mischievous deeds, scampering about trying to frighten the chickens and goats of the village, seemed preposterous. His spirit, despite transcending from the physical world, had to be pensive and profound like he was. I couldn't imagine it floating noisily in the empty corridors or outside in the open fields.

"We will see about that. Now, your mind must be absolutely clear. No negative thoughts lingering around; imagine we are in a vacuum and nothing evil can touch us. Also, never question a spirit about how it died, or how you will die…"

"Why don't you ask all the questions?"

"Because it's your grandfather."

"And why do we need his pen?"

"I just thought that we should keep something that belongs to your grandfather if we wish to make contact with him and no one else. It makes most sense, no? So…are you in?"

"Yes, I am in."

"Now sit up straight and focus." He fished out a small white candle from his pocket and lit it with a cheap lighter. I had no idea why we needed the flame but seeing as I had already exhausted his mind and mine with queries, I remained less intrusive.

"This is scaring me, Karan. I hope it turns out well."

"Oh, you will remember this for the rest of your life."

And I did.

The brown board had all the alphabets. He asked me to place my finger in front of his on the upside down lid. Smiling at me, as if for the last time, he began the chant.

"With the permission of the mysterious elements, spirits, angels and Higher Self, we plead to be protected from all negative spirits, entities, energies and influences."

"Are there any spirits nearby that would like to speak to us?" he closed his eyes and gestured me to do the same. "We are curious and would like to communicate. Please assure us of your presence by moving this glass."

Five whole minutes later, the flame of the candle wavered giving us an accurate signal of the entity's attendance. We both took a long breath and accumulated queries in our heads.

"Are you here?' the glass moved.

"How can I trust it?"

"Just trust it. Now let's ask its name," he softly moved the object to the required alphabets while my finger rested to watch the show.

"If you are present, please move this pen. Can you move this pen?"

Transfixed, I stared at the silver pen, somehow hoping the visitor would not move it and I would find a reason to slap shut the board on Karan's serious face. But to our surprise, we both felt as if the pen changed its position a little. Maybe we were seeing things but all I remember is that we felt the pen move.

"Very good…" Karan nodded and his eyes widened like a little child's in a candy store. "Is this your pen?"

I dreaded the answer. Why was I even part of this activity?

The glass, which had now transitioned into an automobile, took us towards "no".

I finally breathed.

"Seems like it's not what we are looking for, please ask it to leave. There is no spirit hovering around in this place, not my grandfather's spirit anyway."

"No, wait, but there is still a spirit…did you live here?" he deliberately moved the glass to the required alphabets again. The spirit said it did. Karan and I exchanged glances.

"How can that be true?" I said with a slight tremor in my voice. "This is ridiculous." I was scared to death, scared that it might be Gulshan's murdered husband, scared that the story might be true.

"Aren't you curious? Don't do that. This will infuriate the spirit."

"Yeah, it would. If there is one to begin with."

This pinched every vein in his body. Without another word, he bade the spirit farewell and folded the board furiously.

"It wasn't me, if that's what you'd like me to say out loud," he said more sharply than he had intended.

"I didn't say it was."

He lowered his eyes and tried to calm himself.

I noticed the bruise on his forehead, I had seen it before but it seemed more conspicuous now, for some reason.

"What happened to your forehead…?"

"I will meet you tomorrow, or whenever you like," ignoring the question, he left me on the roof with ten thousand spirits suspended above my head.

I felt hurt and alone.

***

CHAPTER EIGHT

The next morning we became friends again.

We watched water shoot out of the pipe and fall onto the ground with an incredible force. He released the handle and brought his cupped hands near the source and filled it with the liquid. He threw water on his face. Once. Twice.

"Do you know why your grandfather made this water pump?" he asked as he rubbed the front of his *kameez* over his face to dry it.

Before I could think of an answer, he replied, "Because when he came home during the evenings, his shoes were filled with dirt, grass and mud."

I looked at the wet ground and then at his feet. He wore slippers.

"So he washed up here to avoid arguments with your grandmother. Else she would make him clean the floor."

"How do you know?" I asked, agitated to hear something new about my grandfather from a stranger.

"It makes you jealous, doesn't it? Knowing that perhaps your grandfather was my friend also," he stepped away from the pump. It stopped working and echoing. There were just faint sounds of birds discussing their morning rituals.

"Sometimes he helped me with my homework, right here in the backyard," he smiled and spread his arms, "And sometimes when he found me walking home from school, he offered me a ride of his bicycle and took me back home."

"Wrong!" I got up angrily, "My *dadda* never had a bicycle."

"You don't know anything, Mariam. You only believe in what you hear from people."

I remained silent. He took out a handkerchief from his pocket, wiped his face, then he looked at me and continued, "I didn't want to study, you know, I just wanted to play in the fields and swim in the tube wells all day long, but he told me that I have to."

He moved towards the ladder and then turned to face me again, "He said something like I know how alluring these fields and open space can be, but you must study and become someone. You must challenge yourself, read, and write, and discover….then come back and give something to this place."

Deftly, he climbed up the ladder and jumped on the roof of his house.

I remained still for a while imagining Grandfather, *my* grandfather, stroking Karan's hair with love, taking him for a bicycle ride around the village, sitting in the yard helping with his reading and telling him stories that were new, unheard of, and too complex to be understood by a boy like him.

I felt betrayed. It wasn't fair.

I couldn't share Grandfather with anyone, not even him. My sisters didn't care for him and neither did his wife. But Karan, he spoke of him with a similar devotion and fondness as I did, and it pained me.

From on top of the roof, Karan looked down at his courtyard and waved at somebody.

"Come!" he called out, prying me out of my thoughts, "My mother wants to meet my new friend."

The little three-room quarter had a strong aroma of burning

incense sticks. It was the same aroma that I often smelled in the graveyard. His mother, a radiant looking woman, wrapped a yellow shawl around her head and held the ladder from the lower end so I didn't fall. Next to her feet was a plastic watering can. She was much younger than *daddi* and far more serene.

"Mariam," she ushered me in warmly, "Come have lunch with us."

It was hot inside the kitchen. The sunlight streamed in through the metal bars of the window and touched our foreheads. I introduced myself. She smiled as I spoke, as if she already knew all about me through her son.

Then she told me about herself, beginning with her name. It was one I'd never heard of; a Hindu name, along with which came a whole new set of sounds and more importantly, a secret.

"Prakriti, but now it is Poonam," Karan's mother told me in her melodious voice.

"But now it is Poonam?" I asked in disbelief, "Is it that easy to change names?"

"If you're not happy with yours..."

"Why did you change your name?" I asked, oblivious to the fact that perhaps I was prying.

She lowered her eyes and her lips produced an uneasy smile, "Well, because I had to change who I was."

I watched her grab a ceramic plate from the shelf.

"But I failed. Changing names doesn't help you escape anything..."

"We will move to *Bharat* soon, you know," Karan interrupted, smiling at his mother, who pressed the *roti* with the corner of her *dupatta*.

Bharat. India. I had only seen it in Grandfather's old photo albums and remembered how much I liked it. In places, it looked similar to Lahore, but altogether different as well. I would imagine him walking through vibrant narrow alleys, wearing a purple turban. Sometimes I would picture a *tilak* on his forehead and sometimes he would be riding an elephant, also dressed in a sequined cloth.

"I was born and lived in Delhi before I came here."

"Why?" I asked as she put *saag-paneer* on my buttered *roti*.

"I got married here but *Bharat* is home. *Bharat* will always be home."

"So why are you here now?"

"I came here for my husband and his family. Dev wanted to live here because his grandparents were born here before the Partition. He always thought he had his roots here and this is where he belonged..."

"But now we are returning, aren't we, Mother?"

Her answer was an enchanting smile.

"Why?" I repeated.

"To immerse the ashes of my in-laws and husband in the waters of Ganga," Poonam said.

I looked at her, confused.

"We have come from dust and to dust we shall return," she whispered as if telling a secret. Knitting my brow together, I tried to remember where I'd heard those words before, why they were so familiar to me.

"Why can't you immerse them in the Ravi River?" I asked, referring to the main river that flowed past Lahore.

"Because it's not the Ganga, you idiot. The Ravi is not holy," Karan said quietly.

Later, he showed me three large collared urns draped in a cloth in the basement.

It was a strange reality; I had never seen human ashes before. I did not know that human beings were capable of being condensed into ashes. All the life, its joys, sorrows and experiences suppressed into a small container.

The process of transforming one's physical body into ash was something I had never heard of before; it puzzled me. A living fire ran through my body as I imagined being engulfed in flames. After the funeral, the twins had asked the *moulvi sahib* a rather disturbing question: if they dug Grandfather's grave after a year, what would they see?

He said they would see nothing, but bones. He never said anything about ashes. He never said human beings could also become ashes.

"Have you ever opened the jars and seen the ashes?" was my question to Karan.

"What's to see? We know what ashes look like...grey... fragmented...like silk or powder or smooth sand."

He turned his face entirely away from the urns and looked at me.

"My father's soul is restless. We must immerse these ashes but we can't."

"Why not?"

"It's difficult for us to go back home. This is my father's sixth winter in the basement," he took a deep breath. "No matter how we try, we can never be one of you. I will always be the filthy Hindu boy, and my mother, an untouchable widow."

But even as his eyes were bowed down because of the pain he believed he was causing his father, a faint echo of sinful joy lingered in his voice. His father was closer to him than we could imagine; he was right there, on the first shelf in the basement, in a cinerary urn with *swastika*, it was like he had never left them.

I envied him for a moment.

Why was my grandfather buried in a six feet deep grave while his rested right in front of our eyes?

"Did the board ever bring to you your father's spirit?" I asked.

A flame of delight lit up his face, "It takes two crazy believers to make the board work."

We sat down, withdrawn, in the room full of ashes, old

echoes and strange bliss. That day we realised that we had more in common than the unexplainable urge to communicate with ghosts and dead things. We both had lost someone important and we were too young to realise that that was not the end of things.

***

CHAPTER NINE

Rain made patterns on my red frock. The sky rumbled over our heads like an angry Greek God and the air felt heavy. I glanced towards the metal grey clouds and then at the girls who giggled as the savage lightning split the sky into two untidy halves. They whispered in each other's ears, laughed for a while and then ran towards me. I picked up the chalk and angrily scribbled on my slate. I thought about Karan and the ashes, about Prakriti and her family in India, about Grandfather and his bicycle.

"Mariam, let's go in the rain!" one of the little girls chirped near my ear.

"It's a storm," I replied, "and it is cold."

They were Hamida's daughters. *Daddi* called them most of the afternoons to entertain me when she had friends over. Her friends were old people with oddly-shaped faces. The women wore bright printed *shalwar-kameez* with lots of gold bangles. The men would always give me money before leaving.

"There you go," they would squeeze a twisted green note into my palm, "Buy yourself a doll, a pretty doll like yourself."

Daddi would then take the note away and keep it in her locker saying that she will give it back to me when I grow up.

The girls splashed water and laughed as raindrops fell on their brown skin. I curled up inside and watched them through the glass window. Somebody pulled my braid lightly. I turned around. Hamida stood there, grinning and holding an umbrella.

"I'm going to the tailors to pick up some clothes. Do you want to come?"

The tailor junction smelled of old cigarettes, fuel and cheap perfume. Before she married the wrong man, Hamida was a well-established dressmaker. She told me all her stories as if I were her age, as if I understood her.

"Sometimes loving a man is like loving a cat. You can never be loved back," she snickered as she brought a cigarette to her lips. "When I married him I knew he was like a cabbage, lots of layers. I was ready to unfold. Other than the constant curiosity, there was a prevalent fear that behind the veil of the last layer slept a monster ready to pounce on me. A monster I had hopelessly fallen in love with."

As we walked, she showed me where her shop used to be. A new group of tailors had taken over it now. They all knew her and greeted us as we walked in.

"Each stitch has a voice," she picked up the stitching hoop and needles from a shelf, "There was a time when I would not even use frame, ah, and now I can't see. I am old now and will soon die. I am like a shadow. We are all shadows. One moment we are like dancing shadows on the wall and then, someone turns on the lights."

Chewing hopelessly on a *paan*, the tailor snickered revealing his blood red mouth. Picking up a pair of steel scissors in his ash dry hands, he winked at me.

"When do we leave?" I fidgeted and pulled on Hamida's *dupatta*.

Coming back to reality, she instantly got involved in a senseless banter with the tailor. She threw the stitching hoop at his face and accused him of being a thief for not finishing her clothes on time. The young tailor, now looking like an angry beaver, took out a small blue diary.

"You gave me two weeks! A duration of two weeks, what day is it today?" he scowled, "*Chotay*, what day is it today?" *Chotay* was a twelve-year old boy, who was too engrossed in cutting a shirt, "Sir, Wednesday."

"It's Wednesday, Hamida *appa*, you come on Friday and the clothes will be ready."

"Liar, lying right to my face. I will come on Friday, be sure of that! Come on, Mariam *baji*, let's leave his station. Filthy dog, I have known him for years," she squeezed my hand, "He has always been like this. He was a little boy of five when I first held him in my arms. Stealing spoons from my kitchen, but I didn't mind, he was a child then. Not to mention all the times his mother came to my house to tell me about her husband's affair. She would repeat the same story over and over again, but I never grew tired. She just needed someone to listen. So much I have done for this family."

With a jerk, she let go of my arm and swirled her body to face me. Her eyebrows were knitted and beads of sweat decorated her upper lip.

"You tell me, *baji*. Do people change?" I nodded and then immediately shook my head no and then, nodded again. I couldn't decide the right answer. What answer could a nine-year-old give to that kind of question, anyway.

"No, they don't change, they just become better actors, always remember that."

We were suddenly welcomed by flying rocks and shoes. A huge mass of humans sprung from out nowhere, barefeet and angry. I stooped to prevent my head from being dislocated as the lunatic mob flew past us.

"Catch him!" screamed one of the men. There seemed to be

hundreds of them, anxious and aggressive. I caught a glimpse of a young boy in grey clothes running across a rooftop. The intense sunshine made it hard for me to identify him. He stooped and then reappeared.

"Karan! That's Karan!" I clapped to catch his attention, "Karan…Karan!"

He abruptly stopped and stood still for a while, as if recognising me and then jumped onto another low terrace.

"Oh, quiet! Shh, don't speak!" Hamida slapped my mouth shut and removed me from the sight of the preposterous mob. "Let's leave, Mariam *baji*."

She walked swiftly ahead with me trailing behind. I craned my neck and looked back at the empty rooftops and the narrow lane, where the angry mob of men continued to run after Karan, calling him a thief.

When we reached home, Hamida bolted the door behind us and holding my arm, led me to the kitchen. She looked around vigilantly and then kneeled to bring me closer, "Listen to me, *baji*. How do you know that boy?"

"How do I know which boy?"

"The boy on the rooftop, how do you know him?"

"I met him somewhere, I don't remember."

"Now that you have met him, I beg you, stay out of his way," she turned around and picked up a steel pan for Gulshan's porridge, "They are not the right sort of people."

"The right sort of people?"

"There's too much history here, so much that you would not understand…"

I looked at her with a blank face.

She sighed, nodding her head slowly.

"Just stay out of it, Mariam *baji*," she said in a harsh voice, "…and don't ever tell your *daddi*."

***

Hamida's plea frightened me.

I never mentioned the ashes, I never asked about the Ganga and I didn't see Karan for days.

The afternoons became painfully slow and dull. Gulshan and I spoke more than usual. *Daddi* took me to different houses and I sat on people's *charpoys* with my legs dangling in midair for hours. They spoke about wheat crops and other people's lives; all things I did not care for.

When Father finally came to pick me two weeks later than originally planned, he brought along Abdullah. *Daddi* held him in her arms as we walked through the fields towards Grandfather's tube well. He had never seen anything like it before.

I watched my little brother draw birds on my bedroom wall with chalk. He made small clouds around the sun and then decorated the sky with the letter V, that was his flock of birds.

"Don't ruin the walls, Abu," I said, "Grandfather will be angry."

He turned around as he heard me say a familiar name.

"Grandfather?"

"Yes, Grandfather," I said, "Don't you know he lives here?"

Shaking his head, he stared at me with his wide eyes.

"Haven't you ever seen Grandfather?"

He shook his head again.

"He has a white face and he eats little children. He floats around the corridors and just gobbles them up."

His lips and hands trembled and he dropped the chalk.

"Clean my wall before he comes. Hurry up!"

The four-year-old rubbed his hands frantically over the wall to remove all the stains. I rattled his shoulders and asked him to stop. He was scared but I knew he wouldn't cry.

Abdullah hardly cried. He was a strong little boy.

"Come on. Let me show you *my* Grandfather."

We tiptoed to *daddi's* bedroom. I opened her cupboard and took out an old photo frame from her drawer. The photograph inside was small and dark. I slipped it out.

Grandfather sat on a high chair with a baby in his arms. Behind him was a sugarcane field and in front of him, his *hookah*.

Abdullah leaned over and touched the baby's face and asked me if it was him.

"No, you silly. This is our uncle."

I pointed at the father of the child and said, "Isn't he beautiful?"

He nodded slightly.

***

Hamida took us to a garden and vegetable patch just outside the house. She lifted her purple *shalwar* and walked through rows of lettuce leaves and orange trees. She picked out the ripest lettuce head and tossed it to me. I sniffed it and scanned the patch. It was like a little green forest.

Abdullah squealed and clapped his hands as he pointed at a boy, closer to my age, flying a kite in an open field. I had never seen him before. The yellow kite flared in the soft sunshine.

"It's a blessing, isn't it?" Hamida caught my fixed gaze, "To find a friend in a very lonely place. But you should still keep your eyes open. Every breathing thing in the face of the earth is not capable of our love and friendship. Appearances can often be deceptive."

And that's when she unfolded the mystery.

Karan was the village thief and vandal. It all began a year ago when the neighbours started noticing how their possessions slowly went missing. First, the newspapers and mail started vanishing from their porch, then clothes and kitchen utensils. They blamed ghosts and other mystifying entities, when it suddenly occurred to them what use would a ghost or spirit have for a doormat. He was caught red-handed one night by the neighbour's child. She wailed till her father appeared and saw Karan trying to juggle two saucepans and a plastic cup.

"Now, you don't want to be associated with such a child, do

you? Askar Ameen's granddaughter dwelling on the rooftop with a mischievous Hindu boy…not a pretty picture, is it?"

I looked at her for a long time, badly hurt, and whispered a meek "no".

She bent down to pick up her basket and noticed a tiny dragon fly. "Come here, baby," she let out her hand to Abdullah. He followed her. They enjoyed the insect for a while, and then got distracted by a green parrot, which flew from one branch to another, luring them like the Pied Piper of Hamelin. Their figures became smaller and smaller as they walked away towards the house.

I picked up a withered pink rose fallen on the ground and touched its drying petals. It was the only imperfect thing in the otherwise perfect garden. I looked at it for a while and thought about my friend. A new discovery dawned on my mind – his reason for dwelling on rooftops at midnight when everybody was asleep. He was stealing from my grandfather's house! He had to be stealing, why *else* was he there?

This new realisation brought me sadness and I forgot about the flower.

My heart suddenly plunged.
My grandfather's pen.
He never returned the pen.
Summoning all my strength, I ran back to the house. For me, the pen was important, I had to take the pen back or else Grandfather's spirit would have never forgiven me.

I clambered up the ladder in the *haveli* and jumped down in his yard. I saw him, sitting on the stairs, looking unconsciously at the ground. His feet were bare and dirty and his hair dishevelled.

I stood before him and in a resonant voice that made me tremble, I cried out, "When you die, Karan, the Gods will be so angry. They wouldn't even know which hell to throw you in!"

"Mariam?" he said with his eyes wide open and his lips quivering visibly.

"What is it?' I asked, no longer angry. Something was wrong.
I could almost hear his heart beating wildly in his chest.

"Mariam, the ashes…they're gone."

***

CHAPTER TEN

Ashes everywhere.

Under the steel trunks. Below the sink. Up in the air. Around the burning light. Dispersed like particles of grey sand. Floating in the empty spaces of the heavy room.

The urns shattered on the ground, and shattered along with them were the deep secrets and history of a family. A large crowd descended the dim stairs, inquisitively watching Karan's mother who bowed down and mourned for her husband, whose dying wish she could not fulfill. She mourned because every past memory and its importance were gone. She mourned bitterly because she knew that no one else would mourn for him.

My friend, as if in a trance, sat down on his knees and gently collected the ashes in his hands. His fingers were powdered and grey. A pale stream of sunlight escaped from a window and illuminated a faded photograph. It hung by a loose nail on the yellow papery wall.

I recognised the blurry faces, all three of them.

The voices muttered something in wild confusion. They said

something about *karma* and Karan's rebellious behaviour. They said something about my *dadda* and Prakrati. They said things I did not know and would not have known, had I not been there in the basement that day.

Two hands held my shoulders forcefully and removed me from the scene. It was Hamida. Without my consent, she took me back home. She seized my wrists, exasperated by my actions and said a lot of menacing things, something about disobeying and disgracing my grandfather, something about his spirit trembling with anger and something about our family's honour and integrity. I dared not to speak, dared not to look into her darkened eyes.

It was sheer madness.

I felt upset and confused and angry, all at the same time.

Who could plot such a revenge for Karan's indiscretion? Who could be so mindless, inhuman, destructive? Who took away the only precious thing that they held onto?

I fought with myself for a while but there came the revulsion. I, choking with anger and grief, let out an ear-splitting scream and then began whimpering like a disturbed child.

This was my second memory of feeling pain.

All I saw was Karan's distressed face and the violent scene and all I heard was his mother's howling.

Startled by the outburst, Hamida released me from her grip and assured me she was just protecting me. Moreover, she understood the unexpected emotions that erupted from my heart after witnessing a friend's sorrow. I was a good human being, she said.

"I know you think that in my head I harbour nothing but hatred for them and you ask, who is Hamida to tell me who to love and who to not?" she promptly sat down on her knees and said with a little air of composure, "You might begin to think that I have a prejudice against them but all will eventually make sense to you. There are so many secrets, Mariam *baji,* but I can't be the secret keeper anymore…"

"I, I…saw the photograph…" I began slowly.

Her soul leapt.

"What photograph?"

"The old photograph of Prakrati and Karan…and *dadda,*" I said, barely muttering the words, "What does it mean? Why was he in that photo? Was *she* his lover?"

I couldn't really understand what I had seen or for that matter, what I was asking Hamida. I was just trying to understand the situation the way any nine-year-old would, by asking questions.

She turned away from me, clenching her face in her hands. Then suddenly she put her hands under my chin and lifted it up so I could face her.

"There's just a thin blurry line that separates the innocent world of children from the maddening world of adults. We always forget that. We, the adults, are responsible for this, for this confusion and mess. Mariam…" she said, "Child, don't believe every story you hear. People are judgmental and stonehearted. They don't always know what to say and when to say it. They don't who they hurt and how. What you just saw is only one part of the story. I don't want you to grow up hating your grandfather for all the things that you cannot understand right now. There is nobody in this world that can love you more than him. Keep reminding yourself of that. It *will* come to you, and slowly you will understand."

I remained silent, trying to make sense of what she was saying, and so did she.

After a moment, she mumbled something softly, as if against her better judgment, "She *was* his lover, yes," she said, "But it was nothing like they say…like the people say…trust me, I would know."

After that, we just drowned in our individual thoughts.

Neither did she explain any further and nor did I ask. She was just protecting me from the premature revelations, from questioning my grandparent's relationship and wondering about my grandfather's moral character. But this all meant nothing to me. The photograph was an unexpected blow, but it still didn't stir me as much as the fallen ashes did. To see a friend so badly hurt is what gave me pain.

"Won't you help them?" I asked, "Help them in picking up the ashes?"

She was silent for a few moments.

"I am sure they must have gotten it by now."

I bit my lip.

"Did Grandfather have a bicycle?"

"Yes," she answered, surprised by the sudden and strange question, "Did you ever ride on his bicycle?"

"No," I said, "but Karan did." She held back emotions and said after a great pause, "I know."

***

At night, Father, Abdullah, Hamida and I sat by a fire and watched its embers glow brilliantly against the darkness. Hamida told me that the mother and son immersed the ashes in a flowing river. They travelled on a *tonga* out of the village and no one knew when they would come back. I did not speak but listened to her intently. She told me that very soon I would forget about them and my heart will no longer break from pity and grief.

"I have learned the beauty of childhood now. Every trivial thing holds great significance. Mariam, you are sensitive and vulnerable to everything around you; you notice the changing leaves and all the colours in the rainbow. Every conversation leaves a brilliant imprint on your mind." Hamida held my hand and prayed that when I grew old I would grow a hard shell around myself, "I hope you are unbreakable, Mariam *baji*. I hope you remain strong."

Three days after this conversation, my *daddi* grew terribly ill. Gulshan told everyone that she would die in a day or two because in her dream she met *Munkar* and *Nakir*, the angels of the grave. In their hands they carried all the treasures from the heaven. I asked her what they looked like. She didn't answer but instead only told me what they smelled of.

"Their fragrance is that of roses."

Daddi spent her last week with Abdullah and me. She said that she could hear children laughing in the empty rooms and sometimes she saw an angel descending from paradise to take her with it. As the days wore on, she became paler and weaker. She was like an old photograph, fading, vanishing silently, as the days went by. Seeing her sit suspended on Grandfather's *charpoy* in a state of complete numbness was harder to endure than the terrible thought of her leaving us completely. When she could talk, she would tell us that had seen all that she wanted to see and did all that she wanted to do in her life; that the idea of death might not be easy to swallow but she had lived in fulfillment and regretted nothing.

We were told by the elders that God always heard the prayers of children and were asked to pray for nothing but her easy death. We were asked to beg for mercy and wish for her reunion with her husband in heaven. I deceived the elders by not believing. How could I have prayed for my grandmother's death? How could I have believed that the power in me was not enough to recuperate her?

As she continued to wither, a conscious part of me understood that if I did not plead, she would be in pain and if I did, it would bring me pain, so I decided to do nothing but wait. Wait for time to settle it itself.

But she died soon after. The house lost its colour. Gulshan sat in her bed for days, curled up like a cat in morning fog and Hamida stared out of the kitchen window in disbelief. It was a difficult time for her; she could not believe that she had lost a lifelong friend. For her, everything changed the moment my grandmother took her last breath and closed her eyes forever.

It was very different from when *dadda* died. I didn't really think he died at all. I never saw his body. They just pointed to a wet clump of mud and said that that was him, but *daddi, daddi...* she really died. Her body was wrapped in a white cloth and it lay in the living room for hours attracting mourners.

My mother and sisters travelled to the village once again.

The twins and I were asked to resume the usual practice of fetching water from the water pump. This time we didn't converse at all. We were badly shaken.

There were many unanswered questions. Why does one die? Where is heaven and hell? Does the spirit abandon the body as soon as a person dies? Do all children go to heaven? Is *dadda* waiting for his lover back in heaven? What will *daddi* do there alone?

Aminah picked up a long stick from the ground and pointed at the flying swallow in the open blue sky, "That is Grandmother's spirit," she declared, "Look at her kiss the clouds and escape all the madness."

Fatima and I watched the little bird scour the sky with its tiny wings.

"Look at her transcend into another realm while we're stuck here filling pitchers of water for her mourners."

"Aminah...don't," Fatima said, "Don't make jokes about the dead. We are all going to die someday."

"I know how I will," she replied and got to her feet, "I will die of swollen arms and back pain."

I picked up the fallen stick from the ground and started sketching on the damp earth. I drew drops of water and flying birds.

There was something utterly impersonal about those funerals. The children became invisible. Nobody cared for them. Nobody cared to answer their questions. Nobody told them about heaven, hell, the angels and the spirits. The children just watched the elders break down and pray for forgiveness, and in our case, they just recharged the mourners by feeding them *kebabs* and water.

"You know what, I'm too tired from all this," said the impulsive twin.

A dark flash ran over her face. She was furious. She bent to pick up a brick from the ground and stared at the pump, dramatically. She hit the handle wildly until it twisted and broke miraculously. Amazed at such strength and the strange kind of insanity, I moved backwards to maintain a safe distance.

"There," she said panting, "now no one gets thirsty."

Water sprouted out of the ground with a violent passion. My sisters remained still for a minute and then exited the *haveli* slowly.

The water splattered on the ground, fell on the backs of insects and on the dead bodies of plants. I stamped my foot lightly in the water and imagined two warm faces smiling up at me. I could hear their voices, like bells in a temple far away, laughing freely. I imagined them kneeling down beside a riverbed with large urns in their hands.

A film of dust flowed along the water, as if the ashes they had held onto for years had finally been released, particle by particle. Their spirits were now reuniting with the heavens and Gods.

We have come from dust and to dust we shall return.
Something about that made sense.

***

LAHORE 2007

CHAPTER ELEVEN

The passionate wind carried frail white dandelions and decorated them in my hair. I rode the bicycle onto a muddy track and escaped to a quieter place. The heavy gold sunlight fell warmly on Grandfather's fields. Riding towards the tube well, I got off and dipped my feet in the lustrous water. Taking a deep breath, I let it sink in; a feeling of familiarity enveloped my body. I had missed this sensation of sitting in living, breathing stillness.

From the tube well, you could not see, but only hear the railway station. In the afternoons, it was the busiest. People chattering, mounting and leaving. Porters watching, gossiping and laughing. And the train whistling and rumbling. The sound of the whistle took me back thirteen years.

After my *daddi's* funeral, the family had taken the train back home to Lahore. We had cleaned the house, washed the floors and bolted up the *haveli*. I had locked the door to the rooftop, Father the kitchen, the others made sure that all the bedrooms were clean and in order, and we convened in the main *veranda*. Gulshan was forced to move back into the house of another relative, much younger and less friendly.

Our lips were pursed and our minds, sombre. It must have

been the hardest for my father, but not once did his voice reveal any sense of sorrow or anguish.

He remained silent throughout the journey, revisiting the days when he rode his bicycle gleefully through the fields and the colourful *bazaar*. He had felt a certain comfort then in his childhood, knowing that at home his father would be lighting the fire in the living room and his mother would be putting down a bowl of steaming curry on the table. A comfort that he would never feel again.

It had dawned on me then that that moment of us sitting solemnly in the cabin of the train would never happen again. I would never be eight again and Father would never lose his parents again.

It is a sad reality to understand early that our lives are nothing but a series of fleeting moments, moments that will keep escaping if we do not preserve them in our memories. For memories cannot be stolen. They are ours and ours forever. By preserving Grandfather, his wife and Karan in my memory, I had learned to deceive time and nature. I had stolen them away from everyone and everything. Their memories were to remain mine always.

Hamida had come to the platform to say goodbye. She stood discreetly with a blue shawl around her body. Her eyes were low and wet and on her face was a thick layer of substantial sorrow.

I sat down quietly on the berth and looked out at the lonely figure through the window.

She waved.

I waved.

Both our minds tending to the same thought: it was over. So many things left unsaid, things that only she knew, things that she had heard over the years, things that she was entrusted with, things that she promised to tell me when I grew up.

We began moving. Outside the window, the green world continued to disappear, the faces kept changing and the mud houses became steel and rice factories. I could no longer feel the warm earth, I could no longer smell Grandfather's *hookah* and I could no longer hear Karan's voice in my mind.

Soon, the village was like a dwindling star; a terribly beautiful abstract dream that I prayed I would never forget.

***

After *daddi's* death and Hamida's absence, I finally told somebody about the fallen ashes and the Ganges, and that somebody was no one else but my eldest sister.

Looking into the distance, she said, "I read in a book that the river Ganges flows through heaven, earth and the underworld. If you scatter the ashes in it, the deceased goes straight to heaven. Now see, when Prakrati dies, Karan will do whatever he can to immerse her ashes in the holy water."

I asked her why we didn't cremate Grandfather, the joy of knowing that he would have been in heaven for sure seemed blissful.

She said all good people go to heaven, with or without cremation.

I asked her, "When Karan dies, who will scatter his ashes?"

She didn't reply.

***

As I sat in the fields now as a young woman of twenty-two, years after *daddi's* death, it dawned on me exactly how much time I had spent away from the village. Sadly, it didn't seem to matter, there was no one left to see there anyway and nothing to come back to.

But monsoon had arrived and the Raja's house always flooded. So, for the safety of the ancient furniture and ghosts, Father asked me to come with him to the village. He came every year. Sometimes alone and sometimes brought Abdullah along. This time he thought I should come.

Together, we wrapped every piece of furniture in plastic sheets and dragged it to the corner where we were sure the water couldn't reach. After the task was completed, he went out to the *haveli* where a few men had come to meet him and I went to the fields.

Although I never found out the real truth behind Gulshan's burns, or heard from my friend again, there was still a certain indescribable beauty in the memories of continuous mourning and early childhood losses. A child's world is confusing; he is constantly deceived, deceived about broken relationships, fallen relatives, family history, secrets. All deceptions perpetuated for the sake of keeping him safe, untainted, unharmed from the claws of the outside world.

I was an unusual child and grew into an unusual adult.

I could not let go of things.

There were times when I thought about what would have happened if I had stayed there in the basement, if I hadn't turned away with Hamida. What would have happened if I had asked Prakrati about Grandfather? What would she have told me? What would she have hidden from me?

I got on *dadda's* old bicycle again and rode through the streets. My green *kurta* fluttered as the wind blew with a great passion and force.

I rode by the tailor junction – it still smelled of cheap cigarettes. I rode by what used to be Hamida's house. New faces told me the same story – she hit her husband with a frying pan and took a *tonga* out of the village. She moved back to her mother's house in Multan and no one had heard from her since then. I chuckled and the new tenants looked at me a discomforted look. The idea of hitting a man with a frying pan could have aroused a serious debate if I had stayed for long. I drove by another house I remembered from my childhood – it was a shop now and was much smaller than I recalled. An old woman offered me biscuits, bleach, talcum powder and some free advice.

"If you're lost then take that road, it takes you straight to the city."

I asked her about a boy and his mother. She snickered and said that the village has been free of Hindu since years. It was no longer a filthy place, according to her.

I moved on, and after a while I was indeed lost. A new road unfolded and I decided to explore it. There, I found a certain peace. I rode further and stopped where the world finished, where the waters ended and where lives were different.

It was a graveyard.

It wasn't there when I was eight; I had never been there before. Behind its rusty fence lay countless marble tombstones, scattered carelessly in the ground, as if the dead underneath the beautifully carved Arabic epitaphs had now been forgotten with no one tend to their grave.

That was not how I wanted to be buried.

I didn't want a shrine or a mausoleum but I couldn't imagine lying in a crammed space with dozens of strangers. I wanted my privacy and freedom, even after I was dead. Closing my eyes, I whispered a small prayer for the departed, then turned away and rode back to my grandparents' house.

By the time I reached back, Father was outside, waiting. He had already locked the door.

"I believe you've already said goodbye to the house…or shall I say, to the entire village?"

"Is it hard for you to abandon the house you grew up, every year?" I asked.

"We have to leave some things behind so we can make room for more. Some memories have to be abandoned so that we can build some new ones."

"I think you undermine the capacity of the human mind," I said.

He laughed.

He looked at the bicycle for a moment and then said, "If you think about it, it's just a vacant building that smells of my father's *hookah* and my mother's perfume...but now if you *really* think about it there's no other building in the world that smells of my father's *hookah* and my mother's perfume."

We exchanged faint nervous smiles and then headed for the railway station.

***

Monsoon arrived.

The ceilings didn't leak and the rooms didn't flood but with the unsurprising rains came a series of rather surprising news. One morning Mother announced Anika's engagement to a complete stranger, and the next she confirmed the coming of some unwelcomed guests.

Anika sat on the swing in the *veranda* and stared at the black and white photo of her fiancé. A sober looking man was sitting on a wooden bench near a broken foundation. His head was tilted sideways and he rested it on his hand. His wavy hair were gelled and combed to one side. The pose was debatable – hard to tell whether he were experiencing a mild headache or composing a *gazal* in his head. Anika flipped the photograph upside down and looked at me, her mind distracted with other thoughts.

She was now twenty-five and resembled Mother; both in looks and ideas. She had black hair like Abdullah and I, and an oval face like Mother and the twins. She read books, lots of them, like I did, and we could sit together for hours in the library and not whisper anything. She could be very pleasant and warm and then become isolated and indifferent and in such moments, it was always hard to reach her. Her heart was hidden in a treasure chest. Not I, not anyone else could find the key.

She had studied Economics and as soon as she graduated, Mother began seeking suitors. We played host to many. A month ago, Father ran into an old friend and the old friend happened to have a son. Mother liked the young man instantly and remarked that if she were young and single, she would've given him a chance herself. I mean, what was there not to like? He was an Engineer, had a good family and our father knew his father. Ideal match, they claimed.

A tea party was planned in this eligible bachelor's honour.

"This doesn't feel like it's supposed to feel," said Anika as she lay flat on the swing.

I closed my book and looked at her body sway to and fro. She lay there like a dead body with her hand dangling in the air. In between her fingers was the picture.

"How is it supposed to feel?"

"You know…fairytale-ish."

"There's nothing fairytale-ish about arranged marriages."

"There could be," she said.

"Could be," I echoed without really meaning it.

"Now you see, Mother differs," she sat up, "She says if I let go of all the useless expectations from my head, I'll be happy. She asks me how can I possibly expect much from a stranger? I should take life as it comes. Let it surprise me. Let the strange surprise me."

"A stranger who will be your husband, and you must always expect something from a husband."

Her face fell.

"Look, Anika," I said, "It will only be fairytale-ish, as you so poetically put it, only if we try to make it fairytale-ish."

She passed a confused look and then evading the topic altogether, said, "Well, Mother says it'll be fine."

She lay back again.

It was true, Mother did say that. She also did a lot of other things like ask Anika to tie her hair in a neat braid and to wear lots of perfume when her in-laws arrived for tea. She asked her to walk very gently and to remain completely mum and mysterious. But most importantly, she very sternly asked the rest of us to remain on the rooftop where the sober man couldn't see us.

"Young men tend to go astray," Mother told me in a discreet tone, "*You* don't worry me. It's the twin's beauty that can cause Anika unwanted harm."

***

The day my sister's in-laws were arriving, we were assigned duties early in the morning. Abdullah and I were to fetch biscuits and *samosas* fifteen minutes before the guests were to come. Father was to clean the *veranda* and water the plants. Anika was to take a thorough bath, dress up well and make *halwa* and the twins were to take out the new china, arrange it on the table, and stay out of the way.

So when the family came, the twins and I remained on the roof with Abdullah peeping out from the balcony every now and then. The situation was awkward. The sober-faced man glanced around nervously, Anika fidgeted, the mothers couldn't stop chattering and the fathers sat on the edge of their seats.

I lay on a *charpoy* with my copy of *Wuthering Heights*. Abdullah sat fixing his kite with scotch-tape. He looked a lot like Grandfather did when he was his age, seventeen. I had seen his photograph in Father's brown leather diary and shown it to Abdullah – a tall lean boy with a dusky complexion and a mass of unruly black hair on his head. He had laughed and wished that he remembered at least something about him.

Now, he turned on the radio and the over enthusiastic local jockey played a classic. The singer was Nazia Hasan. The song was from an eighties hit movie, *Qurbani*. Aminah clapped her fair hands in delight and then held her *dupatta* in the air trying to imitate the legend, Zeenat Aman. Now all she needed was a shimmering red dress and a strikingly handsome man watching her lovingly from a distance.

The twins danced around Abdullah for a while, until turned he it off grumpily.

"No one wants to see you both dance," he grumbled.

The twins, whimsical, sharp and exuberant, dwelled in a world of freedom. They were completely spontaneous and beautiful. They could dance and chirp like birds all day long.

"Did you hear about the American aunt?" a voice brought me back to the rooftop.

It was Fatima. She threw a pebble on the ground and then hopped a few steps ahead.

"Which American aunt?" the question intrigued me.

"The one who never came back…"

I shook my head. She was referring to the unexpected monsoon guests.

"You miss out on all the great stories," cried one of them. "You know the one whose husband is Father's elder brother. He died eight years ago…" chimed the other.

"What about her?"

"She is coming to Lahore next week for a few months," Aminah slapped Fatima on her back, when she found out that she had cheated in hopscotch, "Surprise, surprise. I think she has children too."

"She does! She does! A son and a daughter," Fatima almost yelled.

"What does she want now?" I asked.

"Mother thinks she wants her part of the will. I mean, we heard that there are a few lands in the village that were given to her late husband, our uncle, so she is here to learn about them."

"Our uncle, the Artist?" I said.

A sly smile crept on the twin's faces.

The Artist, of course. He was the second most discussed relative after Grandfather. He had his fair share of apocryphal stories. The Artist was our late uncle; our father's brother who estranged himself from his family earlier in his life because of his new ways.

"Her children are growing up; the woman needs an assurance for their happy future," concluded Fatima.

"How do you know all this?" Aminah investigated.

"I overheard mother talking on the phone."

"Why is she coming again?" Abdullah and I asked together.

"She is coming to meet us, of course, her relatives and to learn about the will. I've heard she is bringing gifts!"

"There are many things in America!" Fatima spread her arms, "How far is America? How big is this America?"

Down on the balcony, I saw Anika standing timidly. Next to her was the same thin man with a sober face. He was talking to her in low voice and she was trying not to smile. Standing up, I tried to divert the twin's attention because if they found out the couple was alone, they would have intruded their privacy. .

"So about this aunt," I said, "What's her name?"

"Lubna. Come on, haven't you ever heard her name come up in conversations?"

"I don't eavesdrop like you do. I have developed other habits," I said and began reading again.

Aminah kept a hand on her waist and rolled her eyes, "Yes, like keeping things to yourself and walking endlessly through these halls like a ghost. If you may know, I just happen to have very sharp observation skills. Some would count that as a blessing."

Abdullah snickered.

"Hold my kite, Mariam," he said, "Don't let it go. Slowly release it only when I ask you to."

I concealed my face with the green kite and did as told.

"Isn't this a useless sport now?" Aminah said as the green kite spread itself against the vast white sky. It was an enchanting contrast.

"No, it is not," he said, a little defensive, "You have to learn to control the wind, see which way it blows and watch out for all the enemies that are out there to get you."

"Like I said, useless," she rolled her eyes.

"You both can go downstairs," he said coldly, "Here, Mariam, hold my kite again and don't let it go. I am counting on you."

***

CHAPTER TWELVE

Morning walks were just as crucial as the evening tea. Every day, Anika and I would walk to the nearest park and jog for an hour. There we discussed everything – the weather, politics, family politics, history, family history, religion, our hopes, dreams and secrets.

She wanted to teach at her college for a little while after graduating and I wanted to go abroad for my Masters. Anika wanted that for me, too. She wanted me to go to the west and study what I truly loved – literature and history. We would often joke about travelling to far off places and finding true love. She would say it as a joke and then forget about it, but it was no joke to me. I always bore in my heart a desire to discover new places and learn new things.

After her engagement, she wished to talk about only one subject – the sober-faced man. For a week, her face and her eyes gleamed from pleasure and her voice became soft and merry. Half conscious in the crisp early morning, I would sit on the marble bench and hear her talk about his hair and childhood, about the colour of his favourite shirt and the way he sipped tea, with utmost delicacy. They had met only once but he knew how to conquer her. She was completely smitten.

I think this fascination had little to do with the man himself but it pivoted around the very idea of love; falling in love and being loved in return. Which girl didn't desire that?

One morning, it was drizzling and we had just finished jogging. We sat on a cold marble bench under a tree. Now the subject had changed. She told me that the much-dreaded guests were arriving in two days. She meant our widowed aunt Lubna and her children. Since the announcement of their arrival, there was much anticipation around the household. Our relatives, or the wolves, like my *daddi* used to call them, began dropping by for tea and casually retold the story of a man who went astray and a woman who abandoned her country for vain ambitions.

"You know, a part of me is actually excited to see this aunt of ours," Anika chuckled, "I mean we have been hearing so many stories about her…"

She was right. Like all children, we did grow up listening to many stories. There were stories about kidnapped princesses, genie in lamps and lovers in distress. And then there were other kind of stories; stories about the lives of others – like my grandfather's infidelity and my uncle's possible suicide. Except that those stories were not really stories but gossip and what was this gossip, but just fragments of sad accounts, maneuvered and mutilated year after year for our sinful pleasure.

By listening patiently, I learned that gossiping was not adopted by the bored. Infact, it was an art of discourse adopted by those who had experienced absolutely nothing thrilling in their lives; they had never really fallen in love and eloped, had never explored a new city alone or casually spoken to a complete stranger, and they never dreamt of doing anything extraordinary. They were a dull group of people with dull lives and souls.

"They just found his body on the attic floor," one of my many curious aunts had said. "This is what a foreign land does to you. It makes you lose control."

The wolves never talked about what he painted, his subjects – none of them – nor did any one of them possess any piece of his work. They didn't know what he read, what music he enjoyed or what exactly made him lose control. He was just a shadow that kept shaping and reshaping in their mind.

If it weren't for my devotion to my grandfather or my curiosity towards my uncle, I would have left these stories the way they were, like Hamida wanted me to. But it pained me to hear mocking statements from the wolves about the people they never really knew.

How would these wolves remember *us*? What would they tell their grandchildren?

The drizzling stopped and we began walking back home.

"Sometimes I feel bad for the marginalised," I said.

Anika stopped walking and looked at me.

"What do you mean?"

"I mean, our grandfather, they say a lot of things about him."

A worried look went over her face.

"And why does it matter?" she placed her hands on her hips, "Why does any of this nonsense matter? Does it diminish your love for him?"

It did matter. But I did not say anything.

She turned her face entirely away from me, deep in thought.

"Look, Mariam," she turned around suddenly, "There will come a time when these people will forget about all this, I promise you. All they need is new gossip. One of us will have to screw up really quickly."

I burst into laughter and she brought me close to her face and kissed my forehead.

"You told me Hamida told you something very important

years ago," she whispered, "But remember…don't ever let anyone taint your love for *dadda*. Don't let anyone win."

A smile of relief came swiftly on my lips. She always knew how to bring me back.

***

It was raining heavily when our monsoon guests finally arrived. The white water bombshells landed from the open sky and into our dark eyes. Anika and I stood on the balcony with outstretched palms, trying to catch the raindrops. Mother sat inside with the twins, intensely looking out at the clouds. She had never liked Lubna and couldn't care less for her children. She openly questioned her motives and believed that after her husband's death, she should have returned to Pakistan and reunited with the family.

We heard a horse cry and then the sound of it dancing meekly on the gravel road. My father pushed open the gates of the house as the family made their grand appearance after twenty-four years. The brown animal snorted, came to a halt near Abdullah's feet and shook itself dry of all the rain. From under the covering of the *tonga*, emerged three people. Shielding themselves from the rain, they walked to the entrance of the house.

The woman was in her mid-forties. She slowly removed the *dupatta* from her head with elegance. Her children looked at the hosts reluctantly. One of them was a young man who looked a little older than I was, and the other was a girl, a little younger than Abdullah. They were not like everyone had described. They did not have horns on their heads or a sneer on their faces. The picture was better.

"You came on a *tonga*?" my brother asked excitedly.

"We wanted to come with style, so we hired a *desi* carriage," her son joked, "You know, it's her obsession with *tongas* or anything that's traditional."

Mother gave a low laugh.

The young man brushed away locks of brown hair from his tanned forehead and smiled at me.

His sister waved quietly and fidgeted uncomfortably with a small backpack.

The American aunt walked right towards me, touched my face with her long, slender fingers and kissed my forehead. She leaned in close and whispered, "Do you know whom, you resemble?"

"Muhammad Askar Ameen?"

She smiled faintly as she heard me say her late father-in-law's name.

"Muhammad Askar Ameen," she repeated.

It was going to be an interesting summer.

***

Chapter Thirteen

There is an old lady who lives on the moon. You can see her spinning thread on her spinning wheel. Her isolation and distance from the world has made her a sage. She weaves stories. She knows every wanderer who crosses the grass meadows, she knows every woman who uses her hands to grind grain in the hand mill, she is friends with the little girl who got lost in the corn fields and was never found, and she knows the story of the boy who played flute on the little hill when his lambs slept.

Grandmother always said that if I had been a good girl the moon lady would weave for me a magical blanket and every stitch will be made from a moment of my life, a forgotten moment, a memory. Every stitch would be special. It would be made especially for me.

I looked at the picture of a moon on the cover of a book and traced its boundary with my index finger. Outside, it poured. Lightening struck. The sky crackled. People panicked. I looked outside my window. It was like staring at an abyss.

It was a terrifying night.

In my mind Grandfather's house whirled in that menacing storm. The walls trembled and the floors shook. Troubling thoughts enveloped me instantly: what if there is a flood in the village? What if lightning falls on the Raja's house? What if the rooftop falls down?

"Oh, my God. What if the roof comes crashing down?" I wondered out loud.

My heart sank.

I looked back at the bed. Anika was in deep slumber. Next to her lay an open bridal magazine. I tiptoed to the dressing table and pulled out a drawer. Underneath a few things was a small diary where Anika and I scribbled all the important phone numbers.

Clutching it to my chest, I wore my slippers and crept out of the room. I climbed down the flight of stairs and glided through the corridor. I went to the *veranda* and sat on the swing. The yellow light from the bulb fell on the little pages of the diary. I went through all the numbers, praying that perhaps sometime in the past, I might have scribbled down a useful number of a resident who might still be living in the village.

No such luck. I rubbed my eyes.

Why did it matter to me? Why did that empty house matter to me? There was no Grandmother, or Gulshan, or Karan, so why did its safety matter to me?

I could produce no answer. With a deep sigh, I closed the diary shut. Laying on the swing, I listened to the raindrops as they fell on the trees, birdhouses, flower pots, steel pipes and other places the eye could not see. It was like an unsynchronised symphony.

"I have never seen such a wild storm in my life," said a voice.

I sat up, alarmed to see a figure at the other end of the corridor. I went over.

It was Rizwan. He sat with his head bowed and between his fingers was a half-smoked cigarette.

"So this is what monsoon feels like. It can be a little frightening, can it not?"

He lifted his head to look at me.

"Won't you sit for a little chat?"

"Well, I don't really have much to do right now," I said and sat next to him.

He looked at the diary between my hands and asked:

"Do you write?"

"Oh, no, no, I don't. Do you?"

"No, but I paint."

A small smile formed on my face.

"Yeah, you know, painting houses is always good money."

We laughed.

"No, I do not paint," he said slowly, "but my father did."

I folded up my knees to my chest and made myself comfortable, "Yes, I heard."

"You know…I did paint a house or two when I was nineteen. Now, I am twenty six, things change."

He gave a brief smile and looked at the dark clouds.

"Can I ask you a question?" I said.

"Of course."

"What did he paint? Your father, what did he paint?'

Tearing himself away from the clouds, he looked and me and laughed.

"Women, mostly," he nodded, "Goddesses, queens, empresses and horses. Women and horses of all kinds and shapes, in all moods and expressions. He painted his mother too, often."

For a while, we sat in silence.

"What about his father? Did he paint him too?"

"No, not really."

I nodded.

"He drew other things though. You should come to

Washington some day. A lot of his work is hanging around the house. Do you travel?"

"No. But I will someday."

"That's determination! I knew there was something different about you."

We exchanged smiles.

"My grandfather...I mean our grandfather...wanted me to travel around the world and study and explore and meet men."

He laughed, "Now that's a man I wanted to meet! Travel where?"

I said I did not know yet.

"You should come back with us."

"Come where?"

"America, Washington. You will like it. I know it."

I told him that I had applied to many universities to study further but wasn't sure if I was going or not.

"You can always stay with us," he smiled, "You know you're welcome."

In my heart, the desire burned some more. I contemplated the notion more sincerely.

He killed the cigarette and blew smoke in thin air. They had been around for three days now and this was the first time we had spoken. We sat together and watched the rain soak and destroy things. He told me about his life, boarding school days, girlfriends and past drinking problem. He told me how estranged his father was from his family in the last years of his life. He would shut himself in the attic and draw sketches of women, some clothed, some nude, some laughing, some dying. Though Rizwan didn't seem the kind to admit it, his father's estrangement seemed to provoke in him a bitter indifference. When he talked about him, it was almost as though he was recounting an acquaintance or someone he had just heard about, not his own father.

"He often drew strange faces and fields bathing in moonlight," he said, "It was his childhood home, I think. Have you been there?"

I told him I did many times but said nothing more.

I did not tell him anything that night, about myself, or the others, but just listened. I listened to stories about the life and death of the elusive Artist and of my American aunt.

***

CHAPTER FOURTEEN

His finger caressed the delicate neck of the bird. It closed its eyes as a warm, familiar hand touched its body. It was in pain and he felt it too.

I watched him kiss its head and place it back into the cage. Then, he stood with his back towards me, looking out of the window at the houses, big and small, and people, happy and lonely and the sun, red and orange setting in the fathomless purple sky.

In that complete silence, it felt as if I could hear his heart palpitating madly and his soul stirring from the awake of this foreshadowed grief. It was not the bird that made him sad but the fact that he had so much faith in its recovery. He had promised the owner, a neighbouring boy that it would survive against all odds.

That was my little brother – the nurse, the healer of wounded birds and cats. There was something in his touch, my mother would say, certain warmth that could fix any broken wing or limb. She said the same thing when he was a child; she said his laughter could heal her broken heart.

He began nursing when he was seven. It was a pigeon with a

broken wing that he had picked it up from the graveyard and kept it on his windowsill. He fed it. He nursed it. He bathed it.

When the bird recuperated and flew away into the heavens like a majestic revived phoenix, Abdullah cried for three days. He felt deceived. No one could console him; no other pigeon could take a place in his heart.

It is hard to explain to a privileged child the difference between freedom and captivity. For him, the world functions differently, all rains bear fruits and all men are free. He catches a golden bird and puts it inside a gold cage. He watches it grow, captivated, unaware that with its beautiful body comes a pair of wings that can set it free.

After that first betrayal, he never cried again and dozens of birds began to fly from our rooftop. As he watched the birds fly away, he smiled and laughed, and in tucked carefully between that laughter was the pain that he could never recover from.

When he was fourteen, Father built for him a small room, a *barsati* on the roof. There he spent most of his summer days. My sisters and I, the intruders, would parade into his abode during the monsoon showers. We played Ludo. We ate mangoes and *pakoras*. We told stories. We played the radio.

But when it did not rain, it was just him, his radio, and his pets.

He returned to the neighbour's swallow and opened its cage.

I told him that it was in great pain and it was okay for it to die. He nodded and continued to pet the little thing.

With that, I looked at the shifting clouds. The sound of *azaan* penetrated into the air from countless directions. We glanced down at the street beneath us. Men assembled in groups and began walking towards the mosque. Father was there; he waved up at us.

A smile broke out on Abdullah's face. It was not the waving that pleased him but something far more interesting. He had found something in the sky.

"Look, Mariam," he said, jovial.

An abandoned kite was sailing in the high wind. The red dot moved back and forth and our eyes kept following.

Out of all the Ameen children, we were the most sensitive and wilful. It was our failing, really. Little things left deep impressions in our hearts; things that should be sifted touched us the most. We remained cuddled up in our thoughts and were selfish in our dreams, we could listen to people in wilful silence but at the end of the day, we did what we wanted, what our hearts desired.

My brother was quiet, honest, and kept himself away from the empowering world of fiction and rumours. I, on the other hand, was even quieter but very much entrapped in the world of gossip and stories. But regardless of growing up in a same place, around the same people, we both had very different childhoods. In mine, the people I enjoyed evaporated into thin air and in his, Mother was pleasant, relatives were kinder and the sweets were tastier. I was raised on my grandfather's wisdom and he, on Mother's love and kindness.

He was very young when *daddi* died, even younger when *dadda* passed away. When *daddi's* corpse lay in the living room compelling women to wail and pull out their hair, Abdullah sat in a corner drawing trees and doves.

Children are not judged if they don't mourn at funerals even when they recognise the pain and horror like I had. I remember that I had so badly wanted to cry, but felt guilty for not being able to shed a single tear for my grandmother. That guilt burned my heart, and slowly metamorphosed into a hidden rage. I so badly wanted to let it out – this anger, this pain I felt for my grandmother, for Karan, for Prakriti. But somehow I couldn't let it out and couldn't let it go. I kept it inside me, where it multiplied until one day it finally let itself loose.

I released the pain for the first time when I was nine years old, by hitting Abdullah on his little shoulder. We sat doing our homework on the kitchen table when he suddenly stood up and began drawing on a wall, as was his habit. I lifted my head and saw his flock of birds. It was the same picture that he had made in *daddi's* room.

The Raja's house rushed back into my head, followed by the sound of water rushing from the pump. The voices returned – *daddi's*, Hamida's, the woeful sounds of women wailing as they beat their chests like drums in mourning, the hushed whispers of the men as they narrated stories from my grandfather's life…it all flew back at me disguised innocently as Abdullah's chalk birds. And all of a sudden I was overcome by guilt. Of course, it upset me that they were no more, but what upset me far more than that, was the fact that I had not been able to shed a single tear for either of them. Abdullah's birds reminded me of that guilt and, more than anything, this confrontation made me angry. Not knowing what else to do, I lashed out violently at the only person I could.

"You!" I cried, my voice echoed a great temper.

He turned, and then resumed making the letter V.

"Are you deaf?"

I struck him sharply on the shoulder, making him drop the colour pencil. He did not react, just stood there like a wax statue.

I smacked him harder and then harder until his eyelashes started fluttering and his lips began to quiver.

"Rub it!" I cried, "Rub all of it!"

He did not rub it, instead ran away, mortified at such callousness from me. I heard the thudding of his little feet bolt down the corridor. He sobbed as he ran away from me, thus creating an eternal distance between our lives. Sensitive as we were even as children, we never bonded after that episode. He had his own people, and I had my own company.

Abdullah now went to the *barsati* to get his *topi* and sandals for the *namaz*. I watched him for a while. At times, I prayed his memory was duller and deceitful unlike mine. He returned, placed the *topi* on his head and passed me a comforting smile.

I was convinced, he remembered nothing.

***

CHAPTER FIFTEEN

Grandfather always said that there are two kinds of children, one, who choose to remain stuck with their parents' identity and second, who are clever enough to find their own. But it was often the latter that suffered.

He had both.

The older son, my father, took the easy road. He studied what my *daddi* wanted where she wanted, married whom she wished and then did what she had prayed for – ran a small business of carpets and was left in charge of a few lands in the village. The younger son, however, had a mind of his own. He changed his major twice, went to college in a different city and later in his life, moved to Washington D.C. and became an artist.

His wife, whose motives for the summer visit were still ambiguous, struggled to get more into accord with the new place and people. She felt drawn out during family gatherings when the conversations revolved around unfamiliar people and subjects. I saw her trying to blend with relatives during the wedding preparations. She pleased them with the only three things that they adored; gossips, stories and gifts.

According to Aminah's promising research through eaves-dropping, she had had a hard life. At twenty-one, she was married to my father's brother who was a heart patient and rumours said that her family was never told about his illness but we had heard a different tale, which said, that they were so in love that she didn't care. It was difficult for her to raise two young children all by herself in a foreign land. She told everyone that she now ran a small store by a petrol station. Noor was joining an art school and Rizwan worked in advertising.

Once during evening tea, she placed her hand on my arm and said tenderly, "I must speak to my other parents. Take me to the graveyard."

"But it is very far away."

"Let's go tomorrow then, just you and I."

So we hired a car for the day and drove out.

When we arrived, I slowly walked out, but my aunt marched ahead excitedly. Dust flew from under our feet as we jumped over a mountain of bricks and unused garden tools at the entrance of the graveyard. We reached the family graves. Lubna put her hand on her mouth and pondered for a long time. I gave her a moment alone and sat on the bench where I often sat with Grandfather.

The smell of the incense sticks was stronger than ever, it burned my nostrils. Dried rose petals were scattered on various graves. Round and round the birds flew, fluttering from one spot to the other, pecking, conspiring and judging the intruders.

My aunt looked back at me, a small smile contracted her rosy face. I rose slowly and stood next to her.

"My husband wanted to be buried here, next to his parents," she said.

I spoke after a while, "Then why didn't you bring his body here?"

"They wouldn't let us bring the body here," she crushed russet leaves under her clogs, "It's tragic I couldn't fulfill his only wish. But oh, these dying people and their wishes. They float away into the other world and just don't care what perils they push the living into. My father wanted to buried in Berlin next to his first wife but of course my mother never kept her promise."

I remembered Prakriti and the ashes, Karan's dismay and the unfulfilled promise.

"*The bishop orders his tomb,*" I muttered.

Apart from the birds, we were the only moving objects in that space. We walked around for a while, silently scrutinising the graves. Some were abandoned, some adopted by caretakers, some had ordinary headstones with extraordinary prayers engraved on them, and some with grand headstones and epitaphs breathing regret and sorrow.

"It is such a brilliant and frail thing, this human life," I said, "Grandfather used to say, Mariam, never take off your shoes because life is a never-ending journey. You will meet people that will take your breath away and you will see places that will surprise you. You are a free spirit. And when this all ends, there is another glorious world above, waiting for you. We will all be free there."

She remained quiet for a moment but then she uttered, "I don't know what the Book says but I tell myself that when I leave this place, it will be a good thing because I will have another chance. I will have another chance to meet my husband and start a new life, and this time we will do it right."

We filled the empty bowl with water for the birds and placed it near the head of Grandfather's grave. It read:

'In the name of God, most Gracious, most Compassionate'
Loving son, husband and father
Muhammad Askar Ameen

Lubna plucked a cheerful *motia* flower and smelled it, "They do have a beautiful smell, transports me back to my childhood when my sisters and I made garlands for our dolls."

We walked out of the cemetery through its muddy track and

got into the car. She wanted to go to the *bazaar*. Lahori *bazaar* in broad daylight is full of colours and activities. It was that day, too. Women and children walked fast through the glimmering alleys. There were jewellers with their dazzling collections, half naked, bald mannequins with sequenced cloth pieces, scattered signs of dentists, palmists, whitening creams and beauty salons. Merchants, craftsmen, shopkeepers, hawkers and little labour boys kept the market running.

In the air were a mixture of smells; *paratha* rolls, burgers, *jaleebis* and *samoosas*.

"You don't find such things there," Lubna yelled over the noise, "The colour, the animation, the spirit."

A man on a cycle flew from nowhere barely hitting me in the gut with his steel handle. He said something about young girls never watching and sped into a neighbouring alleyway. Lubna still remembered a shop her sister and mother went to when she was seventeen.

"I dreamt about that shop, it had the most amazing *kundan* imitations," she said in my ear.

We got lost in the narrow alleys for a while. Some said that the shop had moved to another alley and some said that the family who had run the business had moved away to Karachi. Lubna did not give up. She finally hunted down the place. In the shop, a group of sad looking men sat around a black and white television set watching a cricket match. Their lunch boxes were opened on the counter, ignored, and the store smelled of peas and mutton. It took a while to get their attention.

"This place seems smaller," she said, "Memory deceives you."

There remained a big grin on her face.

She bought *kundan* imitation earrings, suits made of *lawn* fabric, a jar of homemade pickle and herbs for a tonic.

"I feel seventeen again," she exclaimed as we went back home.

***

CHAPTER SIXTEEN

When Lubna showed a desire to travel to the village, it was obvious that I was to accompany her. It was more obvious that the twins wanted to come along and relish Rizwan's charming company.

This sudden impulse to travel turned many faces and raised even more eyebrows. Mother had her own theories. Maybe the callous aunt wanted something from the ancestral home or maybe she wanted to look at the family lands. It seemed like an unusual wish for a woman who had fled for a "new world" years ago, abandoning her family and in-laws, to suddenly express such a sentimental request.

The twins and I were given duties – we were to keep our eyes and ears open at all times and the person to bring back home the juiciest gossip was to win Mother's preference. The twins were good at this, but then, so was I. I was used to observing and seldom being observed. Mother knew that I would fail to supply the apt results from the expedition because unlike the twins, who were good with words and dramatic performances, I unknowingly guarded whomever the wolves hunted. It was a habit that had developed in me over the years.

Mother's plan failed miserably when the twins remained fixated with Rizwan all through the train ride. Upon reaching the village, the group went exploring the fields and played in the tube well while Lubna and I walked around the house.

I strolled through the *haveli*, the one where the twins and I had collected water. I looked at the rooftop, the one where Karan and I met, and the empty space where he kept the ladder that separated our two worlds. I looked at the low wall that separated *daddi's* house from Prakriti's, the wall that seemed so high and forbidden as a child. Behind that wall still remained the place where Prakriti told me she changed her name to escape her past; the place, where the ashes fell and where I imagined Karan would eventually come back to and perhaps write to me, after years and years.

I touched the wall and looked around; the *haveli* hadn't flooded, it never flooded. It was like it had some sort of a protective shield around it or perhaps it was just the ghosts mopping floors, placing buckets and cleaning windows while mourning for their dead keepers.

We walked around and discovered that the rains had in fact left little messy reminders in every corner of the house. The *veranda* where *daddi*, Gulshan and I soaked up the sun was covered in leaves, corpses of flowers, fallen branches and twigs. There were small islands of water inside the corridors and the ceiling in *daddi's* room was damp.

Lubna looked at herself in *daddi's* mirror and brushed a strand of greying hair from her forehead. She glided, touching dusty shelves with her slender fingers and looking at old photographs. She lifted a frame and looked at the black and white image inside it. Her face held no expression.

The room held no value in her life and the people in the photographs had become strangers. I asked myself the obvious, why had she really come? What did she long to see after all these years?

I asked if she remembered the house.

"I lived her for two years after the wedding," she said and looked away from the mirror, "The guest room used to be my room. It still has some of my things, actually."

I nodded.

"You said you wanted to go find the twins. You can go," she smiled.

I concluded from this abrupt dismissal that she wanted to be alone; to collect the remainder of her things, perhaps. I responded with a brief smile but did not move.

She smiled a little more.

Still, I did not bat an eye. Neither did I show any inclination of leaving.

It was simple; I did not want her to be alone in *daddi's* room. I was afraid that if she stood long enough the room would consume her smell, the smell of her sugary perfume. A room should always smell of its inhabitant and should always tell its story. The room should have always smelled of *daddi's* cologne and Grandfather's *hookah*.

So she simply walked out of the room and into the guest room and I went out of the house.

The sun looked lazily at the slumbering fields. The air was cool and the smell of parched earth was sweet and warm. The rail lines were quiet and now and then, blew a gust of strong wind, blowing dust, leaves and all the broken things. Where the fields ended, brown houses rose serenely, children played and animals rested under shades of trees.

At a short distance, three colourful figures strolled, hand in hand, frolicking, squealing, and relishing each other's presence. They were hopping towards the tube well, which at that time was filled with cool water.

The impulsive twin threw back her head, her cheeks flushing with great joy, and laughed loudly. Her *dupatta* fluttered in the air, she held it and pinned it to her side. She took hold of Rizwan's hand again and clutched it in a momentous grip, a loud declaration of her newly found sentiments.

Aminah had become passionately fond of Rizwan and all that he represented. I, on the other side, did not know yet what to feel about the stranger.

The wind blew the dust from the ground and I lost the figures.

I took off my shoes, picked up a long stick from the ground and began walking away, feeling the earth beneath my toes. I touched the leaves and flowers in my path as I walked along, humming and wandering like a child would in a garden.

I didn't form intimacies as quickly as my sisters. I observed. I weighed and then when I was intrigued enough, I took my chances. It was not inside of me – the bright spark of spontaneity, a flare of impulsiveness and the acute sense of risk and adventure. I had what Anika called "a dry soul". She thought this "dryness" would smother me, suck away my youth and spirit. What kind of an eight-year-old calls a graveyard their favourite place and an old distraught man, their hero?

That is why, she said, Grandfather wanted me to travel and see places. She said that I thought too highly of myself, that I was buried under a thick wall and it was hard for men to reach me. She was afraid that one day, the right man would walk away from me. I responded that if he would walk away, he was not the right man.

I sat on a dry patch of land, crouched and drew with the stick on the ground.

Love and marriage was all anyone was talking about, I thought. Grand preparations were taking place at home. When we were young, these kinds of grand celebrations were special for two reasons. One, there was plenty of sweet food, *methai*, *halwa* and *methay-chawal* and second, there were plenty of good films on the cable. We would sit together in front of the television with plates of *biryani* and *halwa* and watch lovers cry, sing and finally unite in rain before the curtains fell. The world conspired, the nature reacted, the director intervened, but we knew that the lovers would get to each other one way or the other.

It made sense to the wolves when the characters on screen flirted, cheated on their spouses and fell in love with people they ought not to. It was ironic that they even shed tears for them, yet Grandfather never made sense to them. In their minds, he was to remain a vulgar man.

"Love, Mariam," Grandfather had said to me once, "This indescribable phenomena makes us great, strange, and sometimes even horrible in the eyes of the world. But we *must* love, regardless of what people say."

Lovers could be silent. Lovers could be afraid. Lovers could be Grandfather and Prakriti. Lovers could be imperfect.

"Prakriti," I said out aloud. I had not said her name out aloud in years. So foreign it seemed on the tongue now; the sounds, so sharp.

I pushed hair away from my forehead and let the sunshine kiss my skin. So blissful and frightening is silence, this naked isolation when you just belong to yourself, when your fears, known and unknown, despairs, old and new, and secrets of the heart lie before you, exposed and vulnerable. So strange was this silence.

I threw the stick on the ground and realised what had really happened; coming back to the village had filled me with an extraordinary sorrow. The more I thought of it, the more it began to swallow me whole. I promised myself that I would never return. The feeling of loss confirmed that there was nothing more for me here.

Familiar voices broke me away from my thoughts. The figures were walking back now.

"Is this what you do when you're bored?'

They had come to where I sat. I kept a hand on my forehead to dodge the rays.

The speaker was Rizwan, "Haunting the corridors at midnight, wandering aimlessly in the fields during the day."

"That's all she does, wander aimlessly in and out of her mind," said Aminah with a jeer in her voice, "I wish Noor would have come out on this beautiful day. I don't think she likes being here much."

Rizwan's face lit up in a wonderful smile. He wasn't thinking about his sister, he was staring at me with profound interest.

"Sometimes I worry about you. It must be difficult being a loner in a house full of such vibrant people."

Aminah punched his shoulder playfully.

"There is nothing to worry about," I said softly and stood up.

I was still frustrated. I began to walk back into the fields where I had removed my shoes. Rizwan followed me, leaving the twins behind. None of us spoke for some time. He walked alongside me, looked at my muddy feet and then at my face. I didn't know what he was thinking but around him, I found myself more self-conscious than I would have liked. Maybe it was because I didn't understand him completely but I wanted to. He was like a character from a book, a mysterious man from another land, a man who was ought to be family but felt nothing like family, invading our private lives and thoughts. Parts of his character, both hidden and revealed, aroused in me an unwelcomed curiosity.

I wanted to talk to him more and I wanted to talk to his mother, who showed great interest in me.

He came closer to me and brushed off a blade of grass from my shoulder. We exchanged a brief smile. He was irresistibly cheery during the day, but at night, from my window I often saw him smoking alone, isolated and pensive. My presence would go unnoticed as he sat unguarded in darkness, without that signature spirit and joy of life that people in the house liked him for. I, on the other hand, liked him for his silence and broodings, for his map-like mind. In the cover of darkness, he would shrink in the chair and gently caress his forehead with tip of his fingers for a while and then eventually stand up and walk away.

He was a tall man like his father, had dark eyes like his father, a "wheatish" tone like his father, and yet he was nothing like his father.

When he was nine, he was sent away to boarding school. His parents had a good, happy life. The Artists' work sold well, Lubna had a decent job, so the money was not a problem. College days were a blur, he laughed and said. He only remembered girls and alcohol, lots of alcohol. When he went back home after his first year, his father was a changed man. He was weaker, quieter and restless. He barely spoke to the family, barely showed his face, even. He remained in the attic, sometimes painting and sometimes just sitting. His disinterest in life bore down on Lubna and the kids, and the house became perpetually tense; the Artist's passivity became their unravelling.

"And then one day, just like that, he died," he said, "I had just turned eighteen."

He looked down at the ground.

"We did not know what to do for the longest time. Whom to call, whom to tell? Neighbours? Friends? Family? It was a strange funeral."

"Talk about strange funerals," I had said.

"Do you remember Grandfather's funeral?'

"Yes, very vividly."

"How was it?"

"Strange. I did not feel anything except the pain in my arms from fetching water for the mourners and the kitchen. The body was never brought in the house where the women and children sat. In the evening, I asked my father if I could see his face for one last time and he said I would see his face but not now, not in this life."

Rizwan kept looking at me, thoughtful

"And only then did it hit me. He had died. He had really died and my father would never take me to the graveyard. How else was I to meet him? *Where* else would I meet him?"

"You possess an uncommon ability of attracting people," he said suddenly, bringing me back to the present.

"As long as you understand that this is not my motive, I think it is fine," I said without looking at him, "My sisters, however..."

"Your sisters are like birds, beautiful and fearless..."

"...Good summer distraction for you."

"We're cousins, after all," his face said that he knew full well of my sisters' infatuation.

"This doesn't bother them, trust me."

"Well, it isn't about them. It is about you. They were raised believing in different things."

He nodded.

"If you won't open up and learn to trust people, you will miss on some of the greatest things in life."

"Grandfather used to say the same thing," I said, "He wanted me to make friends, and so does Anika." Grandfather kept to himself and this is why he was the way he was.

"Ah, our scandalous *daddajan*," said Rizwan.

"We shouldn't talk that way about people we don't know."

"But you did know him. What was so great about him, Mariam?"

"I don't know, Rizwan..."

"I guess sometimes we find heroes in the most ordinary people. We don't know why we love them but we do. There has to be some extraordinary element in them, and there has to be something extraordinary in you too, for finding it and always remembering. It is a pathetic life without mentors and ideals. Ask me, I'd know."

I watched him closely with curiosity. He picked up a rock from the ground and threw it straight ahead. His hair was wet from bathing in the tube well and his face shone from the sunlight.

"I understand I know nothing about your...our grandfather,'

he said, "but from what I've heard from people, he was very much like his distraught son or rather, his son was very much like him."

"How can you say that?"

"I say a lot of things," a faint smile seized his face.

After that day, we didn't have the chance to talk properly for a long time. He was seldom alone and when he was, I chose not to disrupt his silence and mediation.

The girls were ascending into the fields. I left him in their merry company and returned to Lubna.

***

At home, my elder sister struggled with a secret. She was getting married in a month and was thrilled, until she felt the sober-faced man was hiding something from her. When I returned, she took me to the empty *barsati* and told me she was having doubts and doubts are ill when your wedding is arranged.

The man behaved indifferently in her solitary presence, like she did not matter, like the task of getting married was too burdensome for him. It was against Mother's wishes that she met him alone but her impulse was to meet him in person and inquire about his behaviour.

So we snuck into a park one morning. I sat under a tree and watched my sister take a seat on a bench farther away. The sober-faced man held Anika's arm and then gave her a gentle hug. They talked and then she watched him leave the park. I walked towards her.

"What is it?" I asked

Anika looked at me with tears in her eyes, "He came to tell me that he loves someone else."

My heart stopped beating for a moment. I could not say anything.

We went back home in silence and I watched Anika suffer; drown into complete sadness. So many sleepless nights. To pacify her, I would lie down with her and hold her hand. We wouldn't talk. I just didn't know what to say

She told me that she would soon confide in Mother. When she did, Mother picked up the nearest glass from the shelf and threw it at her feet in anger. The glass jug smashed in a hundred unfriendly pieces near her trembling toes. Tears flooded my sister's eyes and she stammered but again, Mother had a lot to say.

"When a parent asks you to stay away, you stay away!"

She wasn't furious about the fact that Anika's husband-to-be had a lover but she was angry that Anika had the audacity to see him alone. She believed it was better if she hadn't found out and with time her husband would have forgotten this supposed lover.

"But he asked me to…" she whimpered.

"It takes a minute for a man to crumble a woman's respect!" she grabbed the *dupatta* that was draped around her head to signify. "Do you know what this means? Do you know what your grandmother meant when she said the word *izzat*?"

She would use it endlessly whenever she wore her *burqa* and she also when asking us to stay away from strange men she called "vibrant snakes".

Anika took a step backward.

"I won't hit you, Anika, I wouldn't dare hit you!" Mother said, "but you have no idea what you've done. Wouldn't it have been better if you hadn't found out? That's why we say, stay away."

Anika concealed her face and cried in her *dupatta,* "He is marrying me because he has to, not because he wants to."

"Don't be silly. No one is that desperate. He is not a child. He will admire you after marriage. After all, it is your duty to win over your husband's heart. We shall not discuss this any further. Such humiliation."

"I-I'll be fine,"Anika wiped her eyes, trying to console herself, "After all, it's only a marriage."

No one spoke on the subject anymore.

It was just the two of us whispering in low voices after

everybody slept. We stayed up discussing every book and story we had read about love, marriage, husbands and other women. In the end, we just asked each other the same question over and over again.

"How do you win over a man's heart?"

***

CHAPTER SEVENTEEN

Lubna folded three blankets and placed them in her suitcase. Then she took out from her cupboard an ancient telephone and wrapped it in between the layers of the blankets. On top of everything, she placed two beautifully stitched quilt covers. Those were the things that she had brought back from the village. She had dug into *daddi's* massive trunks in the storehouse and extracted her belongings. She had brought these as dowry when she was a new bride and believed that after all these years, they were still her possession.

When Mother found out, she fumed but did not react much because of Anika's wedding preparations.

The wedding was a grand event; it was as grand as *dadda's* funeral. There were just as many guests and just as much chattering and noise. There was cheering, singing and crying, sometimes all at once. Fairy lights hung like tree branches and the house smelled of fresh petals of rose and *henna*. The low sound of drums echoed through the day. However, summer weddings were wearisome. They required more energy and perspiration.

In the three days of commotion and glitter, Lubna dissolved and became one with the crowd. Her son helped his cousins with the wedding preparations, and her daughter sat in a corner, trying to understand the alien culture that her family said she was from.

The bride looked beautiful. Red bangles shone on her soft *henna* painted hands and she walked around the room leisurely. Mother spoke to the mirror uneasily and wore white studs in her big brown ears. She bent to whisper something into the bride's ear and then left me alone in her company. I straightened her dress, smiled slightly and she signalled to the jug of water that was on a small table next to a bouquet of colourful flowers. I poured some water and her bangles jingled as she indicated me to stop.

Outside, Mother threw her hands in the air and began dancing to a famous folk song. The singer sang about the bride becoming a stranger and the crooning of doves. She sang about the deep bond between a mother and daughter. She sang about the brothers carrying the bride's carriage. As she continued to sing, my sister burst into tears. The song stirred me deeply too. She was leaving me, my sister, beginning a new life, with new people and in a new way.

There were chatters and giggle in the crowd before the band started playing the trumpet and *dhol*. The groom had arrived and it was time for her to go.

I watched the sober-faced man accept the union, say, "*Kabool hai*" from beneath his headdress and saw my sister nod softly. The twins and their friends hid the groom's shoes and Abdullah sang a song.

I sat on the roof in the empty air after the celebrations died down. There was nothing left now, just crushed petals of rose, the scent of cheap perfume and burnt candles. With Anika's departure to her new home, I suddenly realised how alone I had become in a house full of shimmering guests.

I had a dream that night: I sat with my grandfather on a boat that was floating in the middle of a vast sea. I told him about his granddaughter's wedding and his son's children.

Like always, he smiled and didn't have much to say.

***

CHAPTER EIGHTEEN

The afternoon sun streamed through one of the windows and flooded the room with an intense yellow colour. Mother's eyes narrowed with a strange dangerous smile as she went through Lubna's clothes. I stood at the doorway, motionless, gazing at the pile of things she kept tossing onto the bed.

"I don't think we should go through their things…"

There was a puzzled pause.

She lifted her shoulders with a slow shrug, "I know she is hiding something. I won't stop until I find out."

My eyes lit up in horror as she pulled out the blankets and the ancient telephone. It was absurd. Our monsoon guests couldn't imagine what happened in their room when they were not around. I placed a firm hand on the suitcase and shook my head hard.

"Ah!" she exclaimed and pulled out a couple of photographs despite the weight of my hand. She hid them in the folds of her *dupatta* and packed her suitcase like it was never harassed.

I followed her to the kitchen. Her eyebrows rose as she went through their personal photographs.

"She's a chameleon," she whispered, "I knew it!"

"Look, I don't know what happened between you two when we weren't born, but this, Mother, is completely inexcusable."

She thrust the photos in my hand and left the room. I looked down reluctantly. A little square photograph showed Lubna on a beach back home. Her tight rainbow-coloured bathing suit set quite a contrast against the blue green water. The other photograph showed a blonde Lubna in a small white dress with her arms stretched in front of the Empire State building. I felt sorry for her. It must be difficult belonging to two different worlds; she had to be two different people.

When Anika visited a few days later after her wedding, I told her about Mother's brazen act and Lubna's photographs. I also confessed that after looking at the pictures and talking to Rizwan, I had developed a strange desire, a wish to be in foreign land, to be a part of someone else's life for a while and to explore new things on my own.

"We need relationships, roots and boundaries. It's who we are. We have roots, Mariam," Anika said, "Lubna doesn't believe in roots. Her ways are different. She abandons things easily."

I nodded, deep in thought.

"All I'm saying is if we break, at least we have something or someone to fall back on."

I nodded again even though I wasn't quite sure what she meant.

Now every time Lubna brought her pink face in front of me, my mother imagined her in shorts and giggled. On the other hand, the twins, especially Aminah, were quite disturbed when they saw Rizwan's cheesy photos with white girls.

"So what if he has a *gori* girlfriend?" Aminah threw her arms in the air, defensive and wild, "Perhaps people do such things in America…"

"It's not just in America, it's everywhere…" Fatima spoke.

"Oh, shut it, Fati," she sat on the bed and looked at the ground, "I think he likes me."

That triggered it. I had to speak.

"He is just wasting his time here with you; there is nothing here that he can love. His real life is in America, he belongs there."

She stood up dramatically.

"How can you possibly speak for him? Oh, what do you know of love?" she said, "It's the most beautiful feeling in the world..."

"Oh, come to think of it, I can't," I placed hands on my hips, "Because I haven't read the latest romance story in women's digest under your pillow."

"You're saying this because you like him too!"

"I do not like him, believe me."

"Then why do you plan going to America with him? I saw the letter."

"You mean to say, you stole my letter," I murmured.

I placed a hand on my forehead and sighed. She would not have understood. Aminah grinded her teeth and stormed out of the room.

I ran fingers through my hair and sighed.

Fatima tsk-tsked.

"What?" I said.

"Why are you taking it away from her?"

"How can I take away something that's not even there?"

"Let her do her thing, else she will remind you for the rest of her life that you took away her only shot with him."

The night before our fight, I received a letter. It was in response to one of the many applications that I had sent across to American universities for Masters programmes. Aminah stole it and hid it. Then, she showed it to Rizwan because it was hard for her to keep secrets. Rizwan, in return, called my name the same night.

He brought the letter close to my face and said:

"A chance. To be away for a while. To know us, me, study in a new place, with new people...travel...be free...live."

Then he left me to contemplate.

My hands had trembled when I read it.

I was growing older, becoming conscious of the world around me, and what I saw did not appease me. Anika was married, now the twins began seeking partners; things were falling in predictable patterns and I felt misplaced.

It was all too ordinary and *dadda* said that he and I were born to experience the extraordinary.

***

CHAPTER NINETEEN

So in the monsoon of 2007 it was decided that I was leaving to go to America for further education. Lubna was excited and she helped me pack. It was time now for Mother to tell me all about our family's *izzat* and Father and I shared a close moment before I left.

It was twilight. The sky was peach and purple. The sun rose reluctantly from behind the green dome of a mosque. The birds whistled. The clouds became clearer. I rested my head on my knees and looked at the horizon, deep in thought. My father kissed my forehead and asked if I wanted a good luck gift. I said I *did* want a gift but for that he had to exercise his mind and jog his memory; he had to remember what he was conditioned to forget as a child. I asked him to tell me about the time when Grandfather returned from India with his lover. He would have been just seven then.

My father's face unfolded a puzzled look; it was a strange gift that his daughter wanted. Thus he narrated the episode that was told and retold in our family for years:

There were loud cries and exclamations of joy released from the crowd that welcomed Muhammad Askar Ameen at the border. He became clearer and then crossed the border with another woman.

Awful silence.

A clang mistrust and suspicion hung in the air. He approached his father as the dust settled. They hugged and some people took away his bags. His wife, tensed, pallid like a ghost, looked at the closing gates and then at his lover. The other woman looked at the ground, a small bag resting in her arms. Her eyes hung low, not once daring to look up at the wife's frozen face, a broken beauty – fragile, confused and warm.

Askar Ameen kept a hand on his wife's shoulder and before he could utter a word, the other woman rushed out of everybody's sight.

"Nobody had seen her face. Nobody had asked her name. Nobody had asked my father the real story. They abandoned him completely and fabricated different versions of it," said my father.

"But how did he take everything?" was my question.

"He was a changed man. His heart stopped beating. He isolated himself, drifted more and more out of life. Soon, he was nothing but a passive breathing body that I called father and my mother, her husband."

I looked at the blurry sun and then at my father's face. He sat still and his face unearthed no emotion.

"Who was she?" I asked.

"I don't know," he replied.

"Where did she go?"

"We don't know."

"What was she called?"

"I don't know. She just disappeared."

Like Grandfather, I thought.

"Where did they meet?"

"Delhi. She lived there with her family. He was thirty-five and she was much younger, exactly half his age, I think. It was his first trip to India. He went to visit a friend there who took him to a wedding. They met at that wedding."

"Is this why he married so late?"

"No, no," my father laughed, "Your grandfather was a free spirit, a man who had always been wise beyond his years and the kind of man that he was, he felt he needed no companion."

"Until he met her..." I whispered.

"Until he met her," he whispered back.

"So why didn't they marry?" I asked.

"Lovers don't marry. It breaks the illusion."

"It was the families, was it? The families, relatives, religion, the society…"

His reply was a smile, followed by, "It always is."

He thought I should know the rest of the story too, so continued without my asking.

"When your *dadda* married your *daddi*, he told her the truth, just like it was. He told her the story of a Hindu girl whom he had fallen in love with. He did the right thing."

I looked at him. He took a deep breath as he recollected.

"Your *daddi* felt betrayed. She didn't know what to do. But as time passed by, she realised that the past was better left unstirred."

As he said that, I couldn't help but think back to how my mother had told Anika the same thing before she too had gotten married to a man in love with another woman. How she had tried to make her understand that some things were indeed, better left unstirred.

"Were they happy?"

"Yes, for several years but he didn't tell her everything. He didn't tell her that the Hindu girl and him still wrote to each other and that he still loved her. He also didn't tell her it was your *daddi's* beloved Hamida, who like a pigeon, carried the letters."

And the letters. I remembered distinctly a pile of old letters I had once seen in my grandfather's hands. Were those *those* letters? I remembered him burning them one day in the graveyard. I had only watched the little flames swallow each word and memory.

Did he burn them for her, I wondered. To try to forget her. To save her. To save his marriage.

"How did she return with him? What was he doing in India with her?" I asked.

"I don't know," he said, "All I know is that he went to India to meet his friend and returned with her." He looked at me, confused about my intrigue in an ancient love story that was supposed to have no relevance in my life.

But my heart was moved. I did not tell him what I already knew, the things what I had found out on my own, they things they never bothered to really know. For him and the family, the story ended here. For my father and the wolves, the reality was simple – *dadda* was a man who had an affair. For me, the reality was very different, the reality was what Hamida and I shared.

The girl Grandfather had met and fallen in love with in Delhi eventually moved to Pakistan with her husband after she got married. Her husband belonged to the same village as Grandfather. Though he was Hindu and born and raised in Delhi, he chose to move to his ancestor's home in Pakistan. And due to a bizarre coincidence, that house ended up being the one right beside the Ameens. It was a surprise for both the lovers, but then, life worked in strange ways and there it was. Silently, quietly she spent her years living next door to the man she loved. No one but Hamida knew and then only years later, I found out.

Maybe it is true that when two people love each other so madly like *dadda* and Prakriti, a mysterious, mystical force of the universe binds them together forever. No matter how strange and unreal it sounded then, it was the truth and this is what had happened.

Hamida, the eyes and ears of the Ameen household knew everything. She knew the village and its villagers like the back of her hand. When Prakriti had gotten married and moved to Pakistan, she had changed her name suddenly, perhaps to conceal her identity and hope the Ameen household didn't find out who she actually was. But she still could not fool Hamida. It did not take long for her to realise what was going on. I believe she grew up listening to Grandfather's story from his wife. The unspoken affection of the estranged lovers drew her in and just like me, felt she had a role to play. She remained quiet, but as rumour had it, it was she who delivered the letters back and forth between the lovers.

As I sat with my father, I silently recalled every naive discussion I had ever had with Prakriti and Karan in their kitchen. She had told me once that when her husband was very sick, she went to the Ganges and took a dip. She said that that was both her most cherished and saddest memory. I now knew why.

The first time my grandfather went to India, he met Prakriti at a wedding. The second time he went was years after that and had told the family he was going back to India to visit his friend. But actually he had taken Prakriti to the Ganges to pray for her husband's health. Though the trip brought her and Grandfather closer, it also tore them apart forever.

I rested my head on my knees and heaved a long sigh. I felt more pain than I should have.

"Why didn't *daddi* ever forgive him?" I asked my father.

"God forgives but a woman does not."

After a few minutes he asked me, "Why do *you* wish to know all this? Why now?"

Why did I? Why then? What was this incredible obsession to know about the perils in the lives of two lovers who were now gone? I myself did not understand. But I needed to know. I had to.

We remained quiet for a long time. A new sky was born.

"The world is so beautiful and big," he said suddenly, "But where there is the beautiful sun, there are also dark roads. We have always chosen to stay in the light."

"What is darkness for us, Father?"

I knew what he was thinking. The dark was everything the family found unusual and out of the ordinary. As we grew up, we realised that there would come a time when things would start falling in a predictable pattern; a short career, marriage, children, old age, piety and death. This was their light. That was the light he was referring to.

Darkness was everything and everyone else.

Darkness was Lubna.

Darkness was her husband.

Darkness was Grandfather.

"*I* won't come back with a lover, *baba*," I said.

"That's not it, my child."

"Then, what's the matter?"

"I'm scared of sending you off with strangers," he said in his deep resounding voice.

"They're not strangers," I assured, "You've known them all your life."

My father closed his hands over mine.

"You still never know," he whispered and kissed my forehead, "I want you to trust nobody but yourself. Be safe, Mariam. I want you to go there, study, and do something extraordinary with your life."

***

As the airplane you are sitting in cuts through the skies with its wild wings, you feel like you possess a certain power. The buildings shrink and the city lights appear like tiny fireflies frozen in time and space. The entire city is trapped as if in a snow globe and it seems so serene. Peering out of the window, you try to locate your home and imagine your family waving at every flying thing in the sky.

I laid my head back and heaved a breath. To a new time, a new place, a new city, a new family and to new friends. Bathed in this strange new feeling, of change and freedom, of new boundaries and beginnings, my body quivered, now miles away from Lahore. Outside it was all black and blinding as though we were at the bottom of the sea.

Rizwan opened his sleeping eyes and leaned near me, "Are you scared?"

I looked into his eyes before I answered.

Who else had asked me this question before?

Anika.

Saying goodbye to her was the hardest.

We had gone to the graveyard and sat on a marble bench. I wanted to say goodbye to Grandfather and I had wanted her with me. As time passed, I had grown attached to the lump of clay that was his grave, just as Karan had to the urns.

"Do you think they're listening to us?" she asked, looking at the graves.

"I think they have far better things to discuss."

She laughed and then turned serious, "Mariam, what will I do without you? You're my baby."

I watched a pigeon fly away from Grandfather's grave to the shaded area near a mosque. There was strong wind. It was about to rain.

"It's just for a few years. I'm not dying," I said.

"Don't talk about death here," she shook a little, "We might offend them."

I smiled.

"I wish we could take a train somewhere, together, anywhere.'

"I know," I said.

The dark sky glared down at us and roared. We talked gaily till the rain came down to strip our skins and shrink our spirits. Outside, the vendors covered their carts in plastic sheets and the stray cats tried to find shelter under parked cars. My sister and I stood under a blooming *Amaltas* tree. The droplets flirted with the yellow flowers and they fell tenderly on our wet hair and clothes. I took off my blue *dupatta* and spread it over our heads.

"Mariam…Mariam, we should walk home," Anika trembled in the cold.

"But we should wait…" I screamed over the roaring and the rattling.

"You know…I've never bathed in the rain…" she said suddenly, her own words almost surprising herself.

Smiling, I raised my eyebrow at her in wonder.

She walked out from under the shade of the tree and straight into the waterfall. Spreading her hands in the air, she spun around wildly and threw her *dupatta* in the air. I laughed. I had never seen her like this before, so bright, so radiant, so natural and pure.

"This is it, Mariam!" she cried. "You don't know when you'll let the monsoon rain kiss your skin again."

I left my *dupatta* on the ground and stepped inside the curtain of rain. It was everywhere; the sweet scent of the last monsoon rain, the smell of freedom and change.

In the plane, in the darkness of night, with Rizwan leaning in close to me, it hit me. I was really flying away from home, like Abdullah's healed birds. This was it.

There would be no Grandfather in America. There would be no late night talks with Anika. The old lady on the moon doesn't show her face in Washington. Karan's father's spirit didn't wander on those streets.

I had never been so far away…

***

WINE

WASHINGTON D.C. 2008

The stranger finished his second cigarette. November rain pounded heavily against his shoes. He hid under the shade of a dark tree as he fidgeted with a small umbrella. He passed swiftly by shops and restaurants. He walked across an intersection and passed a stone fountain – classical Gods stood frozen in time. Water fell on their cool marble bodies as they stared into the night.

The city streets before him, long and never ending, kept unfolding.

Two girls appeared in a street in short dresses and leather jackets. They fumbled with their bright umbrellas and passed him, laughing at a secret of their own.

The purple sky lit up as the lightning struck, exciting the trees, bushes and sewer rats. The stranger finally got into a cab, giving the driver the name of an art gallery. The driver nodded and drove slowly on the roads of the great American Capital.

The morning had passed by quickly but the night refused to escape. Through the stream of droplets on his window, he looked at the tall buildings, stiff and resilient, standing relentlessly under the rumbling sky. The city seemed dead and deserted in the rain; the only thing alive was the restless nature and blinding city lights. They drove past important monuments, on important roads, slowly, steadily towards the gallery.

The old gallery was bathed in a golden hue. The air smelled sweet, a blend of several perfumes. People walked around in the open space, laughing and chuckling as they discussed books and art, rich countries and exotic cities. Sharply dressed waiters walked around carrying Lucite trays.

He took a glass of wine and sipped it gently as his eyes scanned for any familiar face. The luminous liquid winked and kissed the thin glass. The party was grander that year than any other. There were more people. The music was louder and the night, longer.

Some faces were old and familiar; some were newer and more pleasing to look at. He glided through the hall and smiled at a few faces. The hostess stood besides an oil painting, isolated, weighed down by her own anxiety and nervousness. Between her thin, ageing fingers was a glass of red wine, untouched, forgotten almost like the paintings made by her husband that occupied the walls.

They exchanged greetings and made small talk for a while. He commented on the success of the party and a smile of relief seized her face. That was exactly what she had been wanting to hear; some assurance. She held his arm fondly and took him to a narrow well-lit corridor where she said the rest of the paintings hung. He watched her go back to the rest of the guests. She now walked with a dignified grace, like the anxiety had completely left her company, like she belonged in her own party.

He strolled about leisurely, admiring the art. The women in the paintings were smooth and beautiful; some dark, some pale. They stared at him in wonderment, expecting answers to questions only they knew. Every piece had a different setting – temples, open fields, mountains, mosques, farms...the kind of places one sees in a dream. He studied the work with a great curiosity, spending the time each painting demanded, until a figure caught the corner of his eye.

At the other end of the corridor stood a girl, no older than twenty-three. She stood before a painting, arrested in reverence and awe. He walked a little closer, hoping to get her attention, but she stood, disconnected from the world that surrounded them.

Against all the colour and noise, her stillness was alluring. He knew who she was but they had never met. She was reading a poem by *Rumi*, the Sufi poet, written by the artist in his spidery handwriting underneath a painting. His subject, a nude young woman sat on the golden rim of a wine glass, enticing and enchanting. Her short violet hair was curled to one side, her pale legs were crossed, her left hand was placed just above her knee and the other touched the crystal clear liquid. She had hazel eyes and dewy skin.

"It is like a dream," the girl spoke suddenly.

The man looked at her but she still didn't look back.

"Did you know The Artist?" he asked.

She hesitated for a moment. "He was my uncle."

"So you have met him?"

She smiled, "No, I didn't. I just arrived three months ago."

He nodded.

"What do you think of the paintings?"

"I'm trying to connect with his mind."

"Your uncle's mind?"

"No, The Artist's."

"Nothing will make sense. Nothing will ever make sense. He paints Hermes bathing outside a Buddhist temple... and... underneath writes *Iqbal's* poem. Next, he paints *Chand Bibi*, the Indian woman warrior, on her horse, but instead of fighting the Mughal forces, she is seen battling farm animals. We always look for a deeper meaning, connections in the works of writers, poets, artists, but sometimes, we have to accept that this is it. This is what he produced, nothing less, nothing more."

She bit her lip and whispered, "No, I believe there is always a connection. Perhaps only in the subconscious of their minds but there is always something more. Something troubling them.

Something they wish to tell the world."

He walked a little and pointed at the next painting, "Well, what do you think he meant by this?"

The image revealed an open field, bathed in golden sunlight and filled with wheat crops.

"I know this place," she said, reassured, "I've been there."

He looked at her in amazement, a part of him believing her instantly.

"So what about the first one? Did the woman remind you of someone?"

She looked back at the painting with the wine glass and the young woman.

"I like how her hand touches the drink. It's so nonchalant, just falling into the liquid, like it doesn't even know it's there."

"And…"

"The woman, she is disoriented. I don't know why, but I feel she is. She looks displaced."

"Do you empathise with her?" he asked.

"Don't we all? Are we not all displaced in our own way?"

This is all she said, nothing more. He watched her for a moment and then smiled when their eyes met.

As the night wore on, the conversations became longer and more absurd. The clinking of the glasses and the laughter grew louder. When the party finally died, the girl wrapped a shawl over her dress and walked out of the gallery with her friend. He joined them.

They sat on the stone steps of a deserted house and looked at lanes of new and fancy cars. They remained silent in each other's company and watched as the hostess bade the guests' goodbye and disappeared back inside the gallery.

The friend left their company too. It was now just the two of them.

The stranger smoked and she watched the new roads and

shops from behind the grey smokes screen. He threw the cigarette on the ground and rose.

"I must leave now. Welcome to Washington D.C."

She watched him walk away. Soon, the sound of his footsteps dulled. She sat by herself for some time and watched an old man close shutters outside his shop. His figure also disappeared and his footsteps, too, died after a while.

She picked up the fallen cigarette from the ground and smeared the black ash on her finger. Feeling its powdery texture on her fingers, she admired its darkness. She found herself thinking about a story that often tormented her – a story about a young boy struggling to collect fragments of grey ash that lay scattered on the ground around him. Reminded of the pain again, she pushed it out her mind.

"Mariam?" the hostess peered through the doorway, "We're waiting for you."

The girl nodded, wiped off the ash with her shawl, and went in to help her aunt take down the paintings.

***

CHAPTER TWENTY

The roads were littered with bronze and copper leaves. The air was cool and the feeling festive. A dead leaf fell on my hair. I caught it and looked up at the parent tree. It stood like a relic from an old forgotten civilization. Crouching down, I collected a few leaves from the ground, each with a different colour and pattern, and sealed them between different pages of the book I held in my hand, *Great Expectations*.

Fall never looked so beautiful.

It had all been confusing, the year before when I arrived to America. But this year everything fit perfectly; the people, the places, nature...I understood it. It understood me.

I looked up at the trees. It was as if the world was falling in pieces around me, making place for something much bigger. My friend Judy Baker was a photography major at the university and claimed that this was the period of rebirth; nature was in a transition, the old world was collapsing, making space for a better one.

She wasn't always so optimistic or profound but I noticed that autumn awakened in her a pensive side. I understood completely, winter did the same to me. Not the threatening winter of America but the winter at home, the blissful winter of Lahore. I stood up from the ground and brushed off the bits grass that stuck to my jeans.

Someone called my name, a friend from class who was leaving the coffee shop across the street. I waved back. He said something about catching me in the library later. I said I would text him. This was the same coffee shop where I had met Judy for the first time last year.

The school year was ending, and I still knew very few people in America. Never being the type to go out of her way to interact with people, I remained content with my own company. It had just begun to snow and I sat inside with my coffee and Dostoyevsky. Outside, children played in the snow and adults stopped midway to forget their pains for one moment and to just to admire the sky. I was completely enamoured by it, the snow. I had never seen it before.

Suddenly, I heard a click. It was Judy, sitting a few seats away, holding a camera and beaming widely. I frowned as the stranger violated my personal space.

"I'm sorry," she said suddenly, "You just seemed so engrossed and picturesque, and I just couldn't help myself."

She began talking and soon enough I had found a new friend. She was different than I was, a lot more talkative and outgoing. For the first few weeks, I just listened to her speak about the places that she had seen, the people that she had photographed, the men that she had dated and the things that she had discovered. I felt small and inexperienced, but I allowed myself to feel comfortable in the presence of this new friend. I allowed myself to be open to new things, to new people and places. Over the next few months, I was accompanying her to art exhibits, meeting her friends, making them my own and visiting places that held relevance to her.

It was a good feeling. It was a freeing feeling.

Smiling at the recollection I placed the book with the leaves safely back into my bag and jogged to the bicycle stand. I rode past houses, some big, some small, some coloured and some bare, all standing uniformly in a single file. From atop my bike, I looked at the backyard of a house with a big outdoor swimming pool. Leaves, flowers and twigs drifted calmly in the water. This was Judy's house. I smiled as I thought back to the summer when Judy and I had swum so luxuriously in their pool.

Slowing down, I got off and walked with my bike for a while. My footsteps echoed on the empty sidewalk alongside their house. Mrs. Baker had already started putting up Christmas decorations. Mistletoe hung over the blue door and a few Christmas lights adorned the front of the house. There wasn't much to do since all of her seven children had moved out, some to apartments in and around D.C. and some to different states and countries. Though Judy still lived in the city, she was often busy with her classes at the university.

Mr. Baker loved the Subcontinent and had read every book available about India, Bangladesh, Nepal and Pakistan. He visited India when he was thirty-two and loved talking to me about the temples and the colours of all the spices that were still preserved safely in his head. He would show me photographs from his diary and the *banarasi sari* that he had bought for his mother.

I would tell him about my grandfather – Mr. Baker was fascinated by him. He believed he was still alive and asked me how he was doing whenever I ran into him. I never corrected him and said that he still complained of "that back pain". The discourse remained interesting this way.

A car roared past me and slowed down as it approached a house a few doors down from the Bakers'. I recognised the faces – it was Rizwan with a green-eyed brunette whom I often saw around campus. Running her fingers through his hair and kissing him softly on the lips, she hurried out of the car. The sound of her stilettos disrupted the silent lane. The car sped away again, leaving behind a trail of dust and the pungent smell of fuel.

***

I had been in America for a whole year. My transitioning took time but like water, I made an effort to be flexible, shaping and reshaping myself to surroundings. The first year was hard; everything was different, everything smelled and sounded different. Time and again in that first year, I would remark at all these differences between Pakistan and America. The roads were different, their meaning was different, the buildings and their history was different, and even the family that had eagerly brought me with them, suddenly morphed into different people. Over time, I saw them for what they really were in their true, American lives.

For a while, I spent most of my time studying road maps, making small talk with strangers whom I was to forget later, and roaming around fancy streets and galleries. Rizwan showed me around for the first few days, but then began disappearing with his own friends. Moreover, his unconventional personality that had seemed so appealing to me in Lahore, now often felt impulsive and strange. As a result, I demanded less, and instead, kept to myself, until the end of the first year, when I befriended Judy.

Lubna had begun a PR and Marketing agency when her husband was still alive. In the solitary time he spent painting, she represented important people and organised events. She wasn't very good at the convincing, but her son was. Rizwan, even as a teenager, was able to lure and smooth talk people into becoming their clients. In the beginning, the company ran smoothly, mother and son made a solid team. But the Artist's death changed everything, personally and professionally. Lubna lost sense of her company, investing more time in lovers than work, and Rizwan, he buried his sorrows deep within himself, and instead, adopted feelings of resentment towards his mother. With time, his inclination towards the company, too, worsened and he sought another job, something less demanding and somewhere away from his family.

Lubna didn't like this. She felt misplaced, at home and work. Her faith in the company was faltering and she competed with other agencies for the most competent candidates. Students often interned with her but most of them left after gaining experience and getting into grad schools.

A year ago, she hired me.

Every day after class I'd work with her and then we would go home together. In the office, I sat on a round desk next to a thirty-five-year-old Caucasian man who loved to swing his chair and have discussions with me about race, religion and politics. I handled my aunt's personal documents and notebooks, reminded her of meetings, mails and sometimes travelled with her to events.

At the beginning, she had opened up to me, narrating all her present dilemmas and the time when she believed she could achieve much.

"Time and time again, my husband asked me to leave this company and invest someplace else. I should've listened. Why didn't I listen? Now, I'm so entangled in this world. It is hard to leave. All my dreams are whisking away," she would say.

Hearing her speak like that, I realised how important my presence was to her. My being there was a comfort to her, a living, breathing diary that was available to her at all times to record her sadness and stories. In a way, she reminded me of *daddi* after *dadda* had died; how she had, for a while, found that same comfort in me.

Other than my assistance, she found me to be an ultimate emotional bridge between herself and her son. He and I would meet every other day, and it was a given that I would ask him to reconsider working for his mother. His answers were always predictable. There he was, settled in a nice apartment, an important person in the current company he worked at, and could do as he pleased without his mother's prying eyes scrutinising his relationships and life choices. Why would he have it any other way? And so, when it came to Rizwan, Lubna and I always went on silently.

Her daughter, Noor, had a different career plan as well. She was an artist like her father; a person who could spend hours capturing life on a canvas in all possible shades of green, grey and orange. She had decided recently that she'd soon be moving out of the house to go to art school.

It dawned on me during that time, how different Lubna was now. In Lahore, she was a calm and complacent, a rose-coloured woman, misrepresented and misunderstood by many. In America, her heart was always possessed by a faint delirium. She was always subjected to great anxiety and unease.

But somewhere deep inside, what affected my aunt the most was the very idea that she would be completely alone very soon.

***

CHAPTER TWENTY-ONE

Birds glided in the sky, flapping their tiny wings and swaying their bodies as they became one with the darkening horizon. Dusk was settling, a performance of brilliant colours, and yet the oil painting on the easel still failed to capture its passion.

Noor described the connotation of each colour she bathed her brush in. The sun in the painting was now an abstract green blob suspended with a golden string hovering over five horrid brown hands she called the Earth. Rizwan was right; she was nothing like her father yet. There was still time to grow and learn, to see and interpret the world as an artist.

In the house, the attic was a murky gallery displaying his abandoned work. Charcoal sketches of coloured birds, women, horses and women on horses buried underneath filthy sheets. His pens, his paints and brushes, sketchbooks and reading material placed just like it had been many years ago. It was as though this makeshift studio had been suspended in time, not a thing unchanged, preserving, in a way, the sanctity of the Artist's spirit.

Some of his best work, though, hung in the living room and

in Lubna's office, works worth admiring. I remembered looking at his signature beneath the painting of a woman's eyes. There was a certain delicacy in his handwriting; an unexplored depth.

From the paintings I saw and the bits of conversation overheard and collected, I deduced that the Artist was not a very happy man. He had resigned from life, entrapped himself in a small room and perhaps, found bliss and serenity in his creations. Like a lot of his work, there seemed as incompleteness to him as well. I liked to believe that there was a reason for his feeling this way, a part of the story that no one wished to share with me. No man was born sad.

My aunt sold some of her husband's magnificent work to her colleagues and friends. Maybe that was the real reason she held her annual cocktail cliental parties. Maybe it was not about networking after all. The venue was always the old gallery and the paintings decorating the event were always his. I never asked her why she sold her husband's work but I doubt she would have ever told me.

It required a lot of courage to have her kind of indifference, her kind of negligence and blatant disregard for the Artist's work. These paintings were his love affair and the canvases his mistress to whom he poured out his soul and unravelled his secrets, night after night.

But his wife seemed to understand nothing.

I think it went deeper than that; she *wanted* to understand nothing. If things didn't concern her, she didn't bother with them at all. Her world and love for things was constrained.

It was the evening after Thanksgiving and we were seated in Lubna's den. She was out with a friend and Rizwan had come over for the weekend. Now he sat, watching me with an intense look in his eyes. When I looked back, his face was expressionless and unchanging. Again I looked at him; his eyes remained transfixed and I knew at once that he was thinking about something else.

He was a strange man, Rizwan. He had an air of conceit, certain wickedness in his eyes. He was unpredictable and I was never sure what he felt or thought. He concealed much and told me only what he wanted to tell, the rest was always suspended in the air, for me to deliberate or ignore.

"I'll get this framed," said Noor, the proud young artist, once the painting was complete, "I've been working at it for months."

"I wish I could draw too, for therapeutic reasons, you know," Rizwan played with a paintbrush, "It's not fair that you get the good genes, he was my father too, you know."

"You were never much of an artist or poet. One needs to be sensitive for that," Noor folded her arms.

"Ouch.! That hurt. What shall I ever do?" he rubbed his eyes and then looked at me, "What do you think, Ameen? Does one need to be sensitive to be a poet or a writer?"

"Sensitive, drunk or in love," I said, "Whichever state of mind works."

"I'd prefer drinking over thinking anyway," he laughed and got up from the chair.

"You don't have what a painter should have – curiosity, an insatiable hunger…you give up too easily," Noor continued behind him.

The painting was removed from our sight. I walked to a window and looked outside. Scudding clouds roofed over our heads like a thin quilt of bluish pink shade. I listened to the siblings' debate, half-attentive, half-interested. Noor packed her paintbrushes and other tools in a bag and then went to the other room.

Rizwan and I went out for some coffee. He leaned back slightly and rested his eyes on the book I was holding. Taking it from my hands, he read the title and made a face, saying that I should take life easy.

"I'm not you, I can't take everything easy," I raised my eyebrow.

"Ahh," he said, "You know what your problem is, Mariam?"

I looked with a long, almost sardonic look.

"You feel too much."

"And is that a bad thing?"

"Oh, it's a very bad thing," he replied, mockingly.

There was a silence between us for a moment.

"Well…I can't ignore the demands of my mind," I said.

"Your mind rarely sleeps," he repeated, "You feel too much. This, my love, will only wear you down."

"Wear me down?"

He nodded in approval.

"It's a great burden one carries, Mariam, to think and feel things so intensely."

With that, he rose slowly, hugged me goodnight and we parted ways. He left to see a friend at a bar and I walked out of the coffee shop.

***

Outside, the weather had changed. It was colder. I zipped my jacket and walked on the street, looking at the fresh-faced mannequins outside shops, sale signs and crowds of men and women strolling past me.

I thought about Rizwan's pronouncement: *your mind rarely sleeps.*

His mind was unnatural. He drowned his every pain and unpleasant memory in glasses of wine. It was like an old companion that never failed him. He hardly thought too much, he told me, taking plunges without weighing things. Impulsive.

Whenever misery struck, he chose to sit in a bar and immerse himself in whatever he drank.

He allowed the drink to consume him completely. He enjoyed this feeling of being half-awake and half-asleep, where he could face his demons fearlessly and without any inhibitions. When the demons became stronger, he would waste himself some more, drowning in the medicine till his mind was completely numb. No one in the world could have offered him that kind of unconditional solace and release.

Telling himself repeatedly that the pain of the past was better left unstirred, he chose to bury it deep inside, where no one could access it but him.

Someone else I knew had shared a similar piece of advice with me once.

"The past offers you nothing but pain, someday you will understand this, Mariam baji. It has nothing new to say, or offer. When it knocks, you must not let it enter."

Hamida said this to me when I was growing up.. I remembered the night distinctly. It was a few hours after I heard that my friend and his mother had disappeared, gone somewhere to the city, holding the urns with the remaining ashes close to their hearts. The storm had settled, the village had become painfully quiet and I was washed clean by my tears. Hamida told me that now my friend had become the past and he must be forgotten, in order for me to move on in life.

She had sat near my grandmother's legs, massaging them slowly with almond oil. I had watched her fingers move back and forth in long strokes and her thumbs dig in the skin in circular motions. She drummed on my grandmother's leg just the same way she chopped vegetables on the board in the kitchen, but more gently and with a greater sense of rhythm. My grandmother drifted off to sleep.

I was quiet the entire time, and Hamida had noticed.

"One forgets painful things as time goes by," she said to herself, out loud, so I could hear it too, "It's a good thing. Sometimes there's nothing good in the past. There is just pain. Your friend is gone, the ashes are gone, their memories must now also go…"

She wished to tell me explicitly that my grandfather was a fool to let the past conquer him once again, that Prakriti was a weak woman to choose the past over her marriage, the same past that she escaped once by changing her name and identity.

Her advice had made little sense when I was a child. Only after meeting Rizwan did I fully understand it. I would always think that the lovers' past was beautiful – meant to be unearthed, re-lived and re-imagined. But perhaps I was wrong, for it had caused them nothing but pain. Similarly, Rizwan's memories of his father's death and his mother's philandering had also caused him nothing but pain.

Maybe Rizwan and Hamida were right. Sometimes, clinging onto the past was not the right thing. Sometimes, the past was better left unstirred.

I had to learn to let go of things; let go of Grandfather, of Prakriti, of Karan and the ashes.

***

As the evening wore on, I walked through rows of faces and the cacophony of noises. I sailed like a ghost with no set destination and let my mind wander as it often did in solitude. The bright lights dwindled, the street dissolved into ambiguity and all the sounds ceased. In that state of oblivion, I somehow disappeared from Washington and found myself in familiar graveyard of Lahore.

A light cool wind blew through my hair and a lock of hair fell on my cheek. I was on a marble bench and beside me sat a frail, old figure. We looked at the scattered graves in front of us and were both moved by the spectacle. The figure, my grandfather, heaved a sigh and told me that he had a dream last night, a strange one, where his late mother and grandmother visited him.

His voice trembled as he began, "The human mind is a confusing realm, Mariam. It has a strange obsession with the past. The past is always there, like an unwanted friend, lurking in the basement of our minds. It sits there with all the other things that we have willfully buried – desires, regrets, obsessions and repressed memories. They look for an escape and what better escape than to get a chance to roam freely in your dreams, where you have no control over your mind. What do you dream about, my child?"

I said I didn't remember.

He said he dreamt of long voyages and rivers of holy waters. He said he dreamt of happy lovers and open moors where they could walk till they disappeared.

My grandfather's mind was just abstract and unnatural as Rizwan's, but his had a certain beauty that filled me with a longing to explore its truths and complexities. I now realised that what Grandfather possessed, what he so dearly treasured, was the exact thing that Rizwan craved: company, an escape, an outlet to let out his regrets, desires and obsessions.

I was Grandfather's escape. I had always been his escape.

Somehow he thought his secrets were safer with a child. Children seldom comprehend and with time, forget. I did not. Rather, it had become my life's mission to glue together the brightly coloured scraps of his life, the family myths, and the truths I discovered on my own. And in doing so, gradually developing an understanding of a world that was much larger than mine, a world that belonged to two estranged lovers, a world that was only my grandfather's.

"This is why my mind rarely sleeps," I whispered and stopped at a bus stop, *"Look what you have done to me, Grandfather."*

I checked the time. It was getting late. I wanted to get home before dark. The bus stop was covered in bus routes, timings and maps for people to travel to, to get lost in.

Travelling to different places always made me think of Anika and the railway station. I imagined streams of sunlight spilling across the rooftop, I imagined sitting with her and talking about things that we only knew.

On this cold November night, I thought about my sisters and their lives in Lahore. The weather must have been wonderful back home. Aminah was now engaged to a boy she fell in love with after Rizwan had left. They were thinking of getting her married next year. On the phone, she sounded excited and asked me to tell the news to Rizwan.

Anika was settled with the sober-faced man but her emails remained bland and impersonal, as if she was hiding a pain she wanted to disclose only when we met. She continued our ritual of jogging in the early mornings, though now alone. She wrote that she spent her idle time staring at a fungus growing in the corners of her room. She remained mysterious in her mails. It felt as though with all the distance between us, we had grown from sisters to simply acquaintances, strangers even.

But maybe it was all in my mind; maybe I was reading unnecessarily between the lines. Maybe there wasn't much to think about. Maybe Rizwan was right.

Reality came to me in the form of blinding headlights from a bus. It wasn't mine. I shrugged my shoulders and began walking towards home. I slowed down at an intersection facing a beautiful marble statue of classical nude Gods. Surrounded by lush green trees, the landmark fountain looked holy as it stood silently before the background of the palling sky. Before moving to America, I had read about this statue in books about Washington. Then one day, I had gone out searching for it and found it.

I watched the water flow over the figures, cleansing them.

"Mariam?" I heard a known voice call.

I looked up. It was a colleague from work, Richard White. Running his fingers through his dishevelled black hair, he looked at me warmly.

"I just live around the corner," he smiled.

"So you tell me every time we meet," I laughed.

"Yet you can never take a hint," he winked.

We sat down on a bench.

Richard and I met a year ago at one of Lubna's parties. He was her most prized employee and knew everything about her work.

It had been a long, long week, he told me, riding the elevator countless times at the office, small talk last night at Thanks giving dinner with his family, followed by more small talk this evening with women at a friend's surprise birthday party.

Small talk always tired him. He preferred lighting his cigarette and devouring the world with his eyes as he rested in a corner of some room. He wrote poetry when he was nine and a journal when he was thirteen. He smoked his first cigarette at twelve; his sister gifted him a Marlboro wonderfully wrapped in silver paper. That was the time when his parents got divorced and he wrote three poems every night. He fell in love for the first time when he was in high school but the girl moved away and got married to a much older man by the age of nineteen. Now he saw her flashing her assets on the cover of the new *Playboy*. He didn't miss her much. *Wasn't enough meat on her bones*, he had said when he told me about her.

This evening, we just sat together on the bench, comfortable in each other's company, neither saying much. There wasn't going to be any small talk and I was never one to shy away from silence. I don't know what he was thinking about but he just stared ahead at the falling water and glistening statues. I sank back and allowed myself to relax.

The evening had completely drifted away. The night was falling.

He walked me back home.

***

CHAPTER TWENTY-TWO

At home, Aminah's wedding preparation had come to a stop.

I listened intently as Anika, in hushed whispers, disclosed the reason to me over the phone – Abdullah lost a friend in December. It was during the Eid prayer that a bomb went off in a mosque. Many people died, many returned home broken and many were held for interrogation.

Two months had passed after the tragedy, but our brother failed to recuperate. He remembered and relived every moment, feeling everything so very deeply. He sat in his *barsati* all day and watched the sun come to life and die, watched the restless clouds conspire and form patterns on the changing sky.

Mother wanted him to move on and felt he couldn't if he stayed there. She had always wanted him to settle in America when he was older, get an important job, and establish a good name for the family.

"Mother wants to know if Abdullah should fly out to America or not? It will be good for him to leave Lahore for a while. Will he be happy there?" Anika asked me.

How could I have answered that question?

Sadness had descended upon my family as my brother refused to leave the threshold. Anika made it a point to mention that throughout this grief, the pigeons, the parrots and the swallows kept stopping by.

I changed the subject and asked her how her life had been. I could hear an uneasy chuckle on the other end of the phone.

"Remember when we used to trace lines on our palms and figure out our future?"

I said I did.

"Well, I realised that it's never that simple, is it? How can a few curvy lines on your hand reveal your future?"

She didn't say anything more. And neither did she have to for me to realise that there was something seriously wrong.

***

Mother soon convinced Abdullah to move to America for his Bachelor degree. They zeroed in on Boston and began applications, since there were multiple universities in the vicinity. Anika made sure to always keep me in the loop.

Chemical Engineering, that's what he wanted to do.

As the applications went on the wedding preparations resumed once again.

The news of Abdullah's potential arrival in America and details of Aminah's wedding didn't fill Lubna and her family with the excitement I had hoped. They couldn't deem of the possibility of flying to Pakistan just to attend a three-day ceremony.

My aunt put on her glasses and leaned in as I showed her a picture of Aminah's fiancé on my laptop. Aminah's face was glowing with happiness as her husband-to-be stood beside her, looking shyly into the camera. Anika could be seen in the background without the company of the sober-faced man.

***

CHAPTER TWENTY-THREE

The walls in Richard's apartment were painted yellow. In the living area there was a big wooden bookcase that belonged to his grandfather and a painting that he had bought from the Artist himself.

"He was a man of great patience and mystery," he said while describing her uncle.

The painting was called *The Swan* and was a clear depiction of a golden-haired Leda strangling a seductive bird. Instead of a white swan, the god Zeus was a glistening grey goose and instead of the controversial act of copulation, the fair Leda had won her freedom by overpowering the dominant male. But despite all the poetic license and the Artist's selection of a rather perturbing myth, there was nothing disturbing in his version of the story.

Underneath the painting, Judy sat on a chair with her laptop. She was editing some photographs she took at a party, embedding her watermark into the bottom right corner of each frame. Judy met Richard when I invited her to cover a fashion event Lubna's agency was representing.

Richard returned from the kitchen with three mugs of coffee.

"But where will he stay?" he handed me a mug.

He was asking about my brother.

"I don't know," I replied, "Probably at the dorms."

"But don't you think he should stay with you after all that he has been through?" Judy asked.

I pondered for a moment. This thought had fleetingly raced through my head, but I shoved it away because I knew it wasn't right to ask Lubna for more room. There were times when even I felt like a complete intruder. Those were the days when Rizwan would disappear completely and Noor remained absorbed in her work.

Lubna often brought home Babar, a fifty-six-year-old British-Pakistani that she was presumably seeing. He had separated from his second wife, a twenty-something Canadian-Nepalese woman, two years ago and the two teenaged daughters from his first marriage were studying History at Arizona University.

We met for the first time when I accidently ran into him in the kitchen one morning. The couple was sitting, reading the newspaper. He lifted his head when I arrived. His green eyes glittered as he smiled widely, "So this is Mariam! I've heard a lot about you."

There was a small scar on his left cheek.

"Mariam, this is my new business partner, Babar."

She said that he was supporting and funding Lubna's company for a project. There were times when she felt she should join his automobile company as a business partner and abandon hers forever, but the idea of being a failure didn't entertain her much.

They would often lie down on the couch, nestling, watching television in the den. When our eyes met, hers and mine, she would look away instantly. She felt exposed and feared I'd tell the wolves back home. She had just recently redeemed herself, shed off her previously unholy image in Lahore, and my presence worried her. Even after being around me for over a year, she barely knew me.

The only time I had a proper conversation with Babar was when he was invited for a dinner at home. Rizwan had arrived to meet her mother's new boyfriend and Noor had come home early from university.

Expressionless, I focused on my dinner plate: cold pasta and turkey.

"Is this your first visit to the States?" asked Babar, gently sipping his wine.

"Yes, first visit," I replied politely.

"What do you study here?"

"Language and Literature."

He nodded.

"My eldest daughter, Sasha, wanted to visit Pakistan but I persisted that she stayed here. She is a History major," he began, "I've lived in Pakistan for fifteen years, in fact, my first wife was from Karachi. You've met her, haven't you?" he asked my aunt.

Lubna nodded that she had.

"She is known for her NGO work there. Anyway, I moved to the States when I was sixteen with my stepmother. Perhaps you've heard of my father, he's actively involved in the political front."

I had heard his father's name.

"I didn't know you had a political background," I said, "Would you be joining politics…"

"Ah, not me," he became unnecessarily defensive, "My grandfathers and father were deluded. They made enemies, strange allies…everyone becomes a politician one way or the other in Pakistan, isn't that so? I couldn't get entangled in such a wrecked life. A man shouldn't be judged by the choices his parents make."

The old man took out his cell phone and showed me a picture of a very young woman, closer to my age, standing next to him in front of the Eiffel Tower.

It wasn't his daughter. It was his ex-wife, not the NGO worker but the Canadian-Nepalese. He showed me her picture and said that she was also a student in the same university as I was.

I said I had never met her.

After he left, I had washed the dishes with Noor and then

went to my bedroom. Downstairs, Rizwan had argued with his mother, something about her judgments and choices, something about her getting hurt all the time.

"You know better than this!" was the last thing he said before he stormed out of the back door.

Back in Richard's apartment, Judy called my name, interrupting my thoughts of Lubna and Babar. She flipped her laptop to show a photograph. An old woman lay on a white sandy beach in a wedding dress, around her broken clocks, each set on a different time.

"Miss Havisham?" I said.

"Yes. Something like this," Judy said, "I want to do something like this for my final thesis."

I nodded in approval.

"I will stay with him for a couple of weeks. I have to, I mean after all he's been through," I responded to Richard's question.

"He can always stay with me or Judy before he leaves for Boston. When do his classes begin anyway?"

"He arrives in August and his classes begin at the end of the month, depends on the programme, I don't know."

Richard nodded. The conversation shifted to Lubna. Her company was worsening with time and Lubna's sudden fixation with Babar was playing a big role in everything. Richard had already begun looking for a job in New York. He said he could no longer wanted to deal with this irreverent and dysfunctional family. Unable to change his mind, I had only nodded and said that I would miss his company in the office.

***

Rizwan resurfaced after a few weeks. He didn't come home, but we met at an Indian restaurant for dinner.

"How have you been?" Rizwan asked.

I told him everything was going well for now.

He smiled and then paused for a moment. Then in an almost dejected tone, he said, "You know, there've been rumours that the company might shut down."

I said I was aware.

"You shouldn't believe gossip," he continued

"I know."

Silence.

"You know, Rizwan," I said, "You can always come back…you can work with Lubna again. Things can get better."

"I'm not spending any more time trying to fix her or her life. What about me? What about the things that I want?"

"What is it, Rizwan? What's always troubling you? You've become some modern-day Hamlet."

He studied my serious face and then smiled, "You're wonderful, Mariam, but you need not worry about me. I'll take care of it."

He never liked my questioning gaze; he didn't like the idea of being answerable to anyone. He avoided confrontation at all costs and claimed he no longer even remembered what his real problem was.

But one thing was certain – Rizwan felt a great deal around me. He enjoyed the fact that I would sit with him for as long as he liked and talked about things that only he wanted to. And then he would disappear just as effortlessly as he had arrived. I would never question his pattern nor interrogate him about his life or whereabouts.

Richard, on the other hand, never liked him. He said he was a careless man, a man incapable of love or feeling anything deeper. To that I'd always shake my head, look at Richard with a smile on my face and suggest that perhaps time would change Rizwan.

***

Days later, the news was final.

With a stroke of Babar's hand, Lubna and Rizwan's company's

door closed. Their dreams and company history vanished. The business was wrapped up. Emails were sent to clients with a *"We will be back with something bigger and better"* tagline.

And Babar became Lubna's undying shadow.

Around me, she became needlessly cautious. We seldom interacted. It was like without her folders and laptop in my hands, I was a useless entity to her. She no longer experienced the same connection she had felt with me in Lahore, the same connection that had once made her convince me to move to America. She replaced people too easily, I observed.

I stayed out of her way and spent more time with other people. I tried to stay out of the house as much as possible, mostly to avoid awkward interactions with her. I went hiking with Judy and her friends. I accompanied Mr. Baker to a museum he had wanted to see for the longest time, and I went with Richard to several parties and weddings as his plus one. I stayed long hours at the university library or studied in coffee shops. Anything to stay out of Lubna and Babar's way.

When Rizwan heard the news of the company closing, he drove to the house and got into a heated argument with his mother. Though he didn't want to work with her, he also didn't want her to destroy her own dreams for the whims of a man. His voice became nonchalant and aggressive. He blamed her for everything – his failed education, love life and career. He said something about sinking all of the family and the Artist's money into futile projects. He said something about her choice in men and her constant heartbreaks. He said something about his loneliness and inability to grow as a person.

She talked, reasoned, cried but he left her without listening to a single word.

Hours later, after the dust settled, Lubna asked me if there was still any room for me at the college dormitories. My heart sank. I looked at her stony face, now looking less human and more and more like some evil creature that I no longer recognised.

I understood everything then.

With the company shut down, she didn't really need me.

Her eyes were flickering as she asked me again; I didn't know what to say.

The sinking feeling now transformed into anger. I felt humiliated on many levels.

"I'll leave tomorrow morning, aunt Lubna," I said sardonically and left her walked out of the room.

My time with her in Lahore evaporated from my mind and I pushed away any lingering respect for her. This was new for me, the feeling of rejection and abandonment from someone who was a part of my own family. I had taken her in when the wolves in Lahore had rejected her, and this, she had let escape her mind so easily. It seemed that nothing was important for my American aunt anymore, not her family and certainly not her dreams.

I filled forms for the dorm, wrote a letter to my father asking for some money and made a mental note to look around for a job around campus as soon as possible. The next morning, I moved in with Judy till I was allocated a room. Judy understood and said with Rizwan gone and Noor seldom home, it didn't even make sense staying with the lovers. She was right; their voices rang around the house, intolerable laughter and happiness.

Lubna had become a different person again; someone's lover. She relished this new position, her newly found identity. She no longer wanted to be remembered as a melancholic artist's wife, or a crazy boy's mother. She meant something to someone now. She felt now, at last, so new, so wonderfully young and wanted, that she had forgotten everything else.

But I had wanted to ask her then, who would she be when all these men in her life disappeared? When it would just be her. When she was stripped away of the infatuation with Babar, of the complexities of her relationship with Rizwan, of the lingering memories of the Artist. Who then would Lubna be on her own?

During my time in the house, I had sat in the attic countless times to admire her husband's paintings. They were surreal. I read some of his framed newspaper interviews. He was said to be Godlike. He was called perfect. Opposite to everything she was, but he never left her and I had started wondering why.

Gradually, I formed a bond with all the women and Gods and animals in his work. They were all exquisitely different but reflected the Artist.

There was one that captivated me completely. It was his only painting that showed a couple – a man and a woman squatted on a muddy track in a village, as if awaiting someone or something. The track was swathed in dust, and behind the couple was a sea of green fields. He didn't draw the man's face but the woman had round eyes and a small mouth. She was draped in a red shawl and decorated with jewellery, as if recently married. Her eyes scanned the horizon. The man's face was also turned away from his wife and in his hand was a half-smoked cigarette.

Was this them, I wondered. Was this the caricature of the Artist and Lubna; of their relationship, of the long silences and emotional distance between them?

As I traced the painting's familiar dusty track and field, I was overcome by nostalgia. I missed my grandparents, I missed Anika…I missed all those people who would have never abandoned me like Lubna had.

The night before I left the house, I had looked closely and longingly at every painting and wondered, which out of these Lubna would sell after all this failed. Which part of the Artist's soul would she now trade, without giving it a second thought?

***

Illuminated, scented candles, a sea of rose petals and the bride's fair hands painted with intricate *henna* patterns. Her face glowed with eternal bliss and tenderness. Aminah had gotten married earlier than decided, June. Her in-laws were said to be very impatient.

Lubna asked to see the pictures but I lied and said that I received no email. It took me all of fifteen minutes to pack an entire year in two large boxes.

***

CHAPTER TWENTY-FOUR

Everything else melted away when I saw his face appear through the automatic doors of the airport.

"Abdullah!" I cried out, waving to him from a crowd of people, all eagerly awaiting their loved ones. We looked at each other for a minute before we hugged and laughed, delighted to be in each other's presence again. We carried his luggage together to the cab.

He smelled like monsoon.

He smelled like mother's cooking.

He smelled like home.

I wanted so badly to envelop myself in those smells.

In the cab, he told me stories from back home.

The chief gossip from Aminah's wedding was about a relative who accidently stole a gold bangle, and how the sober-faced man had gotten himself into some business swindle.

Abdullah told me that the monsoon rains were heavier that year and had fallen continuously for days. He had to come down from the *barsati* during a hailstorm and slept in my room.

Grandfather's house finally flooded. Drenched in knee-length water, Abdullah and Father had moved the furniture to drier places, wrapped it in plastic sheets and fixed the leaking walls. They stayed in the village for two nights and in that raging storm, it felt like the Raja's house would crumble completely. I remained quiet, thinking how the indestructible forces of nature can sometimes be responsible for great losses, bringing down mighty rulers and otherwise unconquerable civilizations, rubbing out great legends and their stories. The entire history and story of my grandfather's house could perish with a stroke of an invisible hand and I could do nothing to stop it.

"Mariam, have you ever seen water lizards?" Abdullah repeated his question.

I woke from my thoughts and shook my head.

"I did when he slept in the village. Disgusting!"

I smiled.

"On our way back, we visited the graveyard too. The rains brought in a lot of mess, rotten leaves, twigs, wrappers and other broken things," he said, "We cleaned the place up and then left for home."

Then suddenly, he turned his face and looked out of the window at the adulating clouds, buildings, roads and people.

"Everything is bigger here," he whispered, "And frightening."

"Nothing is frightening," I held his hand, "You'll be happy here, like I have been."

He bit his lip and his eyelids drooped.

"But I'm not like you, Mariam. I'm not strong and flexible like you. Change frightens me." He took my hand.

"We'll be okay, Abdullah. I promise you."

There suddenly evolved a new understanding between us, something that was missing in Lahore. We found it here, in this new place.

***

Abdullah stayed with Judy and me in her apartment. We showed him around D.C. and took him to Boston to see his university. We met Richard consecutively for days and were invited by Lubna's family to Babar's birthday party at his home. We were told that this year, the event was presumed to be a grand one because he was in love again. Abdullah passed on the party and I didn't compel him to go either. He was tired and some sleep would have done him good.

When Rizwan and I met at Babar's party, it had been over a month since I had seen him. He seemed frustrated. We stood in the library, away from all the celebration and noise. He made small talk about Abdullah and pretended to care for a while. Then, he resumed to his drinking and sulking.

"I shall be leaving next week," he said as he sipped his drink.

"Where are you running away to this time?" I asked.

"Philadelphia. Going to stay with a friend for a while. Probably look for work there too."

I nodded.

He took a sip of his drink again and stood with his back towards everything. He looked at the ornaments on the mantelpiece, replicas and gifts Babar had collected from all over the world. I recognised a golden and blue statue of the Egyptian Goddess Isis, a sculpture of the deceptive Trojan horse and a small steel Eiffel tower. There were photo frames, lots of them; some pictures were of his family back in Pakistan and some of his adventure trips around the globe.

I studied Rizwan. He was unusually quiet, as if guarding a horrible secret. As always, he preferred running away to facing his problems. Sadness would often bring out something bitter in him, and this bitterness would appear and disappear. Whenever this intense dark streak re-emerged, he became absolutely dejected and restless.

Lubna entered the room and asked us to join the party. Rizwan turned around dramatically and mocked her. There was a moment of hesitation between the two. In the background, we heard nothing but the light strumming of piano and refined murmurs from the den. It was a superficial and unreal culture that she was entangling herself into and Rizwan knew that she was nothing like them.

Lubna's eyes narrowed towards her son to the point of looking ugly, she pursued her lips and walked away to attend to their guests.

"Do you want to get out of here?" he asked suddenly.

Lubna had had lovers when the Artist was still alive. Towards the end of his life, he spent too much time painting other women, which made her feel neglected and unloved. She had her heart broken by other men, many many times. Every lover took a small part of her away with him, leaving her bare and anxious. It wouldn't be long before Babar completely deprived her of her essence.

"Do you want to go from here?" he asked again. I nodded.

We had driven away from the party now, to a secluded park with a quiet pond. The city seemed deserted, the streets slept in silence. He picked up a large stone and threw it angrily in the water, breaking it as if it were glass. It was an unresolved internal matter and I just happened to be present at a wrong time. My hand on his shoulder pacified him. He smiled slowly.

"I can't save her anymore," he said quietly, "She is too gullible, but I also can't leave her. I feel I owe this to my father."

"She doesn't want to be saved, Rizwan. Maybe she is happy. You owe her this happiness."

"Even if it is for an insignificantly small period of time?"

"What isn't? Is everything not eventually transient?", I asked quietly.

He rubbed his eyes and then kept his hand on his forehead.

"You have to let her go."

"She was never there for me, you know, throughout my life, she was never there for me. And neither was he. They just threw me in boarding school when I was so young, and ever since then…" his voice trailed.

"I know, I can imagine."

He moved away from me and looked hard at the earth.

"Then why do I have this urge to rescue her every time?"

I paused, my eyelids dropped and I whispered, "Because maybe you're a better person than her. Maybe you do have a good heart, maybe you're not as bad a person as you think you are..."

"No Mariam," he interrupted, "That's one thing I'm not – good."

We paused.

"I don't want to be like this, it's not exciting anymore," he confessed.

"You're leaving her, your sister is leaving her too and your father left her. She needs something to cling to. Let Babar be that anchor, even if it's for a brief period of time."

"I've missed you, Mariam," he said softly, "I've missed having someone who doesn't judge me and listens to me."

I didn't speak.

"You shouldn't have just packed your bags and left, you could have called me. We convinced you to come here in the first place, it was our responsibility."

"Nothing was, or is your responsibility. I chose to come here. Besides, I will like the dorm better. It's quieter."

"They are more peaceful. No one can argue about that."

I looked at him for some time and then held his arm, "Come on! You need some distraction. This has been a long night."

He smiled.

"Tell me, where do you want to go?"

"There's a nice bar down the street. I could use a drink..."

We went to the bar and he soon drank his sorrows away. He forgot everything and everyone for the night.

***

CHAPTER TWENTY-FIVE

Abdullah moved to Boston at the end of August. A few weeks after that, Richard and I drove to see him. I noticed that he had a great fondness for Richard. They talked for long hours about his new friends, old friends, the *barsati*, recollections of those long cricket afternoons and the cultural shocks he encountered. They laughed and shared, like two long lost brothers and through their conversations, I gathered that he was doing okay.

"How are you now?" I asked.

"I feel better, Mariam," he smiled widely, talking about the new friends he had made and the courses he was taking. It was the same smile he wore when we played Ludo, during Ramadan as children. When the days felt longer than usual and we did little to pass the time.

He would gently push his playing piece to his starting square without rolling a six on the dice, like the rules said, and Aminah would catch him cheating. The impulsive twin, with a great fury, would hit him with a cushion and he rolled on the carpet, chuckling.

Fasting days were long and tiresome, so my siblings and I would pull out the Ludo board to kill time. Sometimes, I would sit on the kitchen stool and watch Anika fry pakoras and samosas for iftar time, when the family would sit to break the fast. She would ask me to rinse the dishes or wash the vegetables.

"Make yourself useful," she would say, "We can't gossip right now, we're fasting and it's sinful. We have after iftar, don't we?"

With that, she would wink and laugh heartily at her own joke.

During those days, Abdullah and I would often lay down on the swing with our feet dangling in the air, none of us speaking for a long time. Once, when he was eleven and I, fifteen, we sat packing up the Ludo board as iftar time drew near. He said my name and I looked up.

Then, he asked suddenly, "Was it daddi's barsi yesterday, her death anniversary?"

I nodded and put the dice inside a cardboard box.

"Is that why we went to the graveyard?"

"Of course."

"Tell me something about her, our grandmother. I don't remember her," he rested his head on his knee.

I folded the board, lifted my head and our eyes met. I had wanted to say no but then I would have so easily fractured his beautifully curious mind.

"Well, she was wonderful," I said, imagining daddi's face before me, "And she taught us how to protect ourselves from strange men."

"How?"

"By tossing spices in their eyes and running away. Didn't you always wonder why we keep spices powder in our bag packs?"

He pondered, "Yes, but why was she so afraid?"

"I don't know. She said people change, even the good ones. One must always protect themselves."

"Didn't she marry Grandfather? I heard he was pretty strange himself..."

"Abdullah," I had become a little furious, "During your life, you will hear terrible things about him and other people, but you must learn to sift through what is real and what is rumour."

He seemed as confused as ever.

After iftar, Anika and I would sit on the rooftop every day and talk endlessly. I told her about my conversation with Abdullah. At first, she scolded me for being so harsh with him and then suddenly softening her tone, she told me that once she too had asked daddi this very question.

"You did?" my eyes were wide, "But why, Anika?"

"Because I was curious. We are growing up and we should know such things."

She said daddi had thought? for a while and let her fingers run through her silver, wire-like hair.

"I got married because I had to, like my mother had to, like you and your sisters have to and also because I knew that with time I would fall in love with your grandfather," she had said, "Yes, he made some mistakes during his life, but then so did I."

She said that a woman was built to survive. She was built to fight storms, paddle through mighty waves and escape avalanches. She could endure great pains but only if she recognises her strength. Women were strong.

In those days, Anika and I knew a few strong women ourselves but they were made of ink and were imprints on paper. One of them was a recurring face in newspapers. I recalled a huge coloured photograph of the woman; radiant, fierce, unconquerable. She looked into the camera with her bright, fearless eyes, questioning anyone who questioned her strength. On her left shoulder rested a grey shawl with a brown border, on her head a milky white muslin *dupatta* and around her wrist, a golden watch. That was Benazir Bhutto, one of the most famous women in the country.

Then there was the blue-eyed princess of Wales who half smiled on the cover of an old *Time* magazine that Anika and I found in Father's bookshelf. He had saved all the important issues from the nineties. During the village flooding, he had brought these with him along with all of Grandfather's books.

In between the books of Rumi, Iqbal, Ghalib and Manto, lay a copy of a controversial novel by Ismat Chugtai, a woman Grandfather said was too resilient and indomitable for her time. Hence, strong.

There was another strong woman that our mother was particularly fond of, our late aunt Parveen who spent her entire life battling breast cancer. We didn't know much about her but we were reminded repeatedly to pray for her on *Shab-e-Bara'at*, the night of salvation and so, we prayed for a woman we had never met nor seen but whose strength we had only heard about.

After Grandmother's death, I added three more women to the list: my grandmother, who had to endure my grandfather's aloofness for the entirety of their married life, and her two sisters – Gulshan, the blind one who lived with her, and Hamida, and the other mysterious sister who was raped as a young girl.

****

I had kissed Abdullah on his cheek and left his university with Richard.

He still hadn't spoken about his friend's death and I didn't bring it up either. I felt, like me, he must have taken long jogs at night or early mornings walks to think, rethink and then burry those thoughts deep down for the rest of the day. I imagined, like me, he didn't trust people with his thoughts. We both guarded our thoughts like secrets, concealing so they didn't get tainted in the outside world.

"That is a very bad thing," Richard said, "How can you trust yourself with your own thoughts, your own understanding? Can we ever figure out things when we are on our own? We need people, we need friends, Mariam."

He was right, I did need friends. My friend was back home, possibly facing a hard time because of her failing marriage.

Anika.

She asked me if I still lived with Lubna. I had lied and said I did.

She asked me where I worked now. I told her I was now a teacher's assistant and was getting paid quite well. She had told me she was glad.

But I still hadn't responded to her most recent email:

I went to the railway station last week to see off my husband. After he left, I remained on the platform for several minutes looking at the rail tracks, imagining I was waiting for daddi and you were here with me (I pictured an eight-year-old version of you).

I asked a porter when the next train leaves. He said, "Now."

I asked where it was going. I didn't know the place he mentioned. I came back home, feeling empty. All I remember is that I wanted to take that train and go wherever it was going to take me.

There is so much to tell you. So much.

I had read and re-read that email several times but still I had not replied. What could I have written back to her?

***

CHAPTER TWENTY-SIX

Before moving to the States, Afreen was a chef in Lahore. She was a learned woman of forty-six and had three children. Her thin pale hands would move dramatically as she talked about Benazir's assassination, the great elections and the bombings around the country. Whenever she met me, she felt she needed she to release everything from her mind.

"Don't you thank Allah that you're here, Mariam? It's safer here, isn't it?" she said once while handing me my free *chapli kebabs*.

"Perhaps…but my family is there," I replied.

She ran a Pakistani restaurant near the university and we happened to run into each other quite often in departmental stores and pharmacies. She would take me by my arm and we'd talk for hours. We would walk down the street and then towards her restaurant. Like a mother, she would give me food and watch me eat *kebabs* and *nans*, reminding me to tell her repeatedly how well she cooked. On Fridays, she would insist I come to the mosque for prayer. Sometimes, I went in and met the rest of her group but mostly I refused.

She knew that Abdullah had also come to America to study.

I hadn't dared tell her about his friend's death and his sorrow because I knew, unknowingly, she would have relished painting for me the horrifying picture of the accident. She would have told me how a bomber prepares, how *it* goes off, how the bodies scatter in the air and when exactly does the human heart stops beating. Not that she had any malice in her heart, but that was just how she was.

We both knew how things in Pakistan had changed drastically over the years. The difference was that she wanted to talk about it, describe it, question and understand it and I didn't. She wanted to talk about the floods, the fires, the murders, the dirty, dirty political game, and I didn't.

She was going to stay in Washington, she was going to live here and cook here, but I was going to go back. I was going to go back to Lahore, to my city, to my grandparents' city. I didn't want to hear about the fires, bombs and deaths she so conveniently described. I wanted her to talk about the beautiful Lahore – its garden, its people, its colourful *bazaars*, its scrumptious food, its old buildings, its stations, its sights, sounds and colours, but I don't think she remembered any of that. She only wished to remember the wrecks and the heartbreaks.

I sat on a chair in her restaurant and watched her disappear inside the kitchen. We had dinner together that night. I waited for her to lock up so I could bid her a proper goodnight.

The clock ticked on the red wall, six-thirty, it said. I looked at the calendar that hung next to a poster of *Mecca*, November 19th, 2009. Time had flown by. It was fall already. It would snow soon. I would begin work on my thesis soon. Richard would move to New York for work soon. Judy would graduate soon.

My eyes fell on the glass window. Rizwan stood there, waving. I hadn't seen him in weeks.

I waved back, excitedly, and walked out of the restaurant. He put his arm around me, saying he had been looking for me for a long time. I bade Afreen goodnight and drove away with him.

The roads were busy that evening and he was lively, full of a new light. He had reclaimed his previous spirit and energy and I was a little relieved. He was in his element; the same cheery side of him was back, the side that drew my sisters and many other women towards him.

I wondered where he had been all this time and tried a few times to ask him, but he evaded the topic so I too, let it go. In his playfulness, he told me how much he had missed me and how different I was from everyone else that he knew. I looked at him half-expecting a chuckle, a declaration that he was joking. But he remained completely serious.

We stopped at a pharmacy. He had to buy some things. I got lost in the greeting cards and stationary aisle. I thought of sending Anika a card. I knew a handwritten letter would make her happier than an impersonal email, especially when I still hadn't found the right words to respond to her previous confession. I picked up a postcard with a picture of a middle-eastern girl. She stared defiantly as though her piercing sea green eyes could see straight through my soul. She could become anyone's confidant instantly.

"Great choice! This is everybody's favourite," smiled an employee as he walked past me briskly carrying what looked like a new carton of shampoos.

Someone tapped on my shoulder. Rizwan stood, carrying a small brown bag, "Shall we leave?"

"What are you always thinking about?" he asked as we crossed the automatic doors.

I passed him a look, "I'm not always thinking, Rizwan."

"Do you like it here?"

"Of course."

"Would you like to stay here forever?"

"I haven't really thought about it."

"You could think about it now."

He stopped walking and grabbed my arm. We stopped walking. His expression was serious and his eyes looked at me inquisitively.

"I have to figure some things out."

"Figure them out here," he said.

"It's not so simple, Rizwan. There are places there that I belong to. There are people there who need me."

"What about you? What do you need, Mariam?"

"I need those people and I need those places, too."

His released my arm and I began to walk towards the car. He didn't speak for a while but I heard his feet, slowly moving, as if it were too much of a struggle and pain to catch up to me.

"I'm so tired of you, Mariam," he said softly, "I'm so, so tired of you."

I stopped where I was and turned to look at him, "*You're* tired of *me*?"

"Everything you say or do matters to me, changes something in me and so I run away."

"Run away?"

"From you, your influence, because I know you're not here to stay. So I can't allow myself to get used to you being here."

We looked at each other and did not speak. His words rang in my mind. This was his loneliness speaking, and he had begun to grow familiar of it. He was afraid that I would leave him for good, leave him for Lahore, or perhaps worse, leave him for *somebody*.

He had begun to feel that he possessed me, that I was this 'thing' he would call up and go to whenever he was down or angry and everything would be okay. His sounding board; his punching bag.

"I'm very afraid," his voice, almost a whisper, filled the deserted parking lot.

My heart was seared. We had known each other for a while, but we had never talked like this, so honestly. It had always been about him, never me; today he had caught me off guard. I didn't like explaining myself to people, mostly because I myself didn't know what I wanted and why I wanted it. And people, they need facts, they crave logic and my mind had never been able to generate any.

"I don't know what I'll do when you'll leave."

I blinked, taken back, not knowing what to say, "Whatever it was that you did before I got here, I suppose."

I turned my face away slowly.

"Stop there for a minute," he called out softly.

He walked up to me and placed both his hands on my shoulders. An indistinctively foreign feeling crept over me. I felt as though I would stop breathing, yet I tried to remain steady.

"Walk with me," he said, "Let's walk instead of driving. We'll walk, let's go wherever you want to go."

"Rizwan…" I said, my voice faltering.

"Look…Mariam, I enjoy you."

"What do you enjoy about me?"

"Everything."

"That's not enough."

"What do you want me to say?"

"You just need a friend right now, that's all. You don't really mean anything you're saying or feeling."

"You would think I'd know my own sentiments."

I looked at him blankly.

"Why are you so guarded, Mariam? Why do you make it so hard to love you?"

"It's not hard to love me, Rizwan. But I know that you don't. You confuse me with all the other women who lie down beside you too easily."

He smiled sheepishly and came closer, eating the entire distance between us in an instant.

His voice was confident and different. "You're not like those women."

I shuddered.

"I know I'm not."

"So what do you want me to say, I'll say it," he knitted his eyebrows.

"That you will drive us back quietly," I said, "I don't want to wake up tired."

He frowned in frustration, stopped talking and just stared up at the sky. His prolonged silence was pregnant with an alarming violent tenor. I wanted to crawl inside his head and read his mind. What was he thinking about? Did he really mean all this?

Suddenly, he dropped the brown paper bag on the ground and tenderly took both my hands in his. He stroked my palms with his thumb and told me how I had changed him. He said things any woman would have loved to hear but my heart thumped heavily in my chest.

I could clearly name this feeling now. It was the same feeling Anika and I had shared on the railway station many years ago when the chip-seller man creepily encircled us.

I tried to shudder the feeling away.

"Look at me, Mariam," he said kindly, bringing me back to the parking lot. He stroked my cheek.

"What is it?" Fear ripped through my body and I could speak no further.

"Won't you look at me?"

"I want to go home."

He looked at me as if I had severely mutilated his feelings. Shrugging off his hands, I walked towards the car. I heard him groan and call my name. He apologised. I didn't respond. He walked towards me.

"Look at me!" His voice now boomed, striking me from a million directions. He grabbed my arm and swung me around roughly so I could look directly into his eyes, which I now noticed were the same colour as mine. The only difference was they had a flickering light within them that could attract any person.

"I just want you to listen to me," he drew his face closer, "I really like you. I always have and I know you do, too. I refuse to believe that it's just me.."

"What do you know about what I feel and what I don't?"

"Because I know you."

"Trust me, you're not that deep," I slowly took the keys from his hand and he pretended like he didn't notice, "Do you want me to drive?"

This was Rizwan, no one else but Rizwan, I tried to calm myself. Then why was my heart pounding in my chest? Why did I want to escape his company?

I heard *daddi's* voice in my head: *"A man's mind works in miraculous ways. It goes far beyond the perception of a woman. You can never know anyone entirely; not your closest friend, not even the person you wake up next to every single morning."*

Pushing her words out of my mind, I inched closer towards the car. With my back towards him, I tried to unlock the car with shaking hands. I had to do it fast. Somehow I had convinced myself that he could do nothing, but what I dreaded more than anything was what would happen when we were past this moment. I wouldn't be able to look at his face for the rest of my life.

"You know what…I think I'll take a cab…you…" I began

Then suddenly his warm hand touched my waist making my body shiver all over again. He rested his head on my back and remained silent. I dared not move…until I nearly felt his breath on the back of my neck.

I turned around to see that his serious, once handsome face just inches away from mine. With one hand gently caressing my cheek, he used the other to remove the stray strands of hair from my forehead.

"What is it, Rizwan?" I said with a rage alien to my body.

"I am just afraid you will go away, too," he whispered in my ear.

"You can't control people. It doesn't work that way."

"I am not trying to control you."

"Yes, you are."

"What is wrong with you, Mariam?" he said, suddenly becoming angry again, "I am trying to talk to you, why are you always running away?"

I instinctively turned my face away as his fingers softly touched my chin and grazed my jaw line.

"Rizwan…I know you're sad and I'm here for you but…."

I knew I wouldn't be able to restrain him for much longer. He was edging closer to me and it was beginning to make me very uncomfortable. This was not the same Rizwan I had spoken to in the middle of the night in Lahore, a man who trusted a stranger with his secrets, a man who was pensive yet witty and clever and had made me feel somehow at ease. This was a different Rizwan altogether, someone I didn't recognise, a man that allowed his animal instinct to take the better of him, who made me question his motives. In that moment, I truly began to feel afraid of what Rizwan might do to me.

He was a different person and it frightened me.

I pushed his entire body away with all my strength and turned to unlock the car again. He held my arms tightly so I couldn't fight him off, his fingers digging deep into my shoulder making me scream. Feeling his full weight pressing down on my back, I hit his stomach hard with one stiff elbow. He cried in pain and pounded his fist on the window. I slid into the car quickly and sitting on the front seat, tried to gun the engine. Jamming open the door with his right leg, he tried to stop me. Terrified, I tried to scramble across the front seats and escape from the other door.

"Someday you will feel so stupid, Rizwan!" I yelled as he grabbed my left leg, "Stop making this difficult! What the hell is wrong with you?"

"I just want you to listen!"

"Let go!" I pulled his hair as he tried to drag me out of the vehicle, "Somebody help me!"

I was now lying on the cold gravel ground with my fists tightly clutching his car keys. He tried to control my body by pinning down my arms. His lips touched my neck and his hands tried to keep me steady. I felt my cellphone ring in my pocket. I wanted to reach in and pick up the phone, cry into it for help but he would not release my hands. I kicked and shoved, but his grip only became tighter.

"You're hurting me! You're hurting me!"

Snakes, they are all snakes with vibrant patterns."

I could hear a train's whistling blowing.

Bloody snakes. Bloody snakes. Bloody snakes.

"Let go!" I screamed.

My loud scream made him look up to make sure no was around us. With his attention diverted, I kicked him in the groin with all the force that I had managed to accumulate in those last few minutes. I stabbed the key in his neck and ran to where the streets lights flickered a few blocks away.

I ran till my legs felt sore. Then, I took a cab to Judy's house.

I broke the silence around me with a loud knock at her door.

Judy's eyes widened in surprise as she saw my face, "Mariam..."

"I was out walking, coming back here, when you called," I said. "I couldn't pick up. I...I couldn't talk."

She sat me with me in silence and then murmured, "You should wash up and get some rest, Mariam." Then, without asking any questions, she added, "People can be so bad sometimes. People can be so very bad."

I sat inside the tub.

Hot water scoured my skin and the steam began to gently smother me. The air always smelled odd in Judy's apartment. She was smoking in the other room and I could smell it all the way to the bathroom.

I watched the steam rising from the hot water of the shower. It was grey and ephemeral, like the smoke from Rizwan's burning cigarettes. It seemed as if smoke of his cigarette had permeated through the bathroom walls and was trying to smother me. I breathed heavily. Suffocated between the rising steam and stagnant water, I quickly got out of the bath and crawled into bed.

Hours went by as I lay on the bed feeling vacant. My thoughts refused to leave me. The hairs on the back of my neck stood up as I played the night out in my mind. The dim lights and emptiness of the wide, open parking space haunted me.

When sleep finally conquered, I dreamt. I dreamt of fog and smoke, of being smothered and drowning in water. I had not dreamt of water in a long time. For those few painless hours, I was eight again.

***

CHAPTER TWENTY-SEVEN

Waking up is comforting only for the first few minutes before you remember who you are and what has happened.

Fourteen messages from Lubna.

She found his body in a pool of blood in his apartment, his grey shirt drenched in red and his muscles lifeless.

But he didn't die.

He just fell onto a glass table and lost consciousness after he went back home. Someone had tried to stab him in the neck, she said, but they couldn't find the weapon used.

He must have pulled out it.

She was persistent; saying she wanted to see me, ask me what had happened. The answering machine answered all her pertinent questions. I was slowly dying underneath the bed-sheets. His face, passionate and angry, flashed before my eyes. What could I say to his mother?

Judy knocked on the door and entered my room. She tried not to show any worry. Sitting on the edge of my bed, she picked up my phone and scanned the screen.

"Don't you think you should talk to her? Tell her everything that happened before he wakes up and gives some false shit."

"I don't even know what to say anymore," I kept a pillow over my face, hoping to suffocate somehow. "I don't know what to tell her, or whom to trust."

Emotions were meant to be hidden. The world is not a place for advertising your sorrows. I learnt that from my grandfather.

"Call her back and tell her what happened," she took the pillow away, leaving me feeling bare, "I am serious, Mariam. Get up and make that call."

"I am serious too," I said, "I don't know what to tell her."

For me, it was simple.

I was going to forget about it. I had planned on going to collect the remainder of my things from Lubna's house and was hoping to never again cross her path. Everything was settled but this bloody incident from last night had made things complicated. Judy made me some coffee and decided to accompany me to the hospital. She didn't trust me, she said very clearly.

In the waiting room, Lubna looked dazed and dismayed. Her hair was ruffled and her clothes crumpled as if she had just awoken from a nightmare. Noor sat next to her playing with a bandage she had on her index finger.

They rose as we approached. Lubna eagerly took a step forward.

"Mariam, where have you been? I've been trying to reach you!" she spat out, "I don't know what happened…so please tell me…I can't lose my son ."

You lost him a long time ago, I thought.

I wanted to be kind, wanted to pacify but I couldn't even pretend anymore. It's then when I realised that how much I despised them, how much I despised all of them. They lived only for themselves, nothing and no one else mattered for them.

"Why aren't you answering me, Mariam?" she said sternly, "He said you were there. You two were together. Where were you both?"

"Don't worry, he won't die," I said flatly.

"He lost consciousness when he returned home," Noor said, "It might be a drug overdose. They are figuring it out."

His mother stared back me in disbelief.

"You were there, weren't you? He mumbled something about you hurting him. What happened?"

"I...I hurt him?" I said, shocked to my core. Every vein in my body throbbed with anger and disgust.

No one spoke for a while until Noor came forward with a "*did you?*"

"Of course, she did," said Lubna. "He said you attacked him in the car."

All of a sudden, her voice lost all concern and adopted a bitterness and disappointment, as if she had expected me to do something of this sort all along.

"I'm not surprised that he didn't tell you the background story," I spat out the words, "He will tell the truth, if you have raised him well, that is. Ask him what I was doing there."

The American aunt held my shoulders in a firm grip, the kind of grip my mother used on me when I broke her favourite lamp as a child.

"Which version would you like me to please your ears with, his version probably, when I go mad for no reason and viciously attack him, or the truth that he tried to force himself on me and I ran away?"

The mother and daughter gasped.

Lubna let go of my shoulders. The clock stopped for her for a moment.

"You're a filthy liar," she hissed.

I didn't speak.

"After all that I've done for you. If it weren't for me you would probably be married to some old man with a mediocre job back home...I gave you a life."

I stood and listened as she spoke how she raised me, reformed me and how there was always a reason why she never wanted a connection with her husband's family in Pakistan.

"Who are you, aunt Lubna?" I said, "Who are you?"

She looked at me, perplexed.

"You brought me here to work for your godforsaken company because you knew I would give you the affection and service your husband and son didn't. That's all that you've done for me, the rest I've been doing myself."

And before I could say anything else, Judy grabbed my arm and we left.

***

I felt the weight of the world.

Things became slow eventually. Days devoid of company, long isolated moments of disbelief and shame, quick flashbacks and theories on what-could-have-been. My head throbbed for a long time. That's when I learned something about pain. It never leaves you completely. It just deceives you momentarily, by putting itself on a temporary hold.

I saw this in Grandfather and I began to see it in myself. I had to learn how to suppress the pain for good so I distracted myself by going on long jogs, attending parties, making friends and enrolling in diverse academic courses. I needed to be around unfamiliar faces, ones with new stories and different emotions. People who didn't know me and could talk for hours about mundane subjects, strangers who were vaguely interested in me and I, in them. People who didn't call or chase after me once I left the room. I found it hard to trust anyone and so all relations became transient.

But despite this, despite all my efforts, somewhere inside me remained the indomitable feeling of betrayal and unanswered questions about my own gullibility.

Lubna didn't call me for the remainder of the month. She vanished just like her son. But Abdullah and Richard kept calling and leaving messages, asking me where I was and why I wasn't meeting or talking to them. I allowed each call to roll to voicemail, each message to remain unanswered. I needed some time on my own.

I spoke to Anika in my dream and told her everything that had happened. We were both sitting on steps of a ladder and underneath us was the roaring sea. She sat for a long time, dull and unhappy, listening to the waves crash against rocks and other dead things. She told me she wasn't happy either. I made her promise not to tell anyone, especially Grandfather.

I moved out of Judy's apartment and into a dorm room. I needed to return to Lubna's house to gather the rest of my things and after days of contemplation, one afternoon I finally did. To my relief, Lubna wasn't home. There was a slight reluctance on Noor's face as she opened the door to find me standing there, but I didn't need her permission to get my stuff. She let me in. I hurried upstairs to what I had called my room and placed everything in a few large bags. She stepped inside the room.

"You're really moving out?"

"Does that really come as a surprise?"

"No, but I thought you might come back. I was hoping you would come back."

I didn't answer.

"Did you tell anyone about the accident?"

My fingers froze and I looked up at her reflection in the mirror, "Are you guys scared that if I will tell my parents, they will come hunting for your brother?"

"Well, did you?"

"Yes, I did," I lied after a pause. "Did you for one split second try to understand me? That maybe, just maybe, I was not lying, that I didn't have a reason to lie. I have lived with you for over a year, you've known me that much, Noor," I said with more force than I intended.

She didn't speak. I folded the bed sheets, rechecked all four drawers and pulled down a colourful calendar showing Lahore's famous food street.

It felt odd. She had never heard me talk so loud.

"We never talked about it. We never discuss important things in this house. We just shove it under the rug till everyone forgets about it," she said, "He came home, kissed me goodbye and said that he would soon be leaving for another state. A new job. He'll start acting."

"That career might actually work for him," I zipped up the bag and stormed out of the room.

The door to Lubna's room lay ajar. I saw one of the Artist's paintings resting casually against the wall. The nude Mughal empress' penetrating gaze jolted my soul. I felt great sorrow for the Artist and had a sudden desire to lift it up and take it away with me. It's not that anyone would've noticed its absence, but I wanted to sever all connections with the family.

Noor followed me, carrying one of the bags I'd forgotten. We didn't speak until I sat in the cab.

She knocked on the window.

"I get scared, Mariam, when I think about you and that parking lot and everything," her voice cracked, "I know you, but I do also know my brother. I get scared when I imagine what could have happened if you didn't run away from him."

***

CHAPTER TWENTY-EIGHT

Richard was offered a great job in an advertising firm in New York. He was hesitant in the beginning but his decision became clearer when Lubna's business collapsed and I moved into the dorms. He was leaving in a week's time. There was nothing to stay back for.

After a while of self-imposed isolation, I decided to reconnect with him and everyone else. Abdullah was enraged by my disappearance and carelessness. He made plans to come see me in Washington. I left a message for Richard, asking if he cared to join us before he headed to New York.

Afternoon came. When we met, Richard hugged me tight for a long time. He was relieved to see me walking and breathing. I smiled, a little embarrassed. He sat across me with multiple questions. I poked at our lunch of spicy empanadas, avoiding his inquisitive stare. Abdullah also watched me in silence.

"What is wrong with her?" he asked Richard aloud so I could hear.

"I heard that," I said laughing.

"Don't try to be cute," Richard said, "We were seriously worried about you. You can't just disappear like that. I asked Lubna about you and she said she hadn't heard from you in days."

I told them I had a thesis proposal submission and the research was keeping me busy.

"So, I heard you're moving to New York?" I said, hoping to close the topic of my disappearance altogether.

"Lubna nearly had a heart attack when she heard the news," he sniggered, "She thought she could make me work for her boyfriend."

"Well, you always could, you know."

"You know I won't."

I watched Abdullah take a sip of his drink. He looked happy. I was relieved.

He had plans with a friend and so he left right after lunch. Richard and I walked together in a park. I still hadn't told him about the incident, nor was I planning to.

"Thank you very much," he said softly.

"For what?"

"For this day out, it's like I haven't seen you in years."

"I've been too absorbed in things," I repeated.

"You've always been absorbed."

Our footsteps echoed.

"Mariam, when were you going to tell me about Rizwan?" he asked suddenly without even looking at me.

My heart skipped a beat.

"He just got hurt by falling...I think he drank too much."

"I'm not asking about that accident."

I looked him in the eyes and in his voice, traced a sense of betrayal and hurt.

"What are you talking about?" I was surprised to see that my voice didn't shake at all.

"It just hurts that you didn't tell me."

"I didn't tell anyone."

"Judy talks."

"Oh God," I muttered and ran fingers through my hair, "I should've known."

"I spoke to him, just so you know."

I grew pale.

"What did you say? Why would you do something like that?"

"He's an impulsive man…careless. He is not the one for you…"

He turned around and looked at me. "It's getting dark. We should go."

"Richard," I said sharply, "You can't just go around confronting people for me. I can take care of myself, you know. I've been doing it for some time now."

"I regret nothing, Mariam. What happened there was not okay, you are not okay and I want you to keep telling yourself that you're not, so you can drag yourself out of this denial. Can you do that for me?"

I looked at him but said nothing.

The walk home was long and strange, enveloped in awkward silence. We reached the dorms. He turned away and I went inside the building.

***

CHAPTER TWENTY-NINE

It was the last week of November and we were freezing, but still we found ourselves back where we always met: the marble fountain with the classical Gods. I loved this place, no matter what weather.

Despite the cold, we sat there, Richard and I, before he left for New York the next morning. He said New York had more strangers and better parties; I would be happy there. We had shared a laugh.

Neither of us mentioned Rizwan, neither of us brought up our argument from the week before. We just sat together quietly, hoping that no matter how bad things ever got between us, there was always going to be a way back.

He stared at the clouds as they moved across the sky. As dusk settled in, twinkling stars began to appear.

"It's like a map," he said. "The sky, it's like a map."

I smiled.

In my lap slept a blood red rose that Richard had bought for me. I closed my eyes and smelled it, then brought it to my lips and tasted a petal, just as I used to when I was young.

The blinding city lights lost colour. The water fountain disappeared..

A single petal took me back fifteen years.

I saw myself as a young child, sitting on a bench in the village. In my hands was a rose and I tasted its petal. Sweet, with a hint of bitterness towards the end.

In front of me, stood my grandfather, illuminated by brilliant sunshine. He called my name. I smiled, stretching out my hand. Bowing, he accepted it.

"Come now, my little bird."

I jumped on his back and he carried me. We strolled on a muddy path that that opened into an open field. He was tall and very lean but he reassured me he had strong bones; I need not worry about him falling down with my weight. He stopped in the middle; around us was an endless sea of green fields and above our heads, birds flew rapturously in the white sky. Now and again, he took a deep breath and sang a slow song. It was about the wind and a lover, about a mountain and its friend, the blue river.

I stretched my hands and pretended to fly.

He fastened his steps and cried"Fly, my bird! Fly!"

Then he placed me down gently on the ground and inhaled deeply.

We held hands and set off walking straight across the green pasture towards a grand, old Peepal tree. Colossal, it stood, waiting for us. Grandfather pulled out several folded pieces of paper from the pocket of his kameez. He stood under the shade of the tree for a long time, reading the papers. Reading, and re-reading, one after another and then refolding each one.

They were letters. But I didn't know this then.

"What are those?" My eight-year-old self broke the silence.

"It's a story, little bird," he said without looking up, engrossed in the pages.

A parrot sat on one of the old branches. It made a funny noise. I removed my sandals in an attempt to climb. I touched the rough bark and looked up at the wide tree. It was like a mountain I couldn't conquer.

A paper fell from Grandfather's hands near my feet. I picked it up. It was in a language that wasn't familiar, in a writing I didn't recognise. He turned toward me as he heard the crisp sound of paper in my hands.

"Tell me the story," I asked.

"It is not finished, my darling."

"Why is it not finished?"

"Some stories are meant to be incomplete. They are beautiful only when they remain unfinished."

"Well, what is it about?"

"It's about two people who met long time ago and fell in love."

"And then what happens?"

"And then nothing…nothing happens."

He smiled and patted my head. I gave him back his story. He asked me to step away and from his front pocket, extracted a tiny red box of matches. He squatted and lit a fire.

Then, one by one, he burnt the pages.

An unfamiliar expression grew on my grandfather's face. Tears formed in his eyes. I had never seen him like this. We just watched as the flames engulfed every single word. We watched it swallow the whole story like it never existed, like the two people had never met and fallen in love.

We watched the fire swallow the lovers.

I was confused, but there was nothing to say anymore. I was a mere spectator.

After the fire had died, what were left were only black ashes; not a word, not a figure had survived. He crushed the black ash further with his fingers, the only remainders of the story, until they were nothing more than a fine powder. Then, with one mighty blow, he scattered them everywhere, on the ground, on the bottom of the Peepal tree and in the air.

I didn't understand who the lovers were, what the pages said, or how the story ended. And in that moment, it seemed, neither did my Grandfather.

That very same fall, the devastating news of my Grandfather's death shook the family. I never told anyone about the tree, the secret pages, or the unfinished story. While fetching water for his mourners at the funeral, his teary face often flashed before my eyes. After keeping it to myself for a long time, I finally told Anika that I had seen Grandfather cry.

Her explanation was simple.

You must be dreaming. Grandfathers don't cry. Men seldom cry. Only children and women cry.

But I knew what I saw and that was enough.

Richard and I walked away from the fountain. I threw the rose on the ground.

"You don't like flowers?" he bent to pick up my parting gift. He brushed it gently with his fingers.

"It's not that. It just reminded me of something…" I said plainly.

"A bitter memory?"

"A strange memory…"

"Why must you recollect these strange memories?"

"Because I have no control over the things that visit my mind."

"You know that's not true."

I frowned.

"What were you thinking about?"

"Nothing."

I held his arm and we resumed walking. We walked, sometimes silently, sometimes laughing on the little things that made sense to us then. But in between us sat an uneasy tension. I never fully understood what I felt for Richard, I didn't know how to describe it. We went from being strangers to something that had no definition. It was not infatuation exactly, but I had grown very fond of him. He understood me despite the invisible ropes of convention and expectation that held me back. He understood my silence. Most of my life, I had been busy weaving a web around myself, making me emotionally impotent to others. Inside me was an array of well-concealed desires and feelings, which longed to be read. Richard understood this, and he read them silently, unobtrusively.

For a moment then, I regretted shutting him out when I needed him the most, in my time of despair and sadness. Judy was a fine company, a good friend. But Richard, he was extraordinary in his feelings and commitment to people, to me. He was guarded just like I was, and what happens when two introverts collide? Do they dissolve completely in each other's patience and silence, or do they break their glass shells and become new people? I was curious to know the answer myself.

We crossed a church. I knew this road. I knew that a few blocks down was the old gallery where we had first met. He didn't know me then but it hadn't mattered. We had just sat on the stone steps in each other's company.

We got into a cab and towards the dorms.

He looked out of the window at the tall buildings.

"Come to New York with me," he said suddenly.

"What?"

"I mean, for the weekend…with Abdullah. He can meet us there. You haven't seen him in a week and I haven't been to New York myself, could use some company even if it's for three days."

I smiled affirmative. It seemed like a good escape.

***

Eventually though, it was just Richard and me strolling in the Big Apple. Abdullah said that studying for the first semester's final exams had been keeping him too busy. Needing a desperate break from academics, he had planned a weekend out with his friends.

I understood.

Richard's new apartment was in a prime location. If we stood on the balcony, we could almost hear the noisy Times Square.. He opened the lids of the yellow paint tin and then examined the dull grey walls stretched before us. "You're helping, right?" he teased.

In a few hours, we were done painting. We ate at an Indian restaurant then walked through the Bowling Green and towards the Charging Bull. The bronze monster seemed to stare at no one but us with its blank eyes and flared up nostrils. People with painted faces rushed down Broadway, some selling tickets, some all dressed up to attend a musical. After midnight, art was sold at shamelessly low prices, on street corners and bylanes. Artists, subway musicians, lovers strolling the streets and women in fifties diner waitress costumes selling tickets; it truly was the city that never slept!

The night seemed never ending; we sat on the carpet back in his apartment and played cards for an hour. He shook a burgundy coloured bottle and poured us some wine.

"Wine…life, freedom, divinity," he lifted his glass, merrily, "The drink of the gods."

"According to a Persian myth, it was discovered by a woman."

His eyes widened. He picked up the bottle, "Then, to the disillusioned woman who thought this could cure any pain in the world."

"Thank you for doing this," I said.

He looked confused.

"For what?"

"For bringing me here and trying to distract me," I smiled.

Meanwhile, terrible news was waiting for me in D.C.

***

DECEMBER 2009

CHAPTER THIRTY

The week before a frightening snowstorm struck the country, I tried reaching Abdullah. It had been two weeks to my visit to New York and I hadn't spoken to my brother since. From what the news preached, I was afraid that the snow would isolate us, trap us in and bury us for a long time. A correspondence was necessary.

There was no answer.

So instead, I called up Anika casually and when she asked me how Abdullah was doing, I realised the family also hadn't heard from him for some time.

As seconds became hours and hours became days, I began to swallow uneasily. I was forever pinned to my phone and left him several emails.

Two days later, I called up his roommate at college, Chester. From him I found out that Abdullah had been staying over at another friend's house for the past two weeks and had made no contact with anybody. On asking for the friend's detail, he said he had none.

After yet a few more days of waiting and tracing, my heart began to beat wildly in my chest. I was mad at him, for being like me, so careless and mysterious, and I was mad at myself for being so engrossed in things that were so irrelevant and trivial, rather than worrying about where my brother had been.

I walked a lot. I walked in the room, in the hallways and to a coffee shop near the dorms, trying to calm my nerves. I sat inside alone inside the warm café in the evenings, killing time. Where was my brother, I kept thinking, where could he be.

Return to me what I lost because it is what You gave me and placed me with.

I would mutter this under my breath and then look at the lights and the reddening sun.

This is the magic of these bright lights, big city and strange faces, I thought, *it is easy for one to lose significance. You fade away. You disappear and nobody really cares. The cars will keep roaring. The lights will keep burning. People will keep meeting and falling in love. The world will go on.*

If my friends and Abdullah weren't there and I disappeared, no one would know and no one would stop to find. These dark ideas would not leave me alone. I lit a cigarette and exhaled a cloud in the air. I watched the white trail release from the end. I hardly smoked but it helped me when I was nervous or afraid and I was willing to try anything.

I tried blaming Rizwan for diverting my attention and bringing out this sadness in my spirit. I blamed Mother for sending Abdullah here and increasing my responsibility. I began to blame everyone and everything. A classic scapegoater.

The only time I had been this afraid before was when I thought I saw *dadda's* ghost in the corridor. It was the same feeling. *Nerves throbbing. Heart racing.* It was the first time that my own imagination began to frighten me with its potential.

Return to me what I lost because it is what You gave me and placed me with.

I recited the prayer and took a deep breath. Then I thought about the Quran teacher who had taught Abdullah and me this prayer in our childhood.

He always wore a stiff white shalwar-kameez that had been bathed in the soothing scent of jasmine. On his head was a green turban and on his finger a dazzling gold ring, which shone every time he ran fingers through his bushy orange beard. There was a black mark on his forehead, which he often touched and smiled, revealing his broken front tooth.

"Oh, this? This is a sign of dedication and piety. The hell fire will eat up the entire human body but won't be able to touch this."

I had always been jealous of the old man and his mark, especially after he told my sister and me about the fierce blazing fire we could fall into if we didn't stop listening to Junoon, the rock band, on the radio. That's what he loved discussing with us; Jahannam, hell, and the seven gates and the boiling water that the sinners will consume.

Once I sat with him, fidgeting at the end of my seat, distracted as I read aloud from the Quran. A sudden anger rushed to his face. His nostrils flared and his black eyes contracted. He slapped my knee asking me to observe discipline in front of the Holy book. I cleared my throat and started reading again.

"What is it?" he asked.

I stopped reading.

"I've lost something."

"What have you lost?" he asked, a little sternly.

My lips puckered. I moved my leg restlessly.

"Don't move, you child!"

I looked up at him, pale, distressed.

"My china doll…" I said in a low voice.

"Speak up."

"My china doll and sneakers, Qari sahib!" I shouted, stunning him.

The doll was a gift from my grandfather. He sent my sisters and me three nicely bubble-wrapped porcelain dolls. They were delicate and fragile with big doe-shaped eyes and thick golden locks that cascaded down their white backs.

Qari sahib stroked his beard again and then wrote something on a piece of paper, a prayer. I was to recite it daily till I found my things. For a month, everywhere I went, the paper went with me. I *recited before sleeping, while bathing, while studying, while brushing my teeth. I finally found my doll but its angelic face was smashed into pieces.*

A week later, I lost my new shoes. I recited the prayer again but this time, God didn't listen.

I cried for days until Grandfather came to see me. He brought me a new pair and took me to the graveyard to meet his family. The graveyard was our special place. My tears ceased and thanked him for the new shoes. This was the same episode I narrated to the mourners when they asked me at his funeral about the one memory that I was going to hold on forever.

I found the old shoes a month later. It wasn't such a mystery. Abdullah was wearing them. He said Mother had taken them out of my drawer and given it to him. We were the same size. I didn't speak to him for days. He had cried incessantly, begging me to speak to him. I had made him so sad and resentful.

But this was all before I hit him and created between us, this eternal distance.

I ran my hand over my face and rubbed my eyes, trying to shake his little teary face out of my head. I sank in my chair, a heavy feeling of guilt swept over me. The music in the café went on. The people kept on talking and I felt myself dissolving and fading into my own recollections and darkness.

He was so young and it was only a pair shoes. Why was I so selfish? I thought.

I picked up my phone and dialled his number again.

Still no luck. No answer. No ringtone.

It was like the number had never been in use, like my brother had never flown to America and I hadn't seen him in years. I killed the cigarette and tipped the waiter. I couldn't wait any longer.

I had to go down to Boston myself.

***

Richard met me at the university. I hugged him tightly as he stepped out of the cab. My heart was at ease for once.

"Now take a deep breath and tell me what happened…slowly," he whispered and took my hand in his.

I told him how I hadn't heard from Abdullah in two weeks. He didn't call or leave a message. When I tried calling him days earlier, his number was not in use. I tried reaching his roommate and even asked Anika, indirectly, of his whereabouts but no one had heard from him.

"I emailed one of his professors and learned that he hasn't been any attending classes either. For a *whole* month, he hasn't been attending classes for a whole month. He said he couldn't meet us in New York because he had been studying for exams…but…he hasn't been on campus for two weeks now!"

Feeling completely helpless, I repeated, "That's when I drove here to the campus."

He lightly touched my woollen hat and bit his lip anxiously. I had made him afraid, too. He walked away from me a little and looked around the place, everything was draped in a thick blanket of white snow.

"We must go somewhere and talk," he said.

We went inside one of the dorm lobbies where it was warm and noisy.

He asked me if I had asked my family, I hesitated and answered that I had but not openly.

"And why is that?"

"I don't want them to be worried, not yet. Maybe he's gone somewhere with some friends and there're no cell-phone signals there…"

"This is not an episode of *Lost*, Mariam," he kept his hand on my knee to make me stop talking, "Well, actually it could be because a blizzard is coming in. Don't you think you should ask them directly instead of playing mind games?"

"I suppose so," I said briefly.

"All I'm saying is that he might've told someone at home where he was going."

"Why doesn't his roommate know, then? Why doesn't Chester know the name of the friend Abdullah might be staying with?"

"I don't know," he shrugged, "Does it matter?"

"Yes," I stressed, "They lived together for the entire semester… how could he not…"

"Mariam, look, this isn't important. We need to do what we can before we notify the school authorities and make it something serious."

"This is serious!!"

"I know, but…"

"But what, Richard?"

"Mariam, you disappeared for days after you-know-what. But you surfaced after a while. You shut him, me, and everyone else out. Maybe he's here somewhere and will surface also."

"We weren't very close as siblings, is that what you're trying to say?"

"I'm not saying anything except that it should come as no surprise that he didn't tell you where he was going."

I looked at him, perplexed and a little hurt. Deep down, I knew he was right. I just didn't have the courage to believe it.

"Go, call your parents."

I covered my face with my scarf and nodded. He patted and kissed my forehead, thinking he had set my emotions unnecessarily reeling.

"I'll check around with some of the students in the college. Maybe someone will give us a raw clue."

He left. I crouched in front of a big window and rested my head on my knees. The weather was unbearable now. Everything was wrapped under sheets and sheets of white. Neither had I seen so much snow in my life, nor had I seen the skies so angry. It never snowed in Lahore. White flurries endlessly cascaded down to the ground, replenishing whatever snow might have melted.

I looked at my phone. I wanted to talk to Anika, hug her and tell her everything but already I could hear her concerned voice echoing in my head, "Mariam. Mariam, do something please..."

What could I do?

I clutched my face in my hands, wishing I could disappear with him. It felt useless just sitting around so I walked out of the lobby and took the elevator up to the dorm rooms. I found his and knocked on the door loudly.

No response.

The roommate was out, it seemed, but the door was unlocked so I pushed it open.

Chester's side of the room was lived-in, unmade bed and belongings scattered everywhere. Abdullah's side was completely bare and uncluttered. His bed was made, sheets neatly folded. His books lay in piles on the desk. There were two large suitcases containing everything that made him. All his belongings were right there, in that very room.

Quickly, I walked out, shutting the door behind me. I knocked on the adjoining door and then the door next to it. Most of the students had left for Christmas and the remainder, knew nothing. Dejected, I walked back down to the lobby, my scarf tightly around my neck and walked towards the small parking space to find Richard's car.

He wasn't back yet.

My eyebrow knit in thought.

Lubna.

I could have asked Lubna.

But what would she know about Abdullah? She barely wondered about me.

Hurried footsteps walked up to me.

"So, I've asked about fifty students," Richard's eyes gleamed as he lit a cigarette, "Some don't know who he is, some don't care where he is and some only know what we know."

I told him I was going to notify the authorities and call the police. He tried to stop me, saying that I should wait still. There was a chance that he would reconnect. Maybe he needed time.

"Well, he can't have any more time, Richard," I said sharply.

***

CHAPTER THIRTY-ONE

The wind cut people in half. A big fire roared at the centre of the hockey field and the men gathered around it, as if performing an ancient ritual. The police and security guards had assembled there and were dividing the town amongst themselves geographically. There was a small briefing about Abdullah, his name being passed around the crowd for officers to remember before they dispersed to their various locations to begin the search.

I sat on the cold bench, watching their flashlights flicker as they rushed up and down like ants in distress, some were talking on their phones and some were scribbling down things in notepads.

I had been in his room and had looked through his things. They still smelled of him. He was around here, he just had to be.

An officer walked towards us. He leaned forward and said, "You and your friend better go back before travel becomes a hindrance. You could be trapped here for two days, if not more. We will get back to you if we get anything, anything at all."

I closed my eyes in distress and without a single word followed Richard to his car.

***

No call for three days.

Washington D.C. slept under coats of raw snow. It was silent, save the wind that howled and knocked on our windows. Despite being mid-December, it didn't feel like Christmas time. It didn't feel like anything. The fact that the city was snowed in gave it a sense of imprisonment and isolation.

I stayed with Judy, and Richard decided to spend the holidays with us too. He didn't feel like going back to New York for Christmas. I spent those soundless white days thinking about Abdullah. I thought about his childhood, I thought about his odd little habits, I thought about his *barsati* and I thought about his kite flying. My mind was flooded with all the small things that had once seemed trivial.

If I was restless, so were the authorities. A foreigner had apparently disappeared in the streets of their country. So many questions, theories, frightening deductions and inquisitive eyes. What could he be involved in? Was he from any extremist group? Exactly how religious was he? Who else was missing? Was this a case of abduction? A hate crime of some sort? Was he still alive? Did he run away himself?

On the phone, I spoke to a Vincent Burns, an officer from the Boston police force.

"Our search teams are out there. We are trying to track down whatever details we can that connect to your brother. We understand your distress but you just have to be patient, we are doing the best we can," he had said.

Richard said I had to trust them, so I did and waited.

Eventually, they uncovered new details. They found that three other boys were also missing. A dangerous resolve formed in their minds. Inquiries revealed that they took a same class and were last seen together. Nobody had heard from anyone of them.

The families of the missing boys were called in to the station. For the second time that week, Richard and I drove the eight hours it took to get from D.C. to Boston. The Burt family, whose son was also missing along with Abdullah, sat patiently with me. I heard them talking about the other two boys, stepbrothers whose mother had created a scene at the station that morning. She had yelled at the staff and threw things off an officer's table.

"We are printing missing posters and putting them all over town," Mrs. Burt told me. "We just want to know that he is alright. Our son is a good boy."

So is Abdullah, I thought.

The couple rose to leave. She said to me in a warm affectionate voice, "Would you be alright on your own, dear?"

I wanted to cry out to her, tell her that I wasn't going to be alright and that I wanted to rip my heart out and hold on to her for comfort but I only nodded meekly. Her husband opened the glass door for her and she waved back at me before they left.

My hands now quivered at the prospect of telling the whole story to Mother. Only Anika knew at home; I had asked her to keep it a secret, like many other secrets we kept. This, of course, was the biggest of them all.

"This is too much, Mariam," she had cried, "This is too much! You have to do something."

I fidgeted with my bag and listened to the officer tell me that there were no sign of any of them anywhere yet. They'd call some teachers, the school authorities and their friends in the morning.

As we drove back to D.C. I absently gazed out the window.

"So it is true," I said softly as it dawned on me, the ultimate reality, the truth that none of us had spoken out aloud yet, "He has disappeared. My brother is really gone."

***

The week after, I took the train to Boston for the weekend. Slowly, I began pasting posters everywhere in the city, around his university, the streets, local stores and restaurants. They listed every detail, his hair and eye colour, his height, his clothes and his address and mine.

The call records were now also being traced. The boys had been missing for about a month now. The rooms of all the boys were inspected again. The only thing missing from my brother's room was his wallet, Father's wristwatch that he got on his fifteenth birthday and a few of his clothes. He didn't even take all of his cash. It was found lying carelessly in one of the drawers. He was expecting to come back to the dorm.

Anytime I'd walk down the streets, his face stared at me blankly from every black and white poster. Like him, soon my face too, became recognisable. Everyone gave me a low smile or a hug which said, *"Oh, that's the foreign girl whose brother is missing."*

But while the officers and search team performed their duties, I began my own research. I started by seeking help from Chester, Abdullah's roommate. The boy ignored me for days, refusing to see me when I was in Boston. Then he finally showed some shred of mercy and decided to see me before he went home for Christmas.

When we met, I was back in D.C. We met at a coffee house. He looked at me anxiously and then drummed his fingers nervously on the table.

"I don't usually stop at D.C. when I'm on my way home," he said, "I thought you moved to Boston for the search."

"I did but I was asked to return. The snow is terrible. I can't afford to keep staying in hotels. I would have had to look for a place."

He bit his lip.

"And I can't imagine I'm going to say this, but I had to get back to D.C. to put my semester's courses on hold. They were startled to hear my reason. Well, who wouldn't be?"

I had stopped going to work and couldn't ask my father or Lubna for any financial help. I didn't know anyone in Boston, either. If it weren't so painfully cold, I would have camped outside the university and waited for my brother to return.

He nodded.

I said I appreciated what he was doing.

"Abdullah is a good guy, you should know that."

"I know," I whispered.

"He arrived here alone and frightened," he said.

"I know," I repeated, "He went through something very traumatic back home and he was still recovering…"

"Yes, his childhood friend, I know," he said, "He was slowly beginning to get over it, he was fine but lately things had became different again."

I became more attentive.

"He began spending a lot of time with this guy called Max. Max was living in Baltimore with his cousin and was planning to apply to our university for the following year. That's how they met, when he came to Boston to tour the university and soon they became inseparable."

"And the other boys?"

"Yes, Abdullah introduced them to Max. Your brother had something in common with him."

"Like what?"

"He was from your hometown."

"My hometown?" I asked, surprised.

"Yes, and he too, had lost a few friends over the years. Abdullah found in him a relief of some sort. But I haven't even seen the guy.

I'm only telling you all that I heard from the other guys."

I nodded.

"Before his disappearance, the last time we met was after our exams ended. He had a duffle bag over his shoulder and said he was leaving with Max in thirty minutes. They were going to party with his cousin in Baltimore for the weekend."

I guessed this was the same weekend Richard and I had invited him to New York.

"Then they never returned?"

"None of them came back. No one asked me anything because I was away that weekend myself. I'm sorry, I didn't tell you this before. I waited for him to return and call you. I know how this inspection and question-answer stuff works on TV. I guess I just got a little scared. You may think really low of me but there's a grant I'm fighting for…"

I said nothing. He continued to talk about his chances at academic funding.

Massaging my temples slowly, I asked, "Do you know anything about this Max?"

He shrugged.

"You said he had a cousin. Do you know where they lived?"

"All I know is that he has a cousin," he shrugged and hid his face from me, "I'm as curious as you are but I don't want to be involved in any of this mess. I really hope you understand."

I gave him my word and returned to the apartment. I didn't tell my friends anything but just picked up the phone and began dialling furiously.

"There was a guy called Max…yes, you've heard it right, Max with an 'M'. Doesn't matter how I know, Officer, but you have to ask the Burts for any details about this too…maybe their son spoke about him. I don't know about the physical description, nothing at all but I know that he was older than them, maybe thirty, thirty-three and lived in Baltimore….yes, but he came to Boston a lot…the boys went on a trip with him and that's it. No, he didn't study in their college. Max, yes. Please let me know. If you hear anything at all..."

***

The following week I was in Boston again.

Officer Burns put his hands in his pockets and stared at me. He had just told me that Max did not exist. None of the other boys' parents or friends mentioned his name. Their call logs didn't list any unfamiliar number or any number registered to a 'Max'.

It was unbelievable. My brother had just simply disappeared from the streets of America without a trail. I sat in the office with my heart and hands trembling and listened to the officers tell me again that there was no Max. I didn't know whom or what to believe, the boy who shared a few months living in the same room as my brother or the men who were trying everything to locate him.

"Did your brother ever mention an odd group of friends?"

I suddenly woke up to the present.

"An odd group of friends?" I repeated with a perplexed look.

"Friends who were not from his school or friends he made during the first few weeks."

"There was always Chester and a few other friends he mentioned. He was sociable, could make friends everywhere but there were no odd group of friends he mentioned."

"Ms. Ameen, I don't know how to ask this from you," he leaned on his table, "Did you maintain a good relationship with your brother? Were you close?"

"Yes, I think he would tell me everything…" I began.

"Yes, but he didn't tell you about this Max."

"We've traced all their numbers and calls that they've made during the past months and I'm afraid that there's no number that raises suspicion. So here's two things, either Max is a very sly person and he didn't keep any telephonic relationship with either of the boys, or Abdullah came to United States just a few months prior to his disappearance and was not familiar with…"

"Familiar with what? Do you mean that my brother lost his way?" I cut him off, "Took a wrong bus and hasn't found his way back for days? We are not that stupid, Officer."

I tried to control my anger.

"How could you even think…" I bit my lip to seize my temper, "My brother did not just get lost. He would have called, or would have asked for directions. There is one of you in every town, isn't there?"

"That's not what I was saying, Ms. Ameen," he folded his arms and looked at me, remorsefully, "We are as much involved in this matter as you are. But we feel that Abdullah didn't go missing with the other three boys…"

"What do you mean? Then where is he?"

"We will find that out."

His flimsy response made me feel as though I was suspended in limbo, increasingly confusing yet unending.

***

CHAPTER THIRTY-TWO

People get lost every day. There are mysterious jungles, puzzling labyrinths and hundreds of confusing cities to get lost in. The only thing that gets them going, living, is that someone might be out there looking for them, a grieving relative, a torn lover, a curious detective. I struggled to find a way to let my brother know that I was there for him. I was that relative, lover and detective, who was out there looking for him and I wasn't going to give up that easily.

The streets smelled of cinnamon buns and Christmas. The shops were painted in red and white stripes. Festive lights twinkled at a distance, like little bold fireflies in the morning. Shops advertised great discounts and people had already started pouring in.

I walked past a shop that displayed rows of television sets in the window. One of the news channels showed a brief clip – there had been a bomb blast at a press club in Peshawar. The city wasn't very far from home. Years ago, we had attended a cousin's wedding there. I stood outside the window for a moment and watched as the news anchor painted a gruesome picture of the events that had occurred. Disturbed, I walked across the street towards the bus stop. The bus took me past one of the hotels where Lubna and I had once attended a conference together.

The desperation and sadness had made me reconnect with her and I had finally told her about my brother's disappearance. She was my only family here and I felt the need for someone familial.

Her face had changed. She seemed like a fish out of water, dried, weary and restless. Yet her demeanour towards me had softened. Babar had left for a business venture in Paris and she just knew he was not coming back.

"Such relationships don't last, I suppose. They're just made to kill time and remind you, even if for a moment, that you have some youth left in you."

Rizwan had told her the truth about what had happened that night and she felt she owed me an apology. Slowly, she transformed back into the caring relative that had once brought me to America. He, too, apologised and confessed that he had never wanted to cause me any harm. I neither accepted nor dismissed his apology, just simply acknowledged it, now consciously keeping my distance from him. His tragic flaw was that he had no control over his wild emotions, or the emptiness in his life.

Lubna made me call my mother and face her directly. I had negotiated but she thrust the phone in my hands.

"Your mother *needs* to know."

Mother had panicked.

She bellowed and kept ranting Abdullah's name in a chant. In the background, I heard Fatima calming her and Father disconnecting the telephone. I, in turn, had just crashed onto Lubna's kitchen floor with my face in my hands in a faint delirium.

Thinking back to that evening still put my stomach in knots. It had to be the hardest thing I had ever told my family. I tried to distract myself now by looking out of the bus window. Snow. Everything was covered in inches of snow. It was so different from the winter I was used to, the sunny winter of Lahore. But my mind had been so occupied recently that I'd barely thought about how cold and desolate it had become. How easily I had conditioned my body and mind to living in a habitat so unnatural to my being, I thought.

I was going to meet a friend of Abdullah's who lived in D.C. We hadn't met before but he heard about what had happened and called me saying that my brother had left a few things over at his house when they met last.

I got off the bus and began walking towards the coffee shop we had decided on. My body defrosted as soon as I walked inside. The friend wasn't there yet. I took off my hat and gloves and ordering a coffee, sat by the table nearest to the door. Slowly, I emptied a sachet of sugar into the cup and stirred it gently. The spoon created a small whirlpool in the thick brown coffee, which immediately made me smile and think of a story my father had once told me.

Daddi's cousins had come from England with large leather handbags and suitcases. They stayed in the guest room in the village for a week. That was the time when dadda was visiting the city. When he came back, he was startled to see daddi dressed in a long fur overcoat and dress pants. Her hair was pinned up with lily flowers like the English women on the covers of Bronte's novels and her lips were painted red like a rose.

She made him coffee that day and he roared in fits of laughter when he saw her pouring it into a golden English teacup. Tears trickled down her eyes and she pulled out the lily from her hair.

"Oh my darling!" my grandfather laughed, "it's not you, it's not you. You put those English women to shame."

My grandmother had apparently covered her face with her hands and refused to speak to him. He kissed her head and pinned the lily back on, "I hope you have a smart suit for me, so I can dress up like an English man."

"I have," she said, teary-eyed, "It's underneath those blankets."

"And an English hat?"
"No hat."

I was told that he had dressed up like an English man and said, *"Now go get me that coffee, my English woman."*

That story never failed to make me smile.

Just then a hand touched my shoulder and brought me out of my reverie.

I spun around in alarm.

"I didn't mean to scare you," said a face I thought I had seen before, "I suppose you were looking for me."

We shook hands and he sat down across from me.

Mohsin was Abdullah's senior. He had moved to D.C. with his family eleven years ago and then to Boston for university. He was born and raised in Karachi and remembered and loved every detail of his beloved city.

He looked at my coffee cup and then back at me. It was hard to tell what he was thinking. He remained silent for a few minutes and then quietly he said, "You look a lot like Abdullah."

I didn't know what to say.

Noticing my reluctance, he took the hint and continued to speak, "I have his school bag. We played soccer together at the university and he left his bag at my place by accident before the end of the semester. I brought it with me when I came back to D.C. for Christmas. I figured Abdullah would be here visiting you and I'd just return it to him here. But...I didn't bring his bag because I came straight from work. Would you mind if we stopped to pick it up from my studio? It's not far."

"Studio? Have you moved back to D.C. now?"

"Yes, I graduated this year and I paint, hence the studio."

I nodded and followed him to the car. The studio was a ten-minute drive.

It was a small shed-like room with stained glass windows. He opened the door and then led me to a room that smelled only of oil paints and turpentine. I knew that smell. It was the smell of comfort, the smell of Lubna's attic.

"I didn't know you were an art major," I said to break the silence.

"Actually, no. I'm not. This is just a hobby but I needed a studio as a sanctuary."

He walked to a navy blue cupboard and opened it with a click. He took out a medium-sized duffle bag with the college soccer team logo.

"It has some of his things," he said, without looking at me.

I didn't know what I'd find inside, but the dreadful thought of spending yet another minute searching for him without any clues or leads made me unzip the bag regardless.

His shirt, kneepads, a pair of Nike cleats, an ink pen and a small note pad.

This is what my brother was now, nothing but an imprint on his bedsheets and people's mind.

"That's it?" I said.

"Yes, that's it. Will you be alright?" that was not the question he had intended to ask.

"Yes, I'll be fine," I said and flung the back across my shoulder.

He pushed a chair towards me. I remained standing.

"Where do you think he went?"

I tried to analyse the level of discomfort the question contained.

"I wish I knew that, Mohsin. I really do."

"I heard people talking about it on campus. They said maybe your brother went back."

"Went back?"

"Maybe he went back home to Pakistan. He wasn't very happy here."

An angry flame lit in my heart.

"He might not have been as happy as he could have, but he was trying very hard. So was I. He can't just fly back home without even telling me."

"You are his sister."

"I am his sister."

He nodded his head, "Are the police helpful?"

"They're doing the best they can. So am I. I haven't slept in days."

"I understand," he lowered his eyelids, "But you must not trust everyone you meet, Mariam. Don't be surprised if they don't reveal everything to you."

"What does that mean?"

"You knew your brother more than them, didn't you?"

I nodded uneasily.

"Just remember the way they perceive your brother is a little different than what you would like to think."

"What do you mean?" I said in a scarcely audible voice.

"You might think that they're not concerned about finding your brother, when actually they might be more freaked out than you," he said with a grave face. "A young Pakistani boy, the next potential terrorist, hovering in the streets of the Capital. Can you imagine their fear?"

I looked around with my eyes open in surprise.

"My brother is *not* a terrorist. He left Pakistan in the first place because he was traumatised by all that, by that bomb that killed his friend!!"

"*I* know that."

Holding on tightly to the bag, I furiously made my way towards the door. He didn't move a muscle, didn't even try to stop me.

"This happened to us, too, you know," he suddenly spoke, "My family went through the same thing, many years ago."

I turned back slowly. He gestured towards the chair again, knowing that this time I would want to sit down and listen.

"It happened in 2002, when my family was still living in Karachi. My cousin Shahbaz went missing and it was said that he was deported back to Pakistan. But they actually deported him two years *after* they said they had. The things that boy must have gone through…"

"But where was he during all that time?" I asked.

"In prison, dark cells where there's no light, no oxygen, no human contact…and later we heard, they gave him a complimentary prison tour around the country," he scoffed.

I couldn't breathe.

He picked up some raw clay on the bench and started moulding it, refusing to look at me.

"What I'm trying to say, Mariam, is…what if your brother was never lost to begin with…?"

His fingers dug deeper into the soft clay.

"We are never guests of the state but a marching band of suspects under intense and continual scrutiny. The earlier we realise that, the better it is."

I had wanted to break down in his studio and pour out my every repressed sadness and anxiety. But I did not. I tortured myself by sitting there quietly and listening to all the possibilities of what could have happened to my brother. And the only thing that became clear to me by the end was just how utterly alone I was in all this.

***

We walked rapidly between heaps of snow towards his car. Mohsin drove me to the bus stop and gave me his address and studio number for any future help. I crushed the paper in a ball and squeezed it in the pocket of my jeans. He drove back slowly and I sat waiting for the bus, his voice ringing in my ears. I ran a gloved hand over my freezing face as I remembered the framed picture of his cousin he had shown me. I had held the frame and looked at the boy, close to Abdullah's age, same hair and the same look of innocence, standing serenely with his mother.

I considered the story that Mohsin had told me. They arrested

Shahbaz after someone accused him of having relations with terrorist groups. Search teams distracted the father while his son was made to disappear for good. Mohsin said that Shahbaz's father never stopped looking for his son even after he was found dead in some woods, half eaten by animals and insects.

He had stood beside his son's dead body and said without expression, "That's not my son, my son is lost and I will find him."

They buried the body of the boy in their family graveyard in Pakistan and his mother never stopped crying.

I didn't know what to do. Mohsin had thrown me in a dark abyss. *What if he was right? What if I was never seeing my brother again?*

I reached Judy's and knocked on the apartment door. I heard Richard inside, talking on the phone. I knocked hard till he opened, controlling my anxiety and fear. The moment he let me in, I collapsed onto the hard wooden floor in a fit of panic. I removed my scarf and coat, unable to breathe, coughing hard.

He had never seen me this way before, in such a state of paranoia, distraught and miserable. He had always known me as someone who didn't react physically to situations, whose emotions always remained collected. But here I was, helplessly unravelling before him. His scared blue eyes flickered like electric fire as he sat down beside me, clutching my shoulders, wanting to calm me but unable to find the words.

"As a child, I had a friend in the village where my grandparents lived," I cried, "He taught me how to make friends, how it was alright to believe in silly things but most of all he taught me how to be strong. He doesn't know how much I owe him."

My breath evened as I struggled to finish.

"Years later, I went back to find him, to tell him all things about me and my life, only to find that there was no Karan. The villagers had ripped off all the posters of *Ganesha*, broken all the *Krishna* statues, burned down the *tulsi* plants and washed his house with bleach. They took away everything that could serve as evidence to his existence. They gave me no choice but to forget that memory that I held onto and it worked…it worked, Richard. I had no choice but to forget him. People have the power to change everything in your life."

Richard didn't know what to say, he just stared at me. He didn't know about Karan and he didn't quite comprehend the details of our childhood in Pakistan, Karan and mine, of the *Ganesh*, the village, the house. But he saw me vulnerable for the very first time. He looked at me, helpless and sad.

"I don't know if Abdullah ran away with Max or whether he's been imprisoned somewhere," my voice became low, "I'm so alone…and I'm afraid that they will win, they will take away my brother from me just like Hamida took away Karan."

He kept listening, deeply affected by my grief.

"And if he's gone, if he's really gone, Richard, then we didn't even get a chance to say goodbye…"

Richard took a deep breath in.

"I can't do this anymore," he held his head in his hands. "I can't do this to you."

I looked at him in silence.

"Mariam," he said in a voice inflicted with remorse and shame, "There's something you should know."

"What? What is it?"

"I might know where your brother is."

***

CHAPTER THIRTY-THREE

Four days after Christmas and my confrontation with Richard, I received news that both startled and relieved me. They had found the other three boys hiding out in the shady basement of what used to be a strip club in Baltimore. Someone, probably a taxi driver, had seen them skulking about and notified the police of their seemingly suspicious behaviour.

The officers called me in before the interrogation started. We were led into what seemed like a desolated underworld. Everything was dark. The boys sat on a long grey bench with their heads down and mouths stitched shut, as if waiting in line for their turn at the dentists. I scrutinised their faces in the hope that one of them would suddenly transfigure into my brother.

The Burts' son, Paul, a short boy with a discomforted look across his freckled face, was seated along with two other boys-the stepbrothers. They had been taken to the hospital earlier and appeared to have cleared all the tests.

They were brought into a dimly lit room for questioning. I looked through the observation mirror as Officer Burns and another interrogator took their seats. The Burt boy's face showed expression of severe isolation and unfamiliarity. He muttered to himself and then looked at the other boy, who was amused by his reflection in the mirror.

"Paul?" said Burns, "You told us earlier about the little adventure at the store. Would you repeat that for my friend here?"

The second officer passed a practiced professional smile, which made the boy more nervous.

"It was a free weekend. Exams had ended for most of us," he began, "Martin, Vick, Abdullah and I decided to meet some friends in Baltimore."

I held my breath as he said my brother's name with great hesitation and caution. I stood with my arms folded, burying the sudden urge to smash the glass and confront the boys myself.

"Would you name those friends for me, please?"

"Max…this guy Abdullah knew and his cousin who lived in Baltimore. We planned a road trip because, like I said, it was a free weekend and we could use some time off from school."

"Max had his cousin's car and we headed off. We all had our fake IDs. We were going to return in three days. It was taken care of," said the other boy.

They spoke for a long time and they kept scribbling and recording every little detail. He said that Abdullah and Max were particularly close.

"We were returning when we stopped at a nearest gas station."

"And this was when? What time?" Burns asked.

"Around nine."

"Go on…"

"We were a little high. So we stopped at the gas station…"

This is where the real story began.

***

With my back to the room, I looked outside the window at the dark and mysterious night. The officer narrated the incident again, this time only to me. I chewed my nails, blank with confusion. There was not a word that came to my mind. I stood like a corpse, listening to him retell the tale.

The boys just wanted to have fun. No one was supposed to get hurt.

Under the influence of alcohol and drugs, Max dared them to go inside the gas station store and pretend they were robbing it. A pistol was hidden under a rug in the backseat. Max took it out, a shiny new toy. No one knew how to distinguish a real gun from a fake one. Everyone just assumed it was fake. They had no idea.

From their car, they watched two men exit the store. They waited for them to drive away. Then an old woman entered alone. They remembered laughing wildly before they covered their faces with their woollen caps. Max waited for them by the car, smoking a cigarette.

"It was supposed to be a prank. It was stupid, we know. But at the time, we weren't in our right minds to think of the repercussions," the boys had repeated this over and over again.

The woman at the cash saw them enter and suspected danger. She succeeded in calling the police. In sheer frenzy and fright, one of the stepbrothers pulled the trigger, not knowing at all that the gun was real. There were violent screams.

They heard the police siren crying wildly at a distance and ran outside like mad men, only to find that the car was gone. There was no Max.

The police cars neared. They dispersed, and escaped. Abdullah didn't run with them, he was too slow and perhaps he got caught. They all waited for him to reconnect, call them, laugh and tell how he escaped. But there was no call, there was nothing from his side.

Max didn't show up again either. They presumed he ran away before the police approached.

"Ms. Ameen? Ms. Ameen? Ms. Ameen?"

Burns wanted me to react but my mind had ceased to respond.

"It doesn't matter," I mumbled.

"Excuse me?"

The officer looked perplexed.

"Don't you get it?" I turned to look at him, "He doesn't exist. Forget what I told you, forget what Chester told me. There is no Max."

He remained silent.

"The kids made him up to get out of trouble. They're afraid. They're trying to push the blame for something they did, for someone who doesn't exist on someone who they *know* you'll hunt down relentlessly. They made sure of his ethnicity…" I said.

"Max does exist, Ms. Ameen. We met with his cousin…"

I shook my head vigorously and breathed heavily.

"Now, Ms. Ameen," he interrupted and tried to calm me down, "Do you know where your brother went after the store scene?"

I shuddered visibly before answering:

"I do."

"And how did you get to know?"

"My friend confessed."

"Your brother was caught as soon as the police arrived. He didn't contact you when he was asked…instead he called…"

"Richard," I said with an obvious clang of hurt in my voice, "I know he called Richard for help. He didn't call me, his sister. But where is he now?"

"Ms. Ameen, your brother was deported to Pakistan three weeks ago."

"No," I retorted in disbelief.

"We have the deportation records."

"No, this can't be true."

"Your brother arrived in Lahore earlier this month."

"How can you even say that?"

He stood still.

"Then where is he? Why isn't he home?"

"Ms. Ameen," he said, "I don't know that but I'm afraid we'll have to call off the search. I am truly sorry."

"And you knew nothing about this till now? How can that be true, Officer?"

"I am only telling you what we just learned, Ms. Ameen. I understand this is a difficult time for you and your family but there is nothing more we can do."

With that he walked out the room and I remained still, staring into oblivion. Then I wore my jacket and left the place as fast as I could.

Outside there was nothing but fog and heaps of snow. I struggled to walk, to escape to some other world where reality was different. I walked and walked. I walked and prayed that I find a train that could take me straight to Lahore, which could take me straight into my mother's lap and sister's arms.

I couldn't do it anymore. I couldn't be so confused and alone. What was happening? Every fibre in my body throbbed. Now and again came a sharp desire to break down and scream till the wind carried my pain to other part of the world where my family waited.

My knees finally gave in. I tried to walk a little more but found no strength in my limbs. The snow was so thick, so unfamiliar and cruel. I collapsed into a snowbank and screamed as loud as I could. I broke down for the first time in years.

Cry, Mariam, cry. Take it all out.

Like an anguished child I cried loudly into the snow.

I cried for Abdullah's friend who passed away too young.

I cried for my brother and the pain he couldn't escape.

I cried as I felt Rizwan's fingers digging deep in my flesh.

I cried for Karan and the fallen ashes of his father.

I cried for Prakriti, who was compelled to live half her life with a different name and identity.

I cried for Gulshan who spent her life in darkness and could not even see her own sister's face before she was buried.

I cried for *daddi* and the pain she endured for the sake of her husband.

And I cried and cried for Grandfather.

For a moment, I felt free. I felt free from all the pain and bad memories. I felt I could wrestle with the ghosts of Grandfather and Karan. I felt like I had conquered my pain, my past, my mind.

"Oh Abdullah," my words froze in the heavy air, "Where are you?"

***

I spent that night in a hotel in Boston and returned to D.C. the next day.

At night, I went up to the roof of Judy's building and looked for the moon, the same moon that had been following me as a child, the same moon that was home to the spinning woman and the same moon that I imagined Abdullah was also looking at. I spoke to the woman, begged her to weave a spell or send a message across but it wasn't her looking down at me anymore.

I saw only Abdullah's face on the scarred surface.

His disappearance had taken everything away from me.

It had taken everything from my family. Mother saw him everywhere, in teacups, across skies, in paintings, and in markets. She swore that she had seen him standing serenely in the cricket field where he used to play. She said she knew what she saw but he vanished before she could do anything. I understood how she felt because I often saw him, too, between the closing doors of subway trains, perched on benches in parks and in crowds. A part of me wanted to crawl in my mother's lap and sleep, the other wanted to hound the streets like a stray animal.

***

CHAPTER THIRTY FOUR

When Richard and I met again, it was three weeks later at Judy's cabin. It was her birthday weekend. The guests were sprawled around the living room. On the bed lay a woman with her eyes wide open, listening to the wind moan and watching the snow fall in heaps outside the window.

Resting her weight on her skinny elbows, she said miserably, "I hate snow."

Richard glanced at the white universe and muttered, "We need more fire."

"What did you say?"

"I said we need more fire!"

"What are you screaming at me for?" the woman sat up straight, offended and red with temper. "Shut up, Kelly. You've had too much to drink," someone said from across the room.

"I'll get more wood," Richard said, "Would you like to help me, Mariam?'

Reluctantly, I followed him outside.

Gradually the distracting voices subsided as we strode over the doorstep and into the small shed at the back of the house. He turned on the only bulb, which was suspended in the centre of the dingy room. Light fell on old cabinets, fridges, what seemed like a head of a stuffed moose and piles of wood. He picked up an axe and dissected a small tree, cutting little equal pieces of wood for the hearth.

After many long minutes he sat down with his head in his hands and the axe by his side. I found myself sitting further away on a wooden bench, tormented by the thought that he would start talking again. As we sat there, an obvious tension settled between us.

"Mariam...I..."

"Don't," I warned him bitterly.

I stooped to pick up the wood and kicked open the heavy door. I heard him following me.

"I realise you probably don't want to see me ever again."

His voice was muffled. I dropped the tiny logs on the ground and then picked one and threw it at his direction with a loud cry.

"You lied to me!" my voice came stifled as if someone had clutched fingers in my neck, "The time when I needed you the most, you lied to me."

He tried to come forward.

"You knew how important this was for me, Richard," I murmured in my throat, "You lied to me. It's my brother, my brother is missing."

"Mariam, please."

"You lied to me!" this time my voice boomed, "It's my brother! I can't lose my brother."

"I did it for him..."

"For him...what about me, Richard? What about us? What do we represent?"

He looked at the ground, abashed and whispered, "Mariam, listen to me. I know I can't make this right and I regret all that I did. But it was for him, really. I thought the boy needed it."

"Needed what?"

"Comfort, a sense of trust and reassurance. Your family pushed him into this new life. Sent him here when he didn't want to come. Embrace normalcy when he was still grieving. He only surrendered to it because he felt he had disappointed them too much in the past. When he called me, he was scared about losing your trust, so he made me promise not to tell."

"He's a child, Richard. You knew better than to keep his promise."

"He didn't tell me anything about Max or the gun. I was just told about a foolish college prank. He was scared that he would upset you."

I shook my head, "No, no, Richard. All this is not enough." I spoke spitefully.

Dejected, he looked at me. "I would never hurt you, Mariam."

We heard the wind howling, trying to fill the empty void that persisted. We felt the distance between ourselves. Far more than we had imagined, and Richard was persistent on filling it as fast as he could. He was scared that I would leave him. The feeling haunted him.

I was hurt and felt cheated, but reminded myself that I needed to be resilient. Sighing heavily, I faced him.

"Where was he calling from?"

"He didn't say."

"Richard, you were the last person he spoke to," I said with a great discomfort and envy, "Was he happy?"

He looked at the ground and spoke, "I think so."

I looked away.

"It was always you that he chose to talk to, never me," I whispered, "It is as though your understanding and affection always held more importance to him…"

"You know that's not true, Mariam," he said consolingly, "He loves you."

I nodded.

"It's just that…"

"It's just what?"

"You're his family, Mariam."

"And? What is that supposed to mean?" I asked.

He bit his lip uneasily and didn't reply. I thought about what he had said.

I was family.

"Some things are just easier to explain to a stranger. Perhaps he could speak honestly to me because he didn't worry about whether I would be hurt or not, or whether I would judge his predicament."

I paused for a moment. My head was so full. I needed a release, I wanted desperately to think of anything else, even for a moment, but it began to consume me again.

"How do I escape this madness?" I thought out loud. "How can I dodge the feeling that everything that happened was because of me? I wasn't aware and responsible. I wasn't there when he was sad. He must have broken down and missed his friend. I was not his friend. He can be out there, anywhere and I can't do anything to bring him back!"

Silence.

Then he came forward and took both my hands into his, "I'm right here, Mariam. We will bring him back."

I slid my hands out of his and his face altered, "I will bring him back. Not you. But I don't even know where he went. We don't even know where Max went. We don't even know if he's real or not. And Abdullah, what if they killed him or took him away like Mohsin's cousin?"

I looked at him, my face stone cold and expressionless.

He watched me leave and then followed the footsteps that I had crafted in snow. Inside, the birthday girl was pouring wine in everybody's glasses. There was a small toast. I kissed Judy on her forehead and went upstairs to my room to sleep. The guesthouse rocked with loud music and laughter. The party was a good vacation for everyone. It was a good chance to escape the city and the chaos.

I took out a blank piece of paper from my bag and wrote Abdullah's name, next I wrote the time and date I last saw and spoke with him. I made a long arrow and drew a small rectangular box. Around it, I wrote Abdullah and the missing boys' names and in capital letters wrote, MAX. I wrote the date and time of the accident. Then I made another arrow and scribbled Richard's name.

January was ending and I had no answers.

Abdullah's arrest records were found. He was released shortly when it was discovered that it was nothing more than a college prank. No one spoke of the gun. On asking whom he wanted to contact, he took Richard's name and made him promise not to tell me anything. Then he disappeared. That's all I knew, nothing more.

Still, there were so many questions that only Abdullah could answer.

Snow poured down on trees and a half-hidden statue of someone I had never heard of. It looked so scenic. I was absorbed for a while. Some people stood outside the cabin in a group, talking and smoking.

There was a knock at the door. It was Richard. He came to tell me that he was leaving. I coldly whispered goodbye, as if his company scarcely mattered to me anymore.

Abdullah couldn't imagine how many lives he had affected, how many relationships he had destroyed. But what did it matter? What did anything matter now?

But it did matter, everything mattered and we both knew it.

"I wasn't there when he needed me," I whispered quietly.

"It wasn't your fault and could have happened to any family and after sometime…" he took a long uneasy pause, "I'm afraid you'll have to let go."

He was right, I told myself and sat on the bed as tears broke out. A loud noise from his front pocked startled me. He apologised and took out his phone. Looking at the screen, he narrowed his eyes.

"This is an unusual number."

I rose up a little to look into his blue eyes, soaked in excitement and suspicion. My mind processed a thousand things simultaneously. He answered the call and pressed the speaker button so I could hear too.

"Ric…it's me."

I knew that voice. My heart stood still. Stunned by the discovery, I leapt at the phone, almost colliding with Richard. He held my arms firmly.

"Ric…I'm in Lahore with Malik…"

"Hello? Abdullah? Is that you? I heard you, Abdullah!" I cried into the phone.

The speaker didn't speak and then instantly the line was dead.

"He heard me! He knew it was me! Why did he call you?! Where is he?"

"You might've scared him, Mariam," Richard said softly, in a remorseful tone.

I grabbed my coat and went outside. Richard remained in the room, standing still like the lifeless statue. As I walked on the dark snowy path, I cried bitterly. I wept throughout the walk and cab ride back to the city. I didn't know why and where I was headed but I knew that I had to cry, cry loudly. I could no longer quietly swallow my grief. I had to let it all out in order to prevent my heart from sinking and breaking.

***

DUST

LAHORE, JANUARY 2010

My grandfather picked up a fistful of dust from the ground, and threw it into the blistering fire, which died without protest. The wind quickly scattered the ashes of the burned letters, removing them from our sight and for the first time, there appeared on his face, an expression of relief and bliss. It was as if with the obliteration of the letters into mere ash, his soul had finally been set free.

He thought he had destroyed it all in the fire – his history, his pain, his unfinished story, but what he didn't realise was that this release was only transient. The pain would walk home with him, perfectly unharmed within the folds of his skin, the depths of his heart and the essence of his soul and would strike him when he was most vulnerable.

The morning was cool and the place where we sat, under the Peepal tree, was very quiet, overlooking massive green fields. Behind the tree was an orchard that belonged to my great-grandfather. It was home to ripe and colourful oranges, lemons and apples.

Long ago, somebody had tried to burn it down over a decade-old unsettled family dispute. Since then my great-grandfather had placed his charpoy under the Peepal tree and rested on it, swearing to guard the orchard till his dying day. He had planted those trees with his own hands and his son, my grandfather, had climbed and swung on their branches as a child. He wasn't going to abandon the orchard so easily.

We walked inside and sat under a shadow of an orange tree. My grandfather picked up a fallen piece of fruit ripe enough to eat and peeled it open for me.

"How wonderful is this?" he smiled, looking over at the graveyard behind them, "My father is buried just a few steps away from his orchard. It looks as though he kept his promise after all. He watches over it even in death."

I nestled against him.

He kissed my hand and told me how God created earth in six days. He created mountains from a grain of sand, oceans from a drop of sky and the heavens from countless mysterious elements. On the seventh day, God sat on his mighty throne and rested.

I asked him where the living things had come from. He said the angels came from light, the jinns from fire, and humans from dust and water.

It was a baffling discovery for a child; angels were pure and divine like light, jinns were fierce, unpredictable and volatile, thus created from fire, but why would God ever create man from dirt? I asked him if we were really made up of dust.

He rubbed his finger over my arm and said, "Look carefully."

I did as told, looked at my skin. It was slightly brown like wet clay, yellow and rust like the wheat crops. I felt my skin and imagined I was touching tiny specks of dirt.

"But why?" I asked, "Why dust?"

He patted my head and said that water, dust and clay were elements of the earth, that's why we, humans, feel so closely connected to the earth.

I said I didn't understand.

He laughed and said with time, I would.

"Then what did God do after creating us from dirt and dust?"

"Then He gave us a mind to think," he said.

"A mind to think," I echoed.

"And a heart to love," he smiled, "A soul and a spirit to feel, to dance, to sing, to cry and to live."

I had always gotten lost in his words, trying to make sense of whatever he was saying, knowing full well that anything he said was full of hidden wisdom. That the little things he shared with me were always meant to teach me something, to prepare me for life.

After a few brief moments of silence, I climbed on his back and he walked out of the orchard and into the fields. He was muttering something under his breath. By bringing my head closer to his, I heard the faintly whispers.

"We've come from dust and to dust we shall return. We've come from dust and to dust we shall return."

***

CHAPTER THIRTY-FOUR

I washed my hands and face with hot water and looked at myself in the mirror. I surveyed the familiar surroundings, the same as they had always been. Nothing had changed since I left Lahore a year and a half ago, except for myself. My body, my face, my eyes, they had lost their light and life. I seemed to have shrunk into an exhausted, frailer version of a Mariam I didn't recognise.

I met Father in the *veranda* and in silence, we drove out of Lahore and to the graveyard. He was right, *dadda's* grave was indeed in a dreadful state. There were big cracks on the surface and the ink on the tombstone had all but faded.

We sat together on the marble bench, the same one that I shared with my grandfather as a child, and watched the old caretaker apply fresh brown mud on the grave and pat it down with his hands. He said that the winter sun would dry it up. Then he called a local calligrapher to rewrite the name and Arabic verses on the white tombstone. The Artist's palm twisted and turned as he revealed to the world Grandfather's identity and history. He wrote it slowly, he wrote it carefully. When he left, we put a fresh bowl of water out for the pigeons and the swallows, and Father embedded a few sticks of burning incense into the wet mud.

Quietly, we said our prayers.

"Perhaps it was the humidity that caused it to crack, that or the monsoon rainfall," said my father, "Or maybe your grandfather had some unfinished business and tried to crawl out." He meant it as a joke but I felt a sharp pain shoot up my body.

"He wouldn't be happy about this, he wouldn't be happy at all about the way I neglected his grave," he whispered, suddenly sombre, as he fished out some red petals from the bag that I was holding. He sprinkled them and one after another at random and they fell, like brilliant fiery darts, in the centre of the grave.

There was the familiar wind and smell of earth.

There were the cooing pigeons, the fragrance of the incense sticks.

There was the graveyard, my great grandfather's orchard and the great, old *Peepal* tree.

I took a deep sigh. Everything was there, exactly like I had left it, like I had imagined it so many times in so many ways, in the States. It was supposed to feel magical and wonderful, but it did not. Instead, it felt ordinary and mundane and I, in turn, felt more different than I ever had before – completely and utterly lost within that graveyard for the very first time. There was nothing pleasurable about being there anymore. It felt like a malignant disease had conquered my body, sliced my veins in half and crawled icily towards my heart. The feeling of standing there amidst so many withering tombstones was suddenly suffocating and intolerable. It stuck at my heartstrings and I felt pained and sad in a way that I didn't understand.

"What sort of a man takes a child to a graveyard?" I asked myself, "And what sort of a child calls a graveyard their favourite place?"

It made no sense anymore.

As I walked out with my father it dawned on me; the reason why I felt the way I did, why I was questioning my grandfather and his obscure personality. The entire meaning of the place had changed for me. It wasn't because I was now older or had returned home after some time but something else altogether. This graveyard had become a sad reminder that the people we love would eventually disappear into dust. I too, would eventually disappear into dust. Time would try and make us forget them, and time *would* succeed. Their tombstones would decay and the writings would fade into oblivion.

After everything is said and done, a memory remains a treacherous thing…How long does one cling on to the people they've lost? How long could I have remembered my grandfather? How long had it been since I forgotten him and my mind began harbouring other things?

Police stations, reports, strangers, stories, and the cold, cold blizzard; when and where had it all begun? Where had I left him, my grandfather, where were his missing pieces? Did I scatter them with the autumn leaves or did the icy winter wind blow him somewhere far away? I tried desperately to remember the exact moment I had begun to forget his memories, his faint smile, his wisdom, his everything.

My father had forgotten his father, and somewhere in my life in America, I had forgotten my grandfather too and now with time, people and things would make me forget my brother. I would learn to move on, would have to teach myself to function without him. The *barsati* would just be inhibited by old furniture and useless things, his friends would stop visiting, my mother would be distracted with her new grandchildren and my mind would fixate on other trivial distresses. There was simply not enough space and time in the day for advertising and drowning in your sorrows. It demanded attention and life always got in the way.

"Why?" I asked my father as we drove away from the graveyard,

"Why did his grave break down when you were still here?"

He remained quiet for some time. I knew he felt accused, and maybe that is what I wanted then.

"Maybe I didn't love him the way you did. I should have visited more often."

I nodded.

"Did you know the house flooded last monsoon?" he asked.

I said I did.

"I took care of it," there was a sense of pride in his voice.

"You did," I said softly without much emotion.

He nodded and looked straight ahead at the road. There was nothing more to talk about.

I looked out of my window at the passing trees and the children, swinging happily, dancing, eating, enjoying themselves in the sun. I wished that we could just turn back and drive past the graveyard, further to Grandfather's house, to his *charpoy* and *hookah*, his *veranda* and bedroom, to reassure me that was all there, like Father had promised. But with every passing thought, the distance between my grandfather and me increased. We drove far away, back to the city, back to our house, back to being isolated.

Before I walked through our door,, I looked over at our neighbour's house, their gate and windows. Their garden was unkempt, the grass was long and children's toys were sprawled, here and there. From behind a white net curtain on the second floor, I saw two women leer as my father went inside the house. I looked at them for some time and then followed him. He had noticed the gazing.

With a slight pause, he turned around to say, "There have been a lot of these gazes and talks about our family of late. I thought I must warn you."

I replied saying the gazes and talks had always been there, but the only difference was that this time they were directed at us, we were the wolves' current obsession.

He nodded like he understood and then said bitterly, "People believe they're pure, free of sin and that no calamity can touch them. They consider themselves faux-Gods and take it upon themselves as their assigned duty to make other people's lives miserable."

He looked down, remorseful as if he couldn't believe all that had happened to his family in the last few months.

My street and family had ample faux-Gods and they were all great storytellers. Their job was to weave stories in a most dramatic fashion and share them with the rest of the neighbourhood. They never got tired, nor did they ever run out of stories to tell. There was no fun in being discreet. They had to be loud and hurtful, like a performance, in their mockery. They made sure everyone knew who was suffering and why, that who was running away with whom and where, who had kept in touch with his old lover, after all those years, and how. It was their job, at the expense of people's misery and pain, to keep everyone entertained,

This time, the stories just happened to be about us. When we walked down the street, whispers and low laughter penetrated the air. They felt the need to talk about everything that was less than perfect in our home – my lost brother, Anika's failing marriage and, of course, me and all the unholy things that I must have done with the unholy white men in an unholy land.

With time, the family had learned to live with it, the stories and the restlessness that surmounted the insipid air. There was really nothing that could be done to prevent people from talking.

But my father did feel that it was his duty to keep us as far away from the faux-Gods as possible. I was asked not to go out or visit the graveyard anymore. If I were to pray for my grandparents, it was to be done within the four walls of the house, like the other family members. He thought if the family settled and hid in a cocoon for a while, the wolves would find another distractions.

I had not wrestled for my rights then. I had not told him that his relatives did to my grandfather, what the faux-Gods were doing to him. I didn't have that energy and strength left in me anymore.

When I arrived in Lahore, things remained quiet for quite a while until I finally mustered courage to stand up and resume what I had started – the search for my brother. What remained to be unearthed was why he was refusing to surface and reach out to us. But from what the authorities had said, I knew that he was in the same city as I was and I felt it in my heart that he was somewhere very close.

***

Chapter Thirty-Five

We walked in the rose garden, the vacant piece of land used for weddings adjacent of our house. As children, Abdullah and I often looked at it through our window. We enjoyed looking at the grand affairs, the emotional brides and awkwardly quiet grooms. Anika stooped and picked up a rose petal from the ground that the wind had blown near her feet. It was likely from a wedding the night before. She brought it to her nose and smelled it.

Suddenly a dark wave came over her, and her face lost its colour. I knew it reminded her of her own big day when her arms and feet were covered in *henna* and her mind conditioned with promises of a better life. She had worn Mother's red wedding dress, hoping it would bring her the same luck.

My sister took a deep sigh, as if she could still hear laughter ringing through the house and see her husband standing next to a car adorned with flowers and ribbons. To her, it was clear as day, as though it had happened only yesterday. This small petal possessed her. It had much power over her, it had the ability to bring back so many forgotten and suppressed memories. She remembered leaving her house for his, leaving her books, her family, her unspoken dreams and in a way, a part of herself as she forced this metamorphosis on herself in an attempt, naive as it was, to become the object of his desire. The serenity of it all was horribly romantic. Those long solitary hours spent waiting for him, cooking for him, feeding him, and withering away, slowly and quietly, underneath the blanket, while he searched for solace in the arms of the other woman.

She stretched her palm and the petal flew away in search of warmer company. We sat down to relish the winter sunshine and watched as a group of men tore down a large maroon tent erected for the wedding last night. They skillfully folded the vast lengths of colourful cloth and stacked them, along with the long wooden poles that held the tent together, into a truck that stood nearby. They swiftly picked up the chairs, folded the tables, and rolled up the red carpet that had been laid down for the bride's grand entrance and exit. They pulled down a huge, vibrant painting of a peacock meant as a backdrop for where the bride and groom had sat lavishly. They took away all the colour, and the rose garden lay abandoned and bare once again.

"Remember *daddi's biryani*?" Anika said suddenly, her lips forming a small smile, "We would relish the rice and tell her how delicious it was, till we tasted a clove."

I laughed as I reminisced, "We'd spit it out in disgust! It still tastes horrible to me."

"Yes, and what did *daddi* say when we asked why she put it when she knew we didn't like it?"

I couldn't remember.

"She said sometimes we have to taste bad things so we can appreciate good food."

I understood what she was trying to say.

"These are our bad times, Mariam. Now we really know the worth of love and family."

I plucked blades of grass from the ground as her thoughts began to sink inside my head.

"Why couldn't we be the way we were, Anika?" I said, "Why couldn't we just be children? Why couldn't we sit and play Ludo all our lives? Why couldn't things be simpler? Why couldn't I be walking with *dadda* across acres and acres of green land? Why do we have to grow up? This world is so stifling. Sometimes I wish I could just freeze time and trap the years past in a glass globe."

I sighed.

"Your childhood was never simple, Mariam," she responded, looking at me, "Ours was – me, the twins, Abdullah's. You never were simple, my darling. And, why would you *want* to trap that kind of miserable world, the one where you constantly lost someone, in glass and keep it on a shelf, as a reminder for the rest of your life?"

My heart felt heavy as she turned my desire upside down with a single simple truth. I thought about it – the loss of my grandparents inevitable, they were confronted by their imminent demise; how could I have stopped or foreseen that? How could I, as a child, have comprehended the painful cycle of life? Karan's loss was something that made little sense then, but as time passed, I understood better his sense of rejection, displacement and loneliness; he had appeared and disappeared from my childhood like a ghost, with no trail, no answers; there had been no closure. How could I, as a child, have ever come to terms with such a loss? I could have only forgotten it and I believed I had, until my sister brought it up. My childhood was indeed scattered with the loss of many. And now, in my adulthood, it was my brother, lost to us in all senses.

What was I to do? What were we to do? Maybe like Grandfather, the pain could never leave me and it would remain trapped in the folds of my skin. Maybe that was all we could do, enclose it within ourselves and live with it every day. Live with the memory of loss.

"Growing up only drifts us apart, degenerates our mind and body. We no longer understand what it is like to love something with your whole heart without wanting anything back in return, as children do. Why can't we be children again, Mariam? " my sister's flat words brought me back to the dull garden. She stared ahead as she spoke, her eyes looking past everything and directly at nothing.

"I am afraid, Anika, very afraid, that time will make me accept all these loses. Maybe I don't want to do this, maybe I wish to delve deeper and deeper into this feeling."

"Well, this is life, Mariam. We are all born, some live, some suffer and then we all die. We are told that this world is a passing dream and now it has started to feel that way. And the sad part is, we are not even that old yet. There is so much time that is yet to pass..."

Then she crossed her arms over her chest and remained quiet. I looked at her.

With time, like everything else, she was changing, too. There were moments when my sister was delightful and brave and then suddenly a dark shadow would possess her, making her sullen and pensive. Now, it seemed she questioned everything that had once made up her life – why she had so much faith in horoscopes and the lines on her palm that promised to illustrate her future? Why did she marry a man who swore he was in love with someone else? Why did she stay with him for two years, when she was miserable and lost? And when he raised his voice and hand to win an argument, why did she just stand there in front of him, like a corpse?

My heart cried out for her.

I held her hand that morning and apologised.

I said I felt guilty for not being there when everything was falling apart in her life, for all those cold nights she spent alone crying herself to sleep and for all those times he hit and hurt her. She didn't deserve any of this. She was the good daughter. She did everything to appease the family. She was supposed to have it all.

Her face shone in the sun and her loose black curls slithered out from under her *dupatta* and fell on her brown cheek. With a low murmur and a squeeze of my hand, she smiled and said she forgave me.

Then peaceful and amiable once again, she talked about the things she still loved, the things that still made her smile. I knew she was trying hard to start her life again. We all were, then, in the cold January of Lahore.

***

Mother was now a mindless creature. She lived in a different world altogether, a world where there was nothing but endless darkness and shadows. She dreamed in black and white and stammered most of the night. When I asked her of her dreams, I found them mostly disturbing. Abdullah would fall off a cliff into a white wild sea. The sound of his body landing on the rocks and then the waves readily swallowing it, she heard it all.

She waited for some news, a discovery, the moment when the telephone would ring or when someone would hammer on the front door, but for a long time there was no news about my brother. To ease her mind, our relatives would visit her. They stressed that the whole family needed to go on a spiritual journey to cleanse ourselves of the lingering guilt and shame we apparently harboured and the subsequent remorse and pain that followed.

And so we set off one noon, crammed into two small cars, to an unknown destination. The cars stopped in front of a crowded place in the heart of Lahore. We walked by a park. Anika and Fatima walked ahead and I walked slower because of our eldest aunt leaning on my shoulder for support. We left a trail of nine different feet until we realised there was no more of the path to walk on. The trail ended here. The eldest aunt jumped forward to say that she knew another way. No one could argue so we all followed her quietly.

We walked inside a forgotten alley filled with vibrant posters of familiar political leaders, film actresses and brands. There were other kinds of posters made out of cardboard and cloth, advertising promising astrologers, *pirs* and saints with knowledge about lovers, marriage, revenge, fertility and betrayal. A crowd of mostly women and children populated this street. Vendors selling all kinds of religious paraphernalia – *topis*, *tasbeehs*, praying mats and holy water sat chewing on pan. We walked quickly and uneasily.

"What's the matter, dear?" the aunt with abominable orange hair asked Anika. "Are you worried about your husband? Are you seeking a separation? Oh, do tell me."

Anika smiled politely and said that she wasn't.

Relatives are strange people with strange stories to tell. They are able to both love us and misunderstand us at the same time. According to them, our family was cursed, we had lost any connection to God and in order to build that faith again, we needed a man who was close to God.

The man was no one other than a spiritual mentor, a healer – their *mursid*. He was very friendly and courteous and sat on a raised platform with a broad comforting smile. Our aunts became completely different people around him. They were sober and pleasant, much to our surprise. The *pir* chanted a few verses for my mother and Anika, and gave them a list of prayers to recite before going to bed. He kept a hand on Fatima's head and chanted a few more verses in his silky voice for a bright future that included a husband better than Anika's. The eldest aunt hastily pushed me forward and asked him to give special attention to me.

"This is our foreign daughter," she said, "Remember what I told you? Please pray for her."

He beamed at me and spoke softly, "It is only in hard times like these that we miss God and argue with him the most. It is easy to lose faith and blame everything, your fate, your luck, your choices…but the journey to healing will be a lot easier if you take Him along."

My mother said that she agreed. I sighed, realising that this was what she needed, an external force, an outsider's reassurance and trust that everything would eventually be alright, because nothing I or anyone else in the house could do or say would make her happy anymore.

A week later, the aunts came back to check on our progress. My mother's mind was still home to nothing but despair and misery. She rested in her chair, disoriented from the world around her, knitting a sweater since she believed that Aminah would try to get pregnant soon. And Father, he was still the same, there but still not there.

Not much had changed, the aunts observed, disappointed. But they had done their duty to the family. We didn't see them much afterwards.

***

Anika and I began sleeping in the *barsati*. It was cold and we would lie close to each other for warmth on the bed. One night, she asked me about D.C. and I told her everything – about Lubna's family and the Artist's paintings, about Richard and the Bakers, and about the kind lady, Afreen, who ran a restaurant near my university, and my job at the agency. We talked about everything except for our brother and my search for him in the States. We thought maybe if we didn't talk about him, the pain would lessen, the uneasiness would weaken and the *barsati* would no longer smell of him. But we were wrong; it would never stop smelling of him. He was everywhere. There was nothing physical about this familiar smell of our brother anymore, but rather a smell fabricated entirely from our memories of him.

Anika lay and contemplated for a while, trying to envision the streets I spoke of, and then asked, with her eyes still fixed on the ceiling:

"Did you feel alone there?"

"I did, during the first few months but then eventually, I made friends."

"Do you think he felt alone, too?"

I did not respond instantly. I thought and thought about his first days after arrival.

"He had me," I said.

"He was lonely here."

"He had always been a recluse, Anika."

"Like you," she said.

"I am no longer a recluse," I said, "D.C. changed me."

"No, *he* changed you. He changed us all."

With that, she turned away from me and pretended to sleep. Taking a hint, I looked away too, glancing at the walls illuminated by the streetlights outside. There was a calendar that hung from a loose nail, still frozen in time, indicating the month when he had imprisoned himself in the *barsati*.

I sat up and ran my hands over my face. I looked around the room; *his* cupboard, *his* desk, *his* cane chair, *his* books and empty cages *he* used for wounded birds. They were all there encased in his lingering, empty smell. Everything was there, except for him. Too many ghosts lurking in the room.

I called Anika's name and but she did not move.

I wore my sweater, slipped my feet into my slippers and went downstairs, away from the rooftop and the *barsati*, leaving my sister alone once again in the darkness. I sat on the stairs and closed my eyes for a moment. When I opened them again, I saw that in the living room, the lights were still glowing. It was Father.

I walked up and stood at the door. He sat in his chair going through some old photographs. He watched the figures stare back at him in silence. I imagined he was looking at the photographs of his son, I imagined that it was the picture where he stood in front of a flowing river, full of spirit, holding the branch of a tree and beaming with joy.

"There was an infinite distance between him and me," my father said, seeing me standing by the door, "There has always been an infinite distance between me and my family."

"You're just being sentimental," I commented.

"I don't even remember your childhood. I've always been so distant."

"You couldn't have done anything more for us," I consoled him.

"This has been the ugliest winter," he said.

I watched him sigh and shrivel up in his chair.

His mind, like Mother's, was momentarily absent from reality. He looked so old, so weary, drowned in memories, floating in an unseen dream looking for that one grain of hope or any sign that his son was out there and was going to come back. It was like he had been caught in a trap, imprisoned in a cage and his captor had lost the key. I wanted, for my family, to find that key, to find my brother and release them all from this current state of suspended misery.

I watched as the captive placed the photographs back in the album and sank into his chair again.

"What did we do wrong?" he asked, "Why didn't he come back home?"

I held his hands for comfort.

"I don't know. I really don't know. But there must be a reason," I assured him, "And I *will* find it for you."

He kept his hand on mine.

"Do you trust me?" I asked, "If you do then believe me when I say, I won't stop looking for him. I will find him."

He revealed a dozen expressions and said in a reedy voice, "Mariam, of course, I trust you. You said you heard his voice when he called your friend Richard, and he said he is here and that is why you've come back."

I remembered the night when I heard his voice in Richard's phone and cried. I remembered packing my bags for Lahore and calling my family, telling them it was him, I had heard his voice, he was alive. A part of them did not believe me, they thought I was being fooled and so I decided to leave the States for good and resume the futile task of tracing Abdullah down in my country.

"That is why I've come back," I repeated.

He nodded, deep in thought, still wondering about his question: *Why didn't he come back? What did we do wrong?*

"How are things with you, my child?" he asked suddenly, "In

all that's been going on, I realise I've completely forgotten to ask how you are doing…what is going on in your mind?"

He laid his hand over my head and patted down my hair lovingly.

I smiled softly at him.

"To tell you truth, I think I just feel divided. A part of me is still buried within the cocoon I created for myself as a child, and the other half is wild, passionate and curious. I need you to promise me that you will no longer build a tower around us, that you will not imprison us with this seclusion. People will talk, as they always do but we cannot escape or control that. I need this for me, for our family, I *need* to find Abdullah. For that, I must go out, I must ask around for information, I must search for him and you must accept that. I feel he's somewhere here, close to us…" I let my voice trail off.

He contemplated for a while and then spoke very slowly, measuring the weight of his every word.

"I understand, Mariam, at least I think I do. But people who disappear themselves never really want to be found. We can try to hope otherwise, but in the end we know that we should not disturb them. Perhaps this is what he wanted, though I still don't understand why, but may be with time, we *will* understand his choice. Believe me, my child. I say this with a heavy heart."

The tone he used was lifeless, practiced and mechanical, as if the words had been worn out by being repeated many times over. They created a shock that ran through my body and I let go of his hand instantly, letting it fall limp and lifeless in mid-air.

"We don't know this, Father…we must at least try…"

He now placed his hand on my cheek and whispered, "I cannot believe I am saying this, but we have to let him go, Mariam, and that's our little secret."

***

CHAPTER THIRTY-SIX

It was a foggy morning. I sat inside a *rickshaw* and gave the half-asleep driver directions to a stranger's house. Typical to winter mornings in Lahore, the mist had engulfed the roads, canals and the trees. The roads were silent.

I lifted my *chadar* to my face as the cold tried to penetrate through the slits in the doors of the *rickshaw*. The driver chewed on sweet *paan* – a burst of traditional flavours wrapped between layers of beetel leaf – and then straightened one of his many rearview mirrors. I felt his eyes watching me, wondering where I was going at that early hour.

Anika had watched me dress up and prepare to leave before the rest of the family woke up. I told her everything, where I was going and whom I was meeting in the stillness of morning mist.

Adnan Farookh. That was the name of the man whom I wanted to see.

He called me a couple of times, explaining that he was a friend of Mohsin's and wished to see me. When I had asked why, he said it was urgent and could not be explained over the phone. I didn't go the first time he called, nor the second but when he called for the third time, I realised that I had nothing to lose.

Anika showed her reluctance; meeting strangers for the sake of any little information seemed useless and dangerous to her. I told her I had been practicing this art for quite some time now. The argument was brief. She fell silent and I left.

I did not take Father's car because I knew deep down, like Anika, he would not be pleased about my meeting strangers for clues. He would have asked me questions about my insatiable restlessness and indomitable belief that I might be able to find a part of Abdullah somewhere. Thus, I kept it to myself and in doing so, my brother's search became entirely my own mission. I decided not to disclose anything to my parents until I had found something concrete.

The rickety vehicle swayed wildly as we took a U-turn and entered one of Lahore's most posh residencies. A barricade was laid out before us. A traffic warden spat near his feet and then refrained the vehicle from going any further. The driver stepped down, scratching his scalp. The men bickered and reasoned. Slipping out of the *rickshaw*, I handed the man his money and said that I preferred walking.

"It's a long walk, madam!" he began after me, "Oh, Madam! Madam!"

I walked on without looking back.

Before me lay long rows of elegant colonial mansions and grand lawns complete with lush green trees and garden ornaments. I wandered on the long, well-maintained road, looking at the mansions closely, each one so different than the other, so unique in their design and luxury. It was a long walk before I reached my destination. I took out a crumpled piece of paper from my pocket where I had scribbled down the address, and then looked back up at the plaque bearing the name and address of the owner beside the gate. I sighed, unsure of what urgent and secret information I'd discover on the other side.

I rang the bell.

A kitchen boy dressed in a crumpled brown *kurta-shalwar* looked at me with sleepy eyes. I introduced myself and without a word, he went inside to announce my arrival.

"Madam, you may come in!" he called out after a few minutes, from the porch.

I entered from the gate into an emerald green garden. The boy led me inside to what seemed like a study.

"You may sit down," he gestured to the sofa, "Sir is coming."

The interior was kept warm by a burning stone hearth. I sat down on a long leopard-printed *divan*. Every wall of the big room was populated with paintings and photographs hung at different heights and many statues of Buddha and other significant figures, sat on glass tables and wooden shelves. It reminded me of Babar's over extravagant den and his birthday party. If I closed my eyes, I could almost picture myself there; standing beside the small figurines and photo frames that adorned the mantle. I shook my head to remind myself that I was in Lahore, away from the careless people and their reckless natures.

After a minute or two, a young man came inside the room.

"Mariam?" his face lit up, as if he had known me for many years, "I didn't expect you to be here this early."

"I'm sorry, I didn't inform you earlier but this was the only time I could come." I spoke quickly, and nervously.

"I am very happy that you considered meeting me," there appeared a magnetic smile on his face, "Would you at least give me time to make myself a little more presentable? I just got out of bed."

I nodded gently. He smiled and left me alone again.

I walked to a wall and scanned the photographs that decorated it. They were all of the young man – him with important looking old men, him with old women, him with young women and him at a wedding. There was a grand piano in the corner of the room standing against a big window with lush violet curtains. Behind an untidy desk was a cabinet which served as a small library. I ran my fingers over the intricately carved wood.

The kitchen boy returned, this time he was less sleepy and held a tray with a glass filled with orange juice. I asked him what he did there. He did not respond but just rubbed his eyes.

"Why are you up so early?" I asked the boy.

"School," he said quietly.

With that, he placed the glass on a table and walked away with the empty tray.

"His father has been working for us, as chauffer, for thirty years," said a voice from behind me. The young man stood at the door, definitely looking more presentable. He buttoned the sleeves of his shirt and said, "The family lives here in the quarters and I made sure the child studied."

"That's very kind of you."

"I believe we didn't get a chance to introduce ourselves formally." When he spoke, he had slight airs of a worldly accent that was hard to pinpoint.

"You seem to already know me," I said hesitantly.

"Just a little," he smiled.

"Well, Mohsin didn't know me much," I replied, "So you are Adnan Farookh?"

"I am," he shook my hand, "I'm a journalist, I was born in Pakistan, but grew up here, in the States and in Britain."

I released his hand and he continued, "I work for a local channel here, against my father's wishes. He thought I would move to London when I got an offer for a better job a year ago, but I want to stay here for a while and see how things pan out."

He sat down on a chair in front of me. I didn't introduce myself because I felt he was not finished yet. He seemed to be the kind of person that not only enjoyed talking about himself, but was also exceedingly generous with the details.

"I don't know if you know this, but I *do* know you. I have known you for quite some time."

He waited to read my expressions. I pondered, suspicious, wondering if it was true. I tried to identify his face, wondering if I had seen him somewhere.

"I'm sorry...I...I don't recognise you, have we met before?" I asked.

"Don't be stunned. I was in your university in D.C. but I was a senior and left shortly after you arrived. I got accepted at Stanford... for a research post."

I studied his face, not knowing what to make of what he said.

"Next to the campus lake, under the yellow umbrella and adjacent to the student union building, that's where you sat in the afternoons."

I remained still, not revealing any emotion. He didn't seem surprised that I wasn't unnerved.

"You sat with your friend, the photographer, but mostly alone. Sometimes reading, sometimes thinking."

"I don't believe this," I said.

"I don't blame you."

"No, I mean...I don't buy this."

There was a long silence.

"I should say this now, it's the right time," he stood and put his hands in the pockets.

"I'm a good man ....and not a stalker."

"A good man can also be a stalker."

He bit his lip, taken aback by my rebuttal.

"The descriptions of my seating preferences and friends are precise, but I still don't believe you. Who told you all this?"

He looked perplexed for a minute but then began laughing. We were strangers.

"Is this meeting some kind of sick joke?"

"I'm sorry, I was just trying to get your attention..."

"You had it. I woke up at five in the morning just to see you, stranger!" I folded my arms in front of my chest, a little frustrated.

"It was just a..."

"Joke?"

"Yes, a stupid…"

"Yes, it was." My expression was grave and serious.

He looked deeply humiliated when he didn't receive his expected reaction.

"Look…why did you *really* want to meet me?"

"I'm a friend of Mohsin's, like I told you over the phone. Abdullah…I haven't met him personally, but only know of him."

"What is this about? Why have you called me here?"

"I was curious," he explained, "I wanted to meet you in person."

I folded my arms and passed him a steady gaze. He shrugged and emitted a sigh.

"When I heard your story, it rattled me, like it rattled everybody. I was not just startled but a little curious when Mohsin said that your brother just disappeared into thin air. You know how a journalist's mind works. I thought, now that's a story – a young boy travels from Lahore to the United States for a degree and the next thing you know, he's missing and has everyone looking for him. He says he's back in Pakistan yet he hasn't come back home. Why?"

Quietly now, I rose and walked around the room trying to calm my nerves. I didn't want to give an immediate reaction. He had done it now, angered me, and I didn't let him finish his proposal.

"Do you find my misery, this painful chapter of my life, amusing?" I asked.

"I did not say that. You are completely misinterpreting me…"

I shook my head and turned around so he could not see the anger on my face. I heard his heavy, nervous breathing. I walked again towards the wall of photographs and studied them, carefully.

He didn't move from his seat.

There was an old photo from what seemed to be like his boarding school days. I looked at the boys' serious faces and their uniforms. I ran my fingers over the glass, moving them over each of the faces. I couldn't determine exactly what, but something about the boys in that photograph seemed familiar to me. With my eyebrows knit together, I scanned my memory, trying to identify exactly why that particular image stood out to me.

"Mariam?"

The journalist called my name.

I did not answer, instead tore myself away the photograph and walked a few steps towards a large painting that hung near the window. My eyes had not fallen on it before but now as they did, I was drawn in completely. I stood in front of it, enjoying the choice of colours and subject. A woman lay on a wooden swing with her red hair falling all the way down into a vast, vast ocean. In the water were some random objects – a pen, a paper, some kitchen utensils – and what seemed like a child. A small smile appeared on my face as I recognised the signature style of the infamously elusive Artist.

"You have quite an exquisite taste in art," I lowered my eyelids as I waited for him to reply.

"I'm glad you enjoy it. This is my father's study. Everything over here is his, except for that painting. I picked that one out."

"Really…and what exactly drew you to it?" my voice bore hints of sarcasm now.

He stiffened as he realised what I was trying to suggest.

"The theme…"

"The theme," I repeated slowly. "You know, Mohsin does not know I am back in Lahore," I said, curtly. "I am certain he doesn't even know where I live. This leaves me to question…"

He was taken by surprise.

"…who exactly are you?" I turned around.

He studied me before saying simply, "Just a stranger who would like to talk to you."

"I don't converse with strangers."

"The best conversations are amongst strangers, you can talk freely, they don't judge you and for a moment there, you are yourself.'

"A stranger who somehow knows my aunt and uncle. Did she sell this to you, the painting? Did she sell you his painting?"

He stood up and ran fingers through his brown hair, anxious and restless.

"It was a gift...Mariam..."

"How do you know me?"

"Your aunt told me about you and your story," with that, he lowered his gaze and turned away from me, "I should've told you this from the start but I felt you wouldn't meet me then. Lubna told me about your meeting with Mohsin so I took his name, thinking you would not turn me down if I did."

"And did she ask you to watch over me? Do something she was unable to do in D.C.?"

"This hasn't got anything to do with her. I promise."

"Why did you find me?" I said sharply.

"It was fate that allowed me to trace you," he replied, "Do you believe in fate, Ms. Ameen, the fact that people are meant to cross paths for a reason and that in life, there are no accidents?"

"Oh, yes Mr. Farookh, I do believe in fate and destiny...and God and the power of great art and music, but I have recently learned not to trust every walking, living thing!"

My face felt as hard as stone, my breath was heavy and I was livid.

He looked at me intensely. Something I said had touched his heart and it showed on his face, his eyes remained set and his lips quivered a little.

"You know my aunt and I'm sure you know a lot of other things."

"Yes, it is true. She is an acquaintance, my father brought art from her but she has got nothing to do with this. I wanted to find you myself... she only mentioned you because she was worried, I promise you she never asked me to track you down. This decision was entirely my own…"

I didn't speak for a moment and then all the rage that had gradually built up inside me just flew out.

"You want a career break, don't you? You want to sell this story," I said accusingly.

"You really think that low of me?" there was a shade of disappointed in his voice.

"Well, excuse me because I really don't know what to think anymore!" I picked up my bag and began to walk out.

"I know about him, Mariam," he said loudly, "I know about Max and I think I might be able to help you find out where he is."

I turned around immediately, stood stunned for a moment and studied his face. He wanted me to stay, to sit down and talk to him. He hoped that telling me about where I could find Max would compel me to stay. But instead, my eyes fell on his boarding school photograph once again. I looked at it for several seconds and then taking a long, deep angry breath, stormed out of the study.

***

CHAPTER THIRTY-SEVEN

I lay on the wooden swing and swayed to and fro, wondering about the journalist. *What did he want? And what did Lubna tell him? How could he possibly know about Max?*

Two weeks had passed. I kept envisioning myself in his den, his face and his promising eyes when he said he could help me find Max. He had tried talking to me again, tried to arrange another meeting, something less awkward, but I rejected his offer. Anika thought it was foolish of me to go in the first place, to expose myself to strangers in such a way. I had agreed with her then.

I had looked him up after I came home. Google had a lot to share: *Adnan Farookh, a young journalist based in Lahore, working with one of the leading news channel in Pakistan*, it said.

It appeared that his aforementioned academic background was accurate. Furthermore, his father was a writer who had just written his third novel, '*Gypsy love and paradise,*' and was fascinated with themes of women, emancipation and sexuality, among many other things of controversial nature. A scandal website disclosed Adnan's relationship with an Austrian journalist. They remained steady for two years until they decided to put their careers before their love life. It also showed a string of images of Adnan with members of high society, local and international film industries, models and academics, and boasted of his charm and charisma. I rolled my eyes.

I hastily closed the browser and started afresh. I began by typing in: *list of people deported from the United States in 2009….2010…* and *America's most dangerous fugitives*.

After which I repeatedly typed Abdullah's name, then Max's and then Malik, the name Abdullah had mentioned to Richard over the phone.

Nothing of consequence appeared.

I became hysterical and by the end of my research, the browser history read something like this: *Max Malik, Malik Max, Max Malik Baltimore, Malik dangerous man, men named Malik in Lahore, teenagers involved in store robbery, mysterious Max…Boy vanished from Boston campus, teenage student missing from university in Boston, Adnan Farookh, Adnan Max, Adnan and Malik Pakistan, how to find a missing person, Abdullah Ameen, Abdullah Ameen, Abdullah Ameen…*

Frustrated, I slapped the screen shut and rubbed my eyes with my fingers to comfort them. Nothing helped. If only Google could read our hearts and give answers to every question that was maddening our minds. How much simpler would life become? But if I had learnt anything from my life, it was that it was never meant to be simple, never meant to be easy and, in my case, never meant to be comfortable.

Lying on the swing, I stared aimlessly ahead. I could hear Anika move nosily in the other room. I followed the sounds and saw that the room was a complete mess. Her clothes were sprawled everywhere, her things all thrown on the bed and she was trying to pull out a large suitcase from the closet.

"What're you doing, Anika?" I asked startled.

She looked at me in disillusionment and then pointed at the

door. Pulling me inside, she shut it, whispering, "I must leave," she said, "I am taking the next train."

"Why? Where? What's going on? Why are you packing?" I attacked her with questions.

She shook her head vigorously, threw her things in the suitcase and walked around in a mad frenzy. "My husband, he will come for me and everyone will ask me to leave with him. I can't. I need to go away before that time comes."

"But where will you go?"

"I don't know where, I don't care. I just don't want to go home with him. I *need* to be free!"

"Anika," I held her shoulders firmly and she looked into my eyes, "You can't run away from all this. You will fight this, fight him and I promise I will go with you wherever you want."

Her lips worked and tears formed in her eyes.

"I did everything everyone asked me to do. I was a good daughter, then why am I not happy?"

I stared at her in mingled confusion and empathy, as she covered her face with shame.

I took her face tight in my hands and wiped her tears.

"Why are you so afraid?"

"Mariam, I did something terrible. But I can't tell," she muttered, "Not now, I can't tell anyone."

I looked at her, my eyebrows knit together.

"God will forgive, He will understand why. But the man I married won't," she cried.

A part of me broke inside as I found myself unworthy of her trust. "Anika, whatever you did is done now. You can't run away from it," I said, "You can't run away now."

She shook her head madly and burst into tears.

"You don't know…you don't know…" she kept chanting.

She sat on the ground and wept like a child.

"I will be happy," she whispered, "I will be happy if I take that train. Please let me take that train…"

I watched her in silence. She sat trembling before me. I had never seen her like that, so utterly hopeless, so ultimately fragile as if she were a glass vase that had smashed onto the ground and broken into tiny pieces. I didn't know which piece of her to collect first.

She wanted distance, a certain release from the family and herself. She desired freedom, the freedom to be herself, whatever she chose, not someone's trophy wife or an obedient elder daughter or sister. There was an emotional baggage she carried everywhere, her past, her suspended marriage; it lingered with her and was a constant source of inquisition. She was crumbling because she wasn't sure if she should fix her old life or begin a new one; she wasn't sure whether to blame herself and drown in guilt, or blame the circumstance and fate that put her in this position.

"You can never leave me alone, Mariam. Never again," she said in a voice that was toneless yet somehow firm.

"I will never leave you again. I promise." I took her hand in mine.

To calm the tense atmosphere, she asked me to take her to the railway station. She promised she wouldn't leave but just wanted to look at the place, just wanted to be there. She sat by the platform, dull and troubled, no longer fascinated by the train station that once captivated her. She battled the same fearful nostalgia and lingering sadness that I did in the graveyard.

"It's not the same anymore, is it?" she asked and receded down the platform, "Why come here when you know you can't escape? Not yet."

I knew what she meant. There were still some strings that she needed to cut off in order to move on and be free.

Our parents wanted her to give the relationship a chance, to move back with him and try one more time. Anything to keep the wolves from gossiping and not spilling family secrets, even if that meant living the rest of your life in absolute misery.

Anika said she could not do it, neither could she tell her family all that she went through. She said if she did, she would hurt them more than Abdullah had.

From her, I learned that, like Grandfather, the sober-faced man could not leave his old lover and kept going back to her. She couldn't stop him, and he couldn't stop himself. In the empty soulless days, he still wanted her to be his wife, to be around, to bear his children and create a false impression of a happy married wife. She did it, for almost two years, and she could do no more. She wept and told me nothing else, the rest of her pain she kept to herself.

I told her that out *dadda* was nothing like the sober-faced man, that there was so much about him that she didn't know.

She nodded and said, "I can't help myself but think that these lovers must be extraordinary women. They must really be so extraordinary that they make all us ordinary women drown in boring insignificance."

*****

What she feared actually happened. The sober-faced man appeared at our door one day. I was at the market, Father was at work and Fatima and Mother were visiting the *pir* again.

When I returned, I saw a car parked outside the house. It was the same car that Father had gifted Anika at her wedding. I touched the open door and ran inside in horror. I yelled Anika's name. The only response I received was my own voice bouncing back. Suddenly, I heard heavy footsteps, definitely not Anika's, at the far end of the house.

I sprinted up the stone stairs and tried to open the door of our room.

It was locked. I pounded.

"Anika! Anika!! Open the door. Are you in there?"

"Mariam!" she cried and unbolted.

I closed it as soon as I entered.

Streams of bitter tears decorated her reddened cheeks.

"What's going on? Where is he?" I held her shoulders.

"I locked the main door but he still broke in," she stammered. "He is coming here to get me. Mariam, I can't go back. Make him go away, Mariam, I can't go back!"

I hushed her and brought her close to my face, "He won't touch you. I promise you."

Again, I heard the footsteps downstairs. It was him. He was probably looking for her, finding her somewhere, trying to find her room maybe. I couldn't think. Anika's hands were cold. I squeezed them for warmth. After several minutes I decided that we couldn't just sit inside and wait for him to find us. We had to get out of the house, away from him. We crept out of the room and ran downstairs. She shrieked when she saw him standing in the corridor with his feet firmly on the ground and a fierce expression on his face. We ran towards the closest open door of the living room. I made Anika run ahead of me but he sped after her. I followed him and held onto his shirt so she could get time to bolt the door. He pushed me. I fell on the hard ground.

"You don't know what she has done!" he thundered.

"Let her go!"

But he was faster. He forced his body into the door frame so she couldn't lock it.

"You brutal animal!" I shrieked.

I slammed my fist into his shoulder as he tried to grab my sister's *dupatta*. He staggered back and paused, trying to settle his senses. He raised his hand, threatening to slap my face, as his fiery eyes pierced into mine. Every vein in my body ached in fear and pressure, but I didn't look away.

"Mariam, you're getting involved in a matter you don't even know about," he said, "You have nothing to do with us."

"You ungrateful monster, she remained silent for all her life because she is a woman, she won't now. You have given her nothing, but pain. She is my sister and I have everything to do with this!" I said fiercely.

"She cannot leave me. She is my wife."

"You bastard, not anymore."

That was the tipping point. He lashed out with a cry and tried to hit me with his fist. I ducked and his hand hit against the refrigerator. He shook it vigorously to release the pain.

"You know what you've done!" he raged. "Did you tell her what you've done?"

Anika screamed a curse and grabbed a knife from the fruit basket. Sudden confidence possessed her.

"You touch us one more time and I am going to slit your throat!" she hissed as she pointed the knife at him, "and I won't regret it for one bloody second."

"You couldn't do it…" he said mockingly

She ran the blade across her wrist, tearing her skin, "If I can do it to myself, imagine how easy it would be it to slice your throat."

He stared at her bleeding wrists in anger and then stormed out of the room. Anika's hands finally stopped trembling. I put my arms around her body as she cried softly. I tied my *dupatta* around her wrist and cleaned the blood off her fingers.

"Look what you've done to yourself! Why didn't you do something before, Anika? Why didn't you leave him? What person can be so patient with a man like this?" I whispered and rocked her like a child.

"I kept waiting, Mariam, waiting for the right time and it never came."

"How could you be so weak? How could you continue to live this way?"

"It's not that easy. When I came home to meet Mother, I could not imagine looking into her eyes and telling her what I was going through, I couldn't do this to them, to our parents. I could not give them this pain."

"That you were unhappy? That you were kicked…and punched…and…" I swallowed my sentence as I felt my eyes burning with tears, "When will it finally be about *you*, Anika?

What did all this obedience get you?"

She lowered her eyes and cried, "My words throbbed in my throat and every night I told myself that I can live through this, that next morning would be different. You went so far away, Mariam, you went so far away. I had no one."

"But now I am back," a flood of tears gushed down my eyes.

"I lost the baby, Mariam," her whispers followed a muffled cry, "I lost our baby on purpose."

I stroke her hair and calmed her down.

"He was never mine, my husband, he was never mine."

Now my sister was sure what she wanted was a new life, one where she mattered, a life of profound happiness. She was ready to pay the price.

Talaakh, a divorce.

The word was like poison. Mother barely moved and Father listened to her story for the first time. I stood at the doorway watching my parents and sister weep like little children. Whether they were tears of sorrow or guilt, I'd never know.

The morning after that, I helped her pack a suitcase. We went to the railway station and she finally boarded a train.

"Where will you go?" is what I asked her after minutes of dreadful silence.

"To the village," she said, "to the Raja's empty house, to the silence where I will find comfort among my thoughts and myself."

She stepped up the steps and disappeared into the train.

I watched her finally escape to the open fields where she would breathe freely, to a place where no one cared who she was and what she had run away from, to a place that reminded her of our childhood, our grandparents and her happy days. I watched her crawl out and for the first time, find a life for herself. Yes, it might have been empty, very empty, but it was hers.

***

CHAPTER THIRTY-EIGHT

On a chilly February evening, I found myself at Adnan's house again, this time attending a party. Feeling completely out of place, I walked past a group of high society women, dressed in short printed dresses, lighting their cigarettes. They flirted relentlessly with every man at the doorway, talking in their silky voices about food, travel, sex and art. Their own motives were obscure yet they excelled in analysing others'.

I was reminded of Lubna and her lavish parties where she glided around the hall in her ethereal dresses, making small talk with rich men, introducing them to her husband's paintings, and then drinking glass after glass of wine, as if to erase her uneasiness.

The blinds were drawn but there were enough colourful lanterns illuminating the room. Waiters dressed in white *shalwar-kameez* and black waistcoats came in carrying bottles of champagne and flute glasses for a toast. The guests' faces glittered with delight. The sound of glasses clinking together was later followed by performances of the *sitar* and the *rabab*.

"Welcome to our world, Ms. Ameen," Adnan said mildly in my ear, "I mean, welcome to my father's world."

We stood in the living room, where his father was hosting a party in honour of his new book. There was a certain mockery in Adnan's voice and a discomfort on his face. I stood beside him, watching painters, writers and actors light their cigarettes casually in front of the fire. A girl in a see-through black dress walked past me swiftly and then leaned forward to whisper something in his ear. His cheek reddened and he said something back to her in a low voice. The girl didn't seem to like it, anger swept over her face. Feeling rejected and humiliated, she walked away haughtily. Her heels clicked on the marble floor.

I looked at him quietly. He wasn't watching her anymore.

"And is that your father?" I looked at a grey-haired man in a black suit.

"Yes, that's my father. Until last week, he had been in Greece doing research for his next book."

"What does he write about? I'm afraid, I haven't read his work, yet."

"Modern Pakistan and the lifestyle of the elites. Actually, he loves writing about sex, alcohol and the opulent lifestyle that is often not associated with Pakistan," he laughed.

Looking around the room, he suddenly said, "Do you mind if we go from here? Somewhere quieter, somewhere where we can talk? I knew you would call me back."

We went to the same room we had met in on my last visit and he settled behind the desk. Adnan told me this was his father's study but was he was seldom in the country, so he used this as his office.

He lit a cigarette and offered me one. I refused.

"We didn't get to learn about each other properly," he said suddenly, "Have you lived here all your life?"

"In a way, yes. Apart from the strange year or so I spent living in D.C."

He nodded, "I live here now, but I have travelled a lot. And as I told you before, I grew up in several places around the world. I've had four stepmothers and some won't leave me alone, so I tend to move around a lot to please them but mostly its work-related. I'm not very successful yet, I mean, I'm just thirty-three so that perhaps explains why I still live with my father and work for some local channel instead of a fancy broadcasting channel abroad."

I nodded uneasily and tried to comprehend, for the second time now, why this stranger was so comfortable in casually disclosing all these personal details to me. Maybe he wanted me to feel comfortable, to look at him differently, as a journalist who travelled a lot and had many stepmothers, instead of some rich stranger who knew my unpredictable aunt and heaven knew what else about my life and brother.

"You said you knew who I was looking for," I said.

He lifted his face to me but didn't answer.

"How is that possible?" I asked.

He played with a small wooden dice on the table, watching me intently. He was a good-looking man with an angular face and brown eyes that bore a constant fiery spark within them. I imagined his mother to be a stunning woman.

"How is any of this possible? How is your brother's disappearance possible? How is me finding you possible?" he put out the cigarette in an ash-tray carved out from inside the belly of a sculpture a laughing Buddha.

"That doesn't answer my question."

"You're not looking for answers, Mariam."

"I am looking for answers…"

"Then you're not doing a very fine job."

My heart quickened; he was infuriating me again.

"And this is coming from a man who just met me," I snapped.

"Look at me," he leaned forward, "Do I look like a man who is untruthful and dishonest? Like someone who will set you up and play with your emotions? Or on the contrary do I look like a man…"

"You're a media man. You're the child of fabrication and deception," I snubbed, cutting him off.

He smiled, amused.

"We're not all the same, Mariam."

"You're supposed to be diplomatic."

"I'm not a bad person…"

I shrank back in my seat as he waited for me to substantiate.

"I can't distinguish between the two anymore, the good and bad men. Trust me."

"Do I look like a man who is messing with you?"

"What does that kind of man look like?"

We didn't speak for a while but just looked at each other's face, trying to deduce and read each other's mind but there was a failure of connection.

"You are strong, but Rizwan really did shatter something inside of you," he said. "You believe you can't distinguish between people anymore."

For a split second, my face froze as though I didn't want to believe what he had said. Very slowly, I picked myself up from the chair, filled with intense horror and furry as he said his name. A living fire ran through my body, making me stiff like a cardboard.

Of course, he knew Rizwan. How could he only know Lubna and not her son?

But Adnan was unsure about the impact this discovery had on me. He looked at me for a moment, as if he had just let something very important slip out without realising, and then instantly scanned the ashes of his cigarette, edgy and nervous.

Everything made sense now. Everything fit. He was Rizwan's friend. The photograph of the boys at boarding school I had seen earlier now suddenly made sense. Standing next to Adnan in that picture was none other than a young Rizwan.

"Please don't assume things now," he began, "I can explain."

"Take your time," I sat back in a chair, no longer feeling angry.

In fact, I felt nothing at all. Apart from the sudden shock on hearing Rizwan's name, nothing about this situation angered or even surprised me anymore. All I wanted now was for Adnan to just come clean about his intentions on contacting me.

I sighed deeply and then said, "I won't run now. I promised myself that I wouldn't run away from you now. No more. I won't run away from anything now. So you, sir, take your time, recollect yourself and tell me how exactly you think you can help me bring back my brother?"

There was a terrified expression on his face, something that involved disbelief and pity. He stood up and walked around the room, gathering his thoughts and trying to make up for what he had revealed. He opened a window and the music from the *rabab*, haunting and deceiving, wandered in. It made me want to let go of everything and dance around with my hands in the air. It distracted me from my current predicament. I placed both my hands over my ears.

"Did he hurt you?" he asked suddenly.

I remained steady for a moment, and then finally said, "Yes, he did."

He looked at the ground, very pale and then back at me, "I'm so sorry."

He said that in a sincere resonant voice. The voice of the singer grew louder. He sang something about the ruthless world and a common man's struggles. He was pleading, asking God to show that He exists. He threatened to leave Him and look for some other transcendental being if He didn't reciprocate his love.

I chose not to respond or acknowledge Adnan's apology. I did not want it. I no longer wished to continue the conversation and was politely escorted out by the kitchen boy. We cut through the party on our way out. People sang and danced, swaying to the music, barely even noticing my existence as I walked past them.

I stood outside the lavish, well-lit house for a few minutes, so aware of my own being, of the hurt I buried so deep within me. I glanced up to the evening sky. Somehow it looked the same to me, the same colour and an incredibly similar arrangement of clouds as had been on the night I had freed myself from Rizwan's grip in the parking lot. A night whose every detail had engraved itself so firmly in my mind. I cried softly as the *rickshaw* driver took me back home. It was coming back to me, all that I had painfully forgotten. Adnan's words had unknowingly resurrected that horrible evening in D.C.

***

March began.

I didn't hear from him for two months. He disappeared like an extra from a film or a flat character in a novel, but as he disappeared so did my urge of finding my brother. Strangely, I became more curious about this journalist than I was about my brother's whereabouts. I had no lead, no willpower, nothing. I barely moved, barely did anything at all, just lay lazily on the swing and shut out all the activities of the world that surrounded me. I would lie and closed my eyes, pretended that I was in a cradle and the kind lady on the moon was rocking me to sleep.

What else could I have done?

There was no trail to follow, no suspects to question, nothing. I wrote to Richard often. He was doing well and hadn't heard from Abdullah either. He was saving up for a short trip to Lahore and trying to apply for a visa. He said he felt like seeing me, being with me for a while. I encouraged him and said I too, wanted to be with him again. I had forgotten what he looked, smelled like, all the things he said. The irony was that though Lahore was the city I grew up in, I felt more like an outsider than ever. I needed something familiar in this place full of strangers.

The swing sway gently and from the corner of my eye, I saw Mother sitting in the *veranda* with a chubby woman dressed in nauseatingly shiny clothes. She stood out so obviously from the simple background of our home, the gaudy fabric sparkling among the dull accents of its surroundings. She and my mother had many things spread out on the table; tea cups, biscuits, cookbooks and photographs, lots of them, of bachelors in desperate poses. There was a photo of one such man lying in front of tree with a flower in his hands and another who stood in front of a pyramid with his hands on his waist, and yet another one dancing at Aminah's *mehndi*.

Between my mother and I was a massive space of silence and from this hollow void, all emotion and feelings had vanished. We had nothing to say to each other anymore. She remained in Fatima's company and I, in mine. I felt for the longest time, that she blamed me for the disappearance of her little boy. She thought me to be selfish and only care for myself when in the States. It was hard to explain to her about Abdullah and my distance, physical and emotional. She wouldn't have understood.

Pain, somehow, becomes easier to swallow with when you have someone to blame for it. We scapegoat without even realising it, embrace it like second nature. It is always less rational yet far easier to contain this blame and hatred, and project it onto a single person, rather than acknowledging the situation as inevitable. But that was her way of facing the sorrow – blaming me for *allowing* this to happen to Abdullah; and I let her deal with it, even if it was in this way.

The woman she was sitting with was Aunt Ruksana, the local matchmaker and her new best friend. I caught both of the women looking at me and I turned my face away from them entirely. Ruksana was very fond of me and often told my mother that I was quite a catch. She asked me once for one of my best photographs and for my amusement, I gave her one of an eight-month-old me in flowery underwear. She roared with laughter and said that my sense of humour would take me a long way.

Mother now had one, and only one desire – to get me engaged by the end of the month. Apparently there was no space for a divorced woman in the matrimonial market so Anika was out of the picture.

But Mother also had her qualms, like she was certain that I was losing my mind. She told Anika that I didn't just look like Grandfather but I had also started to act like him, unassailable and isolated, and beyond anyone's reach and judgment. That was not a good thing for a woman of my age.

Much to my discontent, a groom was finally selected. I didn't reciprocate, didn't meet him or even come near his family who visited often for tea. My mother realised that she couldn't exercise her will on me so pushed Fatima forward instead.

Fatima didn't react the way I did. She accepted things just as they were, tossed down her way. My sisters' lives were somehow simpler; they were given a sort of code book to follow. A list of what they should and shouldn't do. They didn't deviate and they never doubted this family codebook. They understood that life could never completely be reshaped into what they desired, thus they never desired anything at all. I, on the other hand, could never allow myself to understand this. Aware that though my actions hurt and at times, embarrassed my family, I could never allow myself to live by the conventions prescribed in some obsolete book.

This book that contained rules considered pertinent in our family for years and years, never once altered according to the new world. The code book was meant to define us. It was who we were, a middle-class conventional family with dense unshakeable roots.

I harassed the book by leaving to go to America. I harassed the book by moving in with my foreign aunt, Lubna and not settling down at an appropriate age. I harassed the book by not accepting that my brother was gone and we must move on. And I harassed the book by acknowledging Grandfather's affair and Prakriti's family.

Fatima's engagement was a private, bittersweet event. Anika returned and I asked her not to go back to the village, but stay with me for a while. Lahore felt lonely without her. She said she understood and would stay. She also had an unusual story to share.

A small Hindu family had moved to Grandfather's village and their arrival had caused quite a stir. The only reason why the villagers hushed down was because a man from the family set up a free school for the children. They were moved by this act of kindness.

My sister watched my face turn sore with disgust.

"They should move to the city before they smash their urns and bleach their floors."

"Why should they?" she replied, "They are giving them something, free education. The village needs that. Your friend and his mother gave them nothing. People are selfish."

The engagement was a special moment for Fatima and it was a special moment for me.

I suddenly realised my new position in the family.

I was the newest subject of every conversation – I had become Grandfather.

The distance between my mother and I expanded exponentially, vast like an ocean with no island, no common ground between us. The relatives spun rumours about Anika and me. They wondered why her marriage fell apart and they wondered why I didn't marry, but nothing mattered to us. We just stood serenely and watched our sister exchange rings with her husband-to-be with big smile on her face.

Anika and I had become indestructible.

***

CHAPTER THIRTY-NINE

The next time I spoke to Adnan, it was for a big favour.

Richard wrote to me, saying that he was coming to Lahore and it was final. For a long time, I didn't know how I felt. I could not talk to anyone about it. Around about the same, Adnan reconnected with me. I told him about a friend travelling from D.C. to Lahore, needing a place to stay, and he gave me his word that he would take care of him.

Anika wondered why I asked him, a total stranger, for such big a favour. I told her it was impossible that Mother would agree to Richard staying with us. Adnan was the only other person I knew that would agree to host one of my friends in his home.

She muttered, "Well, you didn't really look for friends all your life, Mariam. This is why one needs friends, for committing crimes and keeping in strangers."

I smiled at her, withholding the fact that Adnan was actually eager to help me; he saw this as an opportunity to win my trust and make me realise that, perhaps sharing the same boarding school as Rizwan did not mean he fostered the same complex mind and desires.

"So you're saying that this journalist is Rizwan's childhood friend and at the same time, he is your stalker?' Richard said alarmingly, over the phone.

"He's not a bad guy...or he doesn't look like a bad guy, anyway...whatever. It's just for a little while. Besides, I want you to find out if this man knows anything. I thought he did at first, but after he blurted Rizwan's name, it raised many doubts. Ask about his relationship with Lubna."

"Now you want me to live in this stranger's house and dig into details?"

I thought about it. When he put it that way, it did seem ridiculous. He was right.

"What sort of a stranger keeps another stranger in his house?"

"Adnan Farookh," I replied, "The rich and possibly spoilt journalist."

"Sounds like your cousin to me."

"He isn't like him."

Adnan's face flashed in my mind.

He baffled me and in that way, he was actually kind of like Karan. I wanted to trust him and but at the same time, I wanted to stay away and scrutinise. I couldn't figure him out and neither could I figure what I was supposed to feel around him.

After Richard and I disconnected, I held the phone to my chest and breathed heavily. A strange nostalgia aroused in my heart after hearing his voice. I still couldn't believe that he was coming here to Lahore. The idea began to frighten me. Would he like Lahore? Would he find me different? Would he be alright staying with Adnan?

I found myself quietly opening all the windows in the room to let in the fresh morning air. The deep yellow sun rays streamed through the trees, creating beautifully shaped shadows on the carpet. There were small figures walking on the street far away, children in tidy uniforms walking wearily to school. I pictured myself standing amongst them in two tight plaits and black shoes. Father calling my name and running down the street; I had forgotten my lunch box again.

I stepped away from the window.

Fatima was lying on the bed. We had started sharing a room. During the night it was good to have some company.

"Why can't your friend stay with us?" she asked.

I remained quiet.

"It's Mother, isn't it?" she instantly guessed, "She doesn't want him here."

"She doesn't want anyone from the States to be here," I said curtly dismissing the subject.

She spread her arms on the bed and closed her eyes as if she was falling into an unknown dream world. I watched her. I had not dreamed in a while. I felt envious as I longed for that parallel universe.

***

It was May when Richard arrived. I went to see him at Adnan's house. To my surprise the journalist opened the door. The kitchen boy was on holiday. His eyes met mine and he smiled.

"I'm only here to meet my friend," I said.

He let me in.

Richard stood up from the *divan* in the study and hugged me, "I am so glad to see you again!"

"How are you?"

"Extremely delighted to see you!"

I hugged him tightly to reassure myself that he was there, that I had not lost a friend in D.C. but he was really here in Lahore, standing in front of me. This was not a figment of my raw imagination. I had never been happier. He kissed my cheek and smiled broadly. We sat for a long time, chatting about everything; his work, Lubna's family, Judy's life and Fatima's wedding, about the past, present and the unpredictable future. It was like meeting a long lost friend.

Adnan came back into the room after a long time. He went to his desk and skimmed through sheets of paper.

"This is the part where I make a special appearance," he said.

I looked at him, unsure of what he meant.

"Did you tell her?" he said to Richard in his refined voice.

Richard took a deep breath and looked at me.

"Tell me what?" I asked, anxious.

They exchanged glances like they shared a secret. I grew more frustrated.

"We've been talking about everything," Richard said, "And he told me how he knew Rizwan."

"I told you that already," I said.

"Yes," said Richard, "And he explained everything to me."

I slid back and folded my arms, refusing to look at either one of them.

"They went to the same boarding school, big deal. What have you both been talking about?"

An interrupted silence fell on both the men. Now, I really felt like an outsider.

"You are right…Rizwan and I met after years when I was visiting a friend in the States, and he told me about you and Abdullah."

My heart both sank and jumped simultaneously as he said my brother's name. I had not heard it in a long time. People refused to say it at all, tip-toeing around it, calling him my brother, my parents' son, as if his name were suddenly a dangerous word, forbidden from regular conversation.

"He told me about Max."

"And you told me you might be able to help me track my brother down…" I said abruptly.

"Oh, I still want to and I feel he was in fact, deported back along with Abdullah," he said. "You can trust me, Mariam," he added, a tone of sincerity in his voice.

I looked at Richard, feeling betrayed, "You've been bonding with strangers, I see. Did you tell him about the call?"

"I *do* know about the call," said Adnan, reluctantly.

Richard kept his hand on mine. It was a sign for me to stop overreacting. I pulled away and ran fingers through my hair in anxiety and then looked back at the speaker. He looked complacent yet anxious, both at the same time. I let out a long sigh.

"Alright, fine. So, can you help me?" I asked, "Can you help me find…Abdullah?"

"I can only try, Mariam."

He handed me a piece of paper. It was a familiar number. I looked at it for a while.

"It's the same number that Abdullah used to call Richard."

He nodded gently.

"But I…I tried to track it down. Nobody uses this number anymore. I even tried to hunt down the district, to get even a single clue…"

He looked at my confused face. He passed me another number.

"I don't recognise this number." I said slowly.

"I went through Richard's phone history and it looks like Abdullah tried to contact him more than once."

My heart exploded from this unexpected surprise.

"Shocking?" he raised his eyebrow, "Richard thought you were calling…"

"I was busy both times I received a call from this number," Richard explained, "I always thought it was you so I called you back instead."

I stood up, frenzied and walked back and forth saying one thing over and over again:

"Oh, Richard, Richard…"

He sat grimly.

"So, what do we do now?" I looked at Adnan.

"I'm already trying to track down what locality this number is from," he said, "Meanwhile, I just want you to keep in mind that there is actually a Max and he might be the reason Abdullah didn't come back home."

"But who is he really, this Max?"

"We'll have to find this out soon. Whoever he is, he played a major part in Abdullah's disappearance and if he is still around, he would certainly know where to find him."

***

Adnan had sources and ways that were far beyond our reach. He worked in the media and knew people that we could only dream of meeting. When it came to procuring any kind of concealed information, we were just ordinary people with ordinary access to ordinary subjects.

His sole idea was to understand Max, whom we now knew was not an allusion or a false persona, or a make-believe figure that the authorities and the boys created to baffle me, but a sore reality. And whoever he was, he influenced Abdullah to a great degree. Max now entered a different sphere in my head. I began envisioning this stranger, fearing him and confronting him in my head.

***

After a restless night of thinking about Max with Abdullah and revisiting over and over in my head the night they played the prank, I went to meet Adnan at his news studio for a private talk. I stood in his makeup room looking anxiously at the clock on the wall. He was not back yet. Two men, probably electricians, stood outside in the corridor watching me with their piercing eyes, thinking I was some intern, or a desperate woman seeking a job in the television industry.

I stood up and closed the door, disappointing them.

It was a sad little room with lots of burning lights. The walls were off white with a few magazine articles taped here and there. I saw Adnan's watch lying on the marble slab. It was a Rolex, and a rather expensive one.

I picked it up and looked at the time and then, tossed it back. It fell clumsily.

"My choice is not that awful now, is it?" said a voice.

I spun around.

"I'm sorry, I was just…" I said.

"Don't be silly, I was just kidding."

Adnan took off his coat and hung it behind the door. Then he picked up a comb and ran it through his brown hair. I stood suspended in the corner.

"The media, it's not like it used to be. This is not why I began working in this industry," he said softly to the mirror, "With time, the journalists are becoming more and more mindless. I just spent forty minutes being a guest on a talk show where all the other guests did was scold and scream at each other. There is no real debate about anything, no real discussions about what is going on in society, in our country. It's all a façade, all useless exposure. They make us sit on their glamorous talk shows like puppets, fighting and gossiping over trivial matters. They've bought us… the media…they've bought all of us."

"So, why do you do it?" I asked.

He looked up at me, brooding, like he had never been asked this question before.

"That's a very pertinent question, actually," he said, still deep in thought, "I guess, it was just this acute desire to do something different with my life. I thought I could change things but as time went by, I became part of the system."

I nodded.

"I didn't want to make a career out of my dad's fortune and I didn't want to live in the same country as my mother."

There followed a long silence.

"Won't you ask me why I'm here?" I asked.

"I am surprised to see you," he said putting extra emphasis on the word *am*, "So why are you here, Mariam?"

"I'm here to tell you that if you're helping me because you

think I'm too fragile and gullible, then you're wrong. I don't need any sympathy from you. I'm stronger than you can imagine and I don't like being used…"

"Oh, I know that," he said taking a step forward, "You're not a charity case. You're just a person I wish to help. There's no personal incentive, I just want to help."

"Why?"

"Because you're strong, Mariam…you're fierce…you refuse to accept this life of mystery…you refuse to sink."

"Still, why?"

"I like you, Mariam. I like everything you represent."

My heart melted with a violent sensation, maybe because no one had spoken to me in that way in a long time. I was used to nonchalance and dramatic silences, indifference and cold shoulders. There was strange warmth in Adnan that I needed just then, sincerity that I yearned for, a certain reassurance in his voice that I could have used in a time like that.

He was waiting for me to respond, looking into my eyes for that glint that would comfort him. I couldn't grant him that joy, not just yet. So instead, I sat down and got to the real reason I was there.

Together we confirmed that Abdullah called Richard twice after my departure. For what reason and why him? None of us knew.

The number he called from kept changing but the locality was somehow the same. The first time he called on Judy's birthday, when I had heard his voice on the phone, he was somewhere in Lahore. For the two other times he called, Adnan was able to track down the specific area. It wasn't a house or a motel but a small tea-shop inside the old city. He also believed that Max and Malik, the name that Abdullah had mentioned to Richard over the phone, might be names of the same person.

"Max in the States and Malik in Lahore," I whispered, "He

must have changed his name to integrate with the crowd in America."

"Yes, it could be. I will try again to ask the concerned personnel who handled their issue in the States to see if he was actually deported, or went somewhere else."

"I still don't understand how someone like Abdullah can just not come back home…"

"There must be a strong reason behind it, Mariam."

He gathered his things and we walked out of the studio, towards the parking lot.

"I'm sorry to ask, did you come on your own?" He scanned the parking space to find my car or any mode of transport.

"No, I walk or take rides," I said, "I don't like to use my dad's car."

"Why not?"

"I don't want my parents funding my mission. They're not equally curious or thrilled."

He laughed, "I see. In that case, let me drop you home."

He reversed the car and I sat there trying to take in all the new information that he had revealed. He said I couldn't just go to the tea-shop right now, not until he had personally investigated it himself. He wanted to see who ran it, and if Abdullah really did call from the place, how often did he come, who else did he call and if the man who owned the shop knew anything. We had to be careful. The slightest mistake and I could lose Abdullah again. He could run away again and I would never know why.

"I don't know why he doesn't want to come back home," I repeated as I watched a guard from his office salute Adnan and push open the giant gates.

"We can find him, right? He called twice; this shows he is safe and he really is here," I asked, looking straight ahead as we drove away.

He seemed suddenly pleased that I had taken him into confidence.

"I really hope so. I'm good at talking. I can talk people into anything," he said, "I talked you into trusting me, didn't I?"

He wiggled his eyebrows up and down.

"I pray you're different than your friend," I whispered.

"Oh, we're very different," is all that he said.

Ahead, the military men scanned people's faces and the interior of the cars. An exasperated policeman spat in front of his Labrador Retriever and then stuck his baton out to stop a motorcyclist from crossing. Roadblocks lay everywhere. A few drivers in the cars panicked. Some cried out saying that they were going to be late.

"I wonder why they're so devoted to their jobs today," Adnan said about the security, "Most of the times they just stand in the corner, chatting or smoking cigarettes as cars pass by them all day."

He called a friend in his office to ask if everything was alright in the city. He 'hmm-ed' and nodded as the voice on the other end explained some things. Then he hung up and turned on the radio. There had been a sudden terrorist attack at a mosque, the newscaster on the radio said.

I looked at Adnan, concerned, and he looked back at me and said, "The attack happened right after the Friday *Juma* prayers…I'll drop you home now. But please stay inside till the storm settles. I'll call you as soon as we can meet."

***

CHAPTER FORTY

The attack was brutal.

People lost their friends, brothers, husbands and fathers. We saw many, wailing and howling on national television, explaining how their loved one died and how untimely and tragic it was. One of these unfortunate people was Basheera *bibi*, our neighbour.

For as long as I remembered, she had always lived on our lane. She came to our house to pay condolences when my grandparents died; she attended Anika's joyful wedding; and came with a forlorn expression when the neighbourhood heard of Abdullah's disappearance. Basheera had always been there to offer her love and affection in both blissful and desperate hours.

But now Anika and I watched her on TV. She had just lost her son in the blast. She stared at the camera blankly, her face numb and her eyes deadened as she allowed the bitter truth to consume her completely. When the media men rattled her body, awakened her emotions and asked her persistently how she felt about her son's death, she began beating her chest, as she cried hysterically for hours,

"My son! My son! Someone bring me back my son! God, give me back my only son."

That day, Lahore bled and so did its people. More heart-wrenching stories surfaced the television and with each new story, a piece of us died. We died many times that day. We died for the many people's fathers, husbands, brothers and sons. We died for all the men who bled and all the women who sat at home and wept like children.

We died, over and over again.

Adnan called me and reminded me to stay inside. He said he would be very busy for a while in the office as the media team tried to cover the event and produce something satiable for the citizens. It could get very dangerous, as it was hard to control the people, who in such times, went on violent protests and rampages around the city.

I called Richard to ask if he was doing alright, he said he was and wasn't frightened at all. I was a little apprehensive that he would pack his bags and take the next flight back to the States, but he didn't and said he wasn't going to either.

Angry mobs roamed the streets like hounds, vandalising buildings, burning tyres and jumping over the police barricades to let out their fury and vent their sorrow. They were unstoppable, angry at this sudden attack. They cursed the government and all the politicians they thought were responsible for the protection of their loved ones. The police, the weaker party, arrived with tear gas and batons after the show was over. The sun fell down and the people were hushed one by one.

The city slept silently through the night.

Anika and I lay side-by-side and whispered softly. She had been to Basheera *bibi's* house with Mother in the evening to pay condolences. She had just returned from the hospital with the body. Anika described the boy's frail body, lying in the *veranda* of her house, hidden underneath a white sheet as women mourned loudly, surrounding it.

"He had just gone to the mosque to pray," Anika said in a low voice, "What did he do wrong? Their mother is a good woman, what did she do to deserve this? She was hysterical; she was beating her chest and howling like an animal in pain. I couldn't believe it myself, her son, the boy that we often saw cycling down the street, playing cricket with Abdullah and coming to our house to borrow sugar, was gone, perished because of this particular anonymous person who decided to blow himself up for the sake of some heavenly favours..."

I turned my face away from her and looked straight at a wall as ghastly details consumed me. I didn't want her to see my face, I didn't want her to see me weep for Basheera *bibi's* loss and wonder what it would have been like for our brother who lost his friend in a similar way.

"Anika?" I asked with my face still away.

"Hmm?"

"What was Abdullah like when his friend died?"

"Devastated. He was devastated. We had lost *him*, in a way."

I close my eyes and imagined his pain, his heart-rending sorrow, and the fact that none of us could actually do anything. We couldn't delve in his mind and take away all his memories of his friend or lie to him and tell him that it was going to be alright.

It was painful, and now I had finally realised it.

***

That night, I finally dreamt again.

I was standing in a familiar place. The trees were swaying viciously with the wind. I crawled onto my grandfather's back and he looked up at the sky. The dark trees were on fire. Someone had set fire to the orchard and the graveyard. Like a wild animal, he ran out through the trees but the orchard didn't seem to end. It was like a perplexing hot maze. The leaves turned to ash and fell on my hair. I would brush them off but they kept falling and falling. It was as if it was raining gunpowder.

I woke up, breathless and sweating and found Anika lying beside me, also awake.

Then minutes before the sun illuminated the sky, she took me to the rooftop. We looked at the city, our city, sleeping serenely like a child that was tired from wailing all night long.

There were no violent mobs.

There were no fires.

There were no pools of blood.

There were no cries.

Men were to resume their daily walks, barricades were to be removed and no one was to mention Basheera *bibi's* name again. It seemed so tranquil in that moment, an artificial peace and silence, it was hard to imagine the city engulfed in chaos just a few hours earlier. It was all over just like that, like a blink of an eye, all the horror and the pain, washed away with a flash of a new morning.

"Look at the morning light, so pure and divine," Anika rested her head on my shoulder, "It is as if there was no fire to begin with, like it was just a terrifying collective nightmare."

Our minds dwelled on the same thing – this was not the city we grew up in. This was no longer *daddi's* Lahore. It was a place filled with sad people and sad stories. It had become a frightening, frightening place.

"Was Lahore always this wild?" I asked Anika. "Was it like this even when we were young?"

She contemplated for a moment and then said, "Maybe it was. Maybe we were just too young to understand all that then."

That noon, I travelled all the way to the graveyard on my own, petrified that amidst the violence and chaos, perhaps someone might have really lit it on fire as well, just like in my dream. I was worried that the mobs might have contaminated the holy ground, knocked down the marble tombstones and chopped the wings of the beloved pigeons. Anika thought this theory to be highly unlikely and far-fetched but that was how afraid I was.

I ran through the gates towards the cold bench and the pigeons. *Dadda* lay safe. He slept quietly under heaps and heaps of dust, and so did his wife, mother and grandmother. I breathed a sigh of relief, confirming that everything in the graveyard was just how it ought to have been. Under the shade of the *Peepal* tree was that terrifying stillness that Grandfather enjoyed. The silence that confronted and questioned me about my deepest desires and secrets yet at the same time managing to, in its own secret way, comfort me.

But I wasn't comforted that time. I was very afraid. I looked at the place where my grandfather burnt the letters, the day he made the decision to forget his love and happiness for the sake of my grandmother. It made me weep. I remembered Grandfather and Prakriti, Karan and the ashes, Grandmother and her blind sister, Gulshan; I remembered and relived every moment that I had the power to recollect; afraid that violent times and volatile people would snatch them away and ultimately leave me with nothing. My memories, my love for my grandfather, my power to remember everything Grandmother said to me, I was afraid it would all slip away.

Since when had I become so afraid? I asked myself.
Since Abdullah's disappearance, I answered.

In the graveyard where the glorious sunlight kissed the fields and trees, I sat alone and wept till the sun finally drowned.

***

CHAPTER FORTY-ONE

Nothing scared Richard.

He was stronger than I gave him credit for. He moved around calmly in Adnan's kitchen wearing his trousers and grey t-shirt. He made coffee and showed me all the pictures that he had taken around the city.

After the attack, Adnan disappeared for a week but I did see him frequently on various news channels. His face would be as sober as ever and his speech, eloquent and precise. He moved his hands a lot as he reasoned with the anchors and other speakers.

Anika and I had watched him on TV together and she had liked him.

"You know, this guy is better than your lover."

She had said this flatly without any particular emotion, as if it were a widely known fact. She meant Richard.

"Richard isn't really my lover, you know. He's free to be with whoever he likes," I replied.

"But he enjoys you and you enjoy him," she had said, "you don't have to put things in black and white boxes all the time,

Mariam. It's alright not to have definite answers and obscure feelings for once. You don't have to hide things from me."

I hadn't replied.

Richard called my name from the kitchen, bringing me back in Adnan's dining room.

"So, what have you brought for me, Mariam?" Richard asked as he sat next to me on the table. He placed a cup of coffee in front of me.

From a bag, I pulled out a brown *shalwar-kameez*. He raised his eyebrow and remained quiet for a few minutes.

"Now, you promise me that all the men in your family will be wearing this at your sister's wedding?" he laughed.

I confirmed.

"Come to think of it, when do I get to meet your family?"

I made sure he met my father the next morning.

Father took him to the place he worked, to the lands that we owned, and later they had *chai* at his favourite place. I don't know what they talked about, neither did I ask them but I believed their topics revolved around the two countries and their different cultures.

Richard liked the traditional breakfasts, the *nashtas* of crispy *parathas* and cold *lassi* that were lavishly spread on the breakfast table each morning during the wedding celebration, and the long rides with me through the city. In just two weeks, he moulded himself to Lahore like I had moulded myself to D.C. in one year.

When the day of the wedding arrived, he was in attendance, standing by my side.

Fatima's was a summer wedding and it was the first time in a while the family had a chance to pretend that they were happy and complete. It was barely a two-day affair. The house was laced with marigold garlands and fairy lights. The rooms and corridors smelled of *henna* and delectable sweet dishes.

On the first day, there was lots of music and dancing. Mother lifted her hands in the air and danced wildly. She danced like the world around her died and she could hear nothing but the music. She spun the same way the earth and the planets orbited around the sun. She whirled like a dervish in a trance. For a while, it almost seemed as though she had no care in the world. I had never seen her like this before, so carefree, so enchanting.

On the second day, there was good food and chatting.

For me, none of this mattered. The dancing, the music, the food, nothing made me happy. No matter how much we pretended and evaded the questions about Abdullah, he loomed over the entire celebration. It seemed easy for us to dodge his existence, we had all become so good at it, selecting the things we wanted to remember and talk about. It was exactly like Grandfather's case, the wolves and the family spoke about his affair all his life, called his lover names and imagined how they met and what they did. Until the day of his funeral when everyone was silent and not a single person even mentioned his affair or his lover.

Just like that.

And just like that, we chose to denounce my brother's existence.

But still, somewhere along the celebrations, in our hearts we all felt that this was a time when he should have been here, by his sister's side, on her wedding day...

***

Adnan and I met again when he said he found something. The news was bigger than I had anticipated. But what surprised me most was that I was actually glad to see his face after days of no contact, and so was he.

The day after the wedding, our relatives who had travelled from other cities were still around. Tired and still excited about the celebrations, they had stayed the night. I sneaked out of the house in the early morning, before anyone had woken up and went to Adnan's.

He and Richard were already seated in the car when I arrived. They had been waiting for me.

"Get in, let's go," was how the journalist greeted me. I did as told.

I looked at Richard in the passenger seat; he passed a comforting smile. None of us spoke. We drove on one of Lahore's busiest road. We passed *Data Darbaar,* one of the oldest Sufi shrines, sat silently in heavy traffic, passed old buildings, hospitals and the *Badshahi* mosque.

Adnan drove the car inside a day market and then, he pulled over in front of a dim alley. My heart thumped hard as he turned around to face me. I knew he was about to reveal something big, something new that he had found out.

"Malik," he began, "Your brother's friend whose name he took on the phone call to Richard, comes from a very powerful feudal background."

I held my breath.

"I found that out when one of the news channels did a brief report on a missing son of a feudal lord, back in December."

"Around the same time when Abdullah went missing," I said softly.

"They didn't run the news for very long, and like always, something more pertinent occupied its space on news segments. When Richard told me about the phone call, he said Abdullah had taken Malik's name and said that he was in Lahore with him. I grew a little curious. The places where they disappeared from were listed as the same and the timing was accurate. Have you ever seen this Malik…Max's picture?"

"No. The boys said they never had any and the authorities never showed it to me."

"Well, they didn't show it to me either when I approached them. They couldn't leak confidential documents to a stranger who had no personal role in the matter," he gave a small smile, "So I went to the family of the missing son, instead. I said I was a journalist who wanted to cover their dilemma."

"Did they tell you anything?"

"Well, at first they refused to admit they were missing any family members, but I remained adamant and said my news channel itself ran the news months ago. One of the many elders of this big family called me to his farmhouse to meet me face to face, and to understand my persistence in trying to pry into their personal family matter."

"What did he tell you?" I asked.

"He told me that the Malik I had been enquiring about is his son and he was, indeed, in the States and the family did believe that he went missing for a while when they completely lost contact with him. They quieted down when they discovered that he was in a prison for a silly prank that he had been framed for. He is the heir to the family's political legacy and was being pushed to compete in the next elections when he still lived in Pakistan, so they couldn't bring the issue of his arrest into any media light as it would tarnish his public image."

"They told you all this?"

"They did, along with the fact that they would strangle me to death if I disclosed it to any newspaper or channel," he beamed.

I looked at him, with a look of slight apprehension and affection, but he remained calm and content.

"Is he the same person who met Abdullah in Boston?" I asked, "The same person whom my brother somehow trusted over me, planned an ambiguous road trip with and ended up being thrown into a prison for? Is this the same Max? Max, the root cause of all my misery. You believe Max is Malik?"

"I am sure he is."

"And why exactly are we *here*?" I glanced out of the window at the animated city and the roaring cars.

"You'll see why," he said and turned around to drive, "They could hush me down. They could hush all their minions down, and it would have probably worked if your brother wasn't involved and if a team of three people weren't searching for him. But there are always people who can't be hushed down, and we've got to find them."

"And who exactly are those people?" I asked.

"The ones that we call mad and the ones that we abandon because of that madness. They tell the truth, and they will tell you everything."

I looked at him, confused. He had lost me.

"You'll have to wait and see whom I found for you, Mariam."

The very first thing that struck me as I stepped out of the car was the air. The place was filled with substance and stories. The buildings were small and old. Most were two-storey. On the ground floor were the shops and right above them was where the occupants resided. Washed out laundry hung on long ropes on the rooftops. Women stood in their balconies, chattering, hanging laundry and bargaining over daily produce with the vegetable and fruit-sellers below.

We walked into a narrow alleyway, passing old flats, shapeless, faceless with blank windows. We passed by shops with fancy painted shutters and posters of actresses in flattering dance poses. Rows of shops were erected on either side of the lane, selling colourful footwear – *khussas*, sandals and *chapals* – clothes, crockery and glistening jewellery. Pale mannequins stood in front of windows fashioning sequinned clothes for brides and grooms. The women and children with curious faces stopped to notice us as we invaded their community. Men, who sat outside the teashops and food stalls, smoked like chimneys, looking at us with their inquisitive eyes. They watched as three strangers roamed about their narrow lanes searching for answers.

As we went deeper and deeper into the alley, it became darker and darker. There was a fierce energy that I couldn't digest. Finally we reached a place where there were no children, no curious men and no veiled women, just profound silence and a few lonely houses.

"Just down the road is a tea shop," Adnan pointed ahead, "Abdullah's last two calls were made from there."

We walked towards a small house near the shop and Adnan knocked at the door. A woman in her sixties greeted us in an unwelcoming tone. Her face was tired and her expressions undefined. She looked at us with her eyes once full of light and promises. She murmured something that only Adnan's ears comprehended.

Adnan reached for my shoulder and brought me closer to him.

He whispered, "Be strong now, alright?"

My body went numb. I still didn't know what he was preparing me for.

"Mariam…meet Najeeba," Adnan said slowly, "The woman who cared for Max since he was a child, his *ayah*."

***

CHAPTER FORTY-TWO

The interior of the house was shadowy but the small room contained just enough light to distinguish various objects – a lamp with a broken shade that emitted a faint light, a low centre table, a wooden chest covered with a blanket and a steel cupboard with a full length mirror on the front. The carpet was littered with newspapers, shoes and plastic cups. Everything smelled of tobacco and smoke, but there were no *hookahs* or dead cigarettes lying anywhere.

A young girl sat frozen in the corner of the room. Her body shook frequently and she muttered random words, staring at the ceiling. The old woman bent over and handed her some tea, then she glided around the room lifelessly, closing all the small windows that the little room contained.

There were five windows and they all showed a different picture, the white side dome of the grand Badshahi mosque, a balcony that belonged to plump old woman, a tea stall with colourful walls, an empty road and a small building with lots of children.

I looked at the woman and then the girl; none of them spoke.

There seemed to be something wrong with them but then, there was something wrong with all of us.

In that unfamiliar intense silence, I took a deep breath.

There was a heavy energy in the room, a sort of sullen silence and emotional pressure that made me quiver. The air was pregnant with secrets and sadness and as I looked at the woman again, I found it harder and harder to breathe. Never in my life did I imagine that I would meet somebody so closely related to Max, right here in Lahore.

I looked over at Adnan and realised just how strange it was that all of us there were connected to one another in some way, our lives entwined. Richard's path crossed mine for a reason, mine with Adnan, Adnan's with the old woman's, the old woman was someone to that girl and both of their lives were somehow connected with Max, a figment from another world, and somewhere within that perplexing map, lay Abdullah, hidden and, I liked to think, safe.

I looked at the woman and smiled.

She turned her head slowly and whispered to me,

"Would you like some tea?"

"No, thank you."

"You look like your brother."

My lips trembled, "Do you know Abdullah? Have you seen him?"

She scratched her grey hair and shook her head, refusing to speak.

"Where is he?" I asked again, a little louder than before.

She walked away and began combing her the girl's hair with her fingers. She shook her head again, "…don't know. Don't know."

"Where is he?" I screamed out, louder than I had meant to.

The girl gave a low shriek, frightened by my voice, and then hid her head between her knees. The woman looked at me with her eyes wide with horror and disbelief.

Adnan came forward and held my arm. I felt like my body was suspended on a burning flame, every part was in excruciating pain and I wanted to cry loudly to find release.

Why wouldn't she tell me where he was? Why didn't she tell me where he had met him?

"Don't," he whispered as he held me.

"No!" I pushed him slightly.

He released his grip.

"She has to answer me," I looked into his eyes, "She just has to. She is Max's *ayah*, she must know something!"

Richard stood near the window that framed the mosque. He shook his head tragically, asking me to calm myself down. But I couldn't do it; it was beyond my power to act complacent after hearing my brother's name.

I walked to the woman and kneeled in front of her. Sighing deeply, I placed my hand on her knee and told her how I hadn't seen my brother in months and how I didn't know whether he was dead or alive. How nobody knew where he was but Max or Malik, whoever he was. Looking at her helplessly with pleading eyes, I begged her to tell me whatever she knew about either of the boys.

She looked down, her face suffused with warmth and wonder at my outburst. She touched my chin and lifted my face, studying it. Her light brown eyes didn't stray away from mine for a single moment, holding my gaze as if drawing my life out through them. She breathed slowly; every breath was intentional, prolonged. Meanwhile, I remained frozen to her touch, spellbound. A faint smile came across her thin dark lips but she still said nothing.

"She will talk," I heard Adnan say, "Just give her time."

I collapsed heavily on the ground where I sat. My head hung low in my hands. Her very touch had exhausted my being; she had drained me. The pleading and the crying had drained me. I looked at the woman and a dark and gloomy shadow came over me. I realised that she might have seen my brother, whereas I still had not. She must have touched his face and heard his voice, and I still couldn't.

I didn't wish to cry or shriek, not in front of Adnan and Richard. Crying would have surprised Richard because he had always seen the stronger side of me, and it would have confirmed Adnan's belief that I was, in fact, a person in need of desperate help. He had met me in my most fragile form and I hated him for that.

Suddenly, I heard a voice beside me. I lifted my face.

Najeeba was looking right at me. Her lips moved and asked me who I was.

"Nobody," I responded.

"But I was," she said, "My son and I were once somebody in a big, big house."

Her tone became confessional and personal. We became attentive instantly.

"Would you like to listen to a story?" she asked.

***

She had worked for Malik's family for years.

Children grew up and went away, but the nanny stayed. She watched them grow up, leave behind their innocence and delve right into the world of decadence and violence that awaited them. The family was large but she was solely responsible for raising Arbaz Malik and his older brother. Their mother had left them, her children, so easily, when she turned her back on the world of politics and feudalism. She said she had nothing to do with her husband's family anymore. She settled in Paris after which the boys were handed to Najeeba and a stepmother.

The *ayah* now sat in front of our eyes, wiping beads of sweat from the face of the young girl. Muttering to herself, she took out a photograph from a drawer in her closet and then looked at all three of us as if contemplating whom to trust with the precious piece of paper. Then, she slowly walked towards me and showed it to me.

I glanced down at it – a few young boys were standing in an open *veranda*. I could tell that the picture was not that old. Adnan and Richard leaned closer to be able to see the photograph but she dismissed them casually with a wave of her hand, indicating that the picture belonged to her and she would reveal it only to whomever she liked.

With her frail finger, she pointed at the two boys. One of them looked a little like Adnan, he had an attractive face and seemed to be in his late twenties and the other seemed slightly older, he was probably in his mid-thirties.

"This is Arbaz," she murmured slowly, pointing to the younger boy, "And that's his older brother. They were my boys."

My heart stood still.

"This is Arbaz," I repeated and looked hard at the face of the boy, "How old is this photograph?

She looked away and said that it was very old.

"Look at this boy," she pointed at another figure but that one was in the background, half hidden behind a tree, "That's my son."

"Your son," I echoed.

"He worked for the family as a chauffeur," Adnan said softly so only I could hear, "She told me this when I met her for the first time."

"Where is he now?" I asked. I thought maybe if we met her son, he would give us some answers directly instead of making us run in circles. He worked as a chauffer for the family, he must know something, too.

"I don't know," Adnan replied.

I turned my face to look back at her. She was still looking down at the picture, touching the face of her son.

"And Abdullah…" I said, "Do you have any picture of a boy called Abdullah?"

She shook her head frantically and removed the photograph from my sight. I watched her place it back in the drawer, trying to understand this strange world that she had created around and within her.

I waited for her to finish her story, and she did, in bits and pieces, after long painful intervals of time. She said Arbaz was different than his older brother; he was fragile and oversensitive, unfit for the family business and matters. He had no interest in being a politician, carrying out the family legacy he wished to escape. It was easier for him to swim away. He was able to live in a world where he had freedom and choice, because it was his brother who was being prepared to compete for the election seat after his father. As inwardly as Arbaz was, his brother was just as volatile and ambitious, and easily made enemies.

Najeeba's son did not only work for the brothers, but was also their confidante and companion. He escorted them everywhere, to parties, to weddings, to farmhouses, and to meetings. She had one more child, a daughter, who sat with us in the same room. She was called Mehtab.

Najeeba's shawl fell off her head and her grey hair cascaded down her back like a silver river. Her heart was filled with joy as she reminisced about her son and the two boys she practically raised. She looked at me and shuddered with a feeling of deadened nostalgia and fear, as she envisioned and relived every moment in her mind, again. She said it wasn't a difficult life, not at first, but then came a day that changed everything.

Coughing, she asked for water. Adnan poured her a glass from a jug on a table. She drank it quietly and then said:

"Have you ever seen the person you love die before your eyes?"

I shivered a little.

Adnan looked at the ground and then back at me.

The girl cried in horror and covered her eyes.

Her mother quivered and continued the story, one that was much more personal and painful, a story about the day her son was shot dead.

"When the firing happened, everyone heard it. We locked ourselves inside thinking we were safe. We huddled together, praying, just praying it would be over soon. We heard guns, we heard cries and then sirens as the ambulances arrived. The house felt it, too. It shook for days."

"What firing?" I asked, "What are you talking about?"

"One day my son was driving Arbaz Malik's older brother

around and when they pulled the car up in front of the house, two masked men on motorcycles appeared and began shooting and beating both the boys."

She burst into tears.

"Who did they kill?" I asked.

Her eyes dropped as if heavy and drugged. She closed them and swayed her head in dismay.

"They injured the older brother and they killed my son. Their bodies lay on the road before the ambulances arrived. There was blood everywhere, my son's blood had painted the road..." she clutched her face as tears rolled down her cheeks, "My son, my son lay there. Mehtab shook him, she kept shaking his body and calling out his name but he didn't wake up. He just didn't wake up. Why didn't he wake up?"

I watched her break down and cry. A grown woman sat before me and cried like a child would, uncontrollably and overcome by frenzy. She was in pain, so much pain as she remembered her son, hoping and praying her tears might somehow bring him back. I saw myself in her. She experienced the same torture as I did.

Her tired eyes wept and wept for her son.

I had wanted to weep this way for Abdullah so many times in the past few months. I watched her tears form small wet patches on her *dupatta*. I turned away; I could not bear to look at her break down like that.

My brother had not died, but at that moment, he felt just as dead to me as her son did to her.

According to Richard and Adnan, Abdullah was close to us, in Lahore even, but there came times when I did not feel his presence. What I felt was simply a large void where he had once been. The last time that void had truly been full of him was when we were children, before we drifted apart. It was the only time I could remember that I really knew him, appreciated him and admired him for the person he was.

Suddenly, it made sense to me. In that moment of watching

Najeeba cry, I understood everything. Abdullah and I had not been close for years, I did not know him when he came to me America; I never tried to understand the reasons for his hasty departure from Pakistan. I was so self-involved and relied solely on the rationale I received from my mother, from Anika, but not once had I spoken to my brother about it.

I hadn't wanted to make him uncomfortable, exceed the inevitable distance between us by discussing something that upset him but I could have, I should have tried to reach out to him and tell him that I was there for him and that I too understood what it felt to lose someone in this world.

I sat down on a chair and looked at the ground. I heard Najeeba's soft sobbing.

What I realised now was that something like his friend's death must have terrified Abdullah, caused him to flee all the way the America. The same could be said for Malik, his brother's near death encounter could have scared him, causing him to flee to his cousin's house in Baltimore to begin a new life. He and Abdullah must have met in America and understood each other's pain in a way that I never did. I covered my face, as if in shame and disgust.

Richard called my name as I tried to put the story together in my mind.

"When did all this happen?" I asked Najeeba.

"A year ago," she said.

"Then did you ever see them again, Arbaz Malik and his older brother? Did Arbaz Malik come back to Lahore? Did he have a young boy with him?"

She didn't reply, said she didn't know what I was talking about. I walked towards the girl and looked into her eyes. She stared back at me, frightened. She covered her face with her thin hands, trying to shut herself completely from the world.

"Don't be scared," I said softly, "Will you please help me? Have you heard of my brother? Mehtab, will you answer me?"

"She's crazy, she won't answer," her mother called from the other side of the room, "She lost her mind since her brother's death. Sometimes I wish she could die, too."

I covered the girl's ears and stared at the woman in amazement.

"What sort of a mother says that to her child?"

"A mother who would rather see her child die once than suffer endlessly every night and day."

I paused, longing for an explanation.

She buried her head in her knees like her daughter and said, "She hears things, sounds...sounds of footsteps and men screaming...she hears the officers screaming and carrying her brother's dead body off the streets...she hears their hoofs and batons striking against men's bodies...she hears the gunshots and the sound of the cracking skull bones...she never sleeps...now tell me, what sort of a life is this?"

A terrible chill ran down my body as I heard her description.

"I know he visits you, how else would your mother know what he looks like? Or that I look like him," I said, "I will not stop till I find him."

Najeeba didn't respond.

She had drifted to a place where it was hard to reach her.

***

CHAPTER FORTY-THREE

The boat cut through the salty water and headed towards the coast. I rested my paddle and looked at the melting horizon. People laughed like children as they swam swiftly towards the rose coloured lights. I was exhausted but I couldn't stop paddling. I pushed my hair away from my eyes nervously and stood up to see the view. The people kept swimming, moving further and further ahead, and soon their laughter sank below the dark waters. They had reached their stations and I had lost the race. I frantically paddled some more. The sky darkened. The serene reflection of the moon on the surface exploded as I scarred the water with the paddle.

There came a faint buzzing sound in the air, like a thousand mosquitoes were singing above my head. I dropped the paddle in the water and felt the air, then my ears and forehead. There was nothing around me but the buzzing grew louder and louder.

I listened closely.

It was coming from inside me.

I must find the source, I must find it before it kills me.

I stood up and kicked in the air violently, but I didn't know what I was fighting against. I threw my hands around my body blindly to find the insect or insects…because if I didn't, my ears would have bled. I scanned every article of clothing I wore, patting it down vigorously. But the sound was not inside my clothes. It was inside my body. The buzzing lived deep inside my body, indifferent to the world around. It was soft at first, but then picked up volume, becoming louder and louder. I tried to cover my ears to prevent myself from hearing the sound only to find that my ears had disappeared. My nose evaporated, then gradually and slowly so did my mouth and arms.

Desperate, I dived in the water.

I must swim before my eyes disappear, before I can't see anything anymore…I must swim towards the coast.

The moonlight strengthened. Battling with the dark waves, I saw my arms come out of the sockets. It was as if they were made of clay. There was nothing left now, just my face, something similar to a face, bobbing in the waters…fading slowly…dissolving.

"Something's moving in the water!" I heard someone call.

The figure came closer and looked at my sinking face.

It was Abdullah.

He gently scooped me out of water and said, *"Now who will fix you, Mariam?"*

I woke up with a loud gasp on the living room *divan*.

Anika sat in front of the television, watching as some fisherman tried to push a large whale back into the sea. She leaned over and kissed my forehead.

"Oh, my darling," she said, "What did you see?"

"Nothing…nothing," I said, running my hands over my face, arms, neck; confirming all of me was still there in one piece. I shivered. How could I have explained something to her when I didn't understand it myself?

She dusted something off my shoulder and smiled warmly at me.

I hadn't told her anything. She sat, oblivious, thinking that I would eventually tire myself and decide to move on from the search for Abdullah, like the rest of them.

"Do the twins still dream of water?" I asked her.

She removed stray strands of hair from my face and said, "They did not really dream of water, Mariam, only you did. Your mind recreates old memories because you cling to them so desperately."

This filled my heart with insane perplexity.

"I'm sad for losing Abdullah but I'm sadder for losing you. He has taken you away from me. Now, more than ever."

I held her hand and said, "I'll be back, I promise. I just need a little time to figure things out."

She looked at me, waiting for some sort of an explanation.

"I'm finding him for myself, and for no one else," I said, "He owes me some answers and if he asks me to leave him alone, I will do so and never turn back. But I need to hear it from him."

She told me that when I was out earlier that day, a parcel had arrived all the way from Washington D.C. for me. She handed it over and left me alone in its company. I sat down and looked at it, it was a large box and it just had my name on it. I looked at the word 'fragile' written on all sides and tried to recognise the address. It didn't ring a bell.

Finally, I opened it and remained still for a long time. The gift took me miles away back to America. I took it out of the card board box and held it with both my hands, in awe and surprise.

It was the painting. The one I had stood admiring so lovingly at the party in the gallery. My finger touched the subject's nude body and her violet hair; it traced the wine glass upon which she sat perched, and the Artist's spidery handwriting. I brought it close to my chest as if it were a child that needed comfort. Turning it over, I found a small note attached to the back, I knew the handwriting:

"I found her miserably stored in the attic and she called out your

name. I know the Artist didn't know you but I still like to believe that
he painted this for you. I don't know how you will remember me, or if
I have ever given you anything pleasant to remember me by, but I felt
that there is a secret no one else knows that I want you to know. I must
tell you why I do what I do, sell his art, distribute his soul amongst
friends and colleagues, people who seldom comprehend his mind and
craft.

I lost my husband years before he died. He left me for his art
and sacrificed his marriage for his passion. I let him be and looked
elsewhere for affection. By doing so, I lost my son, too.

The Artist always told me to burn down his work after he died.
He said his images consumed him, harassed him, haunted him and
did not let him sleep. He vowed he would never touch a paintbrush in
his next life. He was not a mad man, Mariam, he was just unhappy
in his isolation.

When he left the country, he left his family, too, and no matter
how much he thought of going back to his father's village, he could
not. He felt like going back was like giving up all that he represented
and had fought for. He had told his father that he wanted this, this
freedom, this life in another country, and going back would mean
that he had lost. He could never imagine losing and admitting that he
might be wrong in desiring isolation from his loved ones.

He was a man of great pride and ego, and this ego brought him
nothing but pain.

It stings my heart to give away every living reminder of his
existence, but this is what I have to do, remove him slowly from my life
and watch people take him away from me. I watch the women in his
paintings slowly disappear. The horses, the open fields, barns and the
blue rivers leave my company and settle in dens of other people.

I have no choice, Mariam. I have to do it for him, and for myself,
I need to move on.

For them it is the art. For you it was always the Artist.

Remain in touch, my love (you tend to disappear).

Lubna"

I hung it on a wall where I knew the sunlight fell during the day. It illuminated her hair and porcelain skin.

A part of the Artist had come back home.

***

CHAPTER FORTY-FOUR

The roadside *chai-wala* shook with laughter and then yelled at his little boy for spilling tea at one of his regular customer's shirt. Adnan, Richard and I sat looking at the steel water jug and small glasses that were placed in front of us as courtesy. None of us had reached for the jug, instead we just watched the man chuckle and joke around with his customers.

"*Masala chai*! *Desi masala chai*!" he lured the people in his practiced tone and then turned to us, "*Chai*? *pakoras*?"

We shook our heads in harmony.

"Come along, Azam! Come here!" he shouted rapidly.

His son obeyed.

"Bring the guests some *chai* and biscuits! It is the first time they've come to our shop!"

Azam's father had a stern figure and a very round face. He had a set of yellow teeth and a strange habit of twitching his nose when he spoke. We watched him deal with some of his customers. Azam served us their special tea. His father dismissed him by waving his hand and then sat down with us.

It was time to talk.

"Which of you is Adnan?" he asked and then turned around to make sure that no one was listening in.

"I am," Adnan raised his hand a little.

"Who's the *gora*? Your friend?"

"Yes, he's our friend.'

"How can I trust him? Is he from *Amreeka*?"

"American, yes. Of course, you can trust him," Adnan insisted.

"What if he is a spy? Does he know Obama?"

Little Azam looked over at us when he heard Obama's name. His father gave him a look. Sitting on the floor, far away from us, he took out a small board and blue chalk and began to draw.

"You can trust him. He's with us."

He scanned Richard's face for a few seconds. "*Sahib*, you know the situation nowadays. America this and America that," he kept his leg on the bench and scratched it.

He was hard to persuade but soon the argument reached three conclusions: Richard could be trusted, the *chai* he made was incredible and we were going to keep everything he told us to ourselves.

Then the *chai wala* began, "Habib Qaleem, that's what my grandmother named me but everyone here calls me *kala chai-wala*." He said he was called *kala* because of his unusually dark skin.

He had seen us leave Najeeba's house a day earlier and watched us drive away. He had been giving loans to the mother and daughter for the past year and he knew every little thing about them and their predicament. Now he sat and looked at the half empty glass of tea in my hand.

"Aren't you going to finish that?" he asked, "Did he mess up the recipe again? You see, making tea is a difficult task and I'm sick of this rascal. You know, it has been my family business. My great, great grandfather served tea to Jinnah *sahib* right here! What a beautiful young man he was!"

"Jinnah?" I asked.

"No, no! My grandfather. He wasn't *kala* like me."

He stood up excitedly and sat poised at the place where Jinnah had sat and his grandfather had grown a small tree. "Right here he sat. You see the very famous monument, *Miner-e-Pakistan*, from my shop, so I think he was on his way back and he stopped for tea. Do you not like it?"

I finished it in a single sip and said that I did.

He chucked and leaned closer, "So you want to talk about Arbaz Malik, I see, the devil, the thief…"

"The devil?" my voice cracked.

"He came here last month to see Najeeba. He took her to the doctor," he said. "He's always had a soft corner for this woman, maybe because she raised him when his own mother abandoned him."

"Maybe," Adnan said.

"Does he have anyone with him?" I asked, "A boy? Nineteen…"

He shook his head rapidly and said in a calm voice, "No boy, just him." "But he called from your shop, twice…"

"I mustn't have been around…"

"Please try to remember…anything at all…"

"If I'm lying, you may cut Jinnah's tree. I'll give you the axe."

I took a deep breath and looked at Adnan uneasily.

"Do you know why we're looking for him?" he asked trying to stir the conversation.

"He owes you money, doesn't he?" Habib said and spat on the ground, "He owes me a lot. I've been helping Najeeba's family live and he's a rich man. He promised me back every rupee with a little interest. It's not hard for him. He's a rich man."

Adnan scratched his chin; he knew he had to play it safe. He told Habib that Malik borrowed money a year ago and then sneaked away without repaying. Now he couldn't find him anywhere and his mother doesn't know about his whereabouts.

"This is good, this is good," Habib thought out loud, "I'm not alone in this. We will confront him together. He didn't tell me he came back to town, I found that out by myself, you know. He uses the backdoor to enter now. He never crosses my shop and often comes late at night, when the roads are dead and the activities suspicious."

We all made notes in our head.

"So next time he comes, I suppose you'll call us," I tried to sound as natural as I could.

He folded his arms and nodded his head, smirking.

I looked at both of them, unbelievably. It was still so hard to believe that he had agreed and that I could actually meet Malik… Malik Arbaz…Max and question him about my brother.

I took a deep breath and watched Adnan shake Habib's hand.

How could things fall so easily in my lap? How can a detective solve the entire mystery on finding the first clue?

"But, wait! You have to do something for me too…" Habib snickered.

Adnan thought that he needed money; some greed, some persuasion but the *chai-wala* surprised us all with his intelligence.

"I have seen you on television," he beamed at Adnan, "You're the TV guy, aren't you?"

Adnan was taken aback by this fan.

"You must have a lot of money, isn't it so?"

"How much…" Adnan fished for his wallet.

"Get me on a television show…" Habib giggled.

"What?"

"See, I make tea, excellent shop behind you. Call me as a guest in one of the cooking shows."

"And you'll make tea?"

"Not just plain tea, different kinds of tea…I can make green tea, *masala* tea, white tea, lemon tea, oolong tea, coffee?"

Adnan looked at me and then at the *chai-wala* in amazement.

I stood up casually and walked around his shop.

It was dull from the inside. There were ripped posters of

famous stage dancers and actresses on every wall. There was a small office table at the very end and on top of it was a sign that read, '*Reciption*.'

Adnan and the owner were still engaged in chatting. I walked to the other side of the table and looked around. There was nothing on top of it except for a paper and a crystal paperweight. Gently removing it, I studied the paper. It was just somebody's tab. I opened a drawer; two yellow pens. I turned around, disheartened, and saw the little boy standing just a few inches from me.

I let out a nervous laugh and asked the question that had been haunting me, "Do you have a phone around here? Do a lot of customers make calls?"

He shook his head no and escorted me outside.

***

It was time for Richard to go. That was all the time he had with me. We spent his last evening in Lahore, sitting in a park, away from the journalist, just him and me. We were alone after a long time. There were no classical statues in front of us, no sound of the falling water, no dancing lights of Washington D.C., but large tree trunks and lots of flower beds. The birds were flying away and the butterflies and squirrels had vanished hours ago. Still, there was a magical peace that we both had been craving.

"It was different before," I said gently.

He looked at me for a long time but did not speak. He sat subdued.

"We felt differently before."

"This is just a bad time, Mariam."

"I wish you didn't have to see me like this, Richard, so drained, consumed by grief and pain. You liked me for my strength. You were never meant to see me break down. You were never meant to see every sane part of me perish this way."

He remained still.

"You fell in love with that quiet girl in the art gallery, the girl who felt she knew what she was doing, not this mess," I said quietly.

"Still, I have always loved you," he said after a sigh, "But I'm afraid, you don't feel for me what I feel for you."

"Richard…"

"It *is* true…"

"Maybe I just needed a friend and you were there for me then, like you are now. I know I do love you but I don't think it's in the way that you want me to and whether that's enough. You came here to see me, to help me, and now you see me as a wreck. I don't know how to be happy and alive, and learn to love you more. Learn to love you the way you love me."

"I fell in love with you, Mariam," he interrupted, "I fell in love with a girl who had always been in pain. I met you when you were consumed by your grandfather's memories, by a sense of displacement, by Rizwan and his mother's complicated natures. Even then, I watched you wither and fall apart. So, for as long as I've known you, you've always damaged yourself emotionally. When were you ever happy, Mariam?"

I felt my eyes burn with tears. I wondered about it, all the times when I had been happy and unhappy, memories came rustling back into my mind.

"Never," I replied.

"Then when will you be happy, Mariam?"

"There's nothing to be happy about yet."

"When you were a child, Mariam…you chose to be the unhappy one."

"I lost my grandfather, Richard…and then I lost a dear friend," I said, my heart ringing from sorrow.

"People endure pain all the time but they move on, learn to be happy. That's the right thing to do."

"You don't know what my friend, what Karan endured…"

"Yes, that's true. But what if he forgot you…what if he forgot you the moment he left..."

"He lost everything he loved in a moment!" I burst out crying, "I saw his face, I saw his mother's face and I can't shake them out of my mind, even after all these years, I just can't!"

I held my head in my hands and sobbed. I thought I had forgotten all this, everything that tormented my soul, the day I became fixated with Abdullah's disappearance. Richard's intervention showed me that I was wrong, that I carried the emotional baggage every day, and everywhere. Things that shouldn't have mattered still mattered greatly to me.

"The place inside my head was never quiet. It has always been loud, it is always living and you don't know how painful that is, how painful it is to feel every grief like it were your own."

I paused.

"But it's finally begun to happen...slowly," I suddenly said, "I have forgotten Grandfather. I have forgotten what he smelled like, how he walked, everything he did and said. All I think about is Abdullah."

"Oh, Mariam."

"He doesn't visit me now, not in my mind, not in my dreams," I cried, "He has gone. He has disappeared from my mind like he disappeared from everyone else's the day he died."

Richard hugged me but the weight of anxiety and self-realisation settled on me.

"I didn't even know Abdullah until he went missing. But I knew him, I knew Grandfather."

"In all of this," he whispered, perfectly impassive, "in this constant battle between you and the painful things you choose to remember, you forget the people who want to love you. You can't shut yourself up like this, not anymore. You can't fight everybody off."

I nodded sadly. He was right.

"Don't leave me," I mumbled.

He leaned forward and kissed my cheek gently. He stroked my

hair and whispered, "Don't choose to be lonely, Mariam, and don't choose to be sad. You deserve so much more."

***

One night passed by, and then another.

Habib didn't call.

Richard had left and soon I found myself in only Adnan's company. We would sit with each other for hours in his study. He said we had grown used to each other and would not function properly in the other's absence, I had said that he was delusional and needed to spend more time with the gorgeous women at his father's parties. He would only smile and then swirl around his chair.

Habib finally called and asked us to come at a particular time on a particular day. He said he heard from a neighbour that a man was to visit Najeeba the following night. He presumed it would be Arbaz Malik.

We drove there. The outside world was completely exhausted. Vendors had left with their possessions and the streets were bare as night approached. When we reached, the *chai-wala* made a small fire on the stove and poked it with a wooden spoon. Tiny fireworks sprouted. He kept a small saucepan for tea and waved at Adnan and me. He whispered something in his son's ear and the child took both of us inside to the back of the shop. We climbed a small staircase. On the first floor was Habib's flat.

His wife lay in front of a television and chewed on something.

Adnan and I sat on the roof, hidden from everyone's view.

We could see Najeeba's door.

From our birds' eye view, I watched Habib add tea leaves in water and pat his watchdog, Missile Khan, with his leg. The dog rolled for his master. Then he turned off the stove and sat back and enjoyed his steaming cup of tea. Then he called for his son, who washed the cup in a tap outside, and together they closed the tea shop for the night.

I looked at Najeeba's door again, and found myself prepared for all kinds of odds – anything from running into the wrong Malik, to hearing from Richard that he just met Abdullah in the States. Anything could happen, I reminded myself now and then. Adnan stood tall and attentive, watching an object far away, perhaps the glowing *Minar* or something else in the distance. He raised his arm and said in absolute seriousness,

"There's a kite in the sky."

I rose and followed his gaze. He was right.

There was one small kite, as yellow as a blooming marigold, battling aimlessly against the wind and the heavens. Higher and higher it went, towards the velvety sky and silent stars.

The world died for me as I watched it quiver and fly. My heart trembled with wonderful hope and I couldn't sink the unthinkable feeling that maybe I was closer to Abdullah than I could possibly imagine.

"He enjoyed kites, didn't he?" asked a voice. It was Adnan.

"More than anything else," I said softly, "Before he lost himself."

I heard my friend come closer.

"The government keeps banning the flying of kites. It's the thread that they use for flying the kite…it's so sharp and can be quite dangerous. You know, many people have actually died…" he stopped talking when he realised that I was no longer with him.

"You've come a long way," he said with complete earnestness and put his hand on my shoulder, "I just want you to accept whatever comes your way now. Things change, Mariam, and we have to change with them, else we will remain aloof and unhappy for the rest of our lives."

Before I could answer, Habib came on the rooftop with straightened collars and amplified emotions. The air instantly smelled of *paan* and cigarettes. He brought a finger to his lips, asking us only to listen to him.

"He's here. Did you see him?"

The blood in my veins froze. I shook my head.

"I'll go inside and meet him. None of you will come inside before I take my money back. That was the deal. I don't want him to run away again. Then what you do with him is your business."

With that, he descended. We saw his shadow moving swiftly in the alley towards their door. Our hearts raced as we watched the house curiously. We expected lots of sounds and movements but the air remained still.

Fifteen minutes passed away slowly. Adnan leaned and whispered in my ear,

"I'll go inside now. You stay right here."

I held his arm back roughly as he stood up. I wanted to go with him. A startled look came across his face. Slowly, he shook his head and said that he knew how to deal with such men.

"This is our last chance," he looked into my eyes, "One wrong step and it's over."

His footsteps could be heard going downstairs. He smiled faintly at me before stepping in the dark alley. His shadow walked the long walk and then I heard the sound of the door.

He disappeared inside.

I looked back at the sky; the kite was gone.

I looked downstairs, the dog wasn't resting either.

The first ten minutes were somehow bearable. I paced back and forth impatiently and told myself that Adnan was in there and he could be trusted completely. After ten more minutes, I imagined I heard Abdullah's laughter on a rooftop. This made me descend down the stairs and stand in the mouth of the alley. Twenty minutes later; the feeling became frighteningly intolerable. I walked towards the door and stood outside for some time.

I heard nothing.

Taking a deep breath, I pushed open the door and let myself inside.

***

CHAPTER FORTY-FIVE

Adnan stood still with a man who watched me inquisitively as I opened the door. I stepped inside the room like a hostile intrusive spirit that couldn't be conquered or diminished. There was a heavy silence in the room and it had great power over me but I didn't let myself recoil.

"I didn't know you brought company," spoke the new man, with piercing distinctness.

I looked around where I stood. It was the same littered room where we had met Najeeba and her daughter days before. There was no daughter around but just Najeeba sitting quietly on the carpet stitching a torn shirt. She didn't look up when I came and she didn't look up when the man spoke. She minded her own business, like she didn't wish to get involved in anything that didn't concern her.

I drew closer to look at the man's face.

He was not old, thirty-five maybe, with a tan complexion and a small beard. He wore a grey shirt with a familiar logo on the front. I tried to recognise him but I realised that we had never met before. This wasn't Arbaz Malik. It wasn't the boy from the photographs. A piece of me died that very moment.

The man stood with Najeeba and my friend.

"Who are you?" I asked.

"This is Arbaz's cousin, Sadaan," Adnan told me.

"Well, before this very strange ambush, I came here to clear some debts and visit the woman who served our family for years."

I turned to look at him.

"Abdullah Ameen," my voice quivered as I spoke the name aloud.

It seemed to ring around the room and echo back. No one uttered a word. The man didn't blink.

"Have you heard this name before?"

He looked at me, a light shone in his eyes.

"No, I haven't," he said flatly.

"Please," I persisted, "I know of your cousin."

"Oh, do you?" he seemed taken back.

"You're Max's cousin. My brother knew him and now he's missing."

He nodded and sat back on a chair. He rested his hands on his knees and looked at the ground. I looked at Adnan, who seemed completely calm and in control.

"Tell me something about him," he said.

"What do you mean?"

"Tell me about your brother. I've met many people in my life," he repeated without looking up.

I found myself intimidated by the very question. It seemed he wasn't going to continue if I didn't answer so I said slowly,

"He went missing seven months ago. November 2009 is when I last spoke to him."

"What did you talk about?"

"Why does that matter?"

"What did you talk about?" he repeated without an explanation.

"Our family and a wedding."

"What else?"

"Our grandfather."

Adnan clenched his teeth as the man tested our patience, but I kept answering. His simple questions were taking a toll on me....

"I don't know if he ran away on his own or somebody took him away from us but I need to see him. I want to see him unharmed."

"People don't get lost that easily. Maybe he left because he was looking for something," he said.

"Like what?"

"Freedom."

"He had all the freedom he desired."

"Now, how do you know that?" he rose again, "The last time you spoke to him was in November, you said. And besides, we all have a different definition of the word freedom."

I folded my arms and looked at him sternly, but still engaged in every word he spoke.

"And then there are different kinds of freedom – political freedom...spiritual freedom, emotional freedom..."

"Where is he?" I asked.

My lips trembled and my eyes burned with fury. I wanted to attack him like an animal, rip him apart for torturing my mind. My voice could no longer restrain my emotions.

"You *do* know him," I said.

"Yes, I knew him," he answered in the same subdued tone.

"Where is he now?"

"He doesn't want you to know."

I looked at him sceptically, "I don't believe you."

"I'm afraid you don't have a say in this. You need to respect him and his decisions."

"Why didn't he come back? Why doesn't he want to come back home? "

"Because he was unhappy."

"Unhappy?" I asked, as if confirming that was what he had said.

He nodded.

Tears trickled down my cheeks as I found myself ridiculously attached to the stranger's every word. I thought of my brother's face, simple and beautiful and his dark, passionate eyes. I hated myself for not understanding and being there for him, and being victimised emotionally in the hands of a complete stranger whom I couldn't rebut or pounce on, just because he knew my brother and I did not, just because he felt he had an access to his mind, and I did not.

"Do you know why you're standing here in this house?" he asked suddenly, "Here in this city…this country?"

I looked at him like a child, lost and dazed.

"You're here because he wanted you to be here, with your family," he said, "He wanted you to come back to Lahore. He wanted you to be safe, here and not on your own in a land full of strangers."

"What do you mean?" I heard Adnan ask.

"Why did you come back here?" Sadaan asked me, not looking at Adnan.

"Because he called my friend Richard and told him…." I paused grimly and thought about what the stranger might be insinuating.

Was what he was saying true? Did Abdullah stage all this, pretend he was in Lahore so I could fly back here? But why? What was he running away from? Nothing made sense.

"Why would he want me to come back here? I was happy in America."

"Were you, really?"

I stopped, contemplated and spoke softly, "Yes…"

He smiled.

"If you…or he thinks…that I was unhappy there, then I'm not exactly happy here either. I haven't slept properly in months…I think of little else but him…I don't feel safe and I'm very, very hurt. This isn't my idea of happiness. You should tell him that!"

Sadaan looked at me, still, as if trying to absorb all that I had said, picture me in my pain and agony.

Suddenly, I shook off my dejection and looked at him, resolute.

"Where is he now?" I asked, "Where is my brother? I want to talk to him myself."

He remained silent.

I walked to Adnan and held his arm. He looked at me, as confused as I was.

"Ask him!" I begged, "Ask him where he is. I have to see him now!"

"Why can't Abdullah be here?" Adnan asked.

"What do you want from us?" I asked.

"Look, I want you to go back from the door you came and never return. This woman has seen enough of you both", Sadaan pointed at Najeeba, who was now cleaning the room. She remained in her own world, oblivious of our existence.

"So what about my family?" I said, "What am I to tell them?"

Sadaan stood up gently and walked slowly towards me. His arms were tied at his back and his eyes looked at me severely.

"Tell them something they'll believe. Tell them that before dying, your brother rotted in a dark, dark cell that they build for men like us."

Faces became tense. We could hear nothing but rapid breathing, his and mine.

"No!" I shrieked and went for his throat. "No! You bastard! You liar! You filthy liar!"

Adnan held me back and roared, "Tell us what you know!"

"Abdullah Ameen died six months ago!" he yelled.

"No!" I collapsed on my knees, "No!"

I felt Adnan weaken. His face became white, he couldn't speak.

"I'm sorry, I'm sorry," the cousin said softly, "He killed a woman in the store. The pistol went off. They took him away. I am sure you know the story."

"No, no. I heard his voice…we heard his voice, Adnan, and… and there was no killing…" I stammered as my mind blurred.

Adnan brought a hand to his forehead, petrified to his core.

He didn't know what to say.

"They took him to one of those dark places where time stands still and you don't know who you are anymore."

Adnan accumulated some strength and picked me from the ground. I wailed in his arms and felt him whisper something I couldn't understand.

I leapt up and held Sadaan's collar.

"They lied to you about all their supposed investigations and all you did was waste your time in candle vigils and search parties. I brought you back here," he said as I rattled his collar.

"The call?" I screamed, "I heard his voice!"

"He faked the call. What if Sadaan faked the call?" I heard Adnan murmur.

"You did this to him! Your family did this to him!" I pounded his chest with my fists, "You hollow men! How can you let a child suffer like that?"

Sadaan kept telling me that he was no longer alive and how sorry he was for my loss and that I must understand why the truth was kept away from me.

Madness, it was utter madness.

I was taken back to the cold and lonely Washington nights when I ransacked his room and incessantly questioned every single person that could ease my pain. In my head, I replayed the voices of the other boys and the officers.

I suddenly released his collar as I had an epiphany. Something that I had been ignoring for a long time, a small detail that I had overlooked. I felt like someone had removed a large stone from my chest and my heart burned with a strange hope.

I turned and said to Adnan, "The cousin. He's the cousin… he's the cousin, you said…the cousin…"

He looked at me for some time, confused as he processed the information and then his face visibly relaxed.

Calmly, I faced the man again and repeated all that I knew.

"Max had a cousin. He lived with his cousin in Baltimore. It's you, you are that cousin."

The man's face tightened and grew pale, as if someone had made him remember a sad memory from his childhood.

"There was no murder. I know this." I paced the room hurriedly, "I checked and re-checked and confirmed everything. It was just a prank. After Abdullah was released, he came here immediately…"

"…because *I* brought him to Lahore," Sadaan finished my sentence.

"But why?"

"Because they were going to kill him."

"Who?" I asked.

He looked at me for a long time before saying, "My family."

"Your family? What the hell has your family got to do with my brother? He's just a young boy."

"You don't know of us, I presume. You don't know what we're capable of."

I remained quiet.

"You do know your brother befriended my cousin, right? Max…or Arbaz or Malik, whatever you may know him as."

I nodded.

"And you also know that my cousin and I belong to a family that is…." he took a break, as if struggling for the appropriate description.

"Powerful?" I offered, filling in his silence, "Have lands, businesses, political support, people who are willing to slit their throats for their sake, a family with a sense of authority and unnecessary pride…"

"A family that is dangerous," he finished.

The blood in my veins froze. I asked, "Dangerous?"

"Even sitting in the same room with them is toxic, you enter as yourself and leave as someone you don't even recognise…"

"You mean, they threaten people? Yes, I know," I swallowed as I remembered what Adnan had mentioned about his very first meeting with Malik's family.

Adnan bowed his head in silence.

"Yes," he said, "They threaten, because for them, their family and its safety comes first. They don't care who they trample and kill along the way."

"So what has my brother got to do with any of this?"

He turned his back at me and moved towards a window. I saw him staring far away to a place that was well-lit and festive. Maybe there was a wedding in procession or perhaps some religious seminar, we didn't know and couldn't care less.

"Once we make enemies, we make sure they never witness a blissful day. Your brother befriended Arbaz Malik, my cousin, in America and they soon became inseparable. Do you know why?"

I contemplated for a while and then spoke, still with a great reluctance, "They had some things in common, they were both in pain."

"Exactly," he said, "Your brother was in pain for obvious reasons but Arbaz's pain is hard to describe. In this big family of grandeur, pride, and wealth, he was a very, very lonely. As a child, he watched his mother leave him and never come back. She was a good woman and he liked her, but she couldn't handle it. This family and the raging political scene put her in a great pressure. She was raised abroad, but decided to settle here in Lahore after she got married. But no matter how much she tried, she couldn't find a reason to stay. She loathed everything the family stood for and everyone in it. How do I know this?"

I remained silent and waited for him to tell me more.

"Because there was someone else who felt just like her…my father. My father is Arbaz's uncle, his father's brother. He didn't want to be involved in this culture of feudalism and politics, so he took his family, us, away from all this and we settled in the States for good. In Baltimore, as you already know.

"Arbaz took after his mother; he was sensitive, and wanted to be free from these shackles. His older brother, however, was much more involved with the family. He liked hunting, partying in farm houses, moving around the city campaigning for votes and was preparing to sit on his father's seat for the next elections."

He closed the window and the celebrations were removed from our sights. He sat down on a chair and looked at me, thoughtful.

"Arbaz was free as long as his brother remained in the scene. So he left for America and said he would be back when he finished his education. They let him go…"

"But he was never going to come back, was he?" I asked.

He shook his head and said, "No, and after that night when Abdullah and Arbaz got caught, the news reached Pakistan and the elders of our clan were infuriated. Abdullah was deported immediately but Arbaz was released after a few months. He returned to me in Baltimore, but we never told the family here. He wanted this, he wanted to disappear from their life completely and be able to start afresh without his toxic ancestry following him."

I felt the ground beneath me shake. I tried to imagine Arbaz Malik…Max…The Max, after all that I had just heard, and for the first time felt his agony, his attempt to break free from the ghosts of his past.

"So…so my brother flew back to Lahore?" I asked, almost whispering, choking on my own words as the story was making sense.

"Yes, he did."

I lowered my gaze as sorrow gripped my body and attempted to tear it. I sat down on the carpet, meditated and recollected all that he had said about Arbaz, his violent family and my brother.

I imagined the scenario after the accident with the gun. Arbaz disappeared and his family must have been angry. But were they mad at Abdullah? Why? Did they give him a hard time? Did they harass him in any way? Why didn't he tell me?

"Why didn't he come back home?" I asked even though I was sure I knew the answer.

"Arbaz's older brother, possessive as he was about him, claimed Abdullah to be responsible for the disappearance. They began searching for him everywhere."

"Didn't you tell them?" I stood up and yelled, "You act pretty wise! Why didn't you tell them?"

"You think I didn't?" he rose too, "but once my family sets their mind on something, it is hard to shake it out of their system! They're ignorant. They didn't listen…"

"Oh, no…no…" I murmured and turned my face away so he didn't see me break down. "Tell me. Tell me what happened afterwards? Why didn't he come back home?"

"He just couldn't. For all of you, for the sake of protecting you and your parents and your sisters. It is very easy for my family to load their guns and eliminate every one of you from the face of this planet for the sake of finding Arbaz. That's how upset and serious they really are."

Adnan approached me. I felt his hand on my shoulder. He said a few words of comfort. He understood the seriousness of the matter when Sadaan spoke about the violence his family was capable of, but I didn't care; it wasn't fair.

It wasn't fair. Abdullah did nothing to anyone, he never deemed of hurting a soul. He was a good boy who flew kites, listened to his radio and fixed broken things.

"This is not fair…" I cried softly as Adnan hugged me, "This is not fair."

I felt his hand gently stroking my hair, "I know…I'm so sorry, Mariam."

Sadaan continued, "He is a naïve child, unfamiliar with this dark and tainted world. I flew back to Lahore, as his lookout. I stayed in the family home, mourned Arbaz's disappearance and kept Abdullah out of their sight. He stayed away from your family, because he feared mine would hurt him. And when he said to your friend that he is in Lahore with Malik…he meant me…Sadaan Malik…"

I looked at him and whispered, "So, why here? Why Lahore? Why did he come back to the same city where he knows his life is in danger?"

Sadaan spoke after a moment of silence, "I can't say. But maybe a piece of him wanted you to find him…maybe this place is the only thing keeping him together, a sense of familiarity…his childhood, a time when he had little to worry about…Maybe…"

I lowered my head and closed my eyes.

"Where is he now?" asked Adnan.

"He doesn't want to be contacted. Neither does he want his sister lurking in the streets looking for him. He is safe. I would seriously advise you to start a new life, a life where you remind yourself that you never had a brother."

I walked to him, looked into his steady unblinking eyes and spoke in a clear, unwavering tone:

"…and you tell Abdullah that his sister will not stop looking for him till the last drop of blood in her body dries."

***

Everyone had gone to sleep at home, except for Anika, who sat in the *barsati,* reading. I sat down with her and a painful silence crept inside my body. She continued reading, oblivious of my sadness, preoccupied by her own world, which seemed to get brighter with every passing day. I couldn't hold on to it any longer; this heavy burden I bore had to be shared with her.

I told her everything.

She ceased to move, simply listened to me tell her why our brother did what he did. Her heart felt heavy and she broke the silence by sobbing wildly, repeating over and over that our brother was suffering and there was nothing we could do to stop it. She asked me if there was any way to call him. I said it was up to him to reach out to me, though he wanted us to keep away from everything. Then she said she wished I hadn't found all this out or told her since, in reality, the truth was far bitter that she had imagined. I said I understood and was sorry.

Angry, she threw the book she was reading across the room. It hit the wall with a loud thud and fell on the dusty floor. Then for a moment, she thought, analysed and weighed our brother's options of freeing himself from his predicament.

But there was no answer, no solace.

Infuriated, she ripped off the calendar – the one with Abdullah's scrawly handwriting – from the wall, she took down his posters one by one, and swung all this under her arm, then she picked the bird cages and torn kites and kicked open his closet.

I watched her shove the things inside in a big pile and shut the door, aggressively.

She had done it, removed everything that belonged to him from our sight, taken away everything that reminded us of the little solitary boy on the rooftop.

I watched her sit down and bury her head between her hands. Neither of us spoke. We could only hear the bustling city downstairs and her slight sobbing. We could not bear it, bear the feeling that it was over, that this was it.

She suddenly lifted her face and wiped her tears and whispered, "What if he really is happier this way?"

I told her he was. I was lying and she knew it.

"Maybe he found the serenity that he always wanted."

I silently nodded.

She paused, contemplating the countless possibilities.

"He went away from here to America to escape the madness that prevailed and instead, he ran right into its grip. How ironic is this."

I thought about it for a moment and then said, "Very."

She turned to me wearily, and said that I should stop looking for more answers. If he wanted, he would come out himself. We had to protect him and this is how we could do it, by becoming entirely invisible. She said I should transfer my credits to a university in Lahore, complete my degree and look for a job. We must move on. Life must move on.

I said I would.

She said we lived in a big, terrible world whose activities never ceased to amaze us. She assured me that soon the grief, the urge, the anxiety and everything else that accompanied our brother's disappearance would dissolve, everything that now troubled me would eventually dissolve and disappear and I would be free.

"It will all disappear," she repeated, "And you will be free."

***

CHAPTER FORTY-SIX

Dear Richard,

Father says that we are created for a special purpose, that each of us has an aim. Some have stories to tell, some have lovers to find, others have trains to catch and some keep on walking till the sky ends.

But what about those who have no stories to tell, no lovers to love and no trains to run and catch? What about people like Grandfather, people who choose to drift, drift through life. And what about people like me? Who refuse to see lovers, who miss every train to recovery and who just don't care where the sky ends.

How do these people recover? How can I recover? I am exhausted from being in pain all the time. It can never be washed, not in this life, or in any other. I don't remember what I used to love. I don't remember my favourite novels or songs, my dearest memories or conversations. I don't wish to be close to anyone, yet I'm afraid of being alone. It is becoming more and more difficult every day.

Anika thinks that I should go to the village for some time. She believes it will make me happy but I think the opposite. I cannot go to the village with such a heavy heart.

I went to Najeeba's house again with a faint hope that she would show some sympathy and give me some news about my brother's location, or perhaps Sadaan might have dropped by again. But when I arrived there, I found the house empty!

They have fled. Najeeba and her daughter have gone away for good. Habib's son told me that they went to their village to start a new life. Sadaan had come by to pick them up and asked the little boy to tell me that I must do the same – forget everything and try to move on. I asked Habib where the village was, he gave me a name and then turned away.

That evening, I packed my bag, in haste, not knowing where I was going but that I had to look for the village as Najeeba was my last hope. I thought maybe Sadaan would come visit her someday, or maybe somehow Abdullah might visit…I didn't know what I was thinking, just that I wanted to find that village, find Najeeba and her daughter.

But Adnan didn't agree. He didn't let me go. He believes that I'll lose myself and I have to let everything go. It will take time but I have to start living for myself.

Last night I had a strange dream. I must tell you about it:

In the dream, I am riding a beautiful horse. It is winter; the sky is clear and crisp. From my mouth escapes the soft, white smoke of my own breath. I ride to a place where the hills are grand and the air smells like lemons – zesty, fresh. I feel the horse's skin against mine; it is my friend. We jump over a white fence and fly over frozen meadows. Grass crackles beneath its hooves and the wind touches my face like a gentle mother. It feels as if the hills have eyes and they follow me all the way as I ride to wards a raging sea. Around me is serenity and I hear nothing but the waves crashing against the shore.

I sit there on the sand, feeling small and wonderful.

A stream of people pour into the scene from the left; not all faces are unfamiliar. I see my grandmother and Karan. They walk in a dignified silence and as they draw nearer, I look at their hands; they're holding coal black urns. They stop near the water and scatter the ashes.

They're grey and soft, and they cascade like a wonderful waterfall.
I woke up soon after, feeling completely new.
Mariam

***

Mariam,
Your heart is like a sponge, it soaks everything, takes in everything around it and it feels too much. It constantly needs something to love – a person, a place, a time or a dear memory and it doesn't want anything in return.
But your heart deserves much more than just that. You deserve a life of happiness and better things. You deserve to remember your favourite songs and conversations and books and so much more. You deserve to travel, meet people and write epic poetry.
You should learn to release yourself and let the past be the past.
There is nothing more you could have done.

Richard

***

JULY 2010

CHAPTER FORTY-SEVEN

For as long as he remembered, he had always hated the painting of the black raven in his father's study. It was a dark, twisted sketch that invoked in him nothing but fear and loathing. The cynical bird just sat in mid-air staring at an invisible object.

When he was a child, his father joked that if he kept looking at the painting the bird would twist its neck and stare back at him with its powerful beady eyes. He never took the risk. Now, he stood there, blowing smoke from his cigarette so the bird would disappear behind the thick curtain of smoke and he would never have to see it again.

He walked around in the study, looking at the wooden chairs with their royal blue cushions, the antique bookshelves and decorative lamps. He played with the keys of the piano and smiled at his reflection in a large mirror. The room was too English for his taste; another world altogether and he felt like being a different person in that space.

He picked up a new book from the shelf, the newest addition to the room. He turned it over to study his father's black and white photograph at the back. He sat poised, seemingly highly cultured, with a hand under his chin like he had not a care in the world. His eyes gazed at some distant object, and between his fingers sat a cigar.

His father was not a good parent and he knew it, too. He didn't make false efforts to please his son and he never missed a single one of his book launches or literary festivals to attend any parties or birthdays. But still, he somehow liked him for his honesty.

He fell on a *divan* and looked at the ceiling. It was the last week of June and he hadn't heard from her in eight days. He was right when he told her he had grown used to her presence. He had enjoyed her aura and company, no matter how silent and unnoticeable it was at times. He missed her figure sitting quietly in the corner of the room, sometimes crouching in front of the window, lost in thought, and sometimes lying on the *divan* with a melancholic expression, still lost in thought.

She thought and thought and thought….she told him once that she had thought a lot as a child and now she thought a lot as an adult. It didn't sadden her because this was who she was. Her mind was a solitary realm where no man or companion could enter. There she battled her terrible monsters and storms, drowned and lived through countless shipwrecks, and somehow still retained her aura, her fire, her light. He asked her often to tell him of the things she thought about, what was it that always consumed her, but she would always just smiled, shake her head and whisper:

"Nothing. It is nothing."

He thought maybe if he knew what troubled her, she would enjoy him more and perhaps lend a piece of herself to him, but she belonged only to herself. No man, or place could possess her, dim her essence, take a part of her and leave her forever.

"Adnan *bhai*? There is a phone call for you," called a voice, bringing him back to the refined room with the painting of the raven.

He gently opened his eyes. It was the kitchen boy. He stood in a colourful shirt and checked trousers. He had recently gotten a haircut and had put in an extra effort to comb and gel his hair to the side.

"Who is it?" He asked.

The boy carefully pronounced the speaker's name.

Adnan swiftly sprang up and seized the telephone, leaving the boy alarmed. The child couldn't deem the importance of the caller.

He held the receiver, his heart thumped wildly as he asked, "Is this really you?"

The speaker hesitated but then eventually spoke, "It is me…"

He felt his heart beat fasten. He sat down on the *divan* and tried to take it in. He couldn't believe it.

"Is it really you?" Adnan asked again, "Is this really Abdullah?"

***

Adnan killed the cigarette as he heard a knock on the study door.

The morning was still dark when she arrived. She walked through the door and smiled faintly as her eyes met his. He rose to meet her and then stood quietly in her company. She came forward and threw her arms around him in affection and for comfort.

"Mariam," he whispered softly.

"Abdullah has agreed to see me for one last time," she whispered back and then pulled herself away from his embrace.

"I know. I am the one who received the call and then told you, remember…"

"That is right," she said with a weak smile, "Abdullah called you…he called you and not me…"

Her face became grim as she reminded herself again of the fact that her brother chose to converse with strangers over her. It was never her, she was never in the picture and she didn't know the reason. Did he not trust her? Or was it just that she held such little relevance in his life?

"How did he…what did he sound…" she struggled with her words.

"He sounded okay," he said, "he sounded just fine."

"Good."

Adnan folded his arms and scrutinised her. She sat down on

the *divan* and idly picked up a book from the table. She read the synopsis off the back, studied the cover and flipped through the pages, and then she asked him what it was about.

They talked about it for a while, but then she said suddenly, "Did he…did he ask how I was doing?"

"He did."

"And what did you say?"

"I told him the truth…I told him how miserable you were."

She kept the book back on the table and bit her nails uneasily.

"I feel so small…" she said.

He didn't say anything.

"I feel so small and insignificant, you know. I watch my parents smile, laugh, hide their pain and ignore my brother's existence. They don't even talk to me anymore because they don't know what to say. If I disappear today, who will miss me? Will my parents or my sisters look for me the way I am looking for my brother…I feel this now, this sense of mortality and nothingness."

"We are all small and insignificant in some way, Mariam."

"No," she said, "Arbaz Malik isn't. His family isn't. They are still looking for him, his brother still misses him and Najeeba still cries for him. My brother, on the other hand, is small and insignificant because he is an ordinary boy. He has gone, vanished, he has just disappeared, and people have stopped wondering why…"

"He's not gone…he said he would see you today…"

"He is gone," she repeated.

"Why do you say this?"

"He told you he would see me one last time, didn't he?" she looked up at him.

He lowered his head and couldn't meet her eyes. The answer was a yes.

"After today then, he will be gone. He will leave us completely," she buried her face in her hands, as if wanting to disappear as well.

Adnan kept watching her in silence, finding the right words, a suitable gesture that could lessen her anguish. He had watched her stand up strong and he had watched her fall and crumble, shrivel up in her cocoon, but he had never seen her like this, he had never sensed a sense of clarity in her before. She was realising that after this last meeting, she would have to face the truth, she would have to let him go.

She smiled weakly and said, "I'll go and see him today, but I don't want you to come with me."

His heart felt heavy with the notion that she would be out there on her own. He shook her head.

"You'll let me be," she said.

"Let you be?"

He walked away from her and picked up a picture frame from the desk and looked at it so she couldn't see his eyes.

"I'll let you be, Mariam."

"Adnan…" she began.

"Mariam…" he interrupted.

Sighing, she walked to the window.

She stood still, absorbed in other thoughts. Her hands lay on the windowsill, forgotten and her eyes studied the changing sky.

He was drawn to her then. He had always been but it was then, at that moment, his heart truly fell for her. She gave a broken smile like there were no words in the world to fill the silence between them.

"What are you thinking about?" she asked.

"Just how I came to meet you."

For him, it had begun as a curiosity; a story narrated by a long time friend at a bar – a girl looking for her brother who had mysteriously disappeared from the roads. He thought about it for some days, what a tragedy, what a painful story. This curiosity gave birth to a desire to meet her and then transformed into an obsession to help her. Now, she stood there, in the very same room as he, her heart exploding from bliss because she was meeting her brother, she was walking towards that unity that she had been dreaming about for months.

Where would he go when all this was over? What place

would he have in her life, in her world, in her lonely, complicated world? Where would he go, when it all vanished, the mystery, the adventure, the expectation?

She hadn't thought about it. She was only thinking about her brother.

"I'm so tired," she said suddenly and held her head in her hands.

He looked at her for a long time. None of them spoke. The silence sliced through them. He was afraid of what could happen after she met him, would he come back with her? Would he give her another grim reason for the distance? Would he denounce her completely? Would she ever recover?

"There is a world outside your head and it's time you realise that," he said suddenly.

Tears shone in her eyes. She looked at the carpet instantly. He had never seen cry before.

"Adnan…"

"Mariam, you will listen to me now. When you stopped the clock, many people froze with you and you owe yourself and them, some peace and rest."

She remained quiet.

"And after this is over, promise me that you will start looking after yourself."

Slowly, she slid open the glass of the window. She said she felt suffocated in the room.

"I will do what you say. I think it's time, anyway."

A smile came over his face and he said, "After a few years when things don't work out with anyone, I will rescue you. You could try dating me. I'm not that bad."

She laughed and walked towards him.

She said in a low voice, "We've met at a very strange time, Adnan. It's almost like we needed this tragedy to connect us, bring us closer. Would we have ever met if Abdullah was still here?"

He contemplated but didn't answer.

"It's alright. I'm afraid to answer that, too," she whispered, "I think I'll go now."

"Take care of yourself."

"I will."

"And if you do go missing, Mariam. I promise I will come looking for you."

They smiled and then parted. She looked at the painting of the raven and walked out the door.

He heard her footsteps fade away.

***

CHAPTER FORTY-EIGHT

I had prepared for the moment so many times in my head but when the day arrived, I forgot everything. I forgot what I was to say to him, what I was to ask from him, how I was to cry and plead, how I was to tell him what I felt for him, how everybody felt and how we were was truly sorry for what had happened.

I woke up early that morning and remained still on the bed for a long time. I looked at the ceiling in silence. I thought, revised and analysed the journey, my search for him. I thought about all those painful hours in D.C., those drives to Boston, those talks with the officers, those meetings with strangers, those long walks where I forgot who I was and where I was going, that cold, dreadful winter and that feeling of being utterly alone.

I thought about it all.

Anika had a peaceful sleep. She didn't stir but slept serenely through the hours, while I tossed and turned in the bed. I hadn't told her anything, and I still didn't know why. Maybe her last reaction had frightened me, or maybe I was afraid she would want to come along, and seeing that, Abdullah would never trust me again, or maybe because this was *my* moment. *I* was to reconcile with him first. *I* was to see and talk to him first.

I rinsed my face, picked out nice clothes – a white *shalwar-kameez* with a beautiful yellow *dupatta* and applied a thin layer of *kohl* in my eyes. I opened the dressing table drawer and took out a lipstick – it was a nice, warm colour. Anika had worn the same colour on the day she met the sober-faced man for the very first time. I applied it gently and then looked at my reflection. It seemed as though I was dressed to meet a long lost lover, as if I had lost him in a war and now suddenly received the news that he was alive. I didn't know if he was broken in half or suffered any mental trauma, but I knew that I had to see him and look good.

***

It was a beautiful July morning. The *rickshaw* moved slowly on the roads, as they were still wet from the rain the night before. The smell of parched earth still lingered in the air. I looked outside at the canal, the trees and the cars.

Where were we going?

To a shrine, I answered myself, that's where he wanted to see me. I did not know why and thought perhaps I would ask him this in person, maybe I could begin our conversation this way.

"Why a shrine? Why this shrine?"

I hadn't ever realised there was this element in him, this spiritual angst that out of all the places in Lahore, he chose a shrine as the place he wanted to meet me at.

I stepped out, paid the driver and watched him roar away.

I was early, or maybe late, I didn't know because Adnan said Abdullah never mentioned the time. He just said, "Next week, this day, if she is willing."

Why this day?

Perhaps this could be my very next question.

I stepped onto the marble courtyard. It was too early to visit and pay regards to the Persian saint. The caretaker, who was sweeping the floor with a big mop, stopped to look at me. He approached me and asked me if he could help me with anything. I told him I was waiting for someone. He nodded and moved along.

I looked at the white shrine, the green dome and the tall minarets. Then I sat in the corner of the yard, where I would receive less attention and could look at every face in curious silence. I sat throughout the day with my knees hugged close to my body, my head resting on them. Morning left my company, afternoon passed, and then the lovely evening breeze arrived as I watched the sun melt and dissolve into the sky. Someone said it was going to pour and it was going to be an even lovelier night.

Darkness brought more people and the passion heightened. Hundreds of devotees filled the courtyard. Their faces were swollen with unfulfilled desires and lingering hope and their hands were raised in mid-air.

I watched men in green turbans and white *shalwar-kameez* walk in and out of the shrine compound with a dignified grace. They sat, prostrated, begged and wept. I listened to their secrets, desires and stories and felt that I had lived each and every one of them. I saw in each one of them, my brother. He was everywhere that night, in every child, in every restless man, in every devotee, in every beggar and in every cloud and star.

I went inside to pay my respect, I prayed for Abdullah and for the very first time for myself. I prayed for a peace of mind, for clarity and better understanding.

Soon, the place drowned in the sounds of *Qawwali* and footsteps. The same caretaker from the morning found me standing anxiously and told me that these were the words of the Sufi poet, *Bulleh Shah*.

As the lights and music became more intense, I sat down again and nestled in the farthest corner of the courtyard with my shawl wrapped around my body. The whole day had passed and hundreds of questions settled in my mind: *Where was he? What if he didn't come? What if he came and could not find me? What if it wasn't Abdullah who called?*

I stood up again and scanned every face I could before me. I couldn't leave, I just couldn't leave without making sure that he really wasn't there. The air around the shrine was cool, it could pour anytime. A soothing summer rain.

Closing my eyes, I sung softly to myself, a melody from my childhood,

> *"Oh where did you go, oh lover*
> *The earth still spins and I am here alone*
> *Oh lover, have a heart."*

I imagined that the sky was filled with kites, vibrant kites, red, yellow, green, soaring high into the heavens, away from the world and away from all the madness and chaos.

And just then, I felt someone touch my shoulder.

I remained still.

"Mariam?"

I stopped singing upon hearing a voice that was frighteningly familiar. I slowly opened my eyes. My heart pounded and I could feel blood rushing up and down my body, throbbing in my veins.

"Abdullah…" I said, my voice scarcely audible.

I took his face in my hands and kissed him.

I had found him. I had finally found him. I looked at him as if he were an enchanted creature from a fairytale. There was a bright, mysterious light around him, but there was also something potent. He was beautiful. He was simply beautiful.

He held my hand and kissed it before he murmured in a voice of love, "Go home, Mariam. Think of this as a dream, like it never happened."

***

Then suddenly, like an angry God, the wind stripped the earth bare. It rattled the tin houses and blew dust into the worshippers' eyes. My shawl flew away and I stood on the marble floor with my hand in Abdullah's. We each waited for the other to speak and tried to calm the terribly abnormal beating of our hearts.

"Go home, Mariam," he repeated.

Carefully, then his icy fingertips began to release mine. I did not understand and asked him what he meant, he did not reply. I felt something in my hand, a crisp paper that he said was important to read.

"Don't leave us. Don't leave us again," I cried.

I could see him recoil in horror, the fear that I would not let him go and that I didn't understand what was going on in his life. I told him I did and together, we could figure something out.

"I can't stay for longer. I want you to read this and if you try hard, I'm sure you will be able to forgive me…" is all he said.

"Why didn't you come back home?" I asked. I wanted to hear the answer from him. I wanted to see what he said.

"I had to choose a new life and someday, I *will* find my way back home. But now is not the right time."

"You can't leave again! Do you remember our family?"

"Mariam, please don't."

He couldn't look into my eyes, as if ashamed, as if an internal force compelled him from answering all my questions. He held my hands again and kissed my forehead. Tears trickled down my cheeks as he told me how satisfied and happy he was, spiritually and physically. He said he didn't want anything else and that I shouldn't worry. I told him I was very sorry, but he said he was happy.

"Don't tell them you saw me," he said, "It'll only cause them pain. Let me disappear from their lives in a way that is less painful."

I cried and hugged him. This is what he asked me to do, pretend I had never seen him, pretend it was just one of those dreams where reality doesn't seem so distant.

"Go home, Mariam. Go, for me."

He released me and crept backwards, dissolving into the crowd. I turned my face away, crushed from sorrow, and walked the other way through the stream of strangers.

As I walked, the wind seemed to grow stronger, fiercer, like it was furious at me for letting him go again. It was like a ragging torrent that began to push me towards his direction. My heart ached from the very thought that I had lost him again.

No, I said to myself, *I cannot let it happen yet another time, not in this life, never again. I will not!*

I dropped the paper, still unread and unacknowledged, and followed him.

"Abdullah!" I screamed at the top of my lungs.

The crowd seemed to get larger and denser. It took me a while but I finally saw the back of his head. He was heading inside the shrine to pay his respects.

"Abdullah!" I cried.

My cry was followed by a loud noise.

Suddenly, it was as if the whole sky and the seven heavens had fallen onto the earth and crushed every mountain and being. The noise instantly tore bodies into half, made people wail in agony and run in opposite directions.

"Save yourselves!" cried someone, "Bomb!"

I did not take my eyes off Abdullah. I saw him running towards me. I called out his name again and through the crowd of panicked men, moved towards him.

I watched him trip and fall, and then watched a dozen men walk over him.

"Abdullah!" I shrieked. I feared he would die; the men would kill him. I feared they would crush his body and not care.

"No! No!" I tried to run towards him.

He struggled to stand up but when he did, he fell down once more. I watched him collapse.

In that instant, it was like everything evaporated around me. The shrine, the dusty people, the wind, it all disappeared. I felt like my body was frozen onto the ground but my mind had fallen into a dark, unending, abyss, a parallel world where there was no music, no sky, no birds or mountains. There was no Grandfather smoking his *hookah* in the *veranda*. There was no Karan sharing slices of sweet melon with me on the rooftop. There was no *daddi* smiling at the mud houses from the moving window of the train. There was no Father strolling through acres and acres of green land with his register and ink pen. There was no Anika bathing in the monsoon rains. There was no Richard, somewhere, somewhere far looking at pictures of Lahore and writing about us in his head and there was no Adnan, watching me with affection as I drifted into contemplation.

It all vanished. The meaning, the aim of everything vanished for me the moment my brother's body hit the ground.

And then suddenly, someone held my arm and flipped it around violently. I turned to look into the horrified eyes of a friend.

Adnan.

***

CHAPTER FORTY-NINE

It was all seemingly perfect from a distance.

She stood in the corner of the courtyard, with a look of wonderment and affection in her eyes. Her yellow *dupatta* kept falling off her shoulders and her hair blew in the wind . She held the hands of a young boy, the same boy that I had often seen in photographs, the boy she spoke about so frequently, the boy that had caused her great pain and the boy whose secret she had just learned a few weeks ago. It was Abdullah in whose company she stood. I wanted to go nearer, look at them more closely but I didn't. I didn't want to taint this moment with my presence.

She had asked me not to come there, and I said I wouldn't, but as night fell, I grew anxious. Her sister called and said she left early morning without a word. I assured her she was okay and would return soon.

I watched the boy suddenly retreat and her sobbing as she let him go. In her hand was a piece of paper that she didn't seem to care about. They parted and walked in different directions, and that's when I went away, too.

I decided to drive away and wait for her in my study. I was never to tell her that I was there and about what I saw. I wanted to listen to what she would tell me, maybe she would tell me only happy things, things that mattered or maybe she would break down and tell me another story.

But just as I began to walk away, an ear-splitting sound absorbed everything.

People lapsed into silence, failing to interpret the sound but I knew instantly what it was. Then, with their brains beating wildly out of their heads, they ran loose like mad animals. Their faces grew white and their eyes became wide with fright. The shrine glittered in a strange, exhilarated madness. They ran over children, women and everything that fell in their way, hoping they might get away in time.

I turned around to find her but she was lost in all the dust, screams and hysteria. I called out her name and ran towards the courtyard where I had last seen her.

"Mariam!" I screamed.

After moments of running and panicking, I saw her run towards her brother, who had fallen down. I reached for her and flipped her around. She looked at me as if we had never me before.

"We need to get out now!" I said.

"No, Abdullah is there! We need to get him!"

"Mariam, I will get him! You need to get out before someone crushes us to death!"

She escaped from my grasp and ran away but before she could reach Abdullah, there was another explosion. There was no mistaking the noise that second time.

Again, I lost her in clouds of dust.

"*Taliban*! *Taliban*!" cried a child covering his ears as it stood motionless in the middle of the courtyard. Stained in blood, his mother rushed towards him and picking him up, ran towards the gate.

Someone pulled on my sleeve, a security guard, screaming

half-formed escape strategies in my ear. The police arrived and discussed strategies to tackle the potential suspect, a masked man that was seen going inside the shrine. They wrestled with the crowd, stroked their batons and resorted to aerial firing, creating more panic and hysteria.

There were sirens, lots of them, ambulances, fire trucks and rescue vans rushed in, media vans and people filled the space and more police emerged. Rescue workers carried out the victims by clambering over broken things and shifting them into ambulances.

The entire space outside was filled with cars, everyone stood, spellbound by the tragic spectacle.

"Where did it happen? Inside the shrine?" asked a man.

"Downstairs," he said, "Somewhere near the basement area."

I stood outside the courtyard with the team of eager cameramen and anchors. Together we watched people crushing people, jumping over broken limbs and crying children and women.

"I didn't know you were here!" I heard a familiar voice.

I turned around to find a colleague holding our channel microphone.

I didn't reply but stood there, spellbound by the massacre, trying to find a lead to find her, trying to locate her yellow *dupatta* in the wreck.

My heart burned from the thought that she could have been anywhere and if she had fallen down, nobody would have stopped to pick her up. She could be crushed and forever removed from my life. I pushed aside a few men and ran towards the frenzy.

"Adnan! Are you crazy?" he heard my colleague yell, "We'll cover when it settles down a bit. They're trampling over each other. We've enough to cover!"

I didn't stop to explain. The ground tilted and swayed as I watched men picked up dead bodies or what seemed to be parts of human flesh from the marble floor and place them on stretchers while some just sat on the floor, crying for help. A group of rescue workers pushed me and ran towards a fallen man.

I looked down at him. He wasn't moving. He just bled and bled till the marble soaked in the colour red.

I had never prayed before in my life but that moment, I did.

I prayed for a miracle.

I prayed for her.

I prayed for her brother.

"Mariam!" I screamed.

A thousand other responses.

A thousand Mariams loose like hungry animals in a vegetable patch. It was impossible for her to hear me, to understand, with all the panting, crying and bleating around us. I trembled, scared beyond measure, for her, and for her brother. There was a possibility that another bomber could be amongst us, lurking in the corner, satiating on the right opportunity, ready to decide that we had lived long enough…

A thousand cries filled the air as I struggled through them to find her.

"How many are there?"

"Take out all the women! Children!"

"Close the gates! Close the gates!"

"No, open the gates! Open the gates!"

Near one of the gates, a man grabbed a woman's arm and she cried as she struggled to break free. He was asking her to leave, pushing her outside but she wouldn't listen.

"My brother's in there! Let me go!"

It felt like all my life had narrowed to one point of intense happiness when I recognised the woman: Mariam. I ran over the rubble and glass to reach her. Those were the longest ten seconds of my life. She bit the man and tried to escape. I held her shawl and she fell on the ground.

I called her name and saw her body rise. She had heard me. She stood still, pale, grief-stricken and waited for me to collect her.

"We have to move. I promise, I'll come back for Abdullah," I said.

"He's hurt!" she cried, "You've to help me bring him!"

Her lip bled but she didn't know or care. I cleaned it with my palm and begged her to come outside. She wrestled like a child.

"Look, Adnan! Look at that boy in white clothes! That's Abdullah!"

I looked where she was pointing; several men in white and red, hundreds of them carrying other men in stretchers. As I took her to a safe place, she kept chanting his name.

Women bleated and beat their chests as they cried out the names of their loved ones. They wouldn't move. They said if their husbands and children had died then they should, too, and what better place than the holy shrine. Female wardens threatened to chain them if they didn't reciprocate.

With my all my force I made Mariam sit inside the car. Near the car, a bearded man took Allah's name and swore that there was another masked man inside.

"Is he wearing a jacket?"

"No, there's no jacket!"

Guns were reloaded. Bulletproof shields were brought. Someone said something about teargas. The policemen slowly started disappearing. Some went inside the shrine, some behind the building and some guarded the gates.

"Now listen, Mariam," I held her face in my hands so she paid attention to me and looked nowhere else, "They'll start indiscriminate firing soon."

Her eyes widened and she clutched my arm.

"No, no, no!" she wailed.

"We can't go inside now...we'll wait. What if he ran away? What if he's not inside?"

"No, he couldn't walk, he got hurt! I saw him! Please let me go...please let me go..." she pushed me and ran away before I could stop her again.

I rose and studied the scene. I moved closer back into the crowd and finally saw her, standing about a yard away from her brother. She had found him. They were both gasping for breath. It seemed as if he had been searching for her, too, and now they had found each other. His clothes were covered in dust and blood. She stared at him, without uttering a word. Around them, the world fell apart.

And just then, the masked man came to the scene. I saw him and everyone else did, too. He was standing barely a foot away from Abdullah.

The firing began without any warning. All the sounds in the world grew distant.

Seconds later everything became still.

The police yelled unceasingly that they had taken down the terrorist.

I stood numb for several minutes, praying, believing and telling myself over and over again that they hadn't accidently taken down any other man. The barricades were removed for the rescue workers and firemen to enter and take down the fire, which had started, no one knew when or how. I crossed over the human barricade to get to her.

"Oh my God, oh my God…"

Mariam lay covered in blood, on the ground.

"No!" I held her hand, "You'll be okay! I promise you, Mariam, hold on!"

I looked for the source of bleeding. She had hurt her head from falling on the floor when the police had begun firing, but she didn't look afraid. She laughed a little and then pointed to her left with a trembling arm. I looked behind.

Abdullah.

His lips moved slowly and his face was white. One of his feet quivered for a second and then he lay lifeless. I closed my eyes in dismay and then hid his body from her view by changing my position.

"Let me carry you! We need help here! She's alive, she's breathing!"

"Did you see that…" she whispered, "I spoke to Abdullah…."

"Yes, I'll bring him…"

A rage possessed me. I worked furiously through the maze of people with her body in my shaking arms. Every movement was painful and as I watched her slowly sway her head in agony, I thought I would lose her that day for sure.

The media anchors had now jumped in and one of my friends helped me carry her to the rescue ambulance.

"Don't you hear me, move those people! Don't let that ambulance leave! Move!"

"Adnan!"

"What!"

"I don't think she's breathing anymore…"

I looked down at her face and cried, "Don't you give up on me, Mariam!"

Behind our car, the police celebrated and cheered that they had taken down one of the terrorists. They spoke into the cameras with dust and blood on their faces and their heads held high.

The same night, a sea of men came with water and soap to clean the shrine, pick up the broken glass and remove the rubble. The blood from the marble floors could be washed away, the walls could be repainted and the dome could be fixed, but what of those hearts that were scarred forever and those children who witnessed everything? What of all those who were wounded, those who died and whose loved ones mourned for them now?

Who would fix them?

***

Nation's heroes take down terrorist in Lahore shrine, read the morning paper.

Indeed, they did take down the masked man but along with him, they accidently took down five more people, among them was an old caretaker and a young man named Abdullah.

***

Epilogue

Adnan called, and he said this was the last time.

He was catching a plane to Sudan, where he said he was being sent by the broadcasting channel for research, and he did not know if he would have time to correspond from there. I said I understood.

We had laughed.

We had remained silent.

I had congratulated him.

He had thanked me.

And then we said our goodbyes.

Now, I imagined him packing his bags, dismissing his father's calls and then gliding through the rest of the apartment, surveying the remains of last night's congratulatory party. He said it had been an intimate affair, a few friends, their friends and lots to drink.

I imagined his living room ringing with laugher; there must have been good food and wine, and women, lots of them, some that he worked with and some that he just knew. There must have been toppled chairs and drunken people, discussing life and feelings. And there must have been waiters, gentle and calm, picking up empty glasses and bottles with their delicate hands, pulling down the streamers, popping the purple balloons, putting back the chairs and folding all the tables when all of it was over.

Now, there must be Adnan, all alone in his apartment, in that persistent smell of alcohol and perfume, in the echoes and recollections of last night's gathering, contemplating, not about Sudan but I believe – I know – something far more surreal.

He is thinking about Lahore, its unwinding streets, its

colourful people and he is probably thinking about *her*. He is thinking about what a long way he has come to forget her and those circumstances, those horrible, horrible circumstances. I imagine him thinking about all those things I find myself thinking about, every time after we say goodbye over the phone.

He told me about the time he left Lahore. I had been disappointed that he left, but he said there was no other way for him to begin. He had never thought of coming to London, leaving everything behind and moving to a new country. He imagined he would have been able to establish himself as a successful man in Pakistan and then roam around the globe after a while, show his father that he did not indeed need his favours and money to thrive and have fun.

"I tried, Richard, but everything just changed so suddenly," he said on the phone.

"Lahore changed, the people changed, the meaning and the feeling of being there changed."

I said I understood.

"So, how did your father take it?" I had asked.

There was silence on the other end of the line, but then after a moment, he began.

"So you'll leave?" his father had asked, "Just like that?"

Adnan didn't think it would make such a difference to him. He had only thought about himself. But it appeared he had grown accustomed to his son's quiet presence. He enjoyed having him around, even if it meant sitting and conversing properly only once a year, and that too at his parties and book launches.

"Yes, I have to leave," Adnan had replied.

"But why? Why so soon? Why so suddenly? You're doing well here. You're almost a famous face on TV."

"I'll try my luck in London now…"

"But that's not what you planned."

"Life doesn't really go on set plans, dad."

He had thought for a while and then said, "I know all about that, son. That I can understand. You know when I married your mother I thought we were set and she was the one…"

"Dad, there is a world beyond women, booze and your living room parties," he had said, "And I just got confronted by it. I wasn't prepared. Did I plan for this? Did I plan for this scare, this eternal sense of loss that I will experience for the rest of my life? No. But it still happened. So there are no plans, dad, just people fooling themselves by attempting to design their fates and futures. It makes them feel invincible, even if it's for a transient period of time."

He said his father had remained silent and then before leaving him in his own company, said softly:

"You can't escape life by changing cities and befriending new people. I know I couldn't. My past and my mistakes followed me everywhere, in Greece, in France, in Africa, they followed me everywhere, and they gave me hell."

But, what were Adnan's problems? What was he running away from? What were his mistakes that were to follow him everywhere?

The fact that he befriended an elusive stranger, found himself emotionally entangled in her misery, and after she left, found it hard to accept that he too had to leave her.

He had left the study. He had left Lahore.

Adnan said he spent the first few weeks in London standing by the window, watching the cars, the roads, the people….and thinking about a place that was miles away, imagining he was still in his father's study and when he turned around, he would stare into the eyes of the raven in the painting.

He had begun missing everything.

He had distanced himself from the place and the people, but forgot that distance was nothing but perhaps just as his father had said, a state of mind.

How do we distance ourselves from those past moments and experiences, however surreal, however painful, however trifle, and begin anew, as if just released freshly from the warm womb? How do we get rid of those ghosts, that past life, choices, mistakes, regrets, desires...how do we become new people, with clean slates?

We can't. We can only deceive ourselves by trying to do so.

So, Lahore is real. Lahore burns with memories. Lahore is a storyteller. Lahore breathes and Lahore lives inside him, sometimes like a friend, and sometimes like a bitter enemy.

***

The morning when he was about to leave; his father had asked him one last time the reason for such an abrupt departure. He had told him that he couldn't explain things that didn't make sense to him either. He couldn't describe to him the storm, the torment in his mind when he saw her in his arms, bleeding, fading, still unaware that her brother had died. He could not describe the horror without reliving it.

He couldn't narrate to his father, the time when he went back to his study after that ghastly night and sat on the chair with his head in his hands, recollecting the sounds, the rush, the fury, the heart-breaking scenes that he had just witnessed.

He couldn't explain to him that the very next day when he visited her, she just lay with her head facing the white hospital wall. Her sister didn't let him go inside.

"She said the family had just told her what had happened, what had really happened, that they had lost their brother to unfortunate circumstances," Adnan said over the phone.

"How did she take it?" I had asked as my heart filled with indescribable sorrow.

"She didn't react, she just held her sister's hand and said that she would like to sleep, so they let her be..."

Adnan had left without seeing her face and returned home, only to find his father in the merry company of his tennis partners. He hadn't understood how to tell him about our friend, this strange transcendental being whom he had only known for a few weeks and those few weeks were enough for him. He didn't know how to tell him about her brother and that night when he finally resurfaced.

He could tell him nothing.

The letter, the one her brother handed to her and the one she lost in the dust, remained. Adnan told me about it and kept it with him.

"It lay in my drawer for days. I didn't give it to her family, because it wasn't meant for them. I wanted to place it in her hands and then, walk away, leaving her with it. When I was allowed to see her, it was for a brief moment at her house. We sat on a wooden swing in the *veranda*. She seemed calm and beautiful. She braided her hair in my presence and told me a funny story about her grandmother and the railway station."

They had shared a small laugh and then he had given her the letter. She had said she didn't want it.

"Keep it," she had said softly, "Read it…"

"I can't…"

"Then read it for me. And after that, burn it and immerse the ashes in a river," she smiled.

Adnan did not respond.

He didn't understand what she meant but he didn't ask her anything.

The folded piece of paper sat in his study for a week and he did not touch it because it was not written for him. Then somehow, over time he convinced himself that he was a part of this tragedy, this event. He was a part of Mariam's life and so in some way, this letter was also meant for him.

He had opened it slowly and gently, as if it were a page from the holy scripture, saw Abdullah's handwriting for the first time, studied all the characters and the letters and imagined the pain he was in while composing it. It was personal, very personal, he wrote about how hard it was for him to try to run away from Max's family and try to keep his own safe.

"No one can imagine the pain of living without a definite home, a definite face and a definite name. When I look at the sky and see colourful kites, I remember our roof, I remember my radio, I remember the twins' voices, I remember the birds I had and I wonder if they are still alive... Tell me, for how long do birds live, Mariam?

Max said that it is easy to live without a family and that modern man can thrive without love. But I don't want to be modern, Mariam. I want to be as ancient as Grandfather and his lover.

I know I can't give you back all the time that you have lost looking for me and I can't ask for forgiveness but I can advise you: your life is not complicated. Don't make it any more complicated. I have no choice, Mariam, but you still do. I know you will understand this before it is too late."

After a month, Adnan had wanted to see her again.

He drove to her house and found no one but her father carefully wrapping a stone lamp in newspapers. He acknowledged his visit and offered me tea. Adnan had asked him where everyone was.

"There is nothing here now," is all he said.

He stood in the living room and watched him pack another lamp. He glanced at the rooms; they had all been emptied. There was no one else in the house.

He didn't tell him where they were going and for how long.

So she had left without a trace, without a letter or a word, without a heads-up or a clear warning. He didn't know where and he didn't want to find out. He imagined that like himself, she also wanted to forget the past, bury the ghosts and move on, even if that meant not seeing Adnan ever again.

It was unthinkable at first, but then it made sense – she only existed in his life when her brother did. The search for Abdullah was the only thing that brought them together and now that he was gone, that bond no longer existed and there was nothing new to take its place. This was how they were supposed to meet and eventually part.

"This was the plan," he said to me over the phone.

***

I met June on a cold December night, outside a small coffee shop in New York City. She sat there with her sketchpad, obliviously beautiful, sketching the tall buildings, the wide glittering streets and covering it all with the white falling snow. After a moment of my continuous impudent staring into her drawing, she looked up, full into my face and asked,

"Do I know you?"

I looked back at her, stiff, perplexed. I felt embarrassed, as if I had been glancing at a page of her private journal.

"Yes, I think I do," she said, answering her own question, "We met two weeks ago, when I came for an interview at your company…"

I tried to recall the mentioned week and all the mundane office activities that took place in it. The team had indeed been hiring and there was a line of all sorts of applicants outside the Human Resources office, and I did recall greeting a number of strangers. But that was all I remembered. She might have been there. I must have seen her. I did not remember.

"I do remember," I said, "How did it go?"

"They never called me back," she said as she began packing her stuff, "I don't like you people."

I smiled, "We can be pretty cruel."

Without another word, she stood and walked inside the

coffee shop with me. We sat together, just like that, two strangers with nothing better to do on a Saturday night than discuss the books we had read, the bills we had yet to pay, and the places we had seen.

"So you see, it was Europe where I really, really found myself," she was saying, "I found the artist in me and the actor. The theatre troop I was travelling with wasn't very cool. Believe it or not, they were very narrow-minded…for my taste at least…" she sipped her coffee.

I smiled.

"Tell me, have you travelled much?" she asked.

I told her I hadn't.

"Nowhere?"

"Well, I went to Pakistan once."

Her eyes widened and she chuckled, "And what was that like?"

"I went to see a friend. It was overwhelming."

She asked a few more questions and then, talked in a greater detail about a Pakistani artist whom she had met while she was studying in Syracuse, and then went on to tell me how she was the perfect fit for *Hamlet's* Ophelia but the theatre troop hated her guts and decided to go with somebody named Anna Molly Sue.

We were engaged the next year, but only for a brief period.

She was nothing like the girls I dated or desired. In fact, she was the exact opposite and thus I wanted her. It was difficult to explain to others as well as to myself why I was wasting any time trying to make it work with June, somebody who was so different and much simpler than I was.

After we had separated, I would often frown and say to my friends, "I was in a bad place when June and I were together."

And I was.

My first meeting with June was shortly after Adnan's first few phone calls. I had heard his voice quiver as he unravelled all the details. He was terrified and badly shaken, but I listened to him calmly and after we hung up, I sat down on a couch and lit a cigarette.

I thought about it all – her coming here, his disappearance, my reappearing and the end of the hunt. First my hand began to tremble, my cigarette trailed in disjointed waves and then my head began to explode.

"Oh, Mariam," I whispered as I held my head in my hands.

How I loathed myself for not being there for her!. Adnan told me he wanted to see her but he had no idea where she was. He asked me if I knew anything.

I said I did not.

That year, she really did disappear from our lives, Adnan and mine, like a shadow in the morning sun. And soon, we stopped discussing her and soon, we stopped talking altogether.

A year later, I met June.

And a year after that, we got engaged.

In hindsight, I felt bad for leaving June, for believing that her newness and zest would wake a different person inside me. But it never did, and it looked like there never was a livelier, lighter, version of myself sleeping inside me.

I had always been like this – sullen, boring and pensive.

And so had Mariam.

I had told my friends that I left June because we were too "different". That was the reason I gave them, but in reality, there was another reason altogether that I had kept to myself.

A week before June and I split up, I received a letter. It was from a friend who lived far away, a friend who now wanted to see how I was doing and asked if we could speak.

"Mariam," I said to myself, "Mariam, you irresistible, strange woman."

I didn't reply to the letter. Instead, I just packed my bags and left, one more time, for the love of this strange stranger that I had stumbled upon years ago, at a boring office party in an old art gallery in Washington D.C.

***

The blinds are open now and the lean stewardess asks us to fasten our seatbelts as we near the land. I take a deep breath as we prepare to land; I am back in Lahore, after six long years. I step out through the arrivals gate to find a young boy holding a placard with my name on it.

I walk towards him. He recognises me instantly.

"Hello…Mister Richard," he leans forward, his face is glistening in the sunlight, and his right hand is stretched out to greet me.

"I hope I didn't trouble you," I say as we shake hands and exchange smiles.

"Of course not," he says and we head out towards the parking lot.

From my window, Lahore gently unfolds. She tells me her secrets and stories. She tells me how much she missed me. She gifts me a river of memories.

"You have come on a nice day, Mister Richard," says Hassan as he drives towards a familiar place, "It rained this morning, so the air is cool."

I look outside at a group of students and elderly women waiting at a bus stop.

"It was funny, wasn't it?" he says, "That you called the house to talk to Mariam and found me on the line, instead?"

"I'm glad someone picked it up. I had heard they moved away."

"They did, years ago, but never sold the house. I'm Mariam's first cousin, like I told you over the phone. When they moved out, our family moved in. We moved from a different city and needed a house here and my uncle was kind enough to offer. But you see, they moved away but never really left the place…"

"What do you mean?" I ask as we stop in front of the quiet house.

"It's like their family never left. There are parts of them everywhere, little drawings on the walls from when they were children, a book lying somewhere in a corner, a piece of jewellery, broken bangle on the rooftop, a lonely kite in the *barsati*, old calendars with marked date that hold no significance in our lives….they're always here. It's like the family never left."

A small smile appears on my face. I understand what he meants. I had felt the same when I kissed Mariam goodbye and watched her leave Washington D.C. thinking I would never see her again. But after that, I found her things all over my apartment and in Judy's – her scribbling on random pieces of paper, her books, a scratch she accidently made on the wall from her key chain…I understand Hassan completely.

"But why do you want to come inside when you know they don't live here anymore?" he asks.

"Well, it's like you said, they never really left…"

There is a small steel lock at the gate. He says the members of his family are all at work, so he has to lock the house before leaving to go out anywhere. I watch him fish out the keys from his brown *kurta* and struggle to open the lock.

He opens some windows so the sunlight can lighten the room. I look around, the same familiar living room where once the family entertained the guests for Aminah's wedding. Then, the room had smelled of roses and *henna,* and women had sat on the carpet, clapping, and singing folk songs to welcome the bride into a new household. It all comes back to me in that moment, the laughter, the happy tears, the singing, the persisting jokes about the nervous bride…

"Tea? Coffee?"

"Some tea would be fine, thank you."

I sit on the sofa and look at the murky grey walls and rust

coloured curtains. I hear him speak from the kitchen, his voice is echoing.

"Those things you talked about…" I say.

"What things, Richard *Sahib*?" he calls me that jokingly.

"Their things…her things…that she left behind…"

He peers at me from the kitchen. Behind him, the fire on the stove continues to burn.

"Yes, her books and a diary, and some other things…I think they were in a hurry after…well, you know…they just wanted to get out of here, took all those things that mattered…"

"Well, those things might matter also."

He goes back inside, puts a kettle on the stove and says, "I don't think so, Mister Richard. People change. Things change them…terrifying, ugly things."

I drown into silence, thinking about what he is saying and if there is any truth in his philosophy or not, how much has she changed? How much did the terrifying *thing* terrify her?

He walks into the living room with two cups of steaming tea. Cups in hand, we go upstairs to his room and he pulls out a box from his cupboard. Before he opens it, he pushed back the curtains. The sunlight invades again, everything is ridiculously bright.

"You might find it weird that I have collected these things," he says, "But I am learning photography, so I tend to gather strange things as they make for interesting compositions."

I say I understand, I have a friend who also is into such things.

Inside the box are sea shells, old photographs, colourful frayed wings of unfamiliar birds, another small box full of pot-pourri, some jewellery and other things. He takes out an earring; a delicate silver thing with a crimson drop.

"This is a *jhumka*," he says, "I saw Mariam wearing this on her sister's wedding. I found it in a drawer."

He then moves to his bookshelf and pulls out a small beige leather diary.

"This is also hers," he says and shows me her name inside.

It is her handwriting.

"It's empty," he smiles, "She didn't write anything at all."

I take it from him.

Then he brings to me a yellow kite that he says he never threw away because it didn't feel right, an old CD of a popular *Sufi* pop band, and a book.

"This is all I can find at this time," says Hassan.

"It's okay, it's enough."

"We must leave now."

We drive towards our next destination. It is far from the house. It takes about one and a half hour and Hassan says that we are not even in Lahore anymore. This next place is calmer. Even though it is the first time I have been here, but still a strange sense of unquenched nostalgia lingers in my heart.

It's the family graveyard.

It is exactly how she described it.

We walk under a big tree and Hassan points to an orchard. He says that it belongs to his family. Then we walk inside the graveyard.

I sit on a bench and watch the pigeons pecking near the graves. I meet her grandparents and brother. Hassan hands me a plastic bag of freshly plucked roses. I sit on the dust and place a rose on Abdullah's grave. I tell him how sorry I am.

Hassan waits for me under the big tree. He is standing there with his hands in his pockets and a weak smile on his face.

"Now what?" he asks.

"Now I want you to find me a few things."

I tell him.

He makes a perplexed face and runs to what seems like to be the caretaker's quarters. He returns with a matchbox and box of oil. He also brings with him a bearded man, who is afraid that I, a white intruder, am going to set the graveyard on fire.

I place the things on the ground – the diary, the kite, the *jhumka,* and the CD, and spray some kerosene oil.

"To all those terrifying things that we must leave behind in order to move forward," I say, "To all those mistakes, wrong turns, and bad people, and all that and those we have lost."

I throw the matchstick on the ground and the diary catches fire first, and soon everything else is also taken in by the flames.

"I don't know why we're doing this, but I like it," says Hassan as he sits down and examines the ruins.

Soon, we are left with nothing but grey ashes.

***

We continue the rest of our journey in silence. As we drive for another half hour on a rough road that leads us to a beautiful, little place, Hassan tells me that Fatima got married four years ago to a man in Karachi. She lives there now. I ask about the parents, he says that they still live in Lahore in a new house and are doing quite well now. I say I feel glad.

The next place is where she lives, where she ran off to after all of it was over and the place that I wanted to see for the longest time.

It's the village.

Her grandfather's house.

As we drive to this place, Hassan tells me a great story. He says that here in the village, many many years ago, two children meet on a rooftop. They had both lost someone they loved and found comfort in each other. The boy disappeared and the girl went back to the city. They meet again, sixteen years later when she returns. She found that in her absence, he had returned to the village. He now ran a free school for all the children.

Hassan chuckles as he explains how the teary reunion has been the talk of the village ever since.

"Isn't it a wonderful story?" he smiles and stops the car, "The path is too narrow now, the car can't fit. So you just have to walk straight ahead and you will enter Paradise. You can easily find the unusual looking house."

Evening approaches. The sky above our heads reddens.

Lugging my bag to my side, I ask for a *tonga*.

Hassan finds one instantly. The horse pulls the rusty carriage, galloping on the muddy track, through green fields and towards an unfamiliar sleeping place called Paradise. A man with an unlit lantern stops to look at me. Children laugh and run after the horse. Women return home with pitchers of water on their heads.

I sway my head as I relish the cool evening breeze that is whispering her name, that is telling me that I am exactly like her now; so wonderfully abstract, so calm and simple.

I am her.

The wind trusts me with her stories, stories of a simpler time. A time when two lovers corresponded through secret letters, when two children played under the sweet winter sun, and when a grandfather gently stroked the hair of his grandchild till she drifted to sleep in his lap.

I envision her standing at the doorway, surprised, as beautiful as ever.

"Why have you come here?" she will ask.

I ponder on that thought. My face breaks into a blissful smile.

"I don't know, Mariam," I'll say, "I really don't know."